THE AMETHYST
KINGDOM

ALSO BY A.K. MULFORD

The Five Crowns of Okrith
The High Mountain Court
The Witches' Blade
The Rogue Crown
The Evergreen Heir
The Amethyst Kingdom

The Okrith Novellas
The Witch of Crimson Arrows
The Witch Apothecary
The Witchslayer
The Witching Trail
The Witch's Goodbye

The Golden Court
A River of Golden Bones
A Sky of Emerald Stars

THE AMETHYST KINGDOM

THE FIVE CROWNS OF OKRITH, BOOK FIVE

A.K. MULFORD

HARPER
Voyager

Harper*Voyager*
An imprint of HarperCollins*Publishers* Ltd
1 London Bridge Street
London SE1 9GF

www.harpercollins.co.uk

HarperCollins*Publishers*
Macken House,
39/40 Mayor Street Upper,
Dublin 1
D01 C9W8
Ireland

First published by HarperCollins*Publishers* Ltd 2024
1

A catalogue record for this book is available from the British Library.

ISBN: 978-0-00-858281-4 (PB)
ISBN: 978-0-00-868015-2 (ANZ)

Printed and bound in the UK using 100% Renewable Electricity
by CPI Group (UK) Ltd

Dedicated to my amazing readers all over the world who have been cheering on this series since The High Mountain Court. *I've loved journeying through Okrith with you.*

(And to my mom—I'd ask you not to read chapters 24, 27, 28, and 32, but I know by now that you never heed my warnings.)

CONTENT WARNING

This book contains themes of violence, death, fire, parental loss, depression, suicidal ideation, stampede, as well as menstruation and sexually explicit scenes.

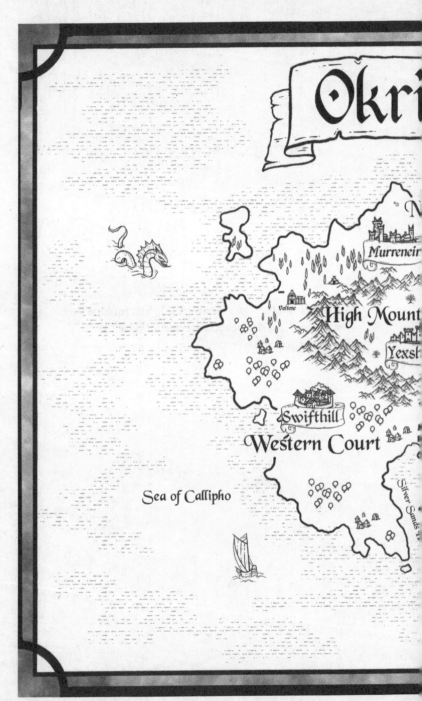

Okri

Murreneir

Valtene

High Mount

Yexsh

Swifthill

Western Court

Sea of Callipho

Silver Sands

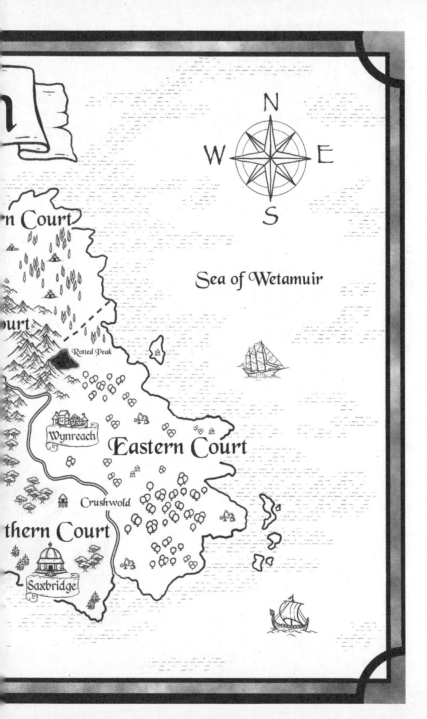

CHAPTER ONE

Wynreach was a hollow version of the sanctuary Carys once knew. Gone was the laughter of her drunken crew, the stories told around campfires after long days of trekking, and the feeling of them side by side in blood-soaked battles. They were all rulers of their own courts now . . . leaving only Carys, the last to claim her crown. But soon she'd be amongst them.

And she wasn't sure how she felt about that.

She glanced at the pinewood and river stone boundaries surrounding the Eastern Court capital. Now manned by dozens of guards, the entire city seemed to move slower in the awareness that a violet storm was coming to the East. The army that her friend and former leader, Hale, had once commanded now held watch at the city gates, watching, waiting . . . for what? Puffs of violet smoke on the horizon? Lion monsters? An army of cursed witches?

Whatever Adisa Monroe had up her sleeve, it was still unknowable. The leader of the violet witches had everyone shaking that her claws would be sinking into their city next. Augustus Norwood had disappeared with Fenrin and Cole from the Southern Court as if they evaporated into the ether. The skies seemed to dim the day they took Carys's brown witch friend—a shift in seasons maybe, or a waking omen of malcontent.

Regardless, a darkness tinged with purple loomed over all of Okrith now.

As the brisk autumn winds whistled through the trees, Carys knew nothing could stay as it was. For better or worse, the realm, and Carys herself, would be irrevocably changed by winter. Maybe by then she'd be Queen of the Eastern Court.

Or maybe Okrith would be burning under the tyranny of an ancient, violet witch.

"You look seriously deep in thought," Bri said. Her words pulled Carys's gaze from beyond the parapet to land on her friend's golden eyes. "Well, not anymore." Carys frowned and Bri chuckled, nudging Carys with her elbow. "It never gets easier, by the way."

Carys cocked her head, her long blond braid sliding over her shoulder. "What doesn't?"

"Being Queen."

"I'm not Queen yet."

"But you will be." Bri nodded, gesturing down to the open courtyard below. "None of these other contenders hold a candle to you."

Carys glanced down at the assembled crowd, counting upward of sixty in her hasty assessment. Some were resplendent in full silver armor that had clearly never seen combat—the pompous sons of Eastern and Northern fae Lords. Others were dressed in modest attire, quiet and stoic. And some looked like frightened rabbits, possibly volunteering to compete just to be able to tell the story to their grandchildren one day. The only person who posed any real challenge was standing tacitly in the corner, her hands clasped behind her back, her sapphire hood pulled low over her face and her totem pouch prominently displayed over the top of her robes.

"What about Aneryn?" Carys asked, tipping her head to the lone figure watching the rest of the group.

"Aneryn is powerful," Bri conceded. "But she's a blue witch. They spook people too much with their visions of the future. I doubt the people of Wynreach would cast their votes for her. Besides, it was *you* who was here in the aftermath of King Norwood's death," Bri said, clapping her on the shoulder. "You pulled the council together and kept the city running. It could've been chaos, but it wasn't, and that was because of you."

Yes, that was all true, but it still meant she was Queen in perception, not name.

Carys's mind flickered back to when she last arrived in Wynreach, of the people calling her name and the children waving in the streets. Over the course of the last two seasons, she'd become a known figure in the Eastern Capital, especially in the human quarter where her halfling sister, Morgan, lived. Morgan and her family had been orchestrating Carys's campaign before the competition was even announced. Morgan was Carys's biggest supporter and in turn, people like her were the reason Carys wanted the crown in the first place.

But wanting didn't mean it was certain, even after all she'd done for these folks.

She stared at the fae Lords in their shining armor again, her doubt turning back to resolve. The last thing Okrith needed was another leader just as wicked and prejudiced as the Norwood kings of old.

Still . . .

"What do they say about counting chickens?" Carys sighed. "Acknowledging my likelihood of winning will definitely make it less likely to happen."

"Oh, is that how it works?" Bri arched her brow. "Since when have you been superstitious?"

"Since an ancient immortal witch stole the mind of our friend," Carys muttered.

Bri glanced back down at Aneryn. "Good point."

The brief warmth that had seemed to blossom in Aneryn had disappeared when Fenrin was taken. They'd kept their relationship secret, Carys only noticing the change in her demeanor now in Fenrin's absence, but it was so apparent that it seemed to cast a pall on the young woman.

"Take care of her," Bri said.

"You know I will."

The head Councilor, Lady Maria Elwyn, raised her hand up to

Carys in a slow gesture that she knew meant the Councilor was beckoning her down.

"Come on." Bri grabbed her by the shoulder and playfully shook her side to side. "Time to win yourself a crown."

They descended the rickety wooden ladder from the parapet down to the stone courtyard. Carys nearly tripped over the uneven ground before righting herself. She straightened, cheeks burning. People would be scrutinizing her more than any other. She needed to be strong yet demure, regal yet likable.

She needed to not stumble like a newborn deer.

She lifted her chin as she took another step. The dusty space in the royal wing of the castle had been neglected for the past several months. Weeds and saplings grew from the dirt between the stones. Soon, this would be the personal reception area of the next ruler, who would use the space to receive their council and honored guests. Now, though, it was ruin, and one filled with people vying for the honor of repairing it all.

And that was something Carys wasn't prepared to leave in another's hands.

The group of contenders gathered around Councilor Elwyn, who drew them toward her through sheer presence alone. Councilor Elwyn had been the wife of the late King Norwood's head Councilor and it was clear from Carys's first meeting with her that Elwyn was twice as smart and thoughtful as her late husband, though she'd never been afforded the opportunity to speak her mind.

When Carys met her, she knew that Councilor Elwyn had been watching, listening, and planning her whole life. Elwyn had everything it took to be head Council for the future ruler, and thankfully, the people of Wynreach had agreed, not a single whisper of protest when Carys had given her the temporary title while succession was planned.

It was Councilor Elwyn who kept the Eastern Court thriving and assembled a group of people to both help and challenge her. But there was only so much Elwyn could do and her requests for a future sovereign had grown more and more desperate over the summer. The

4

people needed a leader—a real leader—and Elwyn had expressed time and again that she was not interested in being the face of the Eastern Court.

Councilor Elwyn's white hair billowed in the breeze along with the skirt of her rust-colored dress. "You have each come here today to contend for the Eastern Court crown." Her voice was deep and soft but carried such charisma that the group seemed to lean in to hear her. "There will be five public trials that you will be graded on before the final crowning vote and the people of Wynreach elect a new sovereign. Three weeks, five contests, one crown." She slowly scanned her gray eyes across the crowd. "You will train for each of these trials together here in the castle. You will dine together, greet the people together, worship the Gods together, and learn about this court together." Her eyes landed on one of the Northern fae—Ivar Halfast—the son of one of the richest Lords in Drunehan. "There will be no in-fighting and no trickery. Whosoever is caught cheating or trying to harm other contenders will be immediately kicked out of the competition. The crown is not about power, but service. To act otherwise is to betray you are here for the wrong reasons. Do you understand?"

The group muttered a collective "Yes," but Ivar only flashed a white-toothed grin.

"Good—"

The carved wooden doors behind them were thrown open, cutting off the Councilor's words. The group whirled as one. Carys lifted on her toes to see who it was but before she could even get more than a flash of the black hair through the crowd, she heard the telltale click of a cane on the stone. Her heart plummeted into her boots.

"Shit," Bri hissed as Ersan Almah, Lord of Arboa, stepped to the front of the group.

"Lord Almah," Councilor Elwyn said tightly. "How good of you to join us."

Bri took a half-step in front of Carys as if she could shield her friend from the blow of seeing him in person after all these years. He had the same shiny raven hair that was pulled into a knot at the nape of his neck, the same beautiful dark eyes and tall, muscular frame.

But his gaze was sharp, the lines deeper at the corners—the only indication of the years that had passed. He dressed in the same attire his father once wore: fitted tan trousers, knee-high leather boots, a billowy white shirt and double-breasted slate-gray jacket over the top. He looked wiser and colder, not the cavalier young fae who rode bareback through the Southern jungles.

She hated the very sight of him.

"Apologies for my tardiness," he said, bowing to Councilor Elwyn and then giving a cursory dip of his head to the rest of the group.

Just the deep rasp of his voice made Carys's body react of its own volition. The sound made her want to cry, pulling on the basest parts of her without logic or thought. How could just the sound of his voice make everything crack open and make her feel like a child again? She thought more solid roots had planted within her, that she'd moved on, but at just the sound of that sonorous timbre, it all felt so delicate again.

She steeled herself. No. She was a fighter now. Her muscles tightened, forcing fire into every corner of her heart.

Ersan rose from his bow. "It seems someone paid off the men at the docks to turn my ship away, but I found my own passage."

Bri apathetically shrugged. "The city is being locked down with the current threats. Can't be too careful."

Carys pressed her lips together to keep from smiling, already knowing it must have been Bri who tried to waylay Ersan's visit . . . but that also meant she knew he was planning on coming. It was such a Bri thing to do, to try and protect her friend by thwarting Ersan's arrival rather than just telling her.

"And who exactly is Lord Almah?" one of the Northern Lords called, derisively emphasizing the word *Lord*. "You sound Southern."

"It won't matter. He'll be gone by next week," another jeered to a round of half-hearted grizzles of agreement.

"Forgive me." Ersan put his hand over her chest and bowed to the group, not contrite in the slightest. "I'm Ersan Almah, Lord of Arboa." He glanced sideways at Carys, his eyes flashing with mischief. She gave him a "don't you fucking dare" look, but his look back to her was unmoved by Carys's entreaty. "And Lady Carys's Fated."

Everyone sucked in a collective breath, their eyes darting to Carys. Her cheeks flamed at the burning touch of their many lingering judgments. In a split second, Bri unsheathed her dagger and took a menacing step toward Ersan. She moved with the stealthy precision that avowed her Eagle moniker, giving Carys barely a breath to grab her friend by the elbow and haul her back.

"You are a queen now, Bri. You can't just go around murdering people," Carys hissed in her ear, struggling to hold her back.

"Watch me." Bri wrenched her elbow from Carys's grip.

"Why don't you all go settle in," Councilor Elwyn called, stepping between Bri and Ersan, seemingly heedless of the knife, her voice rising above the hubbub. "We will discuss the championship details more over lunch."

Carys grabbed Bri again and steered her into Wynreach castle and away from the person they both were two seconds from murdering, the person Carys hated more than anyone in all of Okrith—her Fated.

CHAPTER TWO

S houldn't you be going?" Carys snapped at Bri, who was leisurely lounging across her bed.

"Hey, don't take this out on me, Car. It's not my fault Lord Asshole showed up even after I paid a guy at the docks *five* gold coins to make sure he didn't enter. Besides," Bri shrugged, "my ship doesn't leave until sunset." She popped a grape into her cheek and then picked another. She'd nicked the bowl from the reception banquet after Carys had stormed off at Ersan's arrival. Bri looked around the room, her mouth pinching with distaste. "This place is depressing. It's one step up from a dungeon."

"It's fine."

"It's not fine, but I know what you're saying. A few glasses of wine and it'll be the golden temple of Saxbridge." Bri rubbed the threadbare purple curtain between her thumb and forefinger. "Bet you they're regretting decorating everything in violet-witch purple now, huh?"

"It's still the patron color of the Court," Carys defended as she folded her arms and leaned against her door. The room that she had been appointed as a crown competitor was much smaller than the one she'd stayed in when she was a council advisor. Before, she'd had a whole suite complete with bathing chamber, dining room, and formal lounge. Now, she was in a hall of tiny dormitories just wide enough to fit a single bed filled with clumpy straw and a sliver of window above it. The armoire and a little table with a porcelain washing bowl took up the rest of the room. She wondered if the space had originally been food stores or servants quarters . . . if so, the castle was so lacking in servants after the death of Gedwin Norwood that they had sixty rooms to spare. If she were to become Queen, she'd refurbish this whole wing and make nicer accommodations for her staff like they had in the High Mountain Court and the new Northern Court palace in Murreneir. Just one of the many things Carys would need to change once she became ruler.

And certainly not the most pressing at the moment.

"I think I should delay my departure," Bri said, interrupting Carys's regal daydreams and bringing her back to the harsh reality that her ex-lover and ex–best friend *and* ex-Fated—if there was even such a thing—had now entered into the competition. "I don't want to leave you here alone. With *him*."

"You've got a wedding to plan," Carys countered, inspecting her nails to keep her hands busy when really she wanted to strangle something, or rather, *someone*. "You know—*your* wedding."

"Weddings can be postponed." Bri tossed another grape up and caught it in her mouth. Her words came out muffled as she moved the grapes into her cheeks like a smart-assed chipmunk. "People kind of have to listen to us now." Carys snorted; that was one way to define being a ruler. "And Lina would happily postpone the annoying pageantry for you. We're family. A weird, fucked-up family, but family nevertheless."

"Lina might be fine to delay your nuptials, but she is still trying to pull her court back together after that coup. She needs you by her side more than me," Carys reminded. "I appreciate your concern, but I have this under control. I can handle *him*." She didn't even want to make herself say the name Ersan, let alone his nickname, Sy, which is what she had called him for all of their relationship. Even thinking about being so familiar with him made her stomach sour and her body feel like it was being transported back in time to when they'd been together.

9

"You could hack his other leg off," Bri offered through a mouthful of grapes.

"I didn't hack his first leg off," Carys muttered, hugging her arms tighter to her chest. "He was trapped beneath a beam and I left him there out of spite. His foot was crushed and he would have lost it regardless."

"Minor details." Bri twirled a grape-less stem in her hand. "When he was running in to save your wedding ring, no less."

"Well, I didn't need it anymore," Carys gritted out.

"That's cold, Car, even for you." Yet Bri laughed with an approving nod. "I'm surprised he had the guts to show up here at all."

"I'm not surprised by anything he does at this point. If he can hurt me, he will." Carys pulled the knife out from the belt on her thigh and flipped the blade over and over in her hand. "He lied to me. The fact the Fates decided to punish him for it is not my problem." She loosed her knife, watching it fly across the small chamber and embed into the wood of her wardrobe.

Bri smirked at the soldierly way Carys let out her anger, because it was the same way Bri dealt with her emotions—stabbing things and punching her knuckles into the wall. It didn't really heal anything, but Gods, did it feel good in the moment.

"Why are we even bothering with this competition?" Bri mused. "They should just crown you now. Everyone knows you're going to win."

"Formality, I suppose. When you're appointing a new queen, the ceremony is important—or so Elwyn says. So I still need to win all five of these trials," she said. "Or at least come in the top of each. I need the people to believe in me as a ruler. They need to vote for me."

"They will. Regardless of your performance, their opinions of you won't change over the course of three weeks." Bri plucked up the now empty bowl and rose from the rudimentary bed. She pulled Carys from the doorway with her free arm and wrapped it tightly around her shoulders. "Just don't let the Lord of the Dickheads distract you."

Carys leaned into Bri's hug, resting her chin on her friend's shoulder. The smallest, quietest part of her wanted to cry and beg Bri to stay.

She hated how easily broken Ersan's presence made *her* feel shattered herself, how deeply he riled her just by existing in the same space as her. Instead of admitting the weakness, though—something she was loath to do with even her closest friends—she filled her voice with the confidence of a warrior and said, "I won't." She released her friend and opened her door to let Bri out. "I'll see you at your wedding."

"I'll see you at your coronation first." Bri gave her a wink and added, "Don't die, Car."

She left, and Carys was all alone.

BRI HAD ONLY JUST DEPARTED WHEN A MESSENGER HAD KNOCKED on Carys's door with a note—a farewell note—and Carys had probably scared the life out of the messenger by barking out obscenities and pushing past them down the hall. She'd be late to the competitors' lunch, having not changed or freshened up, not even bothering to pull down the knife still embedded in her wall, but she needed to confront the sender of the note straightaway.

Carys stormed into Councilor Ashby's room, not even deigning to knock. Second only to Councilor Elwyn, Ashby had helped pull the Eastern Court through the tumultuous months without an official ruler, and Carys had always envisioned them being one of her most important guides during her reign . . .

"You're *leaving*?" Carys asked by way of greeting.

Kira Ashby turned, her sage-green eyes softening when they landed on Carys. "It doesn't seem right for me to be here anymore." Her voice was smooth and soft, the sound like a warm blanket wrapped around Carys's shoulders, and despite Kira being denied the role of mother for so much of her son's life, she still was the epitome of maternal.

"You're letting them bully you out," Carys snarled at Kira, instantly feeling guilty for speaking so harshly to such a gentle person.

Kira simply laughed, displaying her hard-won backbone despite her mousy demeanor. Hale's mom had grown more into herself since her banishment had ended. She was one of the first appointments on

11

the new Eastern Court council, one that Carys herself had helped orchestrate. So many of the people who had been wronged by Gedwin Norwood were now filling his old council chamber. It had been strategic on Carys's part, a nonverbal way of communicating to the citizens of Wynreach still loyal to the Norwood throne that change *was* coming.

This—Kira leaving—was a change she didn't want, though.

She and Kira had become close during that time while Carys had helped assemble the council . . . which felt like a minor accomplishment compared to that of her friends. She felt sometimes like the rest of the crew had taken on more important roles in the rebuilding of Okrith: Remy had reconstructed Yexshire from ashes and revived the red witch coven back to a thriving community again; Rua had broken a curse and moved the Northern Court capital; Bri had stopped a coup and was remaking the Western Court; and Neelo had just prevented a whole city from crumbling under the weight of their addictions and yet another mind-controlling curse. They all found their own crowns, their own glory, all the while Carys was back in the East playing nursemaid to a broken kingdom and trying to move along boring endless meetings. The one thing—or rather, two things—that had gotten her through the tedium was becoming close with Elwyn and Kira.

Kira's eyes trailed around her room. She stood and roamed over to the short swords mounted on the wall. She gently selected one and took it down, inspecting the blade and holding the hilt in a way that made it clear she didn't know how to hold a sword.

"I can't believe I'd ever willingly come back here," Kira said, "after everything that's happened."

Carys took another step into the room. "You knew it was the right thing to do for the realm."

"Yes. Just as I know the right thing to do now is leave," Kira murmured, carrying on before Carys could interject.

"I know my presence here brings unease. The council is fully capable of overseeing the trials without little old me." She touched the tip of the sword in her hands to the thick purple curtain. "This place was once my dungeon," she whispered. "It felt good to reclaim it."

To say Kira had been through an ordeal would be an understatement. The elderly fae was easily lovable, gentle yet strong, kind but tough. Yet what she had been through at the hands of Gedwin Norwood was truly horrific and it took a great amount of bravery to return to the place of her torment.

"Did you know?" Carys asked the question she'd been wondering since the Solstice in Saxbridge. "Did you know that Adisa Monroe was your ancestor?"

Kira lowered her sword and walked back over to its mount. "I thought I was only the pawn of kings, not witches too." She sighed. "But now it's clear Adisa Monroe played with my Fate as much as Gedwin did." She glanced up at Carys, seeming to know she was waiting with bated breath. "No, Carys, I didn't know my ancestry. I didn't know who that wild-haired woman was to me even when she was standing on my doorstep."

Carys sucked in a sharp breath. "You'd met her before?"

Kira paused, seeming to consider her words before speaking. "I didn't know her at the time, years ago. I thought she was a traveler lost in a storm." She rubbed her hands together. "I took her in for the night and in the morning she was gone, leaving behind a bottle of perfume." Kira held Carys's sharp gaze. "Blooming amethyst. My favorite scent."

Carys's eyes widened. "And where was the dagger? The one with the amethyst hilt?" She wandered over to Kira and sat on her bed across from her. "Neelo believes it's the key to the immensity of her violet witch powers—a conduit like other talismans."

"That rusty old dagger was at the bottom of my dresser."

"Why would you keep it there?"

"Because I didn't want to see it," Kira said with a shrug. "Or any reminders of Wynreach and my life before I was relegated to a tiny corner of the realm."

Kira stretched up and placed the sword back on its mount, missing one corner. The blade toppled toward the ground. Instinctively, her hands shot out to catch the blade.

Carys leapt over to Kira, already preparing for the sight of blood. Kira wouldn't be the first person to accidentally grab a dropped blade.

But when Carys grabbed Kira's hands and turned them over, her palms didn't even have a line mark on them.

"I'm fine," Kira reassured.

Frowning down at Kira's palms for another beat, Carys finally released the Councilor's hands and dropped back onto her bed. Maybe she was just tired. Maybe the sight of Ersan had distracted her and she didn't see what she thought she saw . . . she pinched the bridge of her nose as Kira sat in the armchair across from her.

"So you kept an ancient, powerful dagger in the bottom of your dresser because it reminded you too much of here?" Carys asked, trying to focus back on getting to the bottom of how the amethyst dagger came into Adisa Monroe's possession.

"Can you blame me?" Kira leaned forward. "I think you and I both know what it is to be hurt by old memories."

Carys stiffened at that. She may have drunkenly spilled her guts to Kira about Ersan one night and now it was apparently coming back to bite her in the ass. She ignored the pointed accuracy of Kira's statement and kept to task. "So Adisa Monroe pretended to be a lost traveler to steal her dagger back from her great-great-however-many granddaughter?"

She hadn't meant it to be an accusation, but realized her tone was not one of gentle inquiry as Kira responded defensively, "She looked like a human. I'm fae. How would I have known she and I were related?" Kira picked at her fingernails, her expression tight with guilt. "The worst part is she seemed nice—a bit eccentric—but nice."

Carys balked. Then said, "That's the least believable part of your story."

"But I'm not lying," Kira said. "I'm no enemy of the East, no matter how I felt about its former king. We'd be kidding ourselves, however, if we think my presence here won't bring suspicion. Too, I fear our closeness might hurt your quest for the crown. You did, after all, encourage my appointment."

"If anyone has concerns with my decisions, they can bring them directly to me," Carys said.

"Listen to you, talking like you're already Queen." Kira chuckled and her smile lines deepened. "How it would reflect on you isn't the only reason I'm leaving . . ." She twiddled her thumbs, her cheeks reddening before finally saying, "It's Timmy. He and I . . . well, he was meant to live in Haastmouth Beach and I guess I was meant to live there with him."

Carys's mouth fell open. "But he's not your Fated." Hale's real dad—Kira's Fated—had died when she was still pregnant with Hale, killed by her former lover, the then-prince Gedwin Norwood. It had been decades since then, but it still made Carys sit a little straighter to hear of anyone moving on from being Fated. It wasn't horror that flooded through her, but rather, hope. If someone could move on from the death of their Fated, maybe she could move on even with him still alive.

"No, he's not my Fated." Kira leaned forward and stared down at her hands, rubbing them together rhythmically as she thought. "But I love him because I *choose* to love him. He makes me happy and I want to be with him." Her smile lines creased again even as she tried to hide her grin. "Stop looking at me like I have two heads."

Carys blinked and schooled her expression. It didn't seem possible. How could anyone move on like that? But excitement also shot through Carys's veins. Maybe it was all just a matter of choice. Maybe she could choose someone other than Ersan and finally get him out of her life for good.

"What was it like?" Carys asked. "Losing your Fated?"

Kira leaned forward, her voice gentle as she patted Carys on the knee. "You already know."

"So much pain," Carys murmured, wringing her hands together, wishing part of her didn't feel compelled to say it aloud. But Kira, of all people, was safe, which made it all that much harder that she was leaving. "Enough to poison every moment of joy."

Kira hummed. "I hate to say, it never goes away. Not fully."

"But you just said you and Timmy—"

"You need to learn to live with the discomfort of two things being true at once." Kira smiled softly. "Which is probably the best advice I could ever give a future Queen. Hurt and love, rewards and punishments, all at once. I feel the pain of Alaric being gone and I let it be there. I let it exist within me. That sorrow walks beside me every day. I cannot turn from it or push it away or else it only amplifies and expands. Sometimes the more you try to be okay, the harder it becomes to be so." She rose from her chair and cupped Carys's cheek. "But joy walks beside me every day too, and I don't try to push away that happiness or love either."

Carys bit the inside of her cheek, trying to keep her cursed eyes from welling. She stood, wishing she could fall apart in Kira's arms just as she wished she'd done with Bri, but again wouldn't allow it of herself. Despite Kira's words, it felt like a lack on her part that she wasn't okay. Carys was a soldier. She shouldn't need any shoulder to cry on. She shouldn't need to cry at all. And yet, it stung knowing that Kira was leaving her too. Her allies and guides were dropping one by one and without them propping her up, Carys was beginning to realize how ill-equipped she was to weather her storming emotions on her own.

"I'll try to remember that," Carys said tightly, her voice thick with unshed tears, even though she was doing the exact opposite even as she spoke.

"The lesson will reach you when it's ready, Carys," Kira said, as if knowing Carys's wayward thoughts. Her pale eyes watched as Carys headed toward the door. "I wish you luck."

Carys bowed her head to Kira and left, feeling further from everything that once anchored her to the world with each step. Gods, she had used Kira to keep her grounded instead of finding her own way, and couldn't help but feel that was the other woman's fault and not hers. She'd wanted to shout at Hale's mother for abandoning her to this competition on her own. She didn't, because a part of her knew it was utter selfishness again. Kira had helped her despite the pain it caused, and now was trying to do the right thing *and* trying to find her own happiness, which she deserved more than anyone after all she'd been through. And yet here was Carys feeling like she was the mountain herself and that everyone should shift their own lives to accommodate her. Instead, it seemed she was nothing but clouds around the peak, and everyone else was wind pushing by her.

Gods, she hated this feeling. She shouldn't need anyone.

She stormed into the shadows of the hallway, hating herself a little more with each step, all while steeling her heart against everything and everyone.

A little voice in her mind echoed out from the darkness: *Focus on the crown. Forget everything else.*

Another voice put it a different way.

Embrace the pain.

CHAPTER THREE

Despite being tainted by the memory of Hale's asshole fake father, King Norwood, the castle of Wynreach was truly a piece of art. Stained glass windows showered the dining commons in a cascade of rainbow colors. Even the tables and chairs were masterpieces—the legs carved in detailed woodwork with animals and landscapes as well as the lion and wave symbols on the Eastern Court crest.

Carys paused as she walked under a banner bearing the court symbols. If she became Queen of the Eastern Court, would she change her crest and, if so, what would she change it to? A lioness perhaps? Simply change out the lion for one without a mane? The waves were an important symbol to the sailors, fishermen, and merchants who called the Eastern Court home. There would probably be discontentment if she took those symbols away. A tree would be appropriate given the artistry of the court's carvers, but the Southern Court crest was already a tree . . .

This would soon be her life: trying to find a way to balance doing the right thing, making her own mark, and choosing the path of least resistance amongst her new people. As Kira had put it, pain and love, always. She hated being reminded of that so soon after her friend's departure.

Carys tried to push those thoughts away and focus first on claiming her crown.

She felt the eyes of many competitors upon her as she strode through the room. In her periphery, she tried to sense if one person in particular was staring at her. She lifted her chin slightly. Ersan was probably watching her from his periphery too, trying to act like he wasn't there just to make her life miserable. Carys threw her shoulders back, acting as if she was already Queen and letting Ersan know he wouldn't throw her off her game . . . though the fact that her mind drifted back to him again and again wasn't a good start.

She found Aneryn seated at the furthest table from the dais, alone. Carys ambled over and dropped into the chair beside her. Two contenders sitting at the table ahead exchanged glances. A silent conversation passed between their eyes and they both reluctantly stood and came over to sit on Carys's free side.

They both bobbed their heads to Carys, nervously murmuring "Lady Hilgaard," and "Lady Carys," at the same time. Carys bowed her head back, not recalling their names but surmising from their brunette hair and olive skin that they were Eastern fae of some distinction. Carys had probably met them at some event or celebration before, but clearly she was more memorable to them than they were to her. They made no introductions either. Instead the two competitors leaned into each other and started whispering between themselves.

"What was that about?" Carys muttered to Aneryn.

The blue witch huffed, holding up her palms until blue flames licked around her fingers and her dark eyes turned sapphire. When Aneryn's eyes landed on the two champions, they rose and scampered off, clearly frightened by her blue magic.

"They want to get close to you," Aneryn said, her steely eyes tracking them across the room until her magic flickered out.

"Why?"

"Because they think you will be elected Queen and they want your favor." Aneryn leaned back in her chair, placing her elbows on the table behind her in a casual position that seemed to ward off any others. "If you become Queen, you will have many positions to fill. Maybe they'll ask to be the captain of your guard or a head merchant or something equally as ludicrous. Becoming your friend in this competition will suit them well if you are Queen."

"If I'm Queen ..." Carys hedged, drawing out each syllable.

Aneryn gave her a sidelong glance. "Don't ask."

"I wasn't—"

"Yes, you were."

"That's really unfair." Carys pouted. "You already know."

"The future isn't certain. The Sight I have sometimes feels more likely than others, but it is never guaranteed. There's only one vision I have so strongly I can smell and taste and *feel* it when I close my eyes." Aneryn's voice thickened and Carys waited silently for her to speak again. "Fenrin with a crown."

Carys's stomach twisted in malevolent knots. She wanted to wrap her arms around Aneryn, but she knew the blue witch wouldn't want it and so she refrained. Carys knew no condolence would be enough for the love that Aneryn had lost when Adisa Monroe stole Fenrin away with her violet mind magic. Because Carys also knew what it felt like to have a loved one ripped away from her for a senseless reason ... many loved ones, in fact. So she didn't say anything and simply sat there and listened.

"It could mean anything," Aneryn continued. "Wearing a crown doesn't necessarily mean he's going to be a king. It doesn't mean the East either, necessarily ... but the vision of him is so unbelievably painful that I wish I didn't have Sight at all." She balled her hands into fists, her blue magic flaring with her anger and heartbreak. Flames licked between her clenched fingers and up her dark blue sleeves, seeming to ignite further the angrier she became. "I don't want to do this without him."

"What? The competition?"

"Life." Aneryn took a long, slow breath even as her voice cracked. She took another breath and she looked as unflappable as usual again. Carys knew that feeling all too well—only permitting herself a moment of weakness, a moment of grief, and then shoving it all down again.

"He was the first good thing I chose for myself. No magic or Fate chose him for me. He was mine. And I will take over this whole moon-cursed court if it means getting him back."

Carys swallowed, taking in each of her words like bearing witness to a curse Aneryn just conjured with her wrath alone. Maybe Bri had been too hasty to dismiss Aneryn's bid for the crown. Her anger alone was incandescent; perhaps she had the aptness to sway public opinion as well. She would certainly make a mighty Queen if she cared for her people even half as much as she cared for Fenrin. Carys shifted her seat on the bench beside Aneryn, wondering if it was a blessing or a curse to be amicable with a strong competitor.

Councilor Elwyn walked in and the rowdy group quieted in a swift decrescendo. Her heeled boots clicked across the floor as she held aloft bundles of spooled cloth in her arms.

Slowly, she hung five pennants from the hooks along the outcroppings in the stone wall behind her. Each of the unfurling pennants depicted the Eastern Court's lion and two waves, but in different postures and colors, along with a single word in regal Ific.

"Over the coming weeks, you will be assessed on the completion of five trials," Councilor Elwyn said in her slow, confident way. She gestured toward the first pennant, depicting a snarling lion, reared on two legs, battling a giant wave. Motioning down the line, she named the theme of the five trials. "Strength. Compassion. Unity. Bravery. Intellect." She folded her hands and turned toward the waiting group. "The future sovereign of the Eastern Court will need all of these qualities in order to successfully rule. It was something your predecessors had been sorely lacking in." She said it with a straight face as if it were a truth and not a snide remark; the group tittered like gossiping courtiers nevertheless. "The first trial, strength, will take place in two days' time. It will be a melee to first blood."

"Fun," Aneryn said flatly. Her gaze scanned around the room, landing on three young fae who were beaming with excitement. "I don't need the gift of Sight to know they won't make it to the second trial."

Carys bit the corner of her lip to keep from laughing.

21

"Look around the room," Councilor Elwyn said. "The first votes will be cast after the strength trial . . . and the bottom half of you will be cut."

A smattering of gasps and angry whispers swept over the crowd. Carys chuckled at their outrage. Did they think they'd get to stay at the palace for all five trials when they couldn't even hold their own in a sparring competition? How many of them were treating this as an excuse to have a good story to tell when they grew old and dine on the palace's food and drink its wine? Many, it seemed.

Well, they better be good with a sword if they wanted a tale for the fire.

"But there's more to rulership than fighting prowess," protested one of the pompous Northern fae—one with immaculate shining armor and the shocked look of someone who had never been challenged in his entire life.

The Northern and Eastern fae were the most represented out of the group of competitors, the Northerners slightly edging out the Easterners, judging by the sea of blond hair amongst the group. That's Northern ambition for you, Carys thought. Conquerors. Arrogant. Mostly pig-headed apart from a few good eggs amongst a rotten bunch. But the entitlement of the Northern fae was truly supreme. It surprised Carys none that so many had come to claim a crown for themselves.

Councilor Elwyn darted her cold gray eyes at the young fae lord. "The East has been at war with one court or another more than it has ever been at peace." She glanced the boy up and down with disdain and Carys smirked at how easily the councilor's look could cut him down to size. "If you do not know how to hold a sword, or at least defend yourself against one, how are you to lead an army?" She carried on before the boy could respond. "Trust me, Lord Everton, if you are not ready for the strength trial, you are certainly not ready for the bravery trial."

"I'm ready," the boy muttered, shrinking down an inch as the group laughed.

"Then it shouldn't be a problem." Councilor Elwyn dusted her hands down her robes. "In two days, there will only be thirty of you left. Until then, you have full use of the training facilities, the library, and the private gardens. That said, any disrespect shown to this competition or to the citizens of this court will result in immediate dismissal." Her eyes found Carys, who frowned at the way the councilor singled her out before saying, "Save your ferocity for the trials."

Aneryn clicked her tongue. "Unlikely."

As Carys elbowed her, Aneryn let out a rough laugh.

Councilor Elywn left out the side door as a line of harried, overworked servants hefting trays of food entered. Carys could feel a set of eyes upon her but didn't turn. "He's watching, isn't he?" she muttered as she stared down at the table.

"Of course he is," Aneryn said without looking in Ersan's direction.

"He's been staring this whole time, hasn't he?"

"Yep."

Carys pushed back from the table and stood. "I'm not hungry."

Aneryn simply nodded and grabbed her cutlery off the table, seemingly happy to be alone again. "All right."

CARYS DIDN'T GET FAR FROM THE DINING COMMONS, HER STEWING anger making her pace outside the doors.

Back and forth. Back and forth.

Gods, she needed to end this. Leaning against the stone archway, she listened as the competitors finished their lunch, paying particular attention to the footsteps of the people shuffling from the dining commons and into the hallway.

When last she saw Ersan, neither of them had been particularly adept at fighting. But Carys had developed her martial prowess in the years of being a solider in Hale's army. She only prayed that Ersan had continued on his highborn trajectory and hadn't invested in his swordsmanship. His wooden leg would surely hinder him in the melee too. At least then the first competition would excise him from her life again.

Waiting, she listened eagerly for the tap of Ersan's cane. When it came she took a deep breath, waiting for him to pass her narrow hiding space between the main entryway and the side corridor.

When Ersan passed, her hand shot out, grabbing him by the collar of his shirt and yanking him into the narrow corridor. She hoped it would leave a bruise on his back as she slammed him hard against the carved wood. In the blink of an eye, her knife was unsheathed from her belt and she stabbed it into the beam a hair's breadth from Ersan's head.

Those dark eyes didn't so much as flinch, as if he'd expected this exact situation to unfold.

"Hello, love," Ersan said with a wink.

"Stop telling people I'm your Fated," Carys seethed, ignoring his cavalier greeting.

"This seems a bit like the kind of intimidation Councilor Elwyn warned us against, no?" His smile was taunting, only incensing her further as his eyes shifted to the dagger beside his temple. "Are you nearing your cycle, then? You were always particularly murderous around that time—"

She yanked him off the column and smashed him back into it again, hoping every nodule along the carved wood left bruises down his spine. Gods, it would feel good to impale her knife into his guts and twist. She pinned him with a venomous look. "I'm not joking! Stop saying we're Fated!"

His scent hit her like a crashing wave, like Arboan clay and blossoming snowflowers and sunshine over the ocean. He smelled like every good memory that now filled her with grief. It made her fist clench tighter in his starched, white shirt. He'd taken every moment of joy. He'd taken everything from her. And she still didn't really understand why.

"But it's the truth. You are my Fated." Ersan's midnight eyes twinkled against his lashes, so thick that from a distance it seemed like they were lined with kohl. His face was still all the same sharp lines, but his strong jaw was now covered in dark stubble all the way up to his defined cheekbones. His straight black hair was just long enough to be pulled back into a low knot at the nape of his neck and stray strands fell across his thick black brows. "Why should I lie to anyone about it?"

"If you weren't here, you wouldn't have to lie. And you shouldn't be here at all," Carys gritted out, yanking her knife free and clenching it in her hand. She debated holding it against his golden-brown skin, wondering how good it might feel to draw blood. "You couldn't just stay gone, could you?"

"You think I'm here for *you*?" Ersan chuckled, his mouth quirking with cruel amusement. "You truly have a sense of entitlement, don't you? Carys, I'm here the same as any contender. I'm here for a crown."

"What about Arboa?"

Ersan shrugged. "Collam will make an excellent lord."

"Collam?" Carys asked incredulously. They couldn't be speaking of the same boy. Ersan's younger brother was a gentle, artistic soul. He was a painter and a philosopher, not a politician. Carys hated that when everything imploded between her and Ersan, she'd lost Collam too. She hated thinking that the boy missed her and their inside jokes and games. She'd abandoned him in some ways . . .

She cleared her throat. It wasn't her fault. Ersan had kept the most important of secrets from her and had never bothered to explain himself in all the years since. Carys pulled Ersan closer only to shove him back again, banging his head into the beam, and shaking his broad shoulders.

He only laughed, the sound grating against Carys and making her clench her jaw. He couldn't even let her have the satisfaction of rattling him a little bit.

"Still got that fire, Car," he said, his eyes trailing down to her mouth. "And it still makes you blind."

Before she could respond, he released his cane and his hand shot out to her wrist that held her knife, immobilizing the weapon. He shoved off the beam, using his size and muscle to pivot Carys so quickly it felt like magic. In another breath, he had her chest pinned to the stone wall across the narrow hallway. He held her knife in one hand and her braid in the other, tugging on her rope of hair and making her stretch up on her tiptoes to arch her head back.

Clearly she'd been wrong about the hindrance of his leg, her hopes of his easy removal from the strength competition now dashed.

His warm breath found its way to her pointed ear. "Do you still like this?" he rasped in a husky lover's whisper.

Carys's stomach flipped and her duplicitous core clenched even as fire filled her veins. "No."

His soft breath brushed against the shell of her ear. "You liar." His nose grazed up her neck. "You think all this perfume in your hair can hide your true scent from me?" He leaned in, his chest pinning her harder until the rough stone bit into her skin and her body pulsed with traitorous desire. "I know you, *Fated.*"

Carys's fingertips dug into the stone, fighting the urge to relent, to lean into his touch. She knew exactly how it would feel—how deft his fingers would be, how skilled his mouth. But then the pain and heartbreak flooded back into her, dousing her desire and filling her with an inky black rage.

"You don't know me anymore," she said, shoving backward and using the hilt of her sheathed sword to push into Ersan's groin—a trick she'd learned from Bri. He pivoted just in time, but she managed to knock him hard in the hip anyway. Without the stability of his cane, he stumbled backward a step. In one smooth movement, she twisted his wrist and snatched back her knife, sheathing it and storming away before Ersan could grab her again.

Carys tsked at the surprise she'd seen on Ersan's face. Clearly, he didn't know her anymore at all. She'd been a working soldier for the last several years, training with the most elite warriors in all the realm. She'd always been a good fighter, but now she had the experience to know how to outmaneuver an opponent not only with brawn but with intellect. The Carys Ersan once knew had died the same day as her father. Ersan might be a trained fighter, but Carys was a *warrior*, and she'd never surrender to him, nor would she ever forgive him for the truths he'd kept from her.

"Go back to your flowers, Lord of Arboa," Carys called over her shoulder, swishing her hips just to taunt him further. "You will never be anyone's king, least of all mine."

CHAPTER FOUR

W hen Carys entered the training rooms the following morning, the sparring rings were packed with contenders, the room teeming with eager fae waiting for their chance to show off their battle skills. Carys couldn't help but wonder what the palace soldiers who normally used the space felt about having a legion of puffed up lords taking over their room. Councilor Elwyn had relegated them out to the western courtyard and Carys had spotted them going through their morning exercises in the wet autumnal mist. She had debated going out and training with them instead. Some of them had become good acquaintances since her time assisting the council, but she knew she needed to put more time into sizing up her competition after being distracted by a certain Arboan lord the day before.

Carys wiped the sleep from her eyes with the palm of her hand. Her back had ached sleeping on the lumpy straw mattress in her chamber and so she'd pulled out her bedroll from her pack and slept on the floor instead. She'd wished it had been in the woods around a campfire with her friends and not on the stone floor of a foreign castle.

Not foreign anymore, she reminded herself.

This place would belong to her soon enough. Soon, she'd finally have a home. Until then, though, there was no court within Okrith that she didn't feel like an outsider in. She had the blond hair and blue eyes of the Northern Court fae, but was raised with the culture, traditions, and accent of the Southern Court fae, and she'd spent most of her adult life with Hale and his crew in the Eastern Court. Not a single one had felt like a homeland to her. Not a single one's inhabitants looked at her like she belonged . . . Only with her ragtag crew of friends, sleeping in the woods, traveling the realm, had she felt whole. She missed their comradery anew as she scrutinized the competition in front of her.

Carys gazed around the group split into their court factions and didn't know which way to turn. She definitely wasn't about to train with the preening Northern fae, and the Southerners were all gathered around Ersan. Being the Arboan lord meant he was rich and powerful in the South, and even if he didn't win the crown, he was still someone to cozy up to. Worse, they all seemed to admire him, which made it even more galling. And it severely limited her options. After the icy reception that Aneryn had given the two brave enough to approach her in the dining commons, it seemed the contenders' willingness to woo Carys had abated too. Now they were all surrounding the favored fae of each of their courts: Ersan Almah was the Southern Court darling, Ivar Halfast the most arrogant and elite of the Northern Court crowd, Sava Dandala was the Western Court favorite, and Falaine Fowler the East's. The only court not represented was the High Mountain Court. While some of the fae had survived all the many years after the Siege of Yexshire, in hiding or in other courts, none seemed particularly keen to reenter the political lives of kings and queens—they had their own courts to rebuild.

The Eastern Court fae seemed the least hostile, but none of them were soldiers in Hale's army and therefore they had strong allegiances to the late King Norwood. Carys glanced at Falaine Fowler, sizing up the auburn-haired beauty—generous curves, strong broad shoulders, and a hard glint in her eyes that belied the softness of her face. She carried herself like a soldier who had seen battle. Carys had probably unknowingly crossed blades with her in one of Gedwin Norwood's many attempts to kill his son and make it look like an accident.

Falaine shot Carys a look so quick she'd have blinked and missed it, but that look said everything: these Easterners were just as much Carys's enemy as the rest of them.

She took a tentative step to her left. The Eastern fae were out, the Northerners were all arrogant pricks, and the Southerners were all scrambling to kiss her ex-Fated's ass . . .

That left the Westerners.

One of their queens was now, after all, Carys's best friend . . . but then would they feel obligated to go easy on her? That would be an embarrassment she wouldn't quickly live down. Besides, not everyone was thrilled with Bri's ascension to Queen Consort . . .

She glanced around for Aneryn, but the blue witch wasn't there, probably because she was a wiser person than Carys.

She should've known better than to visit the training rings the day before a trial anyway. Carys would have plenty of other opportunities to size up the competition throughout the coming weeks. Soon the group would be cut in half and it would be much easier to claim some space for herself.

She was about to turn on her heel when a deep and lilting voice rang out. "Lady Carys."

Turning to the direction of the sound, Carys found a Northern fae with bright blue eyes and white-blond hair smirking at her. "Lord Ivar," she said with a frown of disgust.

She'd met the haughty lord many times over the years at one event or another—weddings, funerals, Equinox festivities . . . fae did love to find a reason to throw a party and lavishly display their amassed wealth. Ivar's fathers were close friends with Carys's own and, had the Fates not intervened, she would've probably been wedded to him. Her stomach tightened at the thought. She knew her younger self wouldn't have said no either—probably even been delighted to be tied to such an important fae. Shame blossomed through her at such a childish thought, spreading along with her burning blush.

"My sparring partners are all lacking," Ivar said, smiling as his crew jeered in protest behind him. He unsheathed his sword and gestured to the white circle painted on the earthen floor below his boots. "I would appreciate someone with your level of skill showing them how it's done."

Tensing, Carys felt the eyes of the entire room upon her. She hated how easily Ivar could goad her into his arrogant display. But maybe a show of her skill would make the others think twice about turning on her in the next trial. If they all left her until last, she'd get through without any trouble at all. Lifting her chin, she decided to demonstrate to them exactly why she would make a good queen.

Also, she really wanted to bash that shit-eating grin off Ivar's face.

She unsheathed her sword and stepped into the ring. "Fine."

The rest of the Northern fae all made space, moving to the wooden benches and leaning in with rapt attention. They muttered bets to each other and Carys couldn't help but roll her eyes. At least the contenders from the other courts had the decency to pretend they were still training, even though Carys could feel the weight of their scrutiny upon her.

Ivar held his sword up to his face and Carys did the same. When his sword dropped, she crouched, ready for his attack. He swiped his sword through the air a few times in a show of frippery that made him look utterly ridiculous. His comrades didn't seem to think so, though, admiring his moves from the corner of the room. She almost laughed at their inexperience. Beauty in battle was meaningless if it wasn't combined with power and purpose, and she was pretty sure Ivar at least lacked the latter.

Carys lunged forward, interrupting his show, and struck him on the thigh where his leather padding protected him from the sting of her steel. Off-kilter, Ivar leaned to the side, dropping his sword arm, and Carys simply held her sword to his exposed neck for a split second to prove her point before retreating again.

"Your lovely choreography means nothing if you can't land a blow," she said, and the room—the whole room, because the other courts had all been surreptitiously watching—erupted in laughter.

Ivar's cheeks reddened with embarrassment and his brow dropped low over his eyes. He rushed forward, all brute force now, and Carys easily danced around him, blocking each of his blows. She waited while he was raining down hits left and right, blocking each one in steady rhythm. Then she ducked, letting the surprise of her missing sword send him off-balance again. She twisted under his sword arm and kicked him in the side, knocking him out of the ring and onto the floor.

The fae from the other courts cheered louder, some even exchanging coins. Carys scowled around the room and the group quieted down.

"I think I shall take my leave now," she muttered, sheathing her sword and walking up to Ivar. She offered him her hand, which she knew would add insult to injury. It was a petty act disguised as chivalry.

To her surprise, Ivar accepted her outstretched hand. She helped him to stand, opening her mouth to say something, when he pulled her forward by their held hands, yanking her into his fist flying from the opposite direction. Her teeth clattered together and cut into her lip as his fist collided with the side of her mouth. The force of the sucker punch made her drop to one knee, one hand flying to her bleeding mouth and the other to her weapons belt.

"Fucking bitch," Ivar shouted. "This crown doesn't belong to a house-less plebe like you. You're a lady in title alone."

She was about to grab her knife and gut him when someone crashed into Ivar and sent him flying. She looked up to see Ersan straddling Ivar, pummeling blows down upon him. Blood sprayed across the dirt floor before three Southern fae grabbed Ersan, hauled him backward, and helped him to his feet.

The rest of the Northern fae leapt up from their bench and unsheathed their weapons. They moved to advance on Ersan, but Ivar stumbled to a stand and held up his hand. They halted as Ivar spat blood onto the ground, his right eyelid already swelling shut.

"You can't blame him for protecting his Fated," Ivar said, looking at Carys with his one good eye. His words hurt more than her cut lip and he clearly knew it by the vicious curl of his mouth. Ivar waved between Ersan and Carys. "The Fates cursed you with that one, Lord of Arboa."

The crowd chuckled and Ersan tried to take a step forward, but his friends held him back.

Carys's whole body burned with rage and embarrassment, but she forced a chill into her voice as she folded her arms and said, "Unfortunately you can't blame the Fates for your terrible swordsmanship and even worse sportsmanship." The crowd "ooh-ed" at the insult. "When you leave this competition tomorrow, Ivar, it will be *me* that cast you out, not the Gods. Remember that."

The crowd broke out into titters of whispered conversations as Carys turned, careful not to let her eyes land on Ersan as she moved. She rolled her shoulders back and stormed off in search of a quieter place to train.

ONE OF THE MANY BENEFITS OF BEING FRIENDS WITH THE FOR-mer crown prince was that Carys knew all the secret nooks and crannies of Wynreach castle. She ventured from the training rings off through the library annex, knowing that if she climbed out the window there, she'd be able to sidestep onto a flat bit of rooftop—the perfect quiet place to train.

But when Carys leapt up onto the roof, she found it already occupied . . . by a certain blue witch.

Aneryn knelt before six tiny objects, the strings of her totem pouch pulled open beside it. A stack of books sat to her right and another two lay open, their pages flipping in the breeze. Her hawk, Ehiris, perched on a weathervane and stared down at Aneryn as if he was studying the witch's actions.

When Carys's heavy boots landed on the stone, Aneryn instinctively reached for her totems. Her hands flared with a burst of fiery blue flames. Whatever magic she was attempting to harness was seemingly just as startled as Aneryn was herself. With a frustrated breath, Aneryn placed her items one by one back into the black leather pouch beside her knee.

Carys assessed the totems as Aneryn put them away: a red ribbon, a seashell, a sprig of dried leaves, a purple stone, a pine cone, and a ball of felted wool.

"I'm sorry," Carys said, awkwardly turning in a circle, unsure if she should climb back down or stay. "I didn't mean to interrupt your prayers."

"I wasn't praying and it doesn't matter," Aneryn grumbled, pulling tight the strings of her totem pouch and placing it back over her head.

What would a witch be doing with her totems out if not praying? Normally the witches laid them out in the light of the full moon and prayed to the Moon Goddess. But not only was it not the full moon, it was daytime, and it all meant that Carys had no clue what Aneryn was up to.

Ehiris made a chirping sound and rustled his wings.

Carys tipped her head to the hawk. "I can't believe Renwick let you bring him."

"Ehiris is my hawk now, not Renwick's," she said in a clipped, annoyed tone. "Normally I leave him in Murreneir, but since I plan on staying here for a very long time, I brought him with me."

Ehiris wasn't the only one ruffling his feathers now. Carys studied Aneryn anew, her confidence chafing Carys's pride. Aneryn was swiftly morphing from an ally to a thorn in her side. Would the blue witch truly try to derail Carys's trajectory? It felt as if the forges were already lit, the smiths already waiting to recast a crown perfectly molded to Carys's head. Why would Aneryn stake such a claim to this place?

Aneryn stood, brushing the dust off her blue robes and turning her flickering sapphire gaze to Carys. The witch seemed to have her magic flaring constantly since she arrived in the Eastern Court as if she couldn't quite keep a handle on her powers. Carys suspected she knew why, her anger slowly ebbing to pity.

"Are you trying to See Fenrin?" she asked. Ehiris took to the skies with a screech as Carys sidled over to the sloping shingled roof and leaned against it.

"I was thinking about Laris, actually, this time." Aneryn let out a long sigh. Laris was her other lover—a mousy green witch from the Northern Court. Aneryn, Laris, and Fenrin had formed a relationship in secret, only uncovered when Carys accidentally walked in on the three of them over the summer Solstice.

"How is she?" Carys offered awkwardly.

"She's doing well." Aneryn stared out at the city. It was the perfect vantage point toward the human quarter. Trails of smoke swirled up into the air from the densely packed houses and Carys wondered if Morgan was busy cooking breakfast.

"It must've been very hard for you to leave her in the South," Carys said, her eyes tracing over the city skyline and out to the Crushwold River in the distance.

"She is apprenticing at the green witch temple. It's the safest place she could be right now." Aneryn swallowed. "Now that Neelo Ember-spear is ruler, Saxbridge is one of the safest cities in all of Okrith."

"I never thought I'd hear someone say that." Shaking her head, Carys thought of the city of debauchery and the many drunken nights she'd spent there with her friends. Gods, what she would give for another night like that: getting lost in the music and laughter and buzzing, light limbs, everything else fading into the background for a little while. "But I suppose it's true."

"Swifthill is a close second, but after the attempted coup last spring, their armies are depleted." Aneryn had stiffened, her words guarded and clipped as if she was an army commander, and Carys wondered how many things the blue witch was keeping to herself these days. How much had she Seen that she was not telling them? "Saxbridge still has the most numbers and has endured the least bloodshed. Yexshire is still rebuilding to its former glory and the North still is a hotbed of allies to the former king."

Interest piqued, Carys glanced at her sideways. "Do you think they'd try something?"

"It depends what you mean by *something*." Aneryn's glowing eyes stayed glued on the horizon. "Do I think the Northerners will try to revolt against fae as powerful as Rua and Renwick? No. But do I think they still believe they have the right to treat witches however they please? Absolutely. I don't want Laris living in the North anymore. One day it will be a friendly place for witches again, but it isn't safe enough for her without me there."

"You are very calculated, Aneryn," Carys said with an approving nod. "And I deeply respect the lengths you'd go to keep your loved ones safe."

Aneryn's eyes flickered at that—the only emotion she seemed willing to show. "I'm not a loved one to her anymore."

Carys's eyes widened and she suddenly felt a terrible guilt for mentioning the green witch. "I'm so sorry," she offered. She opened her mouth to say more but Aneryn waved her hand as if it was ancient history.

"All three of us had terrible childhoods." Aneryn's voice grew softer with every word. "Each in our own ways." She clasped her hands behind her back and lifted her chin. "But Fenrin and I had seen the worst of the world. I shouldn't have expected Laris would want to take on the burden of being attached to either of us, but when it was all three, at least there was balance. With just me . . . she's better off."

"Don't say that."

Aneryn cut Carys a look, blue flames building behind her eyes like tears. "It's true. Why would anyone want this?" She gestured down herself and out toward the city. "I am too fae-like to be loved by most witches. Too witchlike to be loved by most fae. Too fearsome to be loved by humans. Laris was too gentle to handle the world that I live in."

"And Fenrin?" Carys regretted asking as soon as she'd said it—reminding Aneryn of the brown witch she'd lost was only going to pour salt in her wound. But Carys also knew the way Fenrin looked at Aneryn, and that was not the kind of look that would be so easily wiped away.

"Fenrin is just as gentle and kind," Aneryn said. "But he has a fire in him that matches my own. He has struggled, and battled, and suffered." She took a shuddering breath, her eyes glazing over, and Carys couldn't tell if she was imagining the future or thinking of the past. "He was the one to find his mother when she took her own life."

Carys dropped her gaze to her boots, knowing that particular pain all too well. She'd been so little at the time, having experienced something similar. Granted, she hadn't really known what she was seeing . . . but the memories had haunted her—warped and twisting year after year until she couldn't be certain if the image in her mind was what had truly happened or a nightmare of her own making. Her father hadn't talked to her about it, no one in her household had.

"I didn't know," was all Carys could think to say. She wondered if Aneryn knew she was the one to find her mother too.

"I Saw it when I was young," Aneryn said. "I saw that moment when Fenrin found her."

"Gods." Carys sucked in a sharp breath. "How young?"

"I've seen death since the moment my powers awakened," Aneryn said, her memories seeming to drift her further away. "Much more gruesome deaths than that of Fenrin's mother . . . an apothecary has skillful ways of doing such things. But that vision of the lanky blond boy always stuck with me." She swallowed, pausing for such a long moment Carys wondered if she was done speaking. "I tried to See him from time to time over the years, but never did again. That memory remained burned behind my eyelids. I tasted his grief as if it were my own." She looked over at Carys, blue flames licking up from her eyes and swirling into her braided hair. "And then one day there he was, fully grown with that crooked smile."

"You seemed taken with him straightaway." Carys shuffled closer, a soft smile playing on her lips. "But that's because you'd seen him before. Some might call that Fate."

"Witches don't need the Fates to tell them who to love," Aneryn replied. "Fenrin is mine because I wanted him to be mine and I will defy every Moon-cursed fae and violet witch in this realm to bring him back to me." Her voice broke and she cleared her throat. She'd said that before, at dinner the other day, but the vehemence hadn't dissipated because of the repetition. Carys wondered how often Aneryn said these exact words, as if they were a spell the witch was casting over and over. Maybe she could manifest it through that unerring wrath alone.

"How do you plan on getting him back?"

Aneryn glanced back at the stack of books she'd taken from the library and kicked the nearest one closed with her boot. "Like any good witch would: with magic."

"I can help—"

"No," Aneryn cut in. "The fewer people who know my plans, the better." She gave Carys an apologetic glance. "Adisa Monroe has been eavesdropping into too many minds of late. And in the homeland of the blooming amethyst flower, I'm keeping my secrets close. But if you can help me keep the horde of fae lord shitheads out of my way, that would be very helpful."

Carys considered once more Kira's words—being comfortable with two things being true at once. Aneryn was her competition but also someone she cared for—unrequited or no. Fenrin was her friend too and if helping Aneryn meant saving him, then despite the competition their goals were in alignment. Carys would just have to prove herself the undoubted victor.

"I can help with the shitheads." Carys chuckled and bobbed her head. "I'd do anything to help you bring back that crooked smile on Fen's face."

Aneryn's throat bobbed. "Thank you."

Carys narrowed her eyes when a moment of silence passed between them. Aneryn clasped her hands behind her back and stared up to Ehiris circling in the sky. It was only then Carys realized Aneryn was waiting for her to leave to continue with her mysterious work. "I'll let you get back to it."

"Try the gardens," Aneryn said, her eyes dipping from the skyline to the palace grounds below. "The willow tree. No one will bother you there." Carys nodded her head again and turned to leave when Aneryn's voice called after her. "And if you're not searching for peace but rather agitation, he's in the woodshop."

CHAPTER FIVE

C arys's feet found their way to the woodshop seemingly of
their own volition. She didn't want to see Ersan, but there
was still a stinging to her lip and a fire in her veins from
the training ring and she knew she could pick a fight with him. Some
might say it was the thing Carys and Ersan did best. Maybe then she'd
feel a little more settled.

The woodshop sat on the far-eastern side of the palace across a
long open field that looked down onto the city. The grass was grazed
short by a herd of sheep and Carys was careful where she stepped as
she followed the dirt trail that had been worn into the field from many
feet heading to the woodshop.

The place was massive, every inch of it constructed from intri-
cately carved wood. It was like a shrine to the Eastern stylings, from
the heart cutouts of the shutters to the lion paw tracks etched into
the beams above her head. The palace employed twenty woodworkers
who constructed everything from the furniture to the detailed doors
for every room, each one designed to tell a different myth from the
Eastern Court. Despite Carys's room being small, her door was still
exquisite, telling the tale of the boy from Mount Aelusien who slayed
the lion.

She wondered if she should go see that door now—go to her room
and be alone, rather than here. Instead, Carys carefully sidestepped

one of the woodworkers as she entered the shop. All of the staff seemed busy at their work benches as she tiptoed through the side entryway into the main room. A few other visitors dotted in and out, watching the team work on a giant cherrywood armoire from beyond a fenced-off balustrade.

Padding across the floor thick with wood dust, Carys headed to the toy section. Her gaze drifted across the room, searching for one person in particular, but not finding his flash of dark hair amongst the auburns and blonds. Maybe she'd just missed him. Maybe Aneryn was wrong, or more likely, had intentionally misled Carys just to agitate her as promised. Carys squared her shoulders, brushing off the foolish feeling of disappointment. It was probably for the best. She was certain she'd find another way to torment Ersan in the future anyway.

She selected from a basket three miniature carved toys: a horse, a monkey, and an eagle—one for each of her nephews and niece. Smiling, she already knew who would pick what. Molly would choose the horse, Mathew would pick the eagle, and Mark, the silliest of the three, would choose the monkey. Carys debated grabbing a wooden teething ring for the newest addition but that was still a bit premature. She'd be able to have plenty more made for the new baby when she was Queen.

Morgan's husband was a carpenter by trade as well, making fine furniture for the wealthiest and highest-class fae in the city. She wondered if she should get him a job in the royal woodshop . . . though she knew he wouldn't accept and consider it an act of favoritism. Both he and Morgan were too proud to accept that kind of aid anyway. Carys always had to find ways of sneaking them money . . . pretending to leave expensive dresses behind and dropping coins between the pillows of the chairs. Finally, Morgan relented and let her do it without protest. The only thing her sister seemed to actively encourage was the way Carys spoiled Morgan's children. Whenever Carys visited from her far-off adventures, she'd always bring them trinkets, and Morgan smiled each time with genuine thanks.

She supposed the woodshop only being a twenty-minute walk from their house wasn't exactly a far-off adventure . . . but humans weren't allowed to shop there so they'd never visited before.

Soon that would change. One of the many changes Carys would usher in with her reign.

Brushing her braid over her shoulder, Carys ambled over to the woodshop matron and passed her a gold coin. The matron nodded her thanks and went back to helping the other fae perusing the shelves.

Carys turned to leave when she walked smack into a tall figure who hadn't been there the second before. The smell of Arboan clay and sunshine swirled around her, making her ache with nostalgia, remembering the feeling of that hot tropical sunshine on her skin. She savored that scent for one split second, just one, before schooling her features and stepping back.

"What are you doing here?" She scowled up at Ersan, pretending to be surprised to find him there.

Ersan's dark eyes scanned her face and then dropped to the toys in her hands. He lifted the collection of finely carved paintbrushes in his grip. "It's Collam's birthday in a week. I'm sending him some new supplies as a present since I won't be there to celebrate with him."

"You *could* be there to celebrate with him," Carys chided. "All you need to do is get on the nearest ship and go back to where you came from. Or get your ass beat during the melee."

"Where *we* come from," Ersan corrected with an infuriating know-it-all look, ignoring the jibe about the first competition. He always did this—always acted like the smartest person in every room with his stupid inventions and large library collection.

Carys bristled. "I am not Arboan."

"You might as well be for all the time you've spent there." Ersan leaned casually into the beam beside him, though with its small etched waves that circled it, it looked incredibly uncomfortable to lean against. At least, Carys hoped it was. "I'll tell Collam you send your regards in my letter if you like."

"Now you're being cruel," Carys muttered, staring daggers into him. "You know I can't say no to that."

"You always had a soft spot for him." Ersan's knowing smile widened. "He's missed you—"

"*Don't*," Carys cut in. "He knows I had no choice."

"Didn't you?"

Carys swallowed. No. She didn't. Not after what he'd done. She looked down at the figurines in her hands. "Do you know who these are for?"

"Your half sister's children, I presume."

Carys's muscles coiled at the way he said *half sister*, as if her importance in Carys's life somehow counted for less. "I almost missed it," she murmured bitterly. "I almost didn't get to know them at all." It pained her—the flash of their little faces and how much joy each of them brought to her—not being able to watch them grow and learn new things and find new adventures every day. "*You* almost took that from me. Why?"

The muscle on Ersan's jaw flickered and he said nothing.

Carys's laugh was cold and sharp. He never gave her a straight answer, never disclosed the real reason why he didn't tell her about Morgan. No explanation on how he could keep such a life-altering secret from his Fated.

"Tell me, Lord of Arboa," she said tightly. "How would you feel if you never knew Collam, only to discover he existed just now and the person you trusted more than anyone in the world had kept him from you?"

Ersan's eyes narrowed, his face hard. "I'd hate it. And I'd hate the person who kept him from me."

Carys gave Ersan a stiff nod. "Yes. You would."

She sidestepped him and headed for the door, hoping he'd feel even a modicum of the pain that constantly coursed through her. Ersan didn't follow after her. It was all there, laid bare before them. He'd done the worst sort of thing to her and she hated him for it and there could never be any forgiveness between them.

"MOLLY!" CARYS CHEERED, WAVING UP TO THE LITTLE FACE IN THE window. Some of the people milling about the narrow street paused and looked at Carys funny from her crazed overexuberance. "Look how grown you are!"

The little face disappeared, followed by the thundering of footsteps down the creaking wooden staircase. Carys stepped up onto the landing, arms already spread wide, ready for her niece.

"Auntie Carys!" Molly didn't wait to leap into Carys's arms, somehow knowing that her aunt would catch her. Carys could win wars and crowns but winning the love of this little girl was her proudest accomplishment of all.

"Hello, my little love." Carys laughed, squeezing Molly's plump body until she erupted into giggles. That sweet baby scent still clung to Molly's hair and Carys inhaled deeply, knowing it wouldn't be much longer until she, like her brothers before her, lost that baby smell. Luckily another niece or nephew would soon be arriving so that Carys could continue to get her fix.

Carys set her niece down, placing her hand atop her curly golden hair. "Gods, you're nearly to my hip already! You're going to be as tall as me, I reckon. Maybe taller." Molly clapped with delight. "Where are your brothers?"

"They're with Papa in the shop," Molly said, pointing down the road in the wrong direction.

The door opened wider and Morgan appeared, one hand on her slightly swelling belly and the other on her hip. "Aren't you supposed to be training for your first trial?" Morgan asked, arching an accusatory brow.

Morgan had the same bright blue eyes and no-nonsense stare as Carys. Her hair was more golden than Carys's white blond and her face was rounder, her body softer compared to Carys's soldierly, muscled physique. Her ears were slightly elongated but rounded on the top unlike Carys's slender fae ears, but there was no doubt that the two of them were sisters—both in looks and certainly in spirit.

"I trained enough for the day," she said, pointing to the slight bruise where Ivar had hit her. "You should see the other guy."

"If you're getting hit, maybe you need to train some more?" Morgan quipped.

Carys laughed at that. "I thought I'd come bring my favorite niece and nephews some presents," Carys said, winking at Molly's excited expression. She glanced back at her sister, who still guarded the doorway, looking less than enthused. "Aren't you going to invite me in?"

Morgan didn't budge. "This wouldn't have anything to do with the Arboan lord who rumors say arrived at the docks this morning and just entered the competition, does it?"

Carys rolled her eyes. "Would you get off my—" Morgan cleared her throat and eyed Molly, warning Carys to not curse in front of her child. ". . . back. Oh please," Carys said. "Molly is going to be just as fiery as you and I, sooner than you know."

"Fine." Morgan threw her hands up in an exasperated gesture. "One cup of tea and then you need to get back to the palace." Carys snorted. How many people were ordered back to a palace from the human quarter? Morgan leaned down the alleyway, searching for any passersby. "It's not safe for you to be traipsing about Wynreach without protection now that the competition has begun. I wouldn't put it past one of your competitors to pay off some ruffian to injure you before the trial."

"I can take care of myself. I'm perfectly safe."

Morgan pointed to Carys's mouth, but said nothing. Scowling, Carys followed Molly into the kitchen and sprawled into the dining chair—*her* dining chair—the sixth seat at the table that was always Carys's whenever she visited.

"I wouldn't get too cocky about your safety," Morgan warned, making her way back to her rocking chair by the fireplace. Molly climbed up onto her chair beside Carys, watching her aunt with gleeful admiration. Gods, she wished somedays she was half the person that her niece treated her as. "That Lord Fowler's daughter would sooner poison her own stew than lose to a foreigner."

"I can handle the competition," Carys said, her hand dropping to the hilt of her sword. Molly sucked in a breath, her whole body shaking with excitement.

"It's one lord in particular I'm worried about," Morgan muttered.

The kitchen was so small that Carys could lean back in her chair and grab a cup and pitcher of juice from the countertop without rising. She navigated the home as if it were her own . . . it nearly was for how often she resided in it over the past several years. Despite being Morgan's little sister, Carys often felt like Morgan's wayward eldest child for the way her sister mothered her.

"I've got plans for the Lord of Arboa," Carys said, filling her cup.

"Carys Hilgaard—a fighter through and through." Morgan's voice dripped with sarcasm. "You sound so much like some golden-eyed friends I know."

Carys chuckled. Bri and Tal loved Morgan and charmed her as much as they charmed everyone else in their lives. "They send their love, of course, and they lament the fact they aren't here to torture Ersan with me, Bri in particular."

Morgan glanced up from the bowl she shelled peas into and her hands stilled. "Calling him Ersan now?"

Carys's lip curled but she didn't reply. For most of her childhood—and the occasional wine-filled late nights with her sister—she'd called Ersan Almah by the nickname Sy, but that was back when she thought she knew him. Sy had been her best friend, her confidante, her lover . . . Ersan Almah was a stranger to her.

She knew it would hurt him to call him by his full name. She only hoped it hurt a lot.

Reaching over, Carys coiled one of Molly's ringlets around her finger. "When did your hair grow so long?"

She was so close to missing this—to the family she never knew she had. If her father had died an hour earlier and hadn't confessed to Morgan's existence, Morgan would've been lost to her forever. Carys wasn't sure if it was because her father had cheated on his Fated, which was tantamount to spitting in the Gods' faces, or if it was because he'd cheated with a human and sired a child, but her father had kept his halfling daughter a secret her whole life . . . a secret to everyone except Ersan.

Rage boiled below Carys's skin, those old wounds blooming to life anew. Ersan had promised Carys's father to keep making payments to Morgan and her family after he started growing ill. Ersan was to take over seeing the funds reached Morgan after her father's death . . .

and Ersan had also promised to keep Morgan's existence a secret from Carys herself. Carys's father had been "dying" for years before the Goddess finally claimed him. Years when Ersan knew Carys wasn't about to lose her only family like she'd feared, and that more family existed in another court.

On his deathbed, Lord Hilgaard had a change of heart and confessed to Carys about her half sister in the Eastern Court. Carys had left Ersan the same day she watched the light leave her father's eyes. A beautiful new family burst into Carys's life just as she'd left her father and Fated behind. She wished she could leave the memories behind too.

"Car," Morgan said again and Carys realized she'd been far back in her mind, to the humid summer days in the Southern Court, the white flowers of the blooming fields of Arboa, and the first sacred moments of wondering if a friendship was becoming something more . . .

"What?" Carys snapped, lifting her head.

"Sometimes the best revenge is simply to be happy," Morgan said, setting her bowl of shelled peas aside and rising from her chair with a groan.

"Nonsense," Carys said, wishing she could say "bullshit" but knowing Morgan would probably kick her out over it. "I have much more *creative* plans in mind than happiness."

"I have no doubt you do. But it's time to use that creativity elsewhere." Morgan wandered over to the kitchen table and began pulling out the cookware for dinner. "I've got to get the fires lit and the potatoes peeled and—"

"Why don't I stay and help you?"

"No." Morgan whipped her head around and frowned at her sister. "I love you," she added with no small amount of frustration. "But there is a lot resting upon you taking the Eastern Court crown." Her hand fell to her bump again. "Think of my children, of people like me," she said. "Think of what would happen to us if a fae like Ivar Halfast became the new King. What would the life of the humans and halflings of Wynreach be like then?"

"I wouldn't worry about Ivar."

"I *have* to worry about him, and all those like him."

Carys stared at the table for a long moment, shame burning up to the tips of her ears. It was true. She shouldn't be so consumed with her ex-Fated that she couldn't perform to her fullest in the competition. Too much was at stake. She needed to protect her family. She needed to be Queen.

Pushing back from the table, Carys bent and placed a kiss on Molly's head. "I'll leave the presents in the foyer," she said to Molly in a hushed voice. "You help your Ma with dinner and then you can go have first pick."

Molly leapt up from her seat and hustled over to her mother's side, bribed with the promise of a new toy.

Morgan's eyes lifted to meet hers and she offered a half smile to Carys—her silent look of thanks. "Be safe," Morgan said. "And don't allow yourself to be distracted from your purpose."

"I won't." Carys tried to sound confident but she knew the promise rang hollow.

"And don't forget it's your turn to bring desserts to dinner the night of the full moon," Morgan said. "We won't see you back here until then."

Carys knew her sister actually meant "don't come back here until the full moon." Carys knew if she darkened her sister's doorstep before then she'd get another stern talking-to. Since the moment she'd discovered her, Morgan had always been there for Carys. Now it was Carys's chance to take care of her sister in return.

Carys gave Molly a wink. "I'll see you soon. Be good."

Molly waved her chubby little hand at Carys in a way that made her melt and Carys turned and left. That softness of her love for Molly morphing into a ferocity to protect her. Life had always been hard for humans. It had been hard for witches in recent decades too. But the humans had always got the short end of the stick; with no magic and no wealth, they had no power to assume any leadership role within Okrith.

Carys marched down the streets of Wynreach with renewed purpose. This was why she was here. She would be the people's champion.

She'd be her *family's* champion.

SHE WANDERED THROUGH THE QUIET STREETS OF WYNREACH, shutters closing, lamplights flickering above the narrow paths. Carys took a shortcut through a small courtyard in the fae quarter, waving her hands through the fountain's spray as she walked. Ahead of her, a signpost fluttered with hundreds of papers—town notices and decrees. One caught her eye and she yanked it down from its nail and scrutinized the title: Meet Your Competitors.

The scrawling was so small that Carys had to squint to make out the words. Upon the paper was a detailed outline of fifteen competitors and Carys noted how most of the competition didn't even make it onto the notice. But the very first name? Carys Hilgaard. She was cited as the competition favorite with twice as many words dedicated to her, her upbringing, her allies, as any other competitor.

Aneryn too had been cited as a "competitor to watch.": *Will a witch with the power of Sight always be two steps ahead in the competition?*

And, much to her chagrin, Ersan Almah was the last candidate listed, his paragraph squished hastily into the bottom of the page, as if he was an afterthought. But still, his being within the top fifteen could be problematic for Carys. She didn't think he'd be that noteworthy.

"Sizing up the competition?" a feminine voice called from behind her.

She whirled to find Falaine Fowler sauntering through the courtyard. "What in the Gods names are you doing in this part of town?"

Falaine's smile didn't reach her eyes as she said, "Delivering a basket of new blankets to the orphanage."

"Seriously?" Carys scoffed. "You're politicking before the first competition even starts?"

"I'm taking care of my future citizens," she said in mock offense.

"Of course you are." Carys hummed derisively.

"The people of Wynreach are *my* people," Falaine pushed, her auburn hair dancing in the wind behind her as her eyes sharpened at Carys. "I grew up just down the road from here. I know this city and its citizens in a way you never will."

"And how long after the competition will you still care about *all* of your future citizens?"

Falaine tipped her chin to the paper in Carys's hands. "What name is directly below your own?"

Carys didn't bother looking down, already knowing it was hers. Even after the havoc and ruin of the late Eastern King, Gedwin Norwood, people couldn't seem to help but favor someone who acted just like him. The Fowlers and the Norwoods were close family friends. Falaine was just a continuation of the Norwood legacy in so many ways, desperate her softer demeanor and hotter temper. How much sheer confidence and faith the people of Wynreach had in another power-hungry ruler was astounding, history bound to repeat itself. The only hope was this time, the humans would get a vote too.

"The humans know you won't serve their best interest," Carys said.

"Did your halfling sister tell you that?" Falaine's smile turned wicked as she hung on the word "halfling."

"Careful." Carys bristled. "Or I will finish what you started in the training rings."

"It is you who should be careful, Carys Hilgaard," Falaine tittered. "Before you threaten every person in this competition." Her haughty gaze dropped to Carys's split lip. "What would your dear Elwyn say?" She cocked her patronizing head at Carys. "Are you going to get yourself kicked out of this competition before it's even begun?" When Carys didn't move, Falaine rolled her shoulders and lifted her chin smugly. "I didn't think so."

Carys balled up the paper in her hands and threw it to the ground. "I'll see you in the melee tomorrow Falaine," she said, swiftly turning on her heel. "I'll be the one holding a sword to your neck."

CHAPTER SIX

Beautiful door aside, Carys's room was so small she felt like a trapped rabbit. She missed the stars and open night skies that peeked between the forest canopies around their campsites. She missed the exhaustion of a day's trek and the sore muscles of grueling battles. It made it so much easier to turn off her brain then.

She paced back and forth, feeling more irritated by the second, until finally she relented and decided to go find some wine. Fortunately, she already knew the location of the nearest wine cellar thanks to Bri and her bloodhound-like ability to find the closest stash. The main cellar was located right below the grand hall, but a smaller—and more conveniently located one—existed next to the kitchens, filled with cooking wine. It would do in a pinch.

Carys supposed she wasn't allowed to just take the wine in the same way she could when she was a guest in one of her friend's houses. So she grabbed her coin pouch off the narrow wash table and left. Despite the fact that her family home was rubble now, she still had inherited quite a bit of wealth. There were rumors abounding that she'd taken the job as Hale's soldier because her father had left her without a coin to her name, but the truth was she'd safeguarded her riches through Neelo Emberspear, who would deliver her more coins whenever she passed through the South. But better for people to think that she was destitute. All the worst ones would leave her alone if they didn't think they could get anything from her.

The nighttime palace was poorly lit—no one having bothered to light the eerily vacant hallways. Few guards were stationed around the interior. The outer walls of Wynreach city were being bolstered with manpower from the palace defenses. Since there was no ruler to currently protect, many of the guards had been placed on patrols of the outer gates and along the docks of Crushwold River. The whole city seemed to hang in limbo, waiting for a ruler *and* an impending violet witch attack. Wherever Adisa Monroe was in Okrith, her presence was still keenly felt. Whatever she had planned for the other courts, her plans for the Eastern Court would be worse—the homeland of the violet witches. The patron purple colors of the Eastern Court seemed to mock them everywhere, from the lion head pennants that flew over the palace to the violet upholstery and mauve velvet curtains. The calm unnerved Carys more than anything, as if the entire court was bracing for a punch that never landed.

Carys found the cellar with practiced ease and nicked a single bottle, leaving behind a handful of silver *druni* for the kitchen witches to replace the wine with. She tiptoed back up the servant stairwell in the same way she came, reaching the slender corridor where her chambers, and that of four other competitors, were located.

She slunk back toward her room, passing a sliver of golden light. One of her competitor's doors was slightly cracked and laughter echoed out from the room. Interest piqued, Carys crept up to the door to see who was inside. The other four fae who resided on that corridor were all crammed inside Othos's tiny room.

Carys's eyes immediately landed on Ersan sitting on the bed beside Otho, chatting to two raven-haired beauties. Her blood boiled as one passed him a bottle of wine. He took a long swig directly from the bottle before passing it back to her with a wink. Carys realized the four of them were all from the Southern Court. Had she been placed on this floor with them because of that? She blanched. Was Ersan's room on this corridor too? Had she slept last night only a few paces from him without even knowing? She'd imagined she'd heard the click of his cane in her sleep, the sound taunting her . . . now it seemed likely it had been real. She didn't know why but she'd thought Councilor Elwyn would've planned the accommodations weeks ago and that, with Ersan being a last-minute entry, he would be relegated to a far corner of the palace—a broom cupboard or root cellar.

Wishful thinking.

Otho's peeling laughter echoed out the door, pulling Carys closer to the sliver of light. Otho Denton was a highborn fae from Saxbridge. His father was the head of Neelo's council, his family were as rich as thieves, and he had deep ties to all of the prominent families of Okrith, bested only by the connections cultivated by the Lord of Arboa. The two others, Basina and Gabrielle, were twin sisters from the western-most part of the Southern Court near Silver Sands Harbor. They too were from a notable family, though Carys thought they both lacked the combat skills necessary to stay in the competition.

At one point in her life, Carys had considered the twins her friends. Carys had known them her whole life . . . but now, the group was unfamiliar to her. She hadn't spoken to the twins or Otho in years and it was clear Ersan had laid his claim to the friend group in her absence. He always became the leader of every group whether he wanted to or not. People unconsciously seemed to gravitate toward Ersan, and Carys hated that magnetism even more now.

This falling-out with the others had been Carys's fault, though. When she left the South, she'd cut ties to all of them to start a new life in the East. She wouldn't come to the fae fires when they called upon her, wouldn't reply to their letters; everything about their mere existence reminded her of the heartbreak she felt.

The group burst into laughter at something Otho had said and Carys cringed, missing Bri and Tal and Remy and Hale more with each breath. Gabrielle's hand landed playfully on Ersan's shoulder and Carys's muscles tensed.

"Why don't you join us, Lady Hilgaard?" Ersan's eyes lifted, finding Carys in an instant, and she wondered how long he'd known she was there.

Carys's cheeks and lips tingled with a growing blush. She wanted to take a step back and run into the shadows, but instead pushed the door open with a scowl. "Thanks, but I have plans." She lifted her bottle of wine.

"That's sad," Gabrielle replied and the group snickered.

"I just wanted to make sure Otho wasn't being eaten by a pack of wolves with all the grating howling coming from his room." Gabrielle scoffed in offense but Carys kept her eyes hooked on Ersan, a wicked smirk curving his lips.

He grabbed Gabrielle around the waist and tugged her down onto his lap. She let out a giggle as she dropped onto his knee. Ersan arched his brow at Carys, daring her to say something, goading her into a fight like he always did.

Carys put on a fake sweet smile, mimicking Gabrielle's voice. "Enjoy your fun while it lasts," she said, hating the saccharine sound of her mock laughter. "Soon this will be my palace and you will all be bowing to me."

She pulled the door shut behind her and rushed back to her room, the uproarious laughter of her former friends making her stomach tighten into burning knots with each step. The only one who'd seemed unamused by her antics was Ersan. His expression was cold and contemptuous, probably because he knew what a threat to his chances she was. She still couldn't believe he was vying for the crown. The Arboan lord's ambitions had grown since last she knew him. She'd never truly known him at all, she reminded herself, so this shouldn't surprise her.

Carys balled one hand into a fist, the other squeezing the neck of her wine bottle so tightly she thought it might crack. How dare they laugh at her. Didn't they know who she was? She was the closest friend and ally to the kings, queens, and sovereigns of Okrith. They should be kissing her boots. She'd make each of them regret ever laughing at her, already imagining the look on Ersan's bloodied face when she trounced him in the first trial. Her mind wandered to the satisfaction of seeing their defeated faces leaving the competition one by one. Very soon they'd all be scraping and simpering to regain her allegiance. She just needed to stay the course.

Carys pulled out her knife and began uncorking her wine before she even reached her door. She paused at the threshold and swiftly turned back again.

One bottle of wine wasn't going to be enough tonight.

BUZZING WARMTH AND DRUNKEN CONFIDENCE FILLED CARYS'S veins as she stumbled to Aneryn's door. The blue witch opened it before Carys could lift her fist to knock.

"Ooh, spooky." Carys giggled and swayed as drunken tears welled in her eyes. She put a hand to the cold stone wall to steady herself.

Instead of opening the door to let her in, Aneryn stepped out into the hallway and shut her door behind her, folding her arms over her chest and waiting for the question she clearly knew Carys wanted to ask. Ehiris squawked from behind the closed door as if he too was irritated by the interruption to his sleep.

"Is there any way they could've been wrong? Could the blue witch oracles have made a mistake?" Carys asked, her throat burning with too much wine and held-back tears. "Why must it be him? Why must he be my Fated?"

Aneryn's expression oscillated from sympathy to frustration. "You already know the answer."

"Is there no way to break this bond between us, then?" Carys's hand dropped to the hilt of her sword as if she could hack away at the flaring pain in her chest. She wished she could cut out the pain, burn out the infection, find some antidote to the poison that was a Fated mate. She did not want to love him. She didn't want to think about him at all. Surely some witch had a way to erase the memories of snowflowers, Arboan sunshine, and *him* from her mind altogether.

Carys's voice cracked when she asked, "Is there no way to stop feeling like this?"

One eyebrow arched as Aneryn scanned Carys from head to toe, not even a flash of pity on her face anymore. "Did you seriously come here piss drunk looking for someone to stroke your hair and tell you everything you want to hear?" Her voice was so even, so calm, but her words stoked a fire within Carys.

53

"Is that so wrong?" Carys frowned as anger flared in her and she looked around Aneryn to her shut door. "Why can't I come in?"

"Because I am not that person for you," Aneryn said with a steely calmness that made Carys rock back as if she'd been shoved. "I may be your ally, Carys, but I am not yet your friend." The hurt of those words must've been written all over Carys's face judging by Aneryn's reaction. The blue witch scoffed, rubbing her temples, and muttering to the Moon Goddess before squaring her gaze back on Carys again. "Did you know we've met before?"

Carys quirked her brow. "Yes, many times."

"Not with Hale," Aneryn corrected. "Before. In the South. You've met Laris before too." Carys pursed her lips, trying to search her memory but not finding any recollection of Aneryn's green witch lover from earlier. "Your father invited the Lord that Laris's family served to his home on his way to Saxbridge. Being the head green witches to his Lordship, Laris and her parents were forced to travel with him."

Clumsily rubbing the back of her neck, Carys tried to pull up some memory but her past was all a haze. She couldn't remember, so many lords and their human and witch servants had traveled through Hilgaard castle in her youth.

"You were a teenager then—young, drunk, rich, vain," Aneryn continued as she glanced Carys up and down. Carys had the unnerving urge to swipe her stray hairs behind her ear under the blue witch's scrutiny. "I wasn't there but I Saw it. You and your Fated were young, early into your teenage years from what I could tell, but you were already fucking."

Carys winced and decided to ignore that jab, saying instead, "I don't remember Laris."

"You called her a *witch* with such disgust." Aneryn took a step closer and despite being a head shorter than Carys, it felt like her presence made her twice as tall. Blue flames circled Aneryn's fingertips, crawling up her dark skin. "You purposefully spilled your wine on her and everyone laughed. You pointed at her and told everyone else to look. You thought it was hysterical."

"Aner—"

"I don't suppose you would remember," Aneryn said, cutting her off. "It was probably just another drunken party. Just another witch to you."

"I am so terribly sorry," Carys pleaded. "I'm not that person anymore. Believe me. I would never do that now."

"I forgive you," Aneryn said. "But that doesn't make us friends, Carys Hilgaard. First witches were your punching bags, now we're your shoulder to cry on. I won't be your stand-in for Bri. The choices I make aren't from pettiness or grudges, they're from a life of survival and protecting those I love."

"Right." Carys swallowed, anger rising up her throat and wanting to spill out as poisoned words. She wanted to tell Aneryn she was just being a stuck-up bitch, that she was just hurt because Laris didn't want her anymore, that she was just being petty because Fenrin was taken away from her . . . Carys sucked in a shallow breath and pushed the hateful words down.

Aneryn arched a brow, seemingly impressed. She waved her flickering blue hand up and down Carys's body. "I could tell you were playing a part that didn't fit you, even in those visions. You're a better person now, Carys, perhaps even the makings of a good queen, but you will never know peace until you reckon with your past instead of running from it."

"I am not running *from* anything," Carys said tightly. "I am running *toward* my destiny, my crown."

"Okay. Then go run somewhere else." Aneryn turned to her door, walking calmly through it, and shutting the door behind her without so much as a parting word.

Carys squeezed her eyes shut as angry tears spilled from the corners of her eyes. She didn't know why she'd sought out comfort from Aneryn of all people. Probably because Bri wasn't there and Morgan had sent her away and Elwyn was distancing from her to be impartial as Carys was a competitor and even Kira was gone now.

She stormed halfway down the hall. "Well, fuck her, then," she growled. "Stupid, bloody . . ." She let out a snarl, realizing she was being exactly the person Aneryn accused her of being. Gods, when it was all stripped bare, maybe she still was a terrible person, and that enraged her even further.

Anger flamed anew within her and she turned and kicked the wall as hard as she could, bellowing a curse as her boot collided with the stone. She blessed the Gods for making her wear her steel-toed boots, otherwise she'd have shattered all the bones in her foot with that mighty kick.

She rushed back through the shadowed hall to her room as drunken tears slipped down her cheeks. The light from Otho's room still beamed out into the hall and uproarious laughter still spilled out, making her tears fall even faster. When she reached her chambers, she felt blindly for the open wine bottle, nearly spilling it before she snatched the neck. She took a long burning drink, until her body fizzed with warmth and everything raging within her simmered under the pleasant numbness.

She'd hated how right Aneryn was. She wanted the blue witch to replace Bri, Tal, Hale, Remy, Rua, Neelo . . . all of the people she surrounded herself with to keep her moving forward—moving *away*. She didn't like the person she once was, but didn't most people feel that way? She tried on the mask of the mean vapid fae like her father and contemporaries around her. It hadn't fit her at all, but it took incredible heartbreak and suffering to truly shift her away from that old persona and into one of a warrior. But that's all it truly was—yet another mask—and now Carys wondered if she was just searching for a new one: Queen.

Carys took another long swig of her wine, hating herself more with every drink and every breath. She glanced at the array of candles in her miniature hearth, warming the chilled stone room. The frosts of autumn would soon be around the corner. She stared for a long time at the flickering orange flames, knowing she could use her fae magic to contact anyone in that moment. With her power, she could turn the flames a brilliant green and use the magic as a conduit to speak to any fae who had a fire burning on the other end. Each of her friends now had a crown atop their heads and a fae fire room attended by guards day and night should she wish to contact them.

Maybe she could reach out to Rua and ask about the blue witches in Murreneir . . . but what if Aneryn had told Rua about what an awful person Carys used to be and now Rua hated her too? What if Rua had told Remy and now the High Mountain Queen also didn't like her? Neelo and Bri would always be there for Carys, she knew that at least. But talking to Neelo Emberspear through a fae fire would be as good as talking to a brick wall and she knew the Sovereign of the Southern Court would hate every second of it . . .

And then there was Bri. She couldn't contact Bri. The Golden Eagle could read Carys like an open book and she'd probably abandon all of her rebuilding and wedding plans to come back and care for her like a snarky, dagger-wielding mother hen.

Even with a dozen friends and family who would drop everything to come give her a hug in that moment, Carys had never felt more alone. They'd all gone on to their own lives now. Hale's ragtag crew was now scattered to every corner of Okrith, all paired off and happy, and all of the wounds Carys had so neatly hidden up until now started to fester and rot within her.

"Fuck," she hissed, grabbing the neck of her wine bottle and leaving her chambers. She decided to turn her mind from all of the thoughts that plagued her and turn back to the thing that had saved her these last many years: training.

CHAPTER SEVEN

The bottle of wine wobbled on the uneven gravel next to the practice pole. Wrapped in leather and padded with wadding, the battered pole stood resolute as Carys used a wooden practice sword to hack at her stuffed opponent. It was entirely unsatisfying compared to slicing into Hennen Vostemur's battalion of Northern soldiers . . . but it would have to do.

She'd taken to the night, finding the courtyard where the palace soldiers had been practicing while the training rings were swarmed with foreign competitors—the place she should have been training all along. The wine left no room for self-recrimination, though, and she was just happy to see they'd assembled a row of these dummy opponents against the far palace wall.

She thought about the other dummy opponents of hers—the competitors for this throne. A few of the contenders had been on the other side of the battle lines at Falhampton. Carys wouldn't be surprised if Ivar and Prestev were amongst them. How strange that they both thought it appropriate to now be King of the court they'd once raised arms against. They'd be voted out soon enough, Carys hoped. She knew which blood she'd draw first, though, and it wasn't going to be a Northerners.

With an angry puff of air, Carys chucked her wooden sword to the side. It clattered across the stone training ring, echoing in the silence.

Only thin streaks of moonlight beamed into the courtyard, an eerie silver disappearing into shadows.

She unsheathed her real sword from her hip, appreciating the weight of it in her grip, how much it felt like an extension of her arm, the sound it made as it whipped through the air. The cold steel on her palm pulled her back into her body and she had enough sense to remember that chilly autumnal nights should actually feel cold if she wasn't so drunk.

She tossed the sword between her grips but didn't turn it on the padded dummy. She'd have to sharpen it again and she'd be mad at the wasted outrage on her dented steel once she sobered up. Instead, she practiced her form again and again, some of the wine sweating out of her as she went through the motions as she tried to quiet her anger. She wished Bri was there to tell her she was being a fool or Tal to crack a joke or even Neelo to offer her a book with a pointed title like *Quit Being an Asshole*, but instead it was only Carys and her sword and the darkness that seemed to seep into her skin more with every heartbeat.

In a single breath, the air shifted. It wasn't a specific sound or a movement, just a sudden awareness that Carys wasn't alone. The hair prickled at the back of her neck and she knew someone was watching. Her ears strained to hear the sound and, at the light shuffle, she unsheathed the knife on her belt and threw it.

"Gah!" Ersan barked, stumbling into the moonlight from the clinging shadows. He scowled down at the knife protruding from the top of his boot. "What if it had been someone else?"

"Then they'd also have a knife in their boot." Carys sneered as Ersan stooped and pulled the knife free. "But I knew it was you." Only he would be foolish enough to stalk after her in the night.

She reached for her knife, but Ersan yanked it out of his boot and held it aloft. Carys noted he didn't have his cane and wondered if he regretted not having the weapon just in case she unleashed herself at him again. He'd designed a hidden compartment in the handle of it that when twisted correctly produced a needlelike blade.

Had he made any tweaks to the design over the last few years? Ersan could never stop tinkering . . . and that was a random thought. She bounced on her feet as if that would suddenly sober her. She shouldn't care about Ersan's inventions anymore.

"That is a risky game," Ersan said, pulling Carys's focus back to him. "Not everyone has wood beneath their boots."

"It was a risk I was willing to take, obviously. Why are you here, Ersan?" Carys put on a syrupy smile that made Ersan's lip curl, knowing how it would irk him to hear his formal name from her lips. "I thought you were only in this for a crown." Or some dark-haired twin, she didn't say aloud.

"I am. I'm sizing up my biggest opponent." Ersan held up a rumpled sheet of paper in his hand. Even through the shadows, Carys knew it was one of the town crier's notices. So Ersan was keeping an eye on his competitors too . . . He nodded down to the empty bottle of wine beside his boot. "Though you don't particularly seem to have your wits about you currently."

"Is that what outside the dining commons was?" Her mind flashed back to the feel of his chest pinning her to the stone, his hand yanking back her braid. "Sizing me up?"

"Yes. And I'm impressed." Ersan's eyes roved her body and down her arm to her sword. "You've learned some new tricks since last we spoke."

Last we spoke. She hated the way he said it. He made it sound like they were old friends who'd simply lost touch and not Fated mates who were split apart in a brutal breakup by his lies.

Carys shrugged. "I don't care if you're impressed or not."

"Of course you do." Ersan folded his arms over his broad chest and leaned against the padded pole. "Otherwise, why would you be here drunk and alone?"

"Because that's exactly how I want to be," Carys snarled. "You think this has to do with *you*?"

"I think what I think," he said in a way that was as infuriating as everything else about him.

She was surprised words could get past her clenched teeth. "I'd much rather be drunk and alone than dealing with a lying piece of shit like you. Now go."

Ersan laughed, clearly unflustered by her scathing words, and the sound made Carys want to run him through with her sword. "Is that what you've been? *Lonely* all this time?"

"Hardly." Carys scoffed, smoothing her hand over her fitted leathers, her generous hips and muscled thighs. "You think I have any trouble finding lovers?"

Ersan's narrowed eyes seemed to simmer with rage and Carys knew it wasn't from love, but from jealousy, as if she was still his toy and he didn't want to share her.

She cocked her hip to the side, her braid swishing at her back as she tilted her head in a posture she knew would only provoke him further. "Does it make you feel better to think of me pining for you?"

"Yes," Ersan grunted. "But only out of spite." She blinked, surprised he'd be so honest. "I told you I'm not here to win you back. I'm here for a crown. I know I had my chances to explain myself and I didn't take them." His throat bobbed and the muscles on either side of his jaw popped out. "But whatever magic binds us together still makes me hate the thought of someone else's hands on you."

Satisfaction bloomed low in her belly at the perfectly landed blow on his normally steely countenance. Maybe he never wanted her again, but he still didn't want anyone else to have her either, and that was exactly the kind of leverage she could use to get under his skin. It didn't matter that Carys hadn't actually taken any lovers since Ersan—a few drunken sloppy kisses with strangers that had left her wholly unsatisfied had been enough to clear her mind of such notions. In truth, she'd thought maybe she could just satisfy her own urges and never have need of another lover at all. She hadn't even allowed herself to consider missing it, because it was so deeply tangled in the betrayal of this lord in front of her.

Again—not that she'd tell him any of that.

The encounter with Aneryn flashed into Carys's mind. She wondered if Ersan remembered Laris, if he had found a way to atone for their mistreatment of witches that Carys never had.

"We were terrible people, weren't we?" She spoke more to herself, glancing up at the peek of moonlight filtering through the clouds.

"We probably still are, just with older faces, fancier clothes, better connections . . . and perhaps the performance of manners."

Ersan blinked, his brows knitting together for a brief second before smoothing across his forehead again. "I seem to forget that performance when I'm around you."

Carys released a bitter laugh. They brought out the worst in each other. That should've come as no surprise.

"Do you remember a witch called Laris?" Carys's voice wobbled and she cleared her throat as her hand dropped to the hilt of her sword again. "Do you remember me *throwing wine* on her?"

"I don't," Ersan said. "But it doesn't surprise me that I don't. I was always searching for the bottom of a wine bottle back then." He frowned down at the bottle beside his boot pointedly as if Carys had picked up that search where he'd left off. "I had my money, my family, my title, I had you . . . and I was certain that I had earned it all somehow." He shook his head. "I was certain it was because I was better than everyone else, let alone a witch."

"And now?" Carys cocked her head. "You still have your money and title."

With a light flick of his wrist, Ersan embedded the knife in his hand into the pole next to him. "Now I know that we were selfish children. Now I know we deserved the wrath of the Fates." Carys reared her head back, gaping at him and the honesty that seemed to spill from his mouth. She wondered if she asked him right now why he kept her father's secret, if this time he would actually answer her. But then he added, "Now I know that I forfeited all of my chances for happiness for not being brave enough to chase after the right things."

Carys's heartbeat thundered in her ears. "And what were the right things?"

Ersan touched his fingers to his brow in solemn farewell and as he turned he said, "You."

GUARDS RINGED THE AMPHITHEATER THAT SAT ON THE SOUTHERN outskirts of the city. Archers were posted at every lookout, stationed with menacing attention like the stadium was under siege. The stands were so packed with spectators that Carys couldn't even see the staircases that cut through the seats. Not that anyone was sitting. The citizens of Wynreach gathered, all standing, with bated breath, waiting for the first trial to commence. Soon they would have a new ruler. Someone in this battle they would soon crown. Carys knew somewhere in the stands would be Morgan, her husband, and children, cheering for Carys and waving their little purple lioness flags. She wanted to go to them. To give them all a hug. But she also worried—a little—that knowing they were there was a distraction.

It's okay, she thought. *You can do this on your own.*

Carys leaned against the darkened tunnel, waiting for the gate to lift and the melee to begin. The rest of her competitors around her were stretching or bouncing on the balls of their feet or muttering motivational words to themselves. But Carys simply leaned against the dusty brick tunnel, staring at them all, bored. A better future queen would be praying to the Gods or doing something equally moral or pious. But that was not how a lioness behaved.

The anxiety of the looming first trial seemed to grow over the course of the morning. Carys had kept to her room mostly, skipping breakfast to avoid another run-in with Ersan. She didn't want to see the other competitors either since they all seemed determined to pick her as their main target.

Aneryn moved through the sea of competitors to the front of the gate beside Carys. They all seemed to give her wide berth as the witch stepped up beside her. Carys tried not to glance backward, knowing Ersan was somewhere behind her. Judging by the sharp sound of Basina's laughter, he was to the back left of the group, probably more focused on wooing the twins than on the battle. She realized how hypocritical it was for her to judge him for not practicing when she couldn't be bothered to do the same—after that winesoaked night, she'd stayed away from both the sparring circles and the guards' training grounds the following day. Rather it was the *manner* of her distraction that caused her such frustration. This was the curse of being near your Fated. Her jealousy was still an ugly thing even if she never wanted him, even if she hated him with every cell in her body.

"Not preparing?" Carys asked without looking at Aneryn as she tried to distract herself from the jealousy creeping to the front of her mind. "I suppose you've already Seen every eventuality to this battle anyway."

"How many times have I told you Seeing isn't perfect? But yes, I've Seen some of it," Aneryn said with a shrug. "There are a few outcomes I'm more confident of than others, but many are still missing from my Sight. My power isn't an arrow I can just shoot at any target. I See you getting through to the next trial, but I don't See how, if you're wondering."

"I wasn't . . . I'm sorry," Carys murmured. "For everything." She glanced at Aneryn but the blue witch stared out at the assembly of councilors on the dais across the amphitheater. Councilor Elwyn sat with her gentle stoicism at the front center of the group. "I'm sorry we can't be friends."

"I didn't say 'can't be,'" Aneryn corrected. "I said 'aren't.'" She lifted her chin as if she was trying to convince her body to assume a more confident posture but couldn't quite feel it. "It's hard to stand alone, to stand *apart*, and harder still to know the right people to reach out for and lean on. Sometimes you need to face ugly truths within yourself to know which way to turn. The other night, you were turning in the wrong direction."

Carys tried to ignore the sting of Aneryn's words, asking her own stinging question instead. "Was Fenrin the one you'd reached out to?"

"Yes." Aneryn's eyes guttered and she dropped her gaze to her flickering blue fingertips as emotions overcame her. "He *is* that for me. He's still alive."

"Can you See him?"

Aneryn clutched her totem pouch and tucked it under the neckline of her shirt. "No, but I can feel him. I feel his thread of life still here in this world, no matter how obscured by violet smoke he is." Aneryn's hand dropped to the hilt of a dagger on her hip. Carys hadn't even noticed she carried it. It was beautifully carved in silver and gold with sapphires decorating the sheath—she'd wager a gift from Bri. "My vengeance will burn away Adisa Monroe's smoke," Aneryn vowed. "Let's see her magic try to outrun my firestorm."

A shiver ran down Carys's spine at the venom in Aneryn's words, making her study the blue witch closer. "What exactly does that mean? What have you been up to on the library rooftop?"

Aneryn rolled her shoulders back. "If Adisa Monroe thinks she's the only one who can read the ancient spells, she's wrong."

Well, if Carys hadn't been concerned for her before, she certainly was now. "Aneryn, what are you getting yourself—"

The rusted gate creaked as it lurched upward and the crowd roared, drowning out Carys's warning.

Whatever magic Aneryn was talking about would have to wait. The competitors processed out onto the makeshift battlefield as the people of Wynreach erupted in riotous applause. The group spread out across the large oval, kicking up dust from the bare earth below their boots.

Ersan stood toward the front of the oval, closest to the councilors, Basina, Gabrielle, and Otho clustered around him, all wielding the narrow-hooked blades customary of the Southern Court. He didn't turn in Carys's direction, but she had a sneaking suspicion he'd positioned himself directly across from her, not only to keep an eye on her, but also because she couldn't immediately charge him and cut him out of the competition first. Carys tried to put him out of her mind, turning her attention to the Westerners with their battle-axes, the Easterners with their daggers, and the Northerners with their broadswords. Forget Ersan. Dozens of weapons stood between Carys and him now. He was a distraction that she couldn't afford.

Only the most arrogant of fae chose to position themselves around Carys—three from the Northern Court and two from the Eastern Court—Ivar and his gang, Falaine and hers. The rest were smart enough to give her space.

Councilor Elwyn stood from her chair at the back of the dais and walked to its edge. Her white hair was braided in a high bun off her face, but tendrils still curled around her temples, fluttering silver in the breeze as she lifted her deep purple flag into the air and the crowd hushed.

"Upon the dropping of this flag, the first trial will commence," she said over the din. The bowl of the amphitheater was designed to carry her voice up to the crowds, but Elwyn's presence was enough to command their attention as well. When she spoke, people listened, and as Carys stared up at the Councilor, it filled her with sorrow to think of how many years she had to stand silently behind her husband and have her wisdom go unheard. "At the drawing of first blood, the competitor will be out and withdraw themselves from the melee to the steps of the dais." She gestured down to the rickety rudimentary steps that seemed hastily constructed. Carys bet all of the Easterners cringed at its wobbly assembly. To have such bare and untreated wood, no carvings or design, was very un-Eastern-like and was just a minor example of how the Eastern Court had changed without Gedwin Norwood. Carys would reinstate prioritizing the Eastern stylings, probably hiring her brother-in-law to head up the designs. That might be the only similarity between Carys's and Gedwin Norwood's reign.

Elwyn repeated the same instructions a second time as if they were worth repeating. "*First* blood, you will be out and withdraw yourself from the competition on your honor." Elwyn looked each of the competitors in the eye, taking her time with some as if she knew they needed a stronger reminder of her words. When they landed on Carys she held her stare for the longest and she could've sworn she saw the slightest curve of the Councilor's lips before she said, "May the Gods bless the Eastern Court."

"May the Gods bless the Eastern Court!" the crowd shouted and Councilor Elwyn broke her stare with Carys and dropped her flag.

CHAPTER EIGHT

Chaos erupted around Carys as the first competitors blindly lunged and swung into the brawl of clashing swords and axes. Others fled to the walls of the theater as if they could avoid the bloodshed in the giant oval. The walls went straight up, the bottom bench of the stands just beyond reach. If the competitors wanted to run away, they'd either need to have their blood drawn or forfeit and flee to the steps of the dais. The strategy to avoid the battle long enough to make it out of the bottom half and avoid the first trial cull wouldn't garner them any votes amongst the Eastern citizens watching either.

Carys unsheathed her sword and took a steadying breath, knowing she wouldn't need to wait long for the trouble to come to her.

Sure enough, Falaine Fowler and her Norwood cousin—a distant relative of the late King—converged on Carys first. Falaine had her hair braided back in a crown on the top of her head and a stripe of war paint down either cheek. It was enough to make Carys laugh. Falaine looked like a child dressing up as a warrior. She and her cousin had terrible defenses and Carys made quick work of slicing Falaine across the bicep and then, dropping to her knee, Carys sliced the cousin across the thigh.

Falaine looked gobsmacked at the speed with which Carys moved. Perhaps Carys's reputation as a warrior hadn't preceded her as much as she had hoped. Carys winked at Falaine and dropped into a flourishing mock bow before gesturing to the dais. The steps were already crammed with wounded competitors. In a flash, half of the competition had easily been culled and Carys wondered if Falaine would even be cut from the competition at all.

With a heavy string of curses, Falaine and her cousin left the field of battle. Carys didn't watch them long, as there were still combatants about. She searched for Ersan, finding him taking on three fighters of his own, his gaggle of Southern Court friends all in the stands now. Her eyes hooked on his movement, the grace with which he maneuvered his featherlight sword—his speed and stealth. Each of his opponents tried to knock him off-kilter as if his wooden leg would be his weakness, and in doing so, they focused on the one thing Ersan had clearly spent the most energy perfecting. His mind was utter focus and precision. It was glorious to watch. Despite her loathing, Carys couldn't help but feel a begrudging satisfaction as he cut down his every opponent.

She was still distracted when the blade of a Northern soldier whooshed down in front of her. She leapt just in time for it to not make contact. Retreating back another few steps, she lifted her defenses again, preparing to battle the three Northern Lords, who were already splattered in blood—Prestev, Ivar, and Onak.

Carys cut a look to the dais, where more people congregated on the steps while others were being carted off by brown witch healers.

Smart, Carys thought. Cut through the weak ones first, then focus on the bigger competitors. It would gain them more attention too. These three would be in the front of the people of Wynreach's minds after this. They'd stick around for the next trial and probably garner some votes in future competitions too. So now Carys needed to make them look foolish enough that they didn't get too many.

She grinned at the three tall, brawny fae stalking toward her. They wore perfectly shined armor that reticulated like fish scales along their broad bodies. The blood that now splattered across their attire seemed almost too perfectly placed as if they did it themselves after the fact. Their faces were still clean and their shining white-blond hair perfectly combed back.

"If you wanted to make it to the next trial with all your limbs intact, you should have picked an opponent other than me," she said with a wicked grin.

The crowd echoed cheers in the distance, their attention clearly on another fight across the space.

"Yes, I've heard you like to do that," Ivar said with a knowing wink.

Carys rolled her eyes, exasperated. Now wasn't the time to explain that she did not in fact cut off Ersan's leg as all the rumors claimed.

"Carys Hilgaard." Prestev spat at her boots. "An embarrassment to the North if ever there was one."

"I guess I would be, if I *were* Northern," Carys said. "But I'm not. I was once Southern and now I'm Eastern and soon to be a Queen."

She waited for the group to chuckle, knowing their arrogance would get the better of them. When Onak first threw his head back with laughter, she lunged, slicing at the back of his knee where his piecemeal armor didn't cover.

He gasped and dropped, the others turning their heads to watch him. In that brief second of distraction, Carys struck out, knocking Ivar off-balance with her sword. The crowd screamed and cheered, flags moving like waves on a storming sea.

Prestev ran at Carys like a battering ram and she sidestepped him, sticking out her foot to trip him and slicing down his cheek with her dagger as he fell. Carys grinned in satisfaction: she'd been careful not to cut too deep, just enough to draw blood—the perfectly landed strike.

She turned back to Ivar. Now she just needed to draw his blood, and then she could turn her attention to the fight she'd been waiting for this whole trial. She assessed Ivar, contemplating the best method of attack as his eyes widened and he retreated one step, then two.

On his third retreating step he froze, his face paling as he reached up to the back of his neck. When he pulled his fingers away they were covered in crimson blood.

Ivar turned, revealing the small figure of Aneryn standing behind him, her dagger bloodied from where she'd swiped it across the back of his neck. She probably had to stand on tiptoes to do so.

"You witch," he snarled, his pride clearly wounded by the small witch and her tiny dagger. "You don't count."

He lifted his hand to strike Aneryn and Carys lunged forward without a second thought. She brought her sword down on his elbow with all her might. The blade caught the hook of his armor but the force was enough to make a sickening pop and Ivar screamed, dropping to his knees and cradling his dislocated shoulder.

"First blood means first blood, Ivar," Carys snarled. "You're out."

Aneryn hadn't moved, hadn't shown a single second of fear. She watched stoically as the pompous Lord stumbled over to the dais and found a brown witch healer.

Carys wiped the sweat beading across her brow. "Did you know that was going to happen?"

"Maybe," Aneryn said as she surveyed the rest of the group.

In a matter of minutes the battlefield had been cleared of contenders. The dais steps were crammed with people in various stages of injury, from small nicks to massive wounds. Carys's eyes landed upon the last two contenders battling far across the theater.

"Of course," Carys said when she spotted Ersan still standing. She glanced at Aneryn. "Care to make a deal?"

"I already know what you're about to suggest," Aneryn said, holding her dagger higher.

"And?"

"And I think you're a petty fool, but I accept."

Carys's lips curved into a mischievous smile. "Good." She strode across the battlefield with Aneryn prowling along beside her.

Ersan barely had time to lift his head before Carys's sword was coming down on him. The crowd gasped. Ersan deflected her blow, trying to hold his other attacker at bay as well. Aneryn came to his attacker's other side and sliced across the back of his hand.

She shoved him toward the dais. "Out."

The fae cursed but turned and waved to the crowd, who cheered for him as he wandered off toward the steps. He'd made a good showing, and Carys would have to find out his name.

Another time, though. It would probably be in the papers tomorrow.

Aneryn went hard on the offensive, attacking Ersan in a whirl of blows. Whenever Ersan was just about to get the upper hand, Carys would intervene and pull his focus, keeping him from drawing blood. A cat playing with a mouse. He was flagging and she knew it, over-exerting his arms, and with one swift slice, she caught him on his exposed forearm and booted him backward. The crowd erupted into cheers, screaming and chanting her name as Ersan collided into the wall with a grunt.

Carys gave him one long menacing look before she turned to Aneryn and offered her palm. "Thank you."

Aneryn smirked and sliced her dagger across Carys's palm, the smallest nick, barely welling blood. The crowd groaned in disappointment.

"The trial has finished," Councilor Elwyn called. "Aneryn has won."

The crowd soured immediately at the outcome. They booed as they tossed pennants and rubbish into the ring. Carys hadn't realized how hateful the crowd was toward Aneryn until that moment. The fae didn't want a witch Queen and the humans clearly didn't either. There weren't enough witches in Wynreach to make up much of a vote, and those witches were probably very quiet with their support so as not to draw the rage of the others.

"Fucking witch!" one person screamed, throwing a rock at Aneryn. She stepped aside impassively as if knowing the rock was coming.

Carys leapt in front of Aneryn and locked eyes with the human who threw it—a ruddy-cheeked, bald-headed man who had a distinct resemblance to a raw ham. He instantly paled when Carys met his gaze.

"Carys . . ." Ersan warned in the same way he did when she'd jumped off the cliffs over that waterfall that one time . . . and when she'd opened the lion's gate in Queen Emberspear's menagerie . . . and whenever she did something that was equally as foolish. How many

times had she heard that same *Carys* throughout her youth? "Don't."
He reached for her elbow, but Carys was already running forward,
blind with wrath. Ersan didn't get to tell her *don't* anymore, not that
she'd ever listened to him when they were together either.

She wrenched her elbow free and scrambled up the wall, her fingertips digging into the slight crevices in the brick and hoisting herself
into the stands. Covered in flecks of blood and sweat, she stormed up
to the human man and grabbed him by the collar.

"I'm-I'm sorry, my lady, please," he begged as Carys yanked him to
his feet and dragged him to the bottom of the stands, his feet thudding
down the wooden steps. Carys unceremoniously dropped him onto
the bottom step.

"Apologize to her," she seethed. "Now."

Aneryn folded her arms and quirked her brow, only barely amused
at the turn of events.

"Apologies, Lady Aneryn," the man muttered..

Carys turned toward the crammed horde of humans who packed
the lower levels of the theater.

"Hear me now," she shouted. "If any one of you ever throws in-
sults or worse her way, you will have *me* to reckon with. And if ever
I become your Queen, I will remember each and every one of your
faces." She scanned across the crowd and watched as they each cowered back under her stare. "We live here *together*. Remember that."

She leapt back down from the wall into the arena, landing in a
crouch. The crowd was suddenly silent apart from the sporadic smattering of applause.

Aneryn gave Carys a nod of thanks.

"Someone should've called out my behavior long ago," Carys said,
thinking of Laris as she glanced sideways at Ersan. "Both of us."

His eyes tracked her every movement, his face unreadable as she
stalked back toward the tunnel, not waiting for the closing ceremony
to end the first trial. There would be four more trials that she could
use to woo the affections of the people, but her first impression needed
to be one of strength, and so she marched off, feeling the eyes of the
entire crowd upon her, and one set of eyes in particular.

CHAPTER NINE

D espite Carys's best efforts, Falaine wasn't cut from the first trial cull. She'd *just* made it into the top half of contenders and, apparently, the citizens of Wynreach still thought of her as a favorite in the competition. Ivar, Prestev, and Onak had made it through as well. All of them would be terrible rulers for the humans and witches of Wynreach, and Carys was reminded once more of the importance that she held within the competition.

The town papers were all aflutter the following day with play-by-play descriptions of the event and lists of all the names that had been culled. But one contender in particular had the most tongues wagging: Ersan Almah. One paper even proclaimed *Get ready for an Arboan upset.* Carys had immediately thrown that one in the fire. She found it incredibly notable that while the papers reported the winner truthfully, there was very little talk about Aneryn in the articles. The headline that stung the most was *Best of Both: Will the Fated finally make up?* Great, Ersan had not only become a marked competitor, he was opening up the whole city to speculation about their relationship.

At least the halls were emptier, all of the residents on Carys's floor were gone . . . apart from the one she wished was gone the most. Carys hated to admit that she was glad the twins were gone. The image of Gabrielle perched on Ersan's knee was still burned into her mind and she couldn't be faulted if her hands somehow found their way around

Gabrielle's throat in her sleep. Carys would find a way to wash it away, just like she had every awful happy image Ersan had once left there. If she ignored the memories hard enough, and with enough distraction, she could convince herself they didn't haunt her at all.

She sat on her bed, leaning against the headboard and staring out at the flickering firelight illuminating the city. As she dabbed at her cuts with a cloth soaked in poultices, her tongue kept finding the wound inside her lip where she accidentally bit into it at the jarring force of Ersan's block. The battle wounds would heal. She needed to focus on the second trial: compassion. That shouldn't be too difficult. She was the only one who seemed to have any compassion for the humans and witches, at least. Finding compassion for her fae citizens would be the hardest part.

The second trial would commence in three days on the full moon. For this trial, the contestants would all assemble in the grand hall and listen to the citizens one by one, then formulate a plan on how to help the city that they would propose on the day of the compassion trial. The citizens would vote on the proposals they liked best and the group of thirty would be culled to fifteen.

Having spent most of her time in Wynreach in the human quarter, Carys already knew what the humans wanted—mostly, better access to the amenities often excluded by the fae. That and the opportunities for upward mobility. Placing more humans in positions of power and influence would help set this balance. The fae wouldn't like it, but that was to be expected. So long as Carys gave the most influential fae positions too, their discontentment would be relatively quiet. Especially if she dropped a few words about their proud heritage and families' history into conversation. Playing to egos was always welcome with the fae. If Carys was able to get the witches' votes too, any dissent of the fae wouldn't matter as much. The human and fae population was roughly the same size so it would come down to the person the witches favored to tip the vote. But Aneryn was surely going to get the witches' votes, even if she got them quietly. The witches of Wynreach were from all of the different courts. The native coven of violet witches was all gone . . . well, at least so they'd thought.

Adisa Monroe and her descendants were hardly enough to call a coven, though Adisa had plans in the works to rectify that. Neelo had informed Carys that the witch who called herself High Priestess had a spell to give the descendants of her line full violet witch powers. It was why she was so determined to find the *smallest seed*—her youngest heir. With her magic, Fenrin would sire a whole line of full-blooded violet witches, if the prophecies were to be believed.

Carys shuddered, the thought alone making her stomach clench. She had compassion for witches, but not ones that would wipe the rest of the people off the map.

Something flashed in the corner of her eye and Carys peered out to the wall that ringed the city. Torches flickered and flashed back and forth. Were people running? She rose to her knees on her bed and cracked open her window, trying to listen for any sounds of distress.

As she peered down, a figure on horseback rushed up to the palace gate. Something was amiss. She leapt out of bed, grabbing her sword, when she heard it: a bellowing roar echoing off the distant hills. Her whole body prickled with anxious gooseflesh. She'd heard that sound before in the woods outside Swifthill, still remembered the beady yellow eyes and giant dripping tusks.

One of Adisa Monroe's monsters had come to Wynreach.

The city had been waiting for this moment and it was finally here. The violet witch had come to attack the capital at last.

Carys frantically belted her sword to her hip and strapped her knives to her thighs, running down the hall even as her fingers fiddled with the buckles.

"Carys!" Councilor Elwyn shouted, catching her midstride down the hall. She spread her arms wide as if trying to stop a fleeing horse. "The guards can handle one beast."

"No. They can't."

Fear bracketed Elwyn's expression and Carys knew if it had been any other contender, the Councilor wouldn't have put up such a protest. Carys was special to Elwyn, and that was the only reason Carys didn't shove her aside as Elwyn commanded, "Stay in the palace."

Ducking around the Councilor with ease, Carys said, "The guards have never seen a beast like this, I promise you."

"Carys!" Elwyn called after her one last time, but Carys didn't turn. She bolted out the door, running through the city toward the sounds of the creature's roars.

HER LEGS BURNED AND HER CHEST ACHED AS SHE TORE THROUGH the southern banks and toward the city gates. The screams grew louder. Her teeth ached as she dragged the cold air over her bottom teeth with each heaving pant. Whorls of steaming breath trailed after her as she bolted toward an eruption of flames.

"Shit." She ran faster. What had the beast collided into to cause such an explosion? A grain store? A woodshop?

With so many people running amok, Carys feared the panic might cause a stampede. Several houses on the outer reaches of the city were already in flames, whether by attackers with torches or by candles dropped in the panic, she did not know. Carys's eyes darted back and forth, searching for any enemy attackers that might be accompanying the beast, but she saw no one. She scanned the skies for the purple explosions of smoke that had rained down upon them in the Western Court but no violet powders filled the skies either. Was this all Adisa Monroe had planned to claim the city of Wynreach? One monster?

Somehow she doubted it. She would focus on what was before her, though, and deal with what came after . . . after.

When Carys finally reached the outer gates of Wynreach, her heart leapt into her throat. The same unearthly lion creature as she encountered in the forests outside Swifthill prowled through the leather-domed witch houses. The creature had the body of an Eastern mountain lion but twice the size, the tusks of a boar, and the curling horns of a ram, but it was those eyes—those luminous yellow eyes with the vertical pupils of a snake—that truly sent a shiver of fear down her spine. A spear stuck out of the beast's bleeding side and spittle dripped from its snarling maw.

Debris coated the streets, shattered glass and splinters of wood.

The creature had torn through the area, leveling the hide-covered huts and circular buildings. Corpses lay amongst the debris. Downed bodies screamed their wounded cries and others pleaded for aid. Dozens of people ran in every direction, scrambling to get away from the utter chaos that now consumed the city wall.

The beast took a step toward the next building when it paused. It sniffed the air, twisting its head toward Carys as if it had been searching for her. Its vertical pupils seemed to widen as they landed on her. Its giant paws pivoted and padded in her direction, shaking the ground with each heavy step.

Carys's fighting instincts kicked in and she unsheathed her sword and dagger, dropping into a defensive stance. People ran past her screaming, fleeing the carnage, but Carys only moved toward it. The beast's eyes glowed, flashing from their eerie yellow color to a dark shade of violet and back again.

"Is that you, you old hag?" Carys shouted, lifting her blades a little higher. She hoped Adisa Monroe could hear her and watch as she hacked her creature apart. "Are you the puppet master of this beast?"

The creature blinked, letting out a slow breath, steam curling through its thick fur, and Carys swore its lips pulled back into a smile.

A strained voice whispered into her mind and Carys jolted. *It's not her.*

Carys gasped. She knew that voice. It was shredded and raw as if it had been screaming, but she knew the owner of that voice.

Her heart thundered in her chest. "Fenrin?" The beast snorted again. "Gods, Fenrin." Carys's voice cracked and, for a split second, she debated lowering her weapons. "If you are controlling this beast, tell it to turn back."

I can't. Fenrin's voice sounded so weary.

Carys wondered if he still had presence of mind—was still the normal, real, caring Fenrin—even under Adisa's control. She'd thought before that Adisa's victims went completely vacant, just a vessel, when the witch took over their minds . . . but maybe her magic made it so he couldn't do all of the things he wanted to, but he could still think, still be *him*, under all of it.

The streets turned unsettlingly quiet as all the witches fled their quarters, leaving only Carys and the beast—the sound of a cane rapidly tapping the ground sounded behind her—just them and apparently one stubborn asshole.

"By all the fucking Gods." Ersan's voice pulled Carys's attention to her left and the beast roared, the sound so loud it rattled the ground. Ersan held his curved sword aloft with his free hand, pointing it at the beast.

"Don't!" Carys held up her hand, stepping in between Ersan and the creature.

"What do you mean, 'don't'?" Ersan balked, gesturing to the corpses on the ground.

Carys turned back to the beast. "Fenrin, where are you? Are you nearby? Are you watching?"

I am watching.

"You've gone mad," Ersan said to Carys, and she realized he couldn't hear Fenrin's voice in his own mind.

She whirled at Ersan, braid flying. "Shh!"

Ersan's brows shot up. "Did you just shush me?"

"Our petty squabbles can wait one bloody minute," Carys snapped, ready to turn her back on the beast to throttle the Arboan Lord instead. "I'm kind of busy."

If Fenrin was nearby, maybe they could capture him and find a way to reverse his mind control. Surely Aneryn could find a way—

A scream broke through the quiet. "Fenrin!"

Carys turned to see Aneryn bolting toward the lion monster, her blue robes flapping behind her as she sprinted like the Goddess of Death was chasing her. Her whole face was consumed in sapphire flames, only her wide hopeful eyes stood out amongst the burning brilliance of her magic.

"Aneryn, stop!" Carys shouted, holding up her hands and trying to get in front of the determined witch. As she turned, Ersan shot forward, slicing the beast on the leg with his sword. Blood gushed from the wound and Aneryn screamed.

The beast snarled at Ersan, twisting its head and snapping at him. Lunging forward again, Ersan stabbed the beast in the cheek. The creature reared back just as Aneryn reached Carys.

Carys's arms slammed around Aneryn, tackling her to the side.

"No!" Aneryn bellowed. "Let me go!"

"That thing will kill you, Aneryn," Carys hissed, constricting her arms tighter around the flailing witch.

The beast turned to Carys and roared, but Carys didn't let go.

"Go!" Carys shouted at the beast, praying that Fenrin could still see through its eyes, still hear her commands, and still had enough control to obey.

She squeezed Aneryn tighter, the blue witch's magic flaring so bright she had to turn her head away, but she didn't let go. She watched as the beast retreated a step, then two. Her mouth fell open as the monster then turned and ran back out the open city gates and into the pine forests.

"Fenrin!" Aneryn's sobs racked through her. "Let me go, Carys. Let me go!"

"I will not let you run after that thing," Carys said, trying to force calm into her voice even as she battled against Aneryn's flailing limbs. "Friend, ally, whatever we are, I'm not going to let you get eaten by a fucking lion."

"Let me—"

"It's *not* Fenrin."

Her tone was absolute, and still Aneryn cried out. Except her sobs were cut off by a sudden gasp. Her magic flared brighter and her body went limp. Carys twisted Aneryn in her hold, her hand flying to Aneryn's cheek as the witch stared back with wide unblinking eyes. Another sharp breath and Aneryn shot up to her feet but now she was not sobbing and not running either.

"What happened?" Carys asked, scanning Aneryn's body in panic. "What did you See?"

Aneryn swallowed, her voice scratchy from her screams, and Carys thought it sounded so painfully similar to Fenrin's own.

"This wasn't Adisa Monroe's doing," Aneryn panted, dropping her hands to her knees as Ersan rushed over and put his hand on her back. "Fenrin was trying to warn us."

"Warn us of what?" Ersan asked, supporting Aneryn's elbow as if she might collapse again.

Aneryn's eyes darted from Ersan to Carys. "Get Councilor Elwyn." She sucked in another long breath and her panic ebbed to her normal hard, resolute nature. "I know when Adisa Monroe is going to attack."

CHAPTER TEN

They gathered in Councilor Elwyn's chambers. The elderly fae sat on a stately chair by the fireplace in her sitting room. She looked powerful, sitting stoically with the fire at her back as the night drifted into early morning.

Aneryn sat huddled on the chaise lounge, her knees tucked into her chest and her shaking hand holding a glass of water. She looked more riled than Carys had ever seen her, and at every creak in the floorboards and crack of the fire, her sapphire magic flared.

Carys sat close by her side, ready to put her hand on the blue witch's forearm should she need to be pulled out of another vision, which seemed to be now coming thick and fast.

Ersan sat in a chair across from them, pulling his gaze from the fireplace and frowning at Aneryn. "How long before she speaks?"

"You should go back to your room with the other competitors," Carys said with a frown of disapproval.

"You are a competitor too," Ersan shot back.

"This doesn't concern you."

"Was there a giant lion monster in the city?" Ersan's expression darkened. "Yes, there was. So I'd say it does concern me if I am to be King."

Carys scoffed and massaged her temples.

Holding up a hand, Councilor Elwyn drew their attention from each other. "If you two cannot wait for Aneryn to speak, then you can leave. I'm already going to be getting hassled from every person left in this competition that you two were here at all. Be grateful I haven't kicked you out of my chambers." Councilor Elwyn gazed patiently back down at the chaise lounge. "I will not be rushing her."

"I can speak," Aneryn croaked, her voice still raw even hours later. "But I can't understand."

"Your vision?"

At Carys's question, Aneryn's flames flickered brighter again, her expression going vacant, and Carys rested her hand on Aneryn's arm again, seeming to snap her back into her body.

"You could've killed him," Aneryn whispered. "You should have let me go."

"That beast could've killed *you*, Aneryn." Carys shook her head. "We should contact Renwick about what—"

"No!" Aneryn's hands shot to Carys's arms, her fingernails digging in as her eyes narrowed. "Do *not* contact him."

"He'll be concerned," Carys said.

"He'll interfere," Aneryn countered. "Promise me. Promise you'll wait until all of this is over and I have Fenrin back to tell him what's transpired. It's important in ways I can't yet explain. *Please*, just trust me."

Carys's lips curved downward. She didn't feel so confident that there'd be a future where Fenrin was back. And it seemed very likely to Carys that if they were able to save him, he'd be irrevocably changed by the weeks under Adisa Monroe's control, just as his uncle, Cole, had been.

"This is why we need to know what you Saw," Ersan implored, leaning his elbows onto his knees and steepling his fingers in front of his mouth. "Please."

"The night of the full moon," Aneryn said. "That is when Adisa Monroe intends to attack. Fenrin came to warn us."

"And kill a dozen people while he did," Ersan muttered and Carys cut him a sharp look. She drew her thumb across her neck and Ersan only winked back. Aneryn was finally talking; he needed to be fucking quiet.

"The full moon." Elwyn gestured, beckoning Aneryn back to her thoughts again. "That's only three days away." Carys could already see Elwyn calculating in her mind: how long to prepare the soldiers, how long to evacuate the city . . . but she only asked, "What happens?"

"Three, maybe four of her beasts will break into the city," Aneryn murmured. "Along with Adisa herself."

"And Fenrin?"

"No." Aneryn's voice wobbled, that haunted look filling her eyes again. "No, Adisa has sent him away for what he's done. She doesn't know how he managed to defy her."

"That's good, though, isn't it?" Carys asked. "It means he could still be on our side? He could defy her more, maybe even get close enough to kill her?"

Aneryn dropped her chin into her hand. "If Adisa Monroe gives him a direct order, he cannot disobey. He's been testing the boundaries of what her orders will still permit him."

"So Adisa is coming the night of the full moon," Elwyn said. "How do we stop her from getting into the city?"

"You don't." Aneryn's eyes flared again. She brought her trembling glass to her lips and took a long sip, her body filled with so much magic it seemed to strobe through her like lightning. "I've Seen a way to defeat her . . . one where you open the gates and let her in."

"But—"

Ersan tried to interject again and Carys held up her hand, giving him her best glare as she mouthed, "Say one more word and I'll fucking kill you."

Elwyn rolled her eyes at that, letting out an exasperated sigh. Carys bit the inside of her cheek, feeling instantly ashamed of how easily her ex-Fated provoked her. They were no better than when they were teenagers.

"Adisa plans on chaos," Aneryn continued. "She plans on carnage, people fleeing through the streets, herding them into her traps and smoke, the perfect distractions that will keep her beasts rampaging and ruining any coordinated efforts to stop her." Flames flickered from Aneryn's fingertips. "Once the city has been mostly destroyed, only then will she send for Fenrin and place him on the throne."

"I thought you said you saw a way of defeating her?" Carys asked.

"Oh, so it's okay if *you* talk," Ersan muttered, kicking at the tasseled carpet with his boot.

Carys ignored him, twisting to face Aneryn once more.

"I See two futures," Aneryn said. "One where Adisa's beasts kill half of Wynreach and Adisa claims the throne for Fenrin. One where the streets are empty of people and barricades are placed along every side road. The beasts will all be driven straight to the castle and there we will slaughter them and capture Adisa."

Carys's pulse drummed in her ears. She glanced at Elwyn. "If we could pull it off . . ."

"We'd be able to capture the violet witch," Elwyn said, hope seeming to blossom in her expression. "This is the chance that we've been waiting for, to finally secure our people's futures and protect the Eastern Court throne."

Carys wrapped her arm around Aneryn's shoulder. "Is there anything else we need to know?"

Aneryn turned to Carys, the unearthly look in her eyes still flashing behind the sapphire flames, but she seemed more resolute too. "I'm going to find a way to save Fenrin," she said. "I will find a way to undo what his ancestor has done to him."

"I'm sure you will." Carys's brows knitted together in confusion, but she nodded. "Is there anything else you've Seen that we need to know tonight?" Aneryn shook her head. "Would you like to go to bed?" Aneryn bobbed her head, her eyes hooding with exhaustion, and Carys helped her to her feet. "Come, I'll walk with you."

She didn't give Ersan an opportunity to join them as she steered Aneryn back toward the dormitories. They got down the first flight of stairs when Aneryn said, "I don't know which future it will be."

"It will be the good one," Carys assured her.

"It might not be," Aneryn said. "We might all be killed."

"No," Carys insisted. "We will do it just like your vision: open the gates and lead them into a trap."

Aneryn frowned but didn't argue as Carys helped her back to her room. But despite Carys's assurances to the witch, fear twisted in

Carys's gut. As soon as she settled Aneryn back into her room she had somewhere she needed to go, someone she needed to warn.

"CARYS, CALM DOWN!" MORGAN HISSED IN HER HUSHED TONE, glaring at the ceiling above like it might explode.

Carys wheeled her arms, gesturing wildly toward the door, thinking of the beasts she'd just promised were coming. "You don't understand—"

"Not so loud." Morgan slapped her hand over Carys's lips. "I can handle a couple of monsters, but if you wake my kids before sunrise, I will *end* you myself," she snapped. "Now, in a normal voice, what's going on?"

"Aneryn has Seen it," Carys panted. "Adisa Monroe's attack." She pinched her side, suddenly overwhelmed from the midnight sprint through the city. The beast attack had spared Morgan's end of the city and Carys thanked the Gods that the creature had moved east instead of west when it entered the city gates. "On the full moon, Adisa is attacking Wynreach with more of her creatures. At least three by Aneryn's estimate."

"Shit."

Carys was shocked by Morgan's language, but shook it off. "You saw what one did to Witches' Row." Carys wiped the sweat from her brow, finally catching her breath. "Just think what will happen with that many. The whole city could go up in flames."

"At least she doesn't have the element of surprise this time," Morgan said, crossing her arms as her mind seemed to snap into hatching a plan. Morgan was one of the least easily flustered people in the entire realm . . . but right now Carys needed her a little more flustered.

"Aneryn hasn't Seen the whole attack," Carys pleaded. "There could be more. Worse. Aneryn has said she's Seen half the city dead too." Carys noted how her sister drifted closer to her knife rack. "A carving knife isn't going to be enough, Morgs. You *need* to get out of this city before the full moon."

"And go where exactly?" Morgan arched her slender eyebrow in an uncanny likeness to their father. "Where can I travel where I won't be killed for my half-pointed ears? The people in the human quarter know what I am and *warily* accept me at best. If I step foot out of this place, who knows what will happen?"

It only then dawned on Carys how small Morgan's life had been. Being a halfling had meant hiding out in this city her whole life. She'd never really considered it before. Morgan had never seen another town in the Eastern Court, let alone the rest of Okrith.

"You're the future Queen's sister," Carys insisted. "You have my protection."

"What is it like to have all that blind confidence?" Morgan snorted, folding her arms tightly across her chest. "I'm being realistic."

"You can't stay here," Carys pushed. "If we can't stop her, the city might be ashes by the time that violet witch is done with this place. I can't risk it."

"If that happens, then you will be Queen of nothing," Morgan countered. "And your protection won't mean anything to me and my family anyway."

"You could pick any capital in the realm and have a royal welcome from my friends." Carys moved to cross her arms but paused when she realized it was the exact same position Morgan was already standing in. "I have connections everywhere."

"Connections," Morgan muttered. "Your royal friends don't know every citizen in their cities. They may be royalty, but they are young. They don't know how deep the hatred of halflings runs, and if they put us up in their royal accommodations, that hatred would grow even further, and worse, the humans would never treat me like one of their own again." She stared Carys down, her face filled with deep lines from a lifetime spent fighting for herself and then for her family. "I'd be outcast on all sides. We'd be safer in the middle of the forest."

Carys opened her mouth to argue but Morgan cut her off. "No, Carys. If you can't tell me one safe place in all of Okrith, that won't ostracize me from humans or make me the victim of vindictive fae, then I am not packing up my family and fleeing just to wind up in more danger than where I fled from."

Heat rose up Carys's neck to her cheeks. Stubbornness was clearly a family trait. Her jaw tightened, not wanting to say the name, but she thought of her niece and nephews and forced herself to say it anyway. "Arboa." She cleared her throat and shifted her weight. "You'll be safe in Arboa."

Morgan's eyebrows lifted. "It's that serious, then." Her fingers tapped along her forearm, the only indication of her nerves. "For you to even suggest there, of all places, it must be that serious."

"Ersan's younger brother, Collam, currently rules Arboa in Ersan's stead." Carys nodded, cringing more with her every word. "He will protect you, though you won't need it, not in Arboa."

Morgan cocked her head. "And why is that?"

Carys pressed her lips together, warring with the idea of sending Morgan to Arboa with every breath. "Because Collam's father was a halfling too."

Morgan's eyes flared in surprise. Halflings were so incredibly rare. To hear of another one was clearly a shock. Everyone in Arboa knew that Collam had a half-human father . . . though apparently the rumors hadn't traveled further. Ersan's mother's affair with her halfling guard had been the gossip of her generation. She died so soon after Collam's birth that there was no real comeuppance for it and Collam was fae-like enough that the people slowly began to forget he had any human in him at all. It was still scandalous to talk about but it was an open secret within the province. The fact that his father had been allowed to live freely in Arboa, even trusted to become a guard, showed that Arboa didn't think of halflings like the rest of Okrith.

A bud of shame grew within Carys at the many times she'd cursed out the memory of Collam's father. There'd been times in her youth when she'd even drunkenly suggested Collam's father shouldn't have been allowed to *exist* let alone work in the home of a reputable fae family. She was young and arrogant and foolish then, but she'd still said those words aloud, bolstered by the seeming approval of her father. All the fae around her had very rigid ideas of the hierarchy of Okrith, with fae firmly at the top, and Carys had thought she'd gain her father's love and approval by speaking the same way. Little did she know that he'd been funding an illegitimate halfling daughter that whole time—a halfling daughter who was now staring skeptically at Carys.

"No one will bat an eye at you or your family there," Carys promised, then added, "Well, they will probably be distracted by your light hair and blue eyes, but halflings aren't as shunned as they are in the rest of Okrith. You'll be safe there, as much as I'm loath to admit it."

"How big of you." Morgan tipped her head side to side, considering. "It would be nice to meet people who think my eyes are more strange than my ears for once, though."

"There's a merchant ship that sails down the Crushwold to the Arboan markets every morning," Carys said with a definitive nod. "You can leave once the children wake."

Sighing, Morgan shook her head. "By 'merchants' you mean 'pirates,' don't you?"

Carys flashed a wicked grin. "The boys will love it." Morgan rolled her eyes. "Consider it an impromptu vacation. Just give me two weeks away. Please." Carys took a step closer and grabbed Morgan's hand, placing her other on her sister's burgeoning bump. "If anything happened to you all, I wouldn't be able to survive it."

"Ugh. Unfair." Morgan cursed as her eyes misted. "I hate when you do that." She yanked her hand back. "Fine. Two weeks and then we return."

Carys bounced up on her toes with the excitement of a child receiving a present, knowing what a big deal it was for her sister to relent. "Thank you. Thank you. Thank you."

"Maybe with us gone you'll be able to focus more on your competition and defeating that violet witch crone," Morgan added. "And less on a certain Arboan lord."

Her sister's knowing look doused water over all of Carys's excitement. Morgan knew how to crawl under her skin just as easily as any sister. Despite being adults when they first met, they still had the loving jabs and fierce loyalty that a lifetime together would've produced. It was the sort of instant belonging that Carys had yearned for after a lonely childhood of always feeling like she was in the wrong place.

Carys's stomach sank at the thought of sending Morgan away. Morgan was Carys's rock, her anchor that kept her from blowing too far off course. Whenever life got too overwhelming, she knew her sister would set her straight. Without her friends, and now Morgan, Carys felt like a kite with its strings snipped. One by one, every person she turned to was disappearing.

She ground her teeth together. She shouldn't be thinking only of herself.

"Stop clenching your jaw," Morgan chided. "You're going to crack a tooth."

"I'm not."

Morgan opened her mouth and closed it before finally asking, "And what about you?"

"What about me?"

"Are you going to be okay without me here?"

"I don't need you to mother me, Morgs," Carys said, even though they both knew it was a complete lie.

"Well, I will worry for you anyway." She smiled and rested a hand on her belly. "I can't help myself." Her eyes filled with a quiet sorrow. "For the entire time I've known you, you were always filled with strength, but there's a darkness there too—a depth that I saw and knew was a terrifying place that one shouldn't be left alone in for too long. I fear the places you'd go within yourself without anyone around."

Carys blinked at her sister, not knowing how to react to being stripped so bare, so instead she just laughed and waved it away. "You have gotten too broody with this one," she said, gesturing to her sister's bump. "You sound like a mother sending your child off into the world for the first time."

Morgan tried to hide the concern in her eyes with a smile. "Come on," she said. "Have a cup of tea with me before you help me pack up the house."

With a playful huff, Carys followed her sister down the hall to the kitchen. She couldn't believe she was sending her off to the province of her personal enemy . . . but despite her hatred of Ersan, she also still trusted Morgan would be safer in Arboa than anywhere else.

CHAPTER ELEVEN

Carys wandered the halls, looking for what, she didn't know. At first her feet steered her toward the library, but she knew it would be packed with people and the little secret ledge that Hale had showed her those many years ago would probably be occupied by Aneryn. The blue witch had become even more withdrawn over the last two days. Only one more night until the full moon. The stakes were incredibly clear: Aneryn knew this might be the only opportunity to get Fenrin back, but her means of saving him were still murky. Was it as simple as capturing Adisa and killing her with her amethyst dagger? Yeah, that would be easy, Carys thought. Whatever tricks the blue witch had up her sleeve, she kept them to herself, and Carys wondered how much of her vision Aneryn had truly shared.

Despite the looming attack, Councilor Elwyn made it abundantly clear that the competition would continue unhindered. While the guards prepared the city, the competitors were reading old histories of Wynreach and listening to citizen testimonies in the great hall. Many had hypothesized the topic for the compassion trial essays, but Elwyn was remaining tight-lipped until they heard all of the citizens coming forward. After a five-hour session that morning, Carys's brain was mush and she wasn't about to join her competition in the library to make it even mushier.

Instead, she turned toward the kitchens. She'd made fast friends with the green witches who worked there and they'd obliged her in preparing her meals so that she could eat them in her room instead of with the other competitors in the dining commons.

Each day, she drew a little further away from everyone else, and now, with Morgan gone, she realized she hadn't spoken more than a passing word to anyone in two days. She paused at an open window, looking out onto the city. Walls of spiked tree trunks were being erected down strategic roads. Ditches were being dug around the outer walls and barricades covered the port roads. From now on, no one would be coming in or out of the Eastern Court capital. Wynreach was preparing to be under attack.

The hastily constructed plan to lure the beasts and their violet witch mistress into the center of the city was harebrained at best and suicidal at worst. Thus far, Adisa Monroe had evaded every one of her friends' moves. The ancient witch had orchestrated the blue witch armies in the Northern Court without needing to so much as step foot in the North. She had assassinated the Western Court Queen and been nearly successful in inciting a coup. Her attempt to create another poison-minded army in the Southern Court only failed due to Neelo's intervention and even still, she killed the Queen and stole Fenrin away without stepping foot in the castle.

Carys's eyes drifted across the human quarter until they landed on the dilapidated violet witch temple her friends had affectionately nicknamed Lavender Hall. This was once the homeland of the violet witches. Their sacred flower blossomed all along the riverbanks that the city was perched upon. Adisa Monroe would fight for dominion over Wynreach more than any other. Carys sighed. She hoped that meant Adisa Monroe would be pushed to make foolish moves in order to secure her homeland too. If the stakes were higher here, maybe they could shove Adisa Monroe off her back foot and get her to fight them on their own terms.

The sound of a throat clearing made Carys twist back from the window, her eyes landing on Ersan. His eyes widened in his hardened face as he looked her over and Carys wondered what it was he saw in her that caused that flicker of surprise and concern. She forced her face into a steely neutral expression as she dropped her gaze to his outstretched hand and the letter he extended from it.

Carys snatched the note from his hand and looked back up at him.

"I haven't read it." His gaze drifted out the window behind her. "But I know they made it to Arboa safely. Collam is looking forward to hosting them."

Carys's heart ached a little at that. She didn't think she'd miss Morgan as much as she did but she felt her absence like a physical loss, like there was less air in the room suddenly. Everything that kept her moving forward was gone and she felt like she was drifting a little closer into madness with every breath. Gods, she was so weak. She clenched her jaw, forcing down the emotions swinging her from sorrow to rage.

"Thank you," she muttered instead. "For helping her." Ersan shrugged. "I'm surprised—"

"Here we go." He let out a frustrated groan and focused his attention back on her. "You're not surprised. You know me well enough to know I would help her."

"And yet you never wanted to tell me about her, just continuing on with my father's payments to her in secret without me ever the wiser?"

"Yes," Ersan said tightly.

"Why didn't you tell me about her then?"

Ersan just stared at her and said nothing like he always did.

Carys snickered and lifted the letter. "Thanks for this," she said, pushing her way past Ersan.

He sidestepped her, blocking her path. "Weren't you going to the kitchens?" His expression looked frustrated—mean, even—and yet his words were filled with concern. "When's the last time you ate?"

Carys released a short, bitter breath. "It's none of your business."

Ersan opened and closed his mouth, wanting to protest and struggling to find the right thing to say. Carys brushed past him and Ersan took a step after her. Cursing all the Gods, Carys paused to let him speak.

"I want to compete with this famed warrior I keep hearing about," he said as he tried and failed to force levity into his voice. "You've got to be in fighting shape if you want to beat me."

"The next trial is a humanitarian one," Carys countered, continuing to walk down the hall. "I've already proven my fighting skills. But don't worry, Lord Ersan, with the full moon bringing the potential of another attack, I am preparing." Her hollow voice echoed off the stone. "And I will defeat you in the next trial as well."

"Looking forward to seeing you try," he called after her.

She knew he was goading her and she didn't care that it worked. She walked a little faster, head held a little higher, as she contemplated all of the ways she was going to defeat him.

THE THRONE ROOM WAS ACTUALLY ONE OF THE QUIETEST PLACES in the palace these days. Carys found a spot along the dusty rows of heavy wooden banquet tables and pulled out her quill, bottle of ink, and more paper than anyone should need to write a letter. She needed to reply to Morgan's correspondence and make sure the family was settling into Arboa well.

She held Morgan's crinkled letter tight in her grip and she swore she smelled the salty humid air baking off the page. To her surprise, Morgan's first day in Arboa was going surprisingly well. Her normally sarcastic and level-headed sister had nothing but praise for the place . . . well, Morgan's version of praise, which was perfunctory compliments about the architecture and cleanliness. But still, it was a victory. If Morgan had hated the place enough to return, Carys would've been too panicked about their safety to plan with the others for Adisa's impending attack.

The only thing Morgan seemed to disapprove of thus far was its poor carpentry, which she said her husband was already planning on taking care of, giving the local woodworkers lessons in how to better hone their skills. Carys wondered how strange it must be for Morgan— her first time out of Wynreach. It would probably be eased by the delight of her children. Carys already knew they'd love Arboa: swimming in the turquoise waters, running through the blooming fields, waking in the middle of the night to feast and dance. She wished she could be there to see their sweet faces filled with awe.

When she lifted her quill to write that thought down, the doors to the throne room creaked open. Carys expected when she lifted her head to find a servant using the vacant room as a shortcut to the rest of the palace or another competitor wanting to find a quiet space to work, but instead she found none other than Augustus Norwood.

Carys leapt to her feet as he stumbled into the room. His eyes were hooded with drink, a thin cigarette lolling between his lips, his muscled figure wirier than the last time she saw him, and his hair was greasy and matted.

In three steps, Ersan appeared to Carys's left and she stared at him in confusion for a moment before rolling her eyes. He must've been sitting on the garden bench just outside the door. She'd heard someone rustling around out there and had ignored it as one of the palace staff. Now, it was clear Ersan was keeping a close eye on her.

Augustus lifted his hand and mumbled through his lips, still clasping the cigarette. "Calm yourself, Lady Hilgaard, I'm here with a message."

Carys's eyes widened. "How did you get in here? Where are the guards?"

"They ran off to get—"

Councilor Elwyn darted into the room, four guards flanking her either side and her robes flapping behind her like raven's wings.

"Ah." Augustus lifted his hand to her and flourished a bow. "Lord Elwyn's wife, how quaint."

Carys unsheathed her dagger at the insulting way he described the head Councilor, the *shing* of the blade against the scabbard filling the tense silence.

Augustus merely chuckled. "That would be unwise," he said, climbing up the dais and dropping into the throne with a sigh. He ran a finger down the armrest and lifted it to inspect the pad of his fingertip. "You really should have your people dust in here more often. Look at the state of the curtains."

"What are you doing here?" Ersan snapped.

Augustus twisted on the throne, languidly draping his leg over one of the armrests. He narrowed his eyes at Ersan. "Should I know you?"

"No. You shouldn't," Carys said, pressing her lips together as Ersan scowled at her. "But what are you doing here, Augustus? Come to surrender?"

Augustus's shoulder shook with a laugh that ended on a cough. Smoke curled into his white-blond hair as he puffed on his cigarette again. "Hardly."

"And why shouldn't we kill you?" Carys asked as Elwyn cut her a sharp look.

"If you so much as touch me," Augustus said, his beady black eyes scanning the room, "you won't like what comes next. Especially not to your witch friends."

"Fenrin?"

"Your brown witch puppy is still at the mercy of his dear sweet grandmama." Augustus chuckled and Carys cringed at the term of endearment. "If you hurt me, you'll get his head on a spike. Or a roving horde of beasts at your doorstep. Or the smoke that could consume all of your minds in a single breath. Or all of it at once." He touched each of his fingers as he recounted all the ways Adisa Monroe could hurt them. "Oh, or the poisoned blades. I forgot about those." His smile widened. "If that is not enough of a reason, how about I come as a messenger and it wouldn't be very hospitable to kill me when I've come here to help you."

"Help us how?" Elwyn asked, pulling Augustus's gaze to her. It was clear from his look of disdain that he didn't respect Councilor Elwyn's new title.

"Do you have her here, *Councilor*?" he asked, looking around the room. "Fenrin's blue witch lover, is she here?"

"Perhaps," Elwyn hedged.

Amusement crossed Augustus's face. "He whimpers her name at night, *Aneryn, Aneryn!* Like a pathetic lovesick fool—"

"Enough!" Ersan snarled just as Carys unsheathed her sword, now holding a blade in each hand. Carys blinked at Ersan in surprise. He seemed equally ready to decapitate the Norwood prince.

"Ah yes." Augustus snapped as recognition dawned on his face. "This is your Fated, isn't it? That explains this whole angry puffed-up performance . . ." He threw his head back against the satin upholstery and laughed. "Didn't you cut off his leg or something?"

"I did *not*," Carys gritted out through her tightly clenched teeth.

"Your message," Elwyn said again, trying to temper the situation. He held out an open palm to Carys, gesturing for her to sheath her weapons. She did no such thing. "What is it you have to tell us?"

Augustus stood and flicked his cigarette butt onto the stone floor. "The Harvest Moon, of all things, is why I'm here," he said with a bored yawn. "Apparently it is an important time in the witches' calendar, when they need to harvest from their sacred flower. Soon the Crushwold River will be full of seed heads ready to drop next year's crop."

Finally, Carys sheathed her sword and quizzically arched her brow. "That is your message?"

Augustus pulled a fresh cigarette from his pocket and wandered over to the candle lit on the nearest table. "Adisa wants those seeds."

"Why would we give our enemy access to the flower that amplifies her power?" Councilor Elwyn asked.

Augustus turned to her, squinting through the fresh wisps of smoke. "Because she promises not to attack Wynreach if you give her the seeds."

"Gods," Carys whispered, thinking of Aneryn's prophecy and all the lives potentially spared. She glanced at Elwyn, who was frowning at the floor, clearly weighing her options.

When the Councilor's eyes lifted, they went straight to Carys. "What are you thinking?" she asked.

"You defer to her judgment, Lady Elwyn?" Augustus scoffed. "She is not your Queen."

"Not yet," Elwyn said, never breaking eye contact with Carys. The younger woman felt every ounce of the faith that Elwyn placed in her, so confident that she would be the next Queen.

"With those seeds, Adisa might do far worse to far more people," Carys said, thinking of what had nearly happened in the Southern

Court. What if the ancient witch baked the seeds into people's bread or hid them in candle wax or some other sneaky way? What then? She might be able to control every mind in Okrith if she spread those amethyst seeds widely enough. It was too risky. Perhaps it would be better if Carys ordered the entire riverbank of amethyst flowers to be scorched. What control could Adisa have over them without the aid of her sacred flower?

Elwyn seemed to be thinking the same thing, judging by the way her eyes lifted out the window and toward the Crushwold River.

"We decline Adisa's offer," Carys said resolutely, and she swore she felt Ersan shift closer to her.

"So brave," Augustus taunted, taking another long drag from his cigarette. "We'll see how brave you are when this city is being torn apart, your citizens dead, and the High Priestess still gets her seeds. You'll only have yourselves to blame then."

"It's not too late to leave her, Augustus," Carys called after him as he wandered to the throne room doors. "Come back to the side of good, the one that cares about your city and your people."

"There is no undoing what has been done." Augustus shook his head at the floor. "Whatever Fate Okrith befalls, mine and the violet witch's will be the same." He wistfully stared around the room, from the vaulted ceilings to the carved tables to the throne. Finally, he looked at Carys and gave her a mocking wink. "I'll be back on my throne soon, don't drink all the wine."

And with that, he breezed past Elwyn and out the doors, all the guards staring at him like they wanted to chase after him but no one moved.

"I never liked him," Elwyn said, making Carys release a surprised laugh. "Even as a boy. It's good to know I hadn't misjudged him."

"So what do we do now?" Ersan asked.

Elwyn glanced between the two of them, her mouth tightening. "The only thing we can: we stay the course and prepare for a violet witch attack."

CHAPTER TWELVE

The following night was a ridiculous sight—the group of competitors gathered round the hall, poring over sheets of paper, dressed in full suits of armor. The second trial was not at all how Carys envisioned it. They were meant to be writing essays about their plans to help the Eastern Court based on Elwyn's prompts: *How would your reign differ from that of the late King Gedwin Norwood? How do you plan to serve all citizens of Wynreach? What would you want your legacy to be?*

They were meant to have the last few days to plan. But since Aneryn's warning, the night of the full moon was filled with a looming sense of doom. Instead of studying, they'd done everything they could to prepare—to make the city just as Aneryn had envisioned it, but still, no one knew whether they were being clever or foolish.

They'd know by dawn.

Even Carys had protested Councilor Elwyn forcing them to write their second trials as planned on the same night as Aneryn's vision. Trying to focus on word choice felt impossible while they waited for Wynreach to be attacked. Elwyn, however, thought it would be the perfect time to show how well they could work under pressure.

"Being a ruler means coming up with thoughtful decisions under the most intense circumstances," she'd said. "You need to be prepared to rule always, not only when the timing is good for you. The papers are poised to print these essays come the morning, attack or no. More, the people have legitimate problems."

"And we're preparing for the biggest of them," Carys had countered.

"But they need to know there will be a tomorrow. That, once one fight is done, you're ready to take on another right away."

Carys hadn't been able to protest that. One wrong decision might lead a court into an unnecessary civil war. She needed to prove her worth in every possible eventuality.

The city beyond was quiet—not a single laugh or clop of horse hooves echoing through the windows.

Soon they'd all leave for their battle stations across the city, where spiked barricades and pits of tar were strategically placed to herd the beasts—and their mistress—toward the castle. The citizens of Wynreach were instructed to barricade themselves inside and let the creatures past. No pitchforks. No bravado. Let them in quietly and lure them into their trap. Still, Carys thanked the Gods again that she'd sent Morgan away. She'd probably be throwing up with nerves right now if she thought her sister was in danger.

Carys picked at the black ink staining her fingernails as Ivar grumbled. The Northern Lord was incredibly mopey about the fact the second trial was both timed and supervised. It came as no surprise. Carys assumed Ivar had already had a tutor draft up a proposal for him. He probably hadn't even read it, thinking he could just slip it to the printers in place of whatever drivel he was currently writing. Carys pressed her lips together, delighting in Ivar's discontentment. Maybe this time he'd finally be cut from the competition . . . though she doubted she'd be that lucky.

No, Ivar would get a pass straight through the top of the heap, purely from his name and wealth. He looked like a king with his strong jawline, piercing eyes, and serious face that hinted at a knowing smirk. No other skills seemed to matter. He was what the people had always known a ruler to be and, despite the clear need for change, they couldn't seem to get the desire for Ivar on a throne out of their collective minds . . . second only to their desire for Carys on their throne.

Carys shook out her hands and grabbed her quill again, tapping the tip on the ink bottle and starting on her next sheet of paper. She turned Elwyn's prompts over and over in her mind. Each needed to be addressed thoroughly and strategically. Her plans for the Eastern Court needed to be specific yet broad enough that everyone could picture their lives within it—appealing to people who wanted to keep the status quo while still pushing for more equality. Carys needed to be different enough that the witches and humans didn't fear another Gedwin Norwood, yet similar enough that the fae could imagine her as Queen. She stifled a groan as she propped her elbows back on the table. She was no better than Ivar—regal looks, family name, wealth, and allies in every corner of Okrith.

She began writing again, determined that her own work would be of more merit than her inborn advantages.

Councilor Elwyn's chair creaked and her satin slippers scuffed across the floor. She was only one of two people not dressed in armor and she was making her way toward the second.

"We've only just commenced," Councilor Elwyn whispered, her robes draping onto Aneryn's table as she leaned in. "We have two more hours."

"We don't have two more hours. Besides, I'm done," Aneryn said, her eyes glowing so brightly they illuminated her whole face.

Her eyes seemed to be in a constant state of flickering sapphire over the past few days as if magic was seeping out of her uncontrolled. Carys knew whatever she was conjuring for the full moon was deep and powerful. Aneryn hadn't been interested in hearing their plans for capturing Adisa Monroe after the night of the beast attack. She didn't seem to care about the mazelike network through the city to trap all the beasts either. When they tried to ask her if this was all set up like her vision, she'd just vaguely nod. Carys didn't know if that was because the blue witch had already Seen it or because she simply didn't care anymore. Her Sight seemed solely focused elsewhere now.

"This is it?" Councilor Elwyn balked, lifting Aneryn's page. "*Make Fenrin my king.* That's your only plan?"

The room echoed with whispered grumbles.

"I told you she'd side with the witches," Prestev groused to Ivar. "They should've never allowed a witch into the competition."

"If we tell Adisa Monroe her heir will be on the Eastern Court throne," Aneryn said calmly, turning her fearsome gaze to Prestev and making him glance away, "there will be no need for her planned violence. We can pull her into the fold and I can get through to Fenrin."

"That's awfully confident," Ivar spat. "And if you can't we've put an evil witch's puppet on the throne."

"*If*," Aneryn gave Ivar a sharp look, "we promise to put Fenrin on the throne as ruler over all of the East, even the fae, Augustus Norwood will be cut out of Adisa's plans. She always planned on betraying him in favor of Fenrin, though Norwood is too arrogant to see it." Aneryn cocked her head, her mind seemingly floating farther into the future. "Augustus's soldiers will leave with him. There will be in-fighting amongst Adisa's camp. We will create fissures we can turn into gaping chasms until she stands alone." Carys snorted and Aneryn's eyes flashed to her. "You disagree?"

Any other competitor would shudder under Aneryn's powerful glare, but Carys straightened her shoulders and said, "I do. Your whole plan functions under the assumption that Adisa Monroe requires their loyalty, when at every turn we've seen she *takes* it from their own minds. The soldiers fighting for her won't have the ability to deny her. She owns them." Carys hated how Ivar and Prestev tutted in agreement. She didn't want them to be on her side, but she couldn't agree with Aneryn just to avoid that. "Adisa has her poisoned smoke and metals. She has beasts of her own making. She has the amethyst dagger and immortality." Carys shook her head. "She doesn't need loyalty."

Aneryn's bench seat screeched across the stone as she pushed back and stood. "Her entire plan hinges on her youngest heir. *When the blood moon rises and the stars fall, the smallest seed shall be King.*"

"I hadn't heard that first part before." Carys's eyes narrowed. "How do you know that?"

"I've been doing my own research." Aneryn stiffened. "It was the blue witches, *my* people, who told her that prophecy centuries ago." Her fingers flickered a deep blue as she curled them into fists. "It was a blue witch's prophecy that sparked all of the chaos we see around us now. It was my ancestor's words that incited her to act. If she believes Fenrin will one day be King, we make him King now, and all her power will fade along with the completion of that prophecy. There will be nothing more to fight for. No more monsters. No more poisons."

"We cannot just let her win," Ivar growled, his armor rattling as he stood. "Your plan is to surrender?"

"My plan is to end the dying."

"This isn't the answer to my three questions," Elwyn said, calmly cutting above the fray. "An answer like this will see you eliminated from the competition."

Aneryn laughed derisively. "I've already given my real essay to the printers."

Elwyn leaned back, caught off-guard by the statement. "But I've only just announced the questions. How do you even know which printer to deliver them to?"

Aneryn lifted her swirling blue hands and raised her eyebrows at the Councilor. It seemed Aneryn was more than two steps ahead of the rest of them now, her Sight practically consuming her.

Shouts echoed from the distance, interrupting their discussion, and the group tensed, hands reaching for swords, eyes scanning for sudden threats, ears straining to pinpoint the start of the chaos. Carys hated that she wondered, and not for the first time, if Aneryn's love of Fenrin was blinding her to reality. She hated even more that she wondered if they could still trust Aneryn to tell them the truth of her visions. Would Aneryn risk them all in order to save the witch she loved?

"Making Fenrin King is a wiser plan than digging in our heels and fighting an ancient witch," Aneryn said, pulling the group's focus back to her. "I plan on surrendering to Fenrin and Fenrin alone." Another shout rang out and the heavy wooden door creaked open. "Tonight."

A harried-looking messenger rushed to Councilor Elwyn's side.

"There are five beasts outside the city gates. They've come earlier than expected, Councilor." He panted and clutched his side. "And she's here with them. The guards on the north wall have spotted her with that tall blond witch."

Aneryn's magic erupted at the messenger's words. Her whole body flamed a brilliant blue as she whispered, "Fenrin," and stormed toward the door.

"Aneryn, wait!" Carys called, rushing after her. She turned to the messenger. "How old was this brown witch?"

Aneryn paused and the messenger's brow crinkled in confusion. "Early fifties, maybe?" he hedged.

Aneryn's shoulders slumped. "Cole." It was Fenrin's uncle at the gates with Adisa Monroe. Still, hope ignited within Carys that maybe they'd be able to save Cole that night, and Fenrin soon after.

Carys tried to reach for Aneryn's arm, but her entire body was burning like an inferno. Normally Aneryn's magic wasn't hot to the touch, but now the air around the blue witch warped and twisted, burning hotter than a smith's forge. Whatever was building inside Aneryn, Carys feared it might explode.

"I'm not going to him," Aneryn said, her voice strained and distant as Carys snatched her hand back from her burning skin. "It's the full moon. I'm going to my room to pray." Aneryn didn't pause, didn't look back, as she marched out of the room and up the stairs.

Carys wanted to run after her but Councilor Elwyn's hand landed on her shoulder.

"Let her go. Give her some time. Carys," Councilor Elwyn said, pulling Carys's focus back to her resolute face. "We stick to the plan. Are you still patrolling the barricades in the human quarter?"

The breeze from the open door fluttered the abandoned papers off the tables and to the floor. She'd volunteered to protect the area closest to her sister's home. Even with Morgan away, her sister's house and her friends were all still there in the human quarter, and if one of the beasts broke free of their trap, Carys knew she'd fight harder than the rest of the competitors to protect the area.

She took a deep breath. "Yes."

"Then go." Councilor Elwyn nodded and turned back to the messenger. "Open the gates."

THE NIGHT WAS EERILY SILENT, NOT A SINGLE PERSON ROAMED the streets. Not even the stray dogs and cats scavenged, as if even they knew that danger was afoot. Every window was shut, every door closed, and Carys would've thought the city was abandoned were it not for the flickers of candlelight between shutters and the hushed whispers of voices beyond barred doors. She ran in stealth and silence to the barricades stationed just outside the human quarter.

Willing her heavy breathing to silence, Carys dropped into a crouch behind the wall of spiked wood, and waited. Her ears strained to hear the distant growls and clamor in a far corner of the city, but heard nothing. Maybe the beasts would all turn down toward the center of the city as planned, funneled by the blocked roads to the very heart of Wynreach, where a battalion of soldiers waited to pounce upon them. Looking up to the white swollen moon, she prayed to the Gods that the plan would work.

Adisa Monroe was finally here. And they could catch her if she stayed on the right thoroughfare. They could *end* this. Then they'd bar the gates behind her and trap her within the palace walls. Carys's mind roiled, churning through thought after thought of every way this plan could go wrong. It seemed too simple, too easy, and she was beginning to distrust Aneryn's visions. The blue witch seemed too lost in her own mind to be reliable anymore.

A shriek erupted into the night and Carys grabbed the hilt of her sword, the chilly metal biting into her palm and making her take a steeling breath. It sounded like one of the creatures had found a spike pit. The crashing and shattering of glass grew louder, along with the thunder of heavy feet. Fear gripped Carys tighter with the unsettling calm around her clashing with the chaotic distant sounds.

Gods, could three beasts be enough to make that noise? Were there others? It sounded like a stampede. Maybe the other beasts were startled. Maybe they'd bowl over a barricade and go in the wrong direction.

Please not the human quarter. Please.

The thundering sounds faded into the distance.

Good.

She was about to pop up from her crouch to peek between the barricades when a low rumble shook the ground, pebbles bouncing across the street like when a herd of wild horses galloped too close.

Shit.

The thud, thud, thud of heavy paws drew closer, so close she could smell the beast's musky fur and putrid breath like a dead rat left too long in a trap.

A shuddering roar rent the air, the sound so loud that the nearest windows shattered and Carys tipped to the side, releasing her sword to cover her sensitive ears. She heard a few faint screams from behind the closed doors throughout the human quarter.

Thud, thud, thud, the beast stalked closer to the barricade. Then the sound paused and she heard the sniffing. The creature was scenting the air . . . would it be able to pinpoint Carys? She twisted to peek between the slats of wood propping up the spiked posts. The beast was right up against the barricade now—sniffing—searching for her, no doubt, an easy meal to pluck up on its way toward the palace.

Good, she thought. Let it waltz right up to her. She'd stab her sword straight through its yellow eye. Just one more step and she'd be in striking distance—one less beast terrorizing the city. And she hated to admit how much she wanted the acclaim it would bring her too—another victory on her quest for the crown.

But then she heard it—a whimper.

Carys looked over her shoulder, down the abandoned street, and what she saw doused her whole body in ice. A little girl, no more than five years old, stood frozen in the middle of the street, tears welling in her wide eyes.

"Go back inside," Carys mouthed to her, pointing at the nearest door. But all the doors on the street were shut. Wherever this child had come from, it wasn't this street.

A distant, frantic voice called, "Lilly! Lilly!" The girl's mother, Carys presumed, probably frightened out of her wits searching for her daughter during a siege.

"Turn around." Carys twirled her finger, frantically trying to shoo the girl without making a sound and alerting the creature at her back. "Go back!"

But the girl was frozen, transfixed at whatever she saw from beyond the barricade. The beast sniffed the air again and the girl trembled.

Carys held up a finger to her lips, pleading with the girl to remain silent, but when the beast snarled, the girl shrieked, and the world erupted into chaos.

"Shit," Carys barked, rising from her crouch and sprinting at full speed toward the girl as the barricade exploded in splinters.

She didn't turn, didn't look, as she scooped the child roughly up into her arms and kept barreling forward, barely able to keep her feet underneath her. The beast roared again, its thundering paws pounding the ground after them. How in the Gods' names had it broken through that barricade without impaling itself? How was it still alive?

She raced faster, turning down an alleyway in hopes of losing the beast. Wood flew in every direction as the creature took the corner too sharply and tried to chase after them. Carys ducked and weaved through the city square and down another alley, finding a low bridge over a dry riverbed to shelter under.

The little girl shrieked and sobbed in her arms.

"Shh. Shh. It's all right," Carys whispered, sweeping the hair out of the girl's face. Gods, she looked so much like Molly, so rosy-cheeked and small. Her chest cracked at the sight of the girl's terror. "It will be all right, love. It will," she promised. "But we need to stay quiet, okay?"

The little girl trembled like a sapling in a hurricane, but she nodded. Carys heard the beast stalking through the square, hunting them down, and she debated leaving the girl hidden so she could go fight the creature. She looked down into the frightened girl's eyes and knew she couldn't leave her alone. If she didn't kill the creature, it might double back and find the girl out in the open.

"Lilly!" the mother's voice screamed again, much closer this time.

Gods, just shut up, she thought, even as she knew that would have been impossible for her had it been her own kin. Carys peeked round the edge of the bridge and watched as the beast lifted its head in the direction of the sound and took off at a run.

"Mama!" the girl cried.

"Gods," Carys groaned aloud this time, looking back down at the wide eyes of the girl in her arms. "We're going to go find your mama. Just be *quiet*. Hang on tight, okay?"

The girl didn't have time to nod before Carys broke out into a sprint again, balancing the jostling girl atop the lip of her weapons belt as she ran after the creature. She'd never hear the end of it if her friends knew she was *chasing after* a monster instead of running from it.

When they neared the grain stores on the edge of the human block, Carys saw the little girl's mother standing in the doorway of the barn, looking past the beast to Carys.

"Lilly!" she screamed with equal parts panic and relief.

"Shut up and get inside!" Carys shouted back, her voice shredding. "Now!"

Her screams pulled the beast's attention around again and she darted down the side of the barn, the passage so small, she could barely squeeze through. The beast sniffed the air again and stalked back and forth across the barn door as Carys made her way around to the back.

Carys rapped on the massive feed chute out the back of the barn. "We're here," she hissed and the latch to the window beside it flipped open.

The tear-streaked face of the woman appeared. "Oh, thank all the Gods," she sobbed.

Lilly practically flung herself out of Carys's arms to her mother. The woman buried her head in her daughter's hair, squeezing her as she cried and shook.

"Keep this door shut," Carys said tightly. "Keep your mouths shut. Don't open either until the palace guards come to give the all clear. Understood?"

"Come in with us," the woman beckoned with a trembling hand.

Carys shook her head. "That thing is behind the barricades now," she said, unsheathing her sword. "It could hurt a lot of people if I don't kill it. Now, stay inside."

"Th-thank you," the woman wept. "Thank you for saving my baby."

Carys swallowed the lump in her throat at the woman's words, as more shrieks sounded from the other side of the city.

She turned without another word and raced back through the alley to find the beast, but it was already tearing down toward the harbor.

"Shit," she hissed, picking up speed. She trained her eyes on the monster in the distance, leading with her chest and legs burning, so focused—too focused—to realize she was chasing after a different monster . . . and the one she'd first saw was right behind her.

CHAPTER THIRTEEN

The beast's breath made the hairs on the back of her neck stand on end, and Carys slowly turned to face the snarling creature. On giant lion's paws, the beast took a slow, stalking step toward her. Even as her heart raced, she willed herself to think. What was her best course of action right now? A thousand options raced through her mind, varying from ducking into the nearest doorway to attacking with her sword and facing the beast right then and there. But the image of splintering wood and flying debris flashed back into her thoughts. She glanced from side to side.

As the beast took another slow step, Carys knew she couldn't battle it right there. Too many humans were crammed into the townhouses on either side of them. The city was densely packed in this area and any combat would surely destroy their houses, and worse, get some of them killed. No. First she needed to lead this beast away from all the people and into a safer area of Wynreach, then she could end it.

Her mind spiderwebbed, thinking of the city streets as she mapped out her plans. She needed this creature to tail here through streets wide enough that it wouldn't destroy the buildings, but winding enough that it wouldn't easily outrun her . . . and snap her up into its massive jaws.

The beast took another prowling step and Carys knew her planning time had reached its end. Whatever she was going to do, right then, she needed to run.

She turned and bolted down the street, the beast releasing an ear-piercing roar as it chased after her. She willed her legs to run faster, faster, as she darted down Cobblers Row and twisted toward the markets. The beast swiped at her, her skin prickling with the sense of its nearness. Too close.

She sucked in heavy panting breaths as she ducked down the main thoroughfare and left back through the fishmongers' stalls. The beast roared again, only a few paces behind her as she ran.

Moving right, she tried to dart down another side road, but it was barricaded. *Shit. It's not supposed to keep me in.* The thought almost made her laugh, except the paws on the street behind her smothered that emotion. She ran faster, chasing downhill toward the docks. She feigned right again and then swerved left, turning back toward the markets but that path too was barricaded. Gods curse her, this might be it.

She kept running, trying to think on her feet, even as the road was narrowing and there were only a few more streets until she was at the docks. Could she jump in the Crushwold River? The beast surely wouldn't leap after her, would it? Could lions even swim? And even if they could, Carys would be able to climb back up onto the docks more swiftly and run away.

Except there was a chance the beast would abandon its chase and simply turn around to hunt for easier prey amongst the tightly packed townhouses . . .

She was going to curse again, but was sure the Gods wanted nothing to do with this night.

As her boots echoed onto the wobbling docks, Carys held her sword higher, pumping her arms to keep moving. She needed to end this now. She felt the exact moment that the beast landed on the docks, the wood beneath her feet rocking so wildly that she thought she might land straight in the water. Arms wheeling, she regained her balance and kept running.

Don't stop. Don't stop.

The merchant vessels and fishing boats rocked erratically side to side from the waves they created, but Carys kept her eyes focused on the last boat. It was a small fishing vessel, with tattered sails and a weather-worn look about it, but the only thing she needed to see was the coil of rope holding aloft one of the bait barrels.

Go. Go. Go. She willed herself forward, racing toward the fishing boat as the beast barged after her. She'd only have one chance at this. There could be no error.

She reached the boat in three more strides and leapt, cutting the bait rope with her sword. The barrel dropped like a stone and the rope Carys held on to hoisted her up into the air. Flailing her legs, she turned to face the beast as she lurched up to its head height. It reared its head, snapping up at her with its horrible tusks and rancid teeth, but the angle was unexpected and it couldn't quite catch her.

Carys struck out, slicing open the beast's neck. Blood poured from the gaping wound as the beast turned, but its forward momentum was too strong, pulling it sideways and off the docks. With an explosion of water, the creature plummeted into the black water of the Crushwold River.

Carys's chest heaved as she dangled there, watching the burbling water, waiting to see if the creature would emerge. Even with that sliced-open throat, she couldn't be sure. It was a made creature—a monster of an ancient violet witch. Maybe it was just as immortal as Adisa was herself. But the deluge of bubbles slowed and minutes passed with not a single one rising to the surface. Finally, Carys let out a long-held breath and dropped from where she dangled on the rope.

Her hand burned, filled with splintering rough burlap, and her shoulder ached from the sharp jolt upward, but she was alive, and mostly unscathed. She was alive and would heal—again, if she got through the rest of this assault without too much damage. She turned back to the city and all was quiet once more. The brilliant light of the full moon illuminated the human quarter as clear as day as she scoured the cityscape for more destruction. Wherever the other beast she'd spotted was, it was either dead or long gone.

Carys doubled over, placing her hands on her knees and spitting onto the docks, her stomach churning acid as she came down from her panicked run. She only had a moment's peace before she heard a burbling sound beside the boat and fear strangled her again. Leaning over the side of the boat, bile burned up her throat, her entire face flushing red at the horror of what she saw.

There, floating naked with his throat sliced wide open, was Augustus Norwood.

"Wh-what in the Gods' names," she panted, her stomach lurching and bile spilling from her mouth into the black waters.

Augustus Norwood *was* the lion monster? Her mind spun; her legs shook so badly she needed to lean into the railing. Were all of Adisa's monsters actually people controlled by the violet witch? No. It couldn't be . . . none of the others had changed into different bodies after their death. But then how did this happen? Shocked tears filled her eyes. She'd just killed Augustus Norwood.

Carys vaguely registered that someone was calling her name.

She lifted her head, sweeping her braid back over her shoulder as she spotted Ersan bolting down the hill toward her. Carys noted how he visibly sagged in relief when he took her in—alive and seemingly uninjured.

"Carys!" There was something about the way he called her name that made her break into a run before even knowing what he was shouting, but noting by the way he ran that it was enough to be alarmed.

"What is it?" she called, her throat stinging with every word. For Ersan to be seeking her out, it must be bad. "Are you hurt?"

He shook his head, breathlessly pausing mid-street when he realized Carys was running back up toward him. The panic in his eyes quickly morphed to sorrow. "It's Aneryn."

WHEN CARYS JUMPED OUT ONTO THE LEDGE OF THE LIBRARY'S roof, a swarm of people were already there. She gasped at what she saw: Aneryn sprawled across the cold stone, the items of her totem pouch strewn around her along with stacks of old books. Faint blue flames flickered from her fingertips and her closed eyelids. Carys rushed over, dropping hard onto her knees as she checked Aneryn's pulse.

"She's still alive," she said, jolting as Ehiris screeched from the skies. The hawk dove down in sharp strikes and the others all took a step back from Aneryn's body.

"Yes," Councilor Elwyn replied, her hands clasped anxiously in front of her. "But she is in some sort of trance. She can't be roused from it. We've tried."

Carys shook Aneryn by the shoulder, fingers digging in tightly in the faint hope this was all an elaborate ruse. But Aneryn didn't budge, her breathing slow and deep.

"Carys," Ersan murmured from behind her, taking a step closer.

"You've just left her here?" Carys looked around the group of gawking onlookers, pinning each with an accusatory stare. "Someone fetch a brown witch!" She pointed at an elderly fae who stood wringing his hands, his lip curling down at Aneryn as if she were some sort of oddity. "You!" Carys pointed at him. "Go get her a blanket."

The elderly fae looked flummoxed by her request, whether it was because he wasn't used to being given orders or he didn't think a witch worthy of such compassion, she didn't know, but both incensed her.

"We wanted to get the full picture of what happened first." Councilor Elwyn's voice was even and calm, clearly trying to rein in Carys's rising wave of emotions. The rooftop quickly emptied of the other fae as Elwyn looked at them one by one, giving them a silent command to leave. Only Ersan remained behind, his breathing still heavy enough for Carys to hear behind her. Once the rest were gone, Elwyn said, "I should've never let her work on her own projects on the side."

"What projects?" Carys stared up at the gray-eyed Councilor. "You knew about this?" She scanned across the books and piles of totems: beads, feathers, unmarked elixir bottles . . . "What was she doing?"

"She said she was trying to help Fenrin," Elwyn replied, ducking as Ehiris swooped down again. The hawk was clearly distraught over his owner's state but Carys had no idea how to calm an upset hawk. "That she was determined to find a way to bring him back and that if she succeeded, it would help us all."

Carys frowned down at her friend; she'd told Carys just as much. "But she didn't tell you what or how?"

"She kept her secrets close. She seemed hesitant to tell me any more than that."

"She did the same with me," Carys lamented. "She said it was too dangerous for us to know more of her plans." Carys reached to take Aneryn's hands in her own. "An—" She paused when she felt Aneryn's left hand still clutched around something.

Carys didn't know why she didn't alert Elwyn to the object in Aneryn's grip, but some gut instinct told her to keep it quiet. Whatever happened before Aneryn's magic went awry, this was the last thing she'd thought about. Carys waited until Elwyn looked out to the full moon and when the Councilor turned away, she grabbed the item from Aneryn's hand and shoved it in her pocket without looking. She knew Ersan, always tracking her movements, caught it, but she also knew he wouldn't say anything until they were alone. A silent conversation seemed to flow between them, one they'd had so many times in their youth. Whatever Carys's reasons for keeping the item a secret from Elwyn, Ersan wouldn't call her out on it.

Not yet, anyway.

She sat back against the sloping rooftop of the library and picked up one of the heavy texts. It was written in Mhenbic, the witches' language, and Carys had no idea what it said, but the drawing on the borders of each page made her think it was a spell book. Flowers and herbs, bones and stones, decorated the pages, some repeating, others unique like the indigo feather prominently painted across one page. Had Aneryn been casting a spell when this happened? Had she been trying to find a way to wake Fenrin up from his mind-controlling trance and instead cursed herself into her own?

"We did it, though," Elwyn said, turning back to Carys and shaking her head slightly in disbelief. "We captured Adisa Monroe. That wouldn't have happened without Aneryn's Sight."

Carys stared out at the city, now milling about with people despite the late hour. Everyone seemed to have left their homes to inspect the damage and tear down the barricades. "How was Adisa captured?"

"Easily." Elwyn's words were restrained, too cautious to make Carys feel comforted.

"Some might say too easily," Ersan added.

Carys looked between the two of them, reading the words left unsaid. "Do you think she intended on being captured?"

"I think she doesn't care where in all of Okrith she is." Elwyn sighed, folding her hands inside her robes. "I think she can get wherever she needs to go through the minds of others. Perhaps she's exactly where she wants to be, but that doesn't mean we can't use it to our advantage."

Carys shuddered and her whole body throbbed with pain. She hated the way Ersan's posture tightened as if he could sense the exact stinging of cuts and the twang of nearly torn muscles that flooded through her.

Carys suddenly remembered how she was almost eaten by a mountain lion monster . . . one who was actually Augustus Norwood. The adrenaline of finding Aneryn had kept her going, moving forward and ignoring the aches and pains in her body, ignoring the utter fear of seeing that little girl alone in the street and Norwood's naked body floating in the river.

Elwyn pointed out at the far gates, now closed once more. "Aneryn's estimates were off. There were actually nine beasts in all. We only managed to slay three of them . . . one thanks to you." She shook her head in bemusement. "Fifty royal guards to take down two giant beasts, one foolish blond warrior to take down the other."

"If you knew her better, you wouldn't be so surprised," Ersan said, rubbing his hand down his jaw with an amused expression.

Carys rolled her eyes. "I was trying to save a little girl who'd been separated from her mother."

"Well, the people will enjoy that, at least." Elwyn hmphed. "A hero's story if ever there was one—slaying a mountain lion to save a small child, just like the legends of Eastern Kings past. Songs will be sung of their Queen's glory forever."

"If she becomes Queen," Ersan reminded and Elwyn only hummed. Even Elwyn, with all her power and influence, couldn't place a crown atop Carys's head on her own. She would respect her people's vote, even if she and Carys had grown close, but Carys knew Elwyn would spin this tale of her slaying the lion into something worthy of legends nevertheless.

"I need to go collect the competitors' essays before they're due to the printers," Elwyn said. "You still have some time, if you'd like to write more."

Carys let out a little half grunt, not breaking her stare from Aneryn. She and Elwyn both already knew her answer to that. "I've said enough," Carys murmured. "Print what you have." She shouldn't have been surprised that Elwyn was still focused on the competition even in the aftermath of the attack.

"You should go inside at least," Elwyn urged. "Bathe. Rest. I will make sure Aneryn is taken to her room and cared for."

"No," Carys said resolutely, giving Aneryn's hand one last squeeze before rising to a stand. "I need to see that bloody violet witch with my own two eyes."

"I thought you'd say that," Elwyn huffed. She turned to one of the remaining fae lingering by the sloping rooftop. "You gather the essays," she instructed him. "They need to be in the hands of the printer by dawn."

Ersan took a step forward. "I'm coming too."

"No," Carys insisted and he scowled at her. "We can handle this."

His jaw muscles flickered in irritation. "Why must you always do this?"

"Do what?"

"This," he growled, waving between them. Elwyn looked back out to the cityscape, clearly trying to escape their latest bout of childish antagonism.

"Go back to your chambers, Lord Ersan," Carys said tightly, throwing his title in to remind him that they were no longer friends.

His eyes narrowed and she thought he might protest. "Stubborn as ever, *Lady Hilgaard*."

A spark of anger accompanied a flash of lust-filled heat as Carys folded her arms. These fights usually ended one of two ways: with fists or fucking and Carys was not about to let them slip back into their old ways.

It was this strange unspoken thing between them—this odd sense of ownership that Carys, too felt even though she wished she didn't. They might both want to kill each other most of the time, but they also wouldn't let anyone else do it either. Whether they liked it or not, they were still protective of each other. Ersan climbed along the ledge back toward the open library window and Carys turned back to Elwyn.

"Let's go see this witch."

"As you wish." Elwyn sighed, rubbing her hands together. "Though you won't be seeing much of her where she is."

Carys's stomach dropped. "And where is she?"

Elwyn turned slowly to Carys, her eyes filled with warning that where they were about to go would not be pleasant. "The pit."

CHAPTER FOURTEEN

They wound their way down the spiral staircase, deeper into the belly of the castle with every step. The place had never been touched by sunlight, lit only by flickering torches placed so far apart that Carys and Councilor Elwyn had to feel through the darkness for brief spans before reaching the next flame.

"When Gedwin Norwood was King," Elwyn whispered—any louder of a voice would've seemed wrong in the thick, inky blackness—"this place used to howl with the screams of tortured prisoners. I can hear it still." She lifted the hem of her robes as she stepped over an ominous puddle. Water leaked from the cracks in the ceiling above them in a sinister drip, drip, drip. "I still smell the rancid stench of bile and blood."

Elwyn took an instinctive step closer as she spoke and it made Carys puff out her chest and assume the posture of a soldier on patrol. She was grateful for it, actually. Elwyn's fear made Carys push her own aside.

"Hale said his father used to *station* him down here as a boy to teach him a lesson," Carys muttered, thinking how her childhood had been learning archery on horseback and having tea in the gardens around Hilgaard castle. Each of her friends had grown up in the floodwaters of tribulation—Hale, Remy, Bri, Rua, Renwick, even Neelo—and her own struggles and losses were nothing compared to their childhood torments. Carys rolled her shoulders back and shook out her hands. Now was probably not the best time to be thinking of her past.

"I think King Norwood hoped Hale would catch one of the many illnesses being spread amongst the prisoners," Elwyn added, grabbing a torch off the wall. "Here," she said, walking to what appeared to be the end of the hallway and turning to her right. Behind the final beam was a hidden narrow hall that sloped down at a steep angle, the entire length unlit by even a single flickering flame.

"Down there?" Carys swallowed the lump in her throat as she peered down at the sloping floor that led into the bowels of the palace dungeons. Rivulets of putrid water traced down the stones, carving crevices deep into the floor.

"I told you, she's in the pit."

"You put her in a literal pit?" Carys's eyes widened as she stared into the pitch blackness. "I thought that was just a scary nickname for a dungeon cell . . ." She straightened her shoulders and lifted her chin, forcing her body back into a queenly posture—her physical body a gateway to the bravery she sought. If this was to be her palace one day, she couldn't be afraid of its many secrets.

Again she reminded herself she was a warrior, even as she tried not to cling to the circle of light cast by Elwyn's torch. As Carys strained to hear any sound, they walked in complete silence for several minutes, lower and lower until her breath frosted in front of her face. She folded her arms, thrusting her hands into her armpits for warmth. Finally, they reached a door and Elwyn pulled out another key.

"That's five locked doors we've ventured through to get here," Carys muttered.

"You still think it's not safe to keep her here?" Elwyn mused as she passed the torch to Carys and put the key in the lock. The door groaned like an old matron rising from a low chair.

Walking around the curving wall, they hugged the sides as the mouth of the pit appeared in front of them.

Carys's eyebrows lifted as she glanced at Elwyn. "I thought it would be bigger."

Elwyn's face flickered amongst sharp shadows of the torchlight as her lips pressed together. "Its narrowness is on purpose," she replied quietly. "Wide enough for only a single person to sit. Imagine what it was like when five prisoners were thrown in there at once."

"I'm certain they'd be spilling whatever secrets Norwood desired after a few hours down there, let alone days." Carys grimaced, tiptoeing closer to the hole. Judging by the length of coiled rope that hung from the wall, the pit was several stories deep.

A low hum echoed up from the pit and she froze. "Listen to those steps. Confident but delicate," a rough voice called out through the pitch black in an unnerving singsong. "The Lady Hilgaard comes to call, I presume."

"Well, I guess you haven't died down there," Carys gritted out.

"I can't die," Adisa Monroe scoffed as if the mere suggestion was offensive. "And I have plenty of bones down here to keep me company while I wait for my heir to take the throne high above my head."

"We'll see how you feel about that in another few days."

A wicked cackle echoed up the pit, the high-pitched grating noise making Carys grind her teeth. "Silly child. I have lain awake in a grave for *hundreds* of years. You think this pit will scare me?" Her voice disappeared from Carys's ears but Adisa continued, whispering straight into Carys's thoughts. *My mind is still everywhere.*

Carys jolted back, smacking into the cold stone wall. "How?"

"I have my ways," the witch taunted aloud again.

Carys wracked through her memory, trying to think of any way she might have come into contact with the blooming amethyst flower. The plant had been banned from all manner of things since Neelo had discovered the link between the purple flower and the violet witch's mind control, but that didn't mean it couldn't be put into other things.

Because Carys didn't wear perfume . . . and she washed her hair with citrus scents, not floral. How could Adisa Monroe possibly be able to whisper into her mind? The wildflower blooms had all withered this late in the season, soon they'd all go to seed—seeds that Adisa apparently had wanted to claim. Carys's mind drifted to the blooms along the Crushwold River and then to the river itself, which was probably still carrying Augustus Norwood's body downriver unless someone had found him and fished him out. Carys tried to push thoughts of Augustus from her mind, afraid that Adisa might be able to see the image even from within her own memory.

You will never guess how I got into your mind. Adisa's low voice filled Carys's thoughts again, the sensation like a thousand ants crawling across her skin. Then, aloud, "I'm quite content to wait here until your doom befalls you."

"Where exactly is the implement of this destruction?" Councilor Elwyn asked, her back pressed flush against the wall and even in the dimness, Carys could see the sheen of sweat that beaded on her brow despite the frigid temperatures of the dungeon. "Where is your amethyst dagger?"

"With its true master," Adisa called back. "That dagger is his birthright. Fenrin will remake the world with our coven's talisman. 'The blood moon comes, the smallest seed shall be King.'"

Carys bunched her hands into fists at the name of her friend. "Fenrin would never harm us if you hadn't wormed your way into his mind."

"Are you so sure about that, Lady Hilgaard?" The click of the witch's tongue reverberated over and over off the walls. "Maybe I am simply waking him up. Have you actually spent much time getting to know the lad? Or did you glance over him like you do every witch?"

"Fenrin is my *friend*," Carys hissed, taking another step forward. Adisa's cackle was her only response. "He's a good man and you stole his mind from him."

"I didn't toil in my grave for centuries, child, twiddling my thumbs," Adisa said. "I *plotted*, waiting for when the prophecy of my coven's legacy would finally come true. From the moment I was exhumed, I set out to find my youngest heir and place him on the throne of the East. It was time for the violet witches to rise again." She sighed, the clattering of bones indicating she'd shifted her position. "For a long while I'd thought it was Hale Norwood. It made so much sense—a crown prince and a fae to boot, carrying my witch blood in his veins—think of the havoc he could've wrought on this court. When I saw that red star fall from the sky, I knew it was time to act, but when I laid eyes upon Hale Norwood in Swifthill, I realized immediately he wasn't the one. There was another."

"So, you found Fenrin."

"He is the youngest, the true heir, the King. He will usher in the new era of witches upon the Wynreach throne—one of prosperity and supremacy for us." Her voice rose as if summoning a battle cry. "All fae will bow to the violet coven. We shall reign over all of Okrith."

Carys's heart thundered in her chest. "You shall die before you see that day."

"You think that threat scares me? You are all such silly, ineffectual beings. So unimaginative. You simple child, I *welcome* death, if you can find a way to do it." Adisa's laughter was vicious. "The prophecy is already set into motion. My life is inconsequential now. 'The smallest seed shall be King.' I have Seen it. Fenrin *will* sit on the Eastern throne."

"Where is he?" Carys grabbed the hilt of her sword. "What have you done with him? And where is Cole? What did you do to turn your beasts?"

"So many questions." The witch cackled again. "If you'd like to talk about the delivery of my blooming amethyst seeds, then I am happy to share the answers."

"So you can arm yourself with poisoned blades and control the minds of armies of people again?" Carys asked. "I think not."

"Then think again. If you so much as destroy a single one of my sacred flowers, I will bring a reckoning the likes of which this world has never known." The witch's voice was so dark and venomous that Carys held her breath as she spoke. "Well," she considered. "The reckoning is coming regardless, but I'll make you suffer before your end. Now stop being foolish and send someone to collect my seeds."

"Perhaps we should drop the nearest torch into the lot of them." Carys attempted to sound taunting but her voice wobbled. "Maybe we should burn them all."

"Do you not listen? Do it and see what happens. I dare you." Adisa cackled. A yawning sound echoed up the pit. "I think I'm done with our visit. Fare thee well, Lady Hilgaard, Lady Elwyn."

Councilor Elwyn's eyes flew wide and she inched away further— all her stoicism and command disappearing at the sound of her name on the ancient witch's lips.

Rage rose like a cresting wave within Carys. To be so arrogantly dismissed by their own prisoner. The leash to all her restraint snapped and a booming shout erupted from Carys. "Tell me where Fenrin is!" She was met with nothing but silence. "Tell me what you did to turn Augustus Norwood into that beast! Now!"

Elwyn sucked in a breath. Carys hadn't told her about the Norwood prince yet. There'd been no time, but the question came flying out of her as Adisa chuckled.

"I watched through his eyes as your blade sliced open his throat," Adisa said. "Thank you for getting rid of him for me. He was a thorn in my side."

"Are they all people?" Carys demanded.

"No," Adisa said. "But you're a fool if you think I'll tell you which ones are more than the beasts they seem. You have Cole to thank for the magic behind that little trick." Adisa sounded so unsettlingly pleased. "He took a little persuading, of course—"

"Persuading!" Carys screamed, making Elwyn flinch. "You tried to drown him in a trunk on an abandoned ship!"

"He'd already been *persuaded* by then. I had no more need of him." Carys could hear the mocking smile in Adisa's voice, the casual cruelty, and she stepped forward, reaching for her blade.

Elwyn's hand landed on her elbow, tugging her away. Carys wanted to throw the flaming torch into the pit, wanted to boil tar and hurl it down on the witch just to make her suffer. Wrath filled her veins. She wanted vengeance for every one of her friends hurt by Adisa's ancient magic.

She let out a tight growl, her steaming breath curling in front of her face. Punishing the witch would only distract her. The true reprieve from her torment would be finding Fenrin, getting the amethyst dagger, and plunging it straight into Adisa Monroe's heart. Only once Fenrin's mind was free, Aneryn's curse broken, and the people of Okrith safe, would Carys's own mind know any peace.

"Enjoy your pit, Adisa," Carys spat as she turned toward the iron door.

"I will," Adisa sang back.

CHAPTER FIFTEEN

The competitors all slept late the following morning, the dawn ushering in a day of recovery after the attack. But Carys slept little more than an hour, her mind roiling with the memories of Adisa Monroe. She spent the day wandering the city, vacantly assessing the damage and collecting the many papers printed of the competitors' essays.

When she returned to the castle, Carys spent her hours sitting by Aneryn's bedside and ignoring the looming shadow of the Lord of Arboa. Ersan seemed to be tailing her wherever she went but she didn't have the energy to fight him away.

As she sat beside the sleeping blue witch, she read through the different essays quickly, her eyes scanning until she reached Aneryn's. The witch had the longest essay, thorough and exacting. She didn't use pretty language nor did she pander. She was direct in how she planned to assuage any violet witch attacks and why Fenrin should be the people's King. In some ways it was almost a love letter to Fenrin and to her future people.

In the evening, they gathered in the dining commons, summoned by Councilor Elwyn for the second cull. The sun had already dipped from the sky, the days growing shorter with each sunset toward the Winter Solstice. Carys took the same seat she took upon their first induction to the competition, only this time Aneryn wasn't a little blue storm cloud by her side. The mood was tense and far more uncertain than the previous cull. It had been fairly easy to determine who was cut first from the melee but an essay writing competition was far more subjective.

Elwyn held a stack of papers to her chest as she paced back and forth in front of the anxious group. Her eyes drifted over each one of them as if making sure they were all listening before she spoke.

"It has been a harrowing twenty-four hours to say the least," she said, the sentiment met with light chortles and murmuring. "But whosoever wears the Eastern crown must be prepared for such things." She paused, eyeing Falaine, who bristled under her gaze, before she kept walking. "The people of Wynreach are eager too, casting their votes even while sweeping glass from the streets."

She pulled back the papers held against her chest and glanced down at them. "Those whose name I call, please rise and head toward the council chamber. Your next challenge will commence immediately after this." More murmuring broke out through the group but Elwyn raised her hand and they quieted again.

She looked back down at her papers and said, "Carys Hilgaard, Falaine Fowler, Sava Dandala . . ." Carys stood immediately upon hearing her name and turned toward the doors, not wanting to bear witness to the crestfallen faces and inevitable tears. It was time to turn her focus toward the next challenge. Still, she couldn't quite make it over the threshold before the name Ersan Almah followed her out the door.

THE REMAINING COMPETITORS GATHERED IN THE COUNCIL CHAMBERS, cramming around the giant carved redwood table. Maps were held open by smooth river stones, parchment and scrolls littering the table and spilling over the sides.

Councilor Elywn eyed the group, the pinched lines around her mouth deepening. "Given the recent events and the aftermath thereof, the third and fourth trials have been combined into one." She glanced at them one at a time with her serious gaze, daring them to challenge her as the room gasped and murmured. After what they had seen that night, no one raised a voice in protest.

The moon rose low on the horizon out the frosted window, the deep blue sky fading to black as dusk descended over Wynreach. Carys was impressed Councilor Elwyn managed to cull the competition in half again and redesign the competition in only a single day.

Elwyn moved the papers on the table around, turning them out to face different competitors. She was truly a workhorse, cunning and resolute, and Carys wondered again why the Councilor didn't want to become Queen herself . . . probably because she was too smart and knew better. Anyone who wanted this life was a fool.

"The timeline of the competition has changed to meet the rising threat of Adisa Monroe and her beasts. You will be tested next both on your unity and bravery," Elwyn said, as Carys studied the detailed map of the Southern Court on the table in front of her. An amasa tree had been drawn between Saxbridge and Arboa—a signpost of the trails that cut through the jungle—and also where the ruins of her family's castle were located. She'd lived most of her life in the shade of that giant tree. It shaded her parents' graves still. She couldn't go back, couldn't face the destruction of the place. The day it burned down was the dramatic end to her former life.

Elwyn cleared her throat and Carys glanced back up to meet her pale gray eyes. Had the Councilor been waiting for her attention to speak? "Six," Elwyn said, waving a hand across the maps. "Six beasts escaped Wynreach last night, scattering to the wind without their mistress to control them any longer. Now that Adisa is under our control, we must look to the mess her attack has made. These creatures have been sighted all over Okrith, leaving chaos in their wake." She folded her hands together inside her robes. "You will be paired off and each sent to defeat one of them."

The group broke into more whispers and Elwyn gave Carys an apologetic look. Carys had known the next trial would have something to do with these beasts. She'd thought about asking Elwyn to reconsider . . . but she couldn't. Elwyn was the only person Carys had trusted to tell about Augustus Norwood and his shifting form.

They both agreed that it would be better not to share what Carys had seen with the wider group. It would only lead to questions they didn't have the answers to . . . and possibly hesitation when slaying the beasts, which could cost people their lives. Even if some of Adisa's monsters were actually people able to shift between the two forms, which ones were they? And did they have any control over the change or did Adisa control that too? Could she snap her fingers and Augustus would be a lion creature in the blink of an eye? Either way, people or no, the creatures were absolutely lethal and they needed to be stopped.

"You will have three weeks to bring me back the tusk of the beast," Elwyn said. "Whichsoever pair brings back a tusk within that time frame will continue to the fifth and final trial. If you haven't returned by then, you will be removed from the competition. One last thing"— she held up a hand before the group could jump in with questions— "your partner *must* return as well. If you cannot unite against this common foe, you will not have the constitution for ruling."

The group grumbled, folding their arms and shifting their weight as they sized each other up. It felt like that's all they did anymore: continually calculated their odds against their competition.

Councilor Elwyn pulled a scroll out from her deep robe pocket and unfurled it.

"Sava and Alwyth," Councilor Elwyn said, passing Sava a piece of paper. "You will go to Falhampton."

The group grumbled to each other even more at that. Sava and Alwyth were always at odds. Carys wouldn't be surprised if they killed each other before they even got to Falhampton.

She also had a sinking suspicion what that might mean for her.

"That's so close," Ivar was saying. "They won't have to travel as far as the rest of us."

"Are you afraid you can't handle this challenge, Lord Ivar?" Carys taunted. Ivar curled his lip and folded his arms, waiting for his name to be called.

Carys prayed she wouldn't be paired with him. She glanced sideways at Ersan in the corner of the room. Darkness clung to his figure, his arms folded, and his eyes hidden in shadow. He seemed to always be just around the corner over the last few days and Carys hated the feeling that he was keeping an eye on her. She quickly changed her prayer to include not being paired with Ersan either. Avaros would be her pick—he was fast and strong and didn't talk too much. He'd be the perfect hunting companion.

"Selric and Falaine," Councilor Elwyn continued. "You will go to Haastmouth. Ivar and Prestev, you will go to Silver Sands," she said, passing them their piece of paper.

"Silver Sands!" Prestev groused. "How exactly did one of those creatures get that far?"

"You can't put them together!" Sava protested. "They're best friends!"

Councilor Elwyn looked at Sava and arched her brow. "Would you care to travel all the way to Silver Sands instead, Lady Dandala?"

Sava clenched her jaw and looked away. "No."

It would take most of the three weeks riding day and night just to get to Silver Sands and back, let alone to find and kill a monster.

"Antonius and Zetra, you will go to Bradford." She passed them their piece of paper. "Alaister and Ruven, you will go to Raevenport."

Carys huffed. "Rua has probably already slayed every beast in the Northern Court by now with her Immortal Blade."

Ruven shrugged. "Well then, we can collect our tusk from her and have a nice little Northern holiday."

Carys scowled, glancing at the three contenders still unpaired: Avaros, Galen, and Ersan. Her stomach tightened. Either Galen or Avaros would be fine. Galen would be the more annoying of the two, but still fine.

Councilor Elwyn pulled out the final two pieces of paper and gave Carys a look that confirmed all Carys had feared. Carys shook her head, mouthing "please" and Councilor Elywn's lips pulled up to one side, her eyes remorseful.

"Galen and Avaros to Yexshire. Carys and Ersan to Marraden."

Ersan didn't move, didn't even seem to breathe when Councilor Elwyn held the paper out toward him. He didn't take it. Great, he was just as displeased as she was herself. Carys scowled and stepped forward, snatching the paper from Elwyn's waiting outstretched hand.

"Unity," Councilor Elwyn proclaimed. "I will see you in three weeks with your tusks or you will be out of this competition."

"And what if someone has already killed the beasts?"

"Then you will show what a shrewd diplomat and negotiator you are by getting them to give you the tusks."

With that, she turned and left, leaving Carys perplexed at her hasty departure.

Carys immediately began setting a plan to ditch Ersan at her nearest convenience and travel to the southernmost province of the Eastern Court by herself. If the monster was even there, it would probably already be killed by the time she arrived. Maybe she could find a way to chain Ersan to his bed while he slept. Then he'd be there safe and sound when she returned and they'd both advance in the competition. She could beat him in the final trial after that, become queen, and finally—*finally*—be rid of him.

Carys's daydreaming was cut short by Ivar brushing past her. "Good luck to you," he murmured, giving Carys a wink. "You're going to need it."

"Watch yourself," Carys snapped back. "Councilor Elwyn said we needed to return in our pairs, but if I encounter you on a trail outside of Wynreach, you just might find yourself on the wrong end of my sword."

"I have no doubt." Ivar snorted, his eyes roving over Carys's body with unnerving appreciation. "Fortunately we will be taking the northern road and you the southern, but if when I return you'd like to get on the *right* end of my sword, I wouldn't say no."

Ersan shoved off the wall at that, pushing between the two of them. He snatched the detailed map of the Eastern Court off the table and stormed out of the room.

"Your Fated is so easily ruffled," Ivar said. "It's hardly even fun."

Sava came to Carys's rescue, pushing past Ivar and saying, "If you and your tiny sword plan on getting to Silver Sands and back in three weeks, Ivar, you should already be gone."

Ivar scowled, but tipped his head to his fellow Northerners still left in the group and they followed him out. One by one, they all left until Carys stood alone in the council chamber, wishing the floor would open up and swallow her whole.

Before Carys could turn and leave, Councilor Elwyn walked back in. "I was hoping you'd stay behind, or at least come find me in my chambers afterward with your protests," she said, confirming Carys's suspicion that she'd left quickly on purpose.

"Why?" Carys glowered at the map on the table and refused to look at Elwyn. "Why would you do this to me?"

Elwyn sighed, clasping her hands together in her robes. "I'm not sending you south to Marraden just to fight a beast, Carys," she said. "I have something for you, something that one of the guards found on Adisa when they captured her." She pulled a small scroll out of her robes and passed it to Carys.

Carys unfurled the letter, her eyes scanning the message quickly as her mouth fell open.

IT IS DONE, MY KING. MEET ME AT THE MARRADEN CLIFFS TWO *weeks from the full moon. Bring the dagger. -A*

"MY KING?" SHE REPEATED. "THE 'A' . . . DO YOU THINK THIS IS from Augustus or Adisa or someone else entirely? Do they mean Fenrin when they say *my King*?" She scrutinized the page as if it might tell her. "Is this a note for Fenrin?"

"I don't know," Elwyn said "But there's been sightings of a beast down in Roughwater and I thought it best to send you to investigate in the event he is down that way." She wandered back over to the larger map on the table, her eyes trailing down the Crushwold River and to the tip of the Eastern Court. "Whether it is for Fenrin or not, if the amethyst dagger is going to be in Marraden, I need you to be the one to get it. It may be the only way of killing Adisa Monroe. I need the most skillful warrior on the task. We can't risk losing it and

I know you'll put securing the dagger over showing off, unlike the others," she added derisively.

"This could've been planted by Adisa for us to find." Carys rolled the scroll back up and tucked it in her pocket. "This could be a trap."

"It could be." Elwyn nodded. "Which is also why I'm trusting you to handle it."

"And Ersan," Carys added bitterly.

"Look at me," Elwyn said in her soft yet commanding way. When Carys did, she added, "Tell me one other contender more willing to protect you than Lord Ersan." Carys sucked at her teeth as she frowned, the action making Elwyn smile. "You know it's true, even if you hate that it's true. Something about being your Fated still lingers within him. He is the only one I truly trust to keep you safe."

Carys balked. "We can't trust him at all. He kept secrets from me our entire relationship. He's conniving. He's a liar. He's an arrogant ass."

"But he's an arrogant ass who will protect you with his life." Elwyn said it in such a matter-of-fact way that it made Carys seethe. "That's all I'm concerned about right now. Sending my two best competitors to handle this situation delicately, to bring back the amethyst dagger, and," she rested her hand on Carys's forearm, "protecting our future Queen."

"Fine." Carys swallowed, giving Elwyn a cold nod. She already knew it would be a long time before she forgave the Councilor for this, but she also knew she was right. Ersan might want to kill Carys himself, but he'd never let anyone else hurt her. "But I want to see Adisa once more before I go," Carys added.

Carys wondered if Adisa was even still down there. She shuddered thinking of the cold, lifeless place. No guards needed to bring her food or water. Much like Aneryn in her trance, Adisa didn't need anything but her immortal magic to sustain her, and it was beginning to feel like Adisa wasn't even down there at all. Maybe Carys could get a sense of whether this letter was leading her into a trap or not. Maybe the witch would accidentally spill some secret that would give her the upper hand . . . it was at least worth a try.

Elwyn frowned at that but she simply bowed her head. "If that's what you need to do, then go now. You'll need to ride out with the dawn, to return in time." Carys moved past Elwyn, who added, "I hate that so much rests on your shoulders."

Carys pushed open the door. "If I am to be Queen, I fear that will never change."

CHAPTER SIXTEEN

Carys diverted from her course to the dungeons to check on Aneryn one final time and see if some sort of miracle had happened since the morning and the witch healers had come up with a way to pull her from her stupor. But as Carys passed a group of brown witches leaving Aneryn's room, she noted the way they whispered conspiratorially to each other, their brows furrowed in confusion, and Carys knew that they hadn't been able to conjure any miraculous feats.

Aneryn seemed petite lying in her bed—a descriptor Carys would've never used for the witch when she was awake and filled with her normal ferocity. Had she always been so small? Did her sheer presence seem to add another few inches to her somehow? The calm and stillness was unsettling, even when Aneryn was perfectly still before, it felt like a hurricane of magic always swirled around her just waiting to strike.

Ehiris perched on the wash basin beside Aneryn's bed. Apparently her hawk had not moved since Aneryn fell into her trance. The bird wouldn't fly out the window they left open for him. He wouldn't hunt either and Carys feared that the hawk would die of starvation if Aneryn didn't wake soon.

Carys sat on the edge of her bed. "What have you done?" she whispered, staring out at the window above Aneryn's bed, the moonlight beaming into the room. "Is this what you Saw when you walked out of the second trial and went to the rooftop? Did you know that this would be your fate?"

Carys pulled out the totem that she'd secretly grabbed from Aneryn on the rooftop. Ersan, to his credit, hadn't asked her about it, but the way he warily clung to her the last few days told her he wanted to know what was going on. From her pocket Carys produced a scrap of paper and a small purple stone. She smoothed her thumb over the sanded piece of amethyst, carved so perfectly into an orb that she at first thought it was a marble.

On one side of the paper was a note: *I do not withdraw from the competition. A champion will take my place for the next combined challenge.*

Carys furrowed her brow at the succinct statement. So Aneryn must've known that this trance was a risk . . . just as she knew that the next challenges would be combined. But no champion had revealed themselves to take her place. Only Aneryn would be stubborn enough not to yield even when she was unconscious.

Turning over the scrap of paper, Carys found two more words inked onto it, the words smudged as if written with increasing haste: *For Fenrin.*

"'For Fenrin,'" Carys read aloud, holding up the purple orb to the moonlight. "Is this amethyst stone a gift for him? Is it sentimental or is it imbued with some sort of magic?" She closed her eyes and squeezed the stone as if she might feel the thread of magic unspooling from it, but she felt nothing. "Is this just a token of your love? An inside joke?" She shook her head. "What am I going to tell the others? When Renwick finds out, he will probably burn half of the Northern Court down on his way to get here. I know I promised you I wouldn't tell Renwick about what was going on until you were reunited with Fenrin, but I hadn't expected you to be cursed like *this*. If you made me make that promise because you feared this would happen, that is just plain cruel." Carys clicked her tongue bitterly. "I'm sure you did. One step ahead even while you sleep."

Carys twiddled her fingers, not knowing why she even bothered talking to Aneryn at all. Aneryn had been Renwick's personal blue witch since she was a child. He'd always been cold to her in public but incredibly protective of her too, and it wasn't until he allied with the High Mountain Court and he began to let that mask slip that Carys realized that Aneryn was really like his little sister. No one could stand up to Renwick Vostemur like Aneryn could . . . well, except maybe his Fated, Rua. Still, Renwick loved Aneryn fiercely and it would devastate him to learn what had happened to her.

"Should I tell him?" Carys asked, pulling Aneryn's blanket higher and tucking it under her chin. "No. I don't think you'd want me to."

Ehiris squawked as if in agreement, the most life Carys had seen from the bird.

She turned to the hawk and held out her hand. He only stared back for a moment before jumping from the basin and gliding over to her with a single flap of his wings. He perched gently on Carys's hand, his talons pinching but not digging in enough to break the skin. Carys stroked a hand down the soft feathers of his chest and Ehiris leaned in as her hand rose to scratch him under his beak.

"Listen," she said, speaking directly to Ehiris now. "I'm going to send a servant up here with a mouse and you will eat it, understand?" Ehiris cocked his head, one black eye staring at Carys as if in judgment. Carys snorted and shook her head. "Please? It would break Aneryn if anything happens to you. You need to be well for when she wakes up." Ehiris chirped and ruffled his feathers. "I'm taking that as a yes," Carys said as Ehiris hopped off her hand and flew back to the basin.

She sighed and turned to Aneryn, tucking the amethyst stone and note back into her own pocket. "I'm going to find Fenrin in Marraden. I'm going to find that dagger too, and kill Adisa Monroe with it myself. I'll find a way to free him." She said each word with more determination than the last. "I will find a way to save you and become worthy of your friendship, Aneryn. Just hang on until I do."

Aneryn didn't budge but Carys swore she saw the flames around her fingertips flicker a brighter shade of sapphire. Maybe she could hear her after all. Maybe she was still there, right beneath the surface. "Just hang on for me," Carys echoed again as she stood.

Carys turned toward the door, giving Ehiris a final warning nod that he would eat. The hawk just watched like a statue as she left but she didn't have time to continue her one-way battle with the stubborn bird.

She took one step into the hallway before abruptly halting at the person standing in front of Aneryn's door. A raven-haired beauty with pale moonlit skin stood worrying her hands in the middle of the hallway. Carys recognized her instantly. The last time she saw this witch, she'd been hiding under the covers in the Saxbridge palace with Fenrin and Aneryn . . .

"Laris," Carys said, the word barely a whisper.

Laris peeked up at her, emerald magic flickering from her wide saucer eyes in the dim light. Laris's voice came out as a squeak as she said, "Lady Hilgaard—"

Carys held up her hands when Laris made to bow. "Please, just Carys. I . . . What are you doing here?" The question came out more abruptly than intended and she cleared her throat and tried to force a more pleasant expression.

"I have just come from Councilor Elwyn's office," Laris said, her voice soft but her now midnight eyes hard. She was a strange juxtaposition, this green witch—the confidence of her words defied her doe-eyed innocence. "I have come to take Aneryn's place as her champion while she recovers."

Recovers. It was clear from Laris's expression that she knew that wasn't the appropriate word. Still, she had an iron resolve and lifted her chin, defying Carys to question her. She was a mouse with the resolve of a lion, all soft lines and gentle curves, but her eyes bore the same ferocity as the woman she still clearly loved. Maybe Aneryn had pulled that ferocity out of her, given her the confidence to fight. Maybe love could stoke those fires in even the most timid souls. But a champion? That, Carys couldn't envision, piercing gaze or no.

"I don't know if a quest to slay a monster is necessarily the place for—"

"A witch?" Laris suggested and Carys cringed.

"A person untrained in combat," Carys remedied. "Last I spoke with Aneryn, she wanted you to stay in the Southern Court, where you'd be safe."

"I'd rather be whole than be safe," she said. "And I cannot be either without Aneryn and Fen."

"So you chose to come after her? Even after she sent you away?"

"Sometimes we'd rather believe that those we love are incapable of being with us." Laris titled her head, assessing Carys, watching the way her words landed as she continued. "Sometimes it's easier to push them away then watch them get hurt by our side. But I won't be pushed away. Not when they still love me."

A lump formed in Carys's throat. She both respected and admired the witch's determination—foolish or no. Having someone willing to fight for you . . . their love was made of heartier stuff than she'd first assumed.

"I suppose there's no way to convince you to stay behind on this next challenge." Judging from the green witch's resolve, Carys knew it was a moot point. "You shall come with Ersan and me southward, then. We'll protect you."

"I mean this with no intent to offend," Laris said. "But I would rather saw off my thumb with a blunted butter knife than be put between you and your jilted Fated, Lady Hilgaard."

A chortle of surprise escaped Carys's lips. "That is probably wise. Then who?"

"I venture northward to Falhampton with Sava and Alwyth," Laris said. "Councilor Elwyn has assured me they're the least likely to murder me in my sleep, though that is not entirely saying something. I think they fear Aneryn enough not to try, though."

"Even asleep she protects you," Carys offered, feeling the outline of the stone in her pocket. So this was the champion Aneryn had written of in her note—the last person Carys would have expected. Maybe Aneryn could not let go of her lover as easily as she once purported.

Laris shuffled her weight from side to side. The look in her eyes said she didn't want to discuss it further. Carys was standing in the middle of Aneryn's doorway and clearly Laris wanted her to step aside.

"Good luck," Carys said lamely, shifting over and bobbing her head to the green witch. Laris's shoulders bunched around her ears as she dipped her head in return and moved to push past. "And Laris?"

The green witched paused and looked back over her shoulder. "I'm so sorry for the way I once treated you." She wanted to list all of the reasons why she'd acted that way: she was young, she was drunk, she was trying to win her father's approval, she was trying to keep herself above water in whatever way she could . . . Instead, she said, "There is no excuse for my actions. I know I don't deserve your forgiveness, but I promise you I will find a way to make amends."

"Help me save the people I love. Wake Aneryn. Bring Fenrin back to us," Laris said softly. "And I will consider forgiving you."

She walked into Aneryn's room and shut the door before Carys even had a chance to reply. As the door snicked shut so too did the ugly hope that seemed to bloom in Carys only to be cut down again. It seemed as if every time she tried to open a new door—a new friendship, a new outlook, a new resolve—it would be unceremoniously shut on her again. She stood there staring at the shut door, her mind reeling at what had just transpired. It wasn't until she heard the weeping that the broken, mournful sound jolted her back to life.

Two things once again existed at the same time: she was determined to make things right with those she wronged and still beat them at this competition. That started with helping Aneryn.

An ancient magic held Aneryn in her trance and they had no idea how to pull her out of it. But Carys reckoned that one person in the palace did . . . and she was probably cackling to herself right now in a pit below her feet. It was time to go speak with the violet witch.

CARYS STEELED HERSELF FOR THE WALK BACK THROUGH THE DUN-geons, each step down into the inky blackness making her feel a little hollower. The keys to the dungeons jangled in her pocket, clinking against Aneryn's amethyst stone. Carys had debated leaving it in Aneryn's room with her sleeping friend, or giving it to her green witch love, afraid that if the stone was truly magic, she'd be delivering it right into the hands of the most powerful witch in all of Okrith . . . but she didn't want to leave it out of her sight either. Something about the weight of that stone in her pocket kept her moving forward—her way of letting Aneryn know she wouldn't forget about her in all this chaos, that she'd find Fenrin and be the friend and ruler that the Eastern Court so desperately needed.

As she shut the last creaking iron door, she heard a faint sound. It sounded like a grandmother humming while knitting in a rocking chair. Such an unsettling noise to hear in a dungeon. It made the hairs on her arms stand on end. How could Adisa Monroe be so contented to sit in a black void?

When she reached the pit in the floor the humming stopped.

"Lady Hilgaard." Adisa Monroe sounded breezy, delighted even, like Carys had unexpectedly popped by for some afternoon tea. "Coming to visit me again so soon? You must be incredibly desperate to wish for *my* company."

Carys put on her practiced laugh of indifference, the sound too loud in the darkness, reverberating back again and again off the stone. "I am in a castle filled to the brim with people," Carys groused. "The last thing I am is alone."

"Ah, but we both know you can be surrounded by people and still feel the bite of loneliness," Adisa mused.

The thought dropped into Carys's mind like a heavy stone in a deep lake, rippling through her body and filling her with unease. Perhaps that was what drove Adisa to madness. Being alone for so long must have changed her, twisted her already warped mind, made her more of a monster than a sentient being. And Carys hated how easily she understood how such a thing could happen. Already without her friends and family around she felt nudged further and further into chaos and brashness. It felt like she might do anything without them around to bear witness to her being a good person.

But Carys didn't say any of that aloud and she prayed Adisa couldn't hear it either. From the witch's silence, she assumed she couldn't. Instead, Carys said, "I'm sorry. Am I interrupting you from more important matters, like staring into the darkness or being an absolutely horrible person?"

"You can't expect me not to poke at you a little." Adisa's cackle bounced across the room. "You make it too easy. I'm guessing you didn't come here to talk about how sad and broken you are."

Carys reared back at that, her nose wrinkling in disgust. "There is nothing sad or broken about me. I am about to be a queen."

Adisa laughed and Carys realized she was—once again—falling for Adisa's bait.

An unnerving chitter sounded, like fingernails rapping against stone as Adisa said, "You know what it feels like to have everything taken from you just as I do."

"I am nothing like you."

"You'd like to think that, wouldn't you? It makes it easier to cast your judgments upon me when you can't understand why, doesn't it?" Adisa's sigh was light and mocking. "Imagine your losses compounded by centuries. Imagine the injustice. The fury for your people."

"You speak as if everything you do is for your coven," Carys said. "But Neelo told me what was in your journal, Adisa. Your own coven cast you out."

"Because I was the only one brave enough to see the war on witches coming. I needed to use the full force of our magic to save us whether my contemporaries liked it or not," she snarled.

The effects of too much isolation were clear in her words as well as her erratic mood swings. She'd use any excuse, use her own coven— her own bloodline even—as justification for her plans. Perhaps deep down she truly believed what she was saying, but this witch was clearly out of her mind, and someone needed to end her before she caused any more destruction.

"Tell me about your dagger," Carys demanded. "Where is it?"

Adisa cackled again. "Why don't you ask me nicely?"

Carys rolled her eyes. "How about I hoist you out of this pit by your toenails and torture you for the answers."

"But you won't," Adisa sang. "Because you know I won't give them up so freely. I can retreat so far within my own mind that I can't feel your inflicted pain. I can be in the minds of so many others instead. Maybe I'll check on my great-grandson for a while—"

"Where is he?" Carys barked. "Where is Fenrin?"

"The King is a busy man," Adisa said. "He is in many places—gathering allies, creating new beasts, preparing to sit on the Eastern Court throne . . ." She hummed a bit of her tune again. "But I thought you wanted to know about the dagger?"

"I do."

"Then ask me with all of that politeness your tutors schooled you in, Lady Hilgaard. Ask me like you'd ask a fae."

Carys's shoulders bunched around her ears as she gritted out, "Tell me about the dagger . . . please."

Adisa clapped her hands, applauding as Carys's cheeks burned. "What is there to say? It's a dagger like any other."

"We both know that's not true," Carys said. "It's not like any other dagger I've ever seen."

"Like any other fae dagger, perhaps," Adisa mused. "But it is just like all the other ancient witch daggers."

"And what sort of powers did those ancient daggers have?"

"Now, that's actually an astute question."

"So you'll answer?"

"There's not many relics from my days left in Okrith," Adisa said instead, almost musingly. "The fae feared the power of the witches. Most of our talismans were destroyed—buried, tossed in the sea, thrown into the deepest caverns . . . or gifted to undeserving royalty."

Carys froze. "Like the Immortal Blade?"

"Indeed." The sound of bones rattled from the pit and Carys wondered if Adisa was standing. "The Immortal Blade has a sister, with the power of all three of the High Mountain talismans combined."

Carys's eyes flared. The ancient red witches had gifted the High Mountain royal family with three talismans imbued with their power: the Immortal Blade, which could cut down an army with one swing of the sword; the *shil-de* ring, which gave the wearer protection from any harm; and the amulet of Aelusien, which imbued the bearer with the same magic as the ancient red witches.

Carys's whole body tingled with frozen pinpricks. "Your amethyst dagger can do the same as those ancient talismans can?"

"More." Adisa cackled again. "It works for whosoever has been its master even after it finds a new one. Of course, you need to have violet witch blood to unlock its true powers—something I added to its spell-work centuries ago after the red witch coven started kneeling at the altar of the fae. I didn't want the amethyst dagger to fall into fae hands and wield against us. Now it is tied only to its true master's bloodline."

"Gods." Carys shook her head. "So that means you don't need to wield it to be protected by its powers still . . ."

"And unlike the red witches," Adisa's voice turned cold and lethal, "we violet witches don't just give our magic to the fae, nor do we keep our weapons locked away like the foolish High Mountain royals." The bones rattled again. "We *use* our ancient talismans to protect our coven."

A thought flashed into Carys's mind—the moment Councilor Ashby gripped that falling blade. "Is that why Kira wasn't injured in her chambers the other day?" she murmured to herself.

"Now you're starting to understand." Adisa sighed. "She never knew she was the wielder of that dagger until I came to claim it back. What a disappointment she was in the end—no ambition. And her bastard son too. But Fenrin will be the one to bring the violet witch line back to Okrith and resurrect our coven. *He* will wield it to its true potential. The others don't matter."

"I'm going to find Fenrin," Carys said, snapping her focus back to her task at hand. Now that she knew the true power of the amethyst dagger, she needed to find it right away. "I'm going to bring him back."

"There is no *back*." Adisa chuckled. "Or rather, yes, bring him back here. He will be King of the Eastern Court anyway, so it might help if he's already here. I've Seen it. His blue witch lover has seen it too."

"Don't you speak about Aneryn," Carys growled.

"I can help her, if you like," Adisa chided. "All you need to do is release me and I will bring her out of that trance. I've done it myself a few times before, dug so deep into my well of power that it pulled me under before I could expel the force of my magic. She is in terrible pain right now. Release me and I'll help her."

"How?" Carys asked breathlessly. "How did you know?"

"I see through many eyes, Lady Hilgaard," Adisa said. "Some I can control, some I can whisper to, others I can only watch. They don't even realize. Pay heed to that."

"Tell me how to help Aneryn," Carys demanded.

"What did I tell you about you and your commands?"

"Please," she added bitterly.

"Oh, so polite." Adisa cackled again, the sharp sound sending a shiver down Carys's spine. "But no, I think not. We both know you're not going to let me out of this pit, even if it means saving your friend from her torment. These choices are not so easily parsed, hmm? Letting one person suffer to spare another is a game we all must play."

"You and I are not the same." Carys gritted her teeth, hating that with each moment in this dungeon, she felt like she could understand how Adisa got to be the hateful, cruel person she became. Carys wanted it to be unfathomable . . . but somehow she understood.

But she knew not letting Adisa save Aneryn was still the right decision, just as not giving her the seeds was the right decision. Even Aneryn herself would hate Carys for freeing the powerful witch. She patted the amethyst stone in her pocket. First she'd bring the stone to Fenrin and find Adisa's dagger. Then she'd free Adisa only with her dagger held at her throat.

"Enjoy your darkness, Adisa," Carys spat and turned toward the door.

"Enjoy your loneliness, Lady Hilgaard," Adisa called back. "I hope it doesn't drive you as mad as me."

An icy blast of fear shot through Carys. Gods, so Adisa *had* been eavesdropping in her mind. She schooled her thoughts away from her mother, away from all the moments she felt like she was one wayward thought from madness. As she yanked the door shut behind her, it slammed so hard that the sound shook through her chest. She hated the way Adisa had said it like that, as if she was cursing her to a similar fate. But Carys simply turned and marched back up the sloping dungeon steps, Adisa Monroe's jolly humming taunting her all the way.

CHAPTER SEVENTEEN

Carys pulled her cloak tighter around her shoulders, grateful for her horse's warmth as the brisk autumnal winds tousled her hair from her braid. Yellow and red leaves danced in the wind, fluttering to the bright tapestry of forest floor, and she would have noted their beauty if it wasn't for the encroaching darkness that seemed to hang over everything.

Ersan held tight to a map with both hands, flicking it out with his wrists every time the breeze folded its edges. The reins of his horse hung slack across his mare's neck, and yet she walked side by side with Carys's horse without any further instruction. Occasionally Ersan would nudge her with his calf and the horse would straighten its walk. He was the picture of a confident horseman, having ridden since he was old enough to walk—and having ridden even more to make up for walking later in life.

"It shouldn't be too long until we reach the inn," he said, squinting at the map. "Then it will be a few days of camping in the forest before we reach Lord Marraden's manor." He brought his face closer to the map and then held it out again. "If the weather is fine, we can take the coastal pathway, which should cut a day from the journey." He scrutinized the cluster of clouds cutting through the gray haze in the distance. "But if it's going to rain, we should take the inland path through the forest, and pray it's only a light rain and not one of the Southern storms that come this time of year."

Carys rolled her eyes. "How about *I* take the coastal pathway and *you* take the inland road since you're so concerned about the weather?" She leaned toward him, knowing her sweet smile would rile him further. "We can meet back up in Marraden."

Ersan shot her a look as he perfectly folded up the map and tucked it back into the outer pocket of his saddlebag. "As unpleasant as your company is, we will stick together."

"Councilor Elwyn said nothing about staying together."

"But she *did* say that if one of us returns without the other that we'll both be forfeit from the competition." Ersan picked up the reins in one hand again. "I'm not going to risk my crown by you getting yourself killed."

"Your crown?" Carys looked around the forest as if searching for someone to confirm his lunacy. "The papers may favor you as a contender but they still favor me more. There is no world in which *you* beat *me* to the crown."

Giving a derisive snort, Ersan shifted in his saddle. "There's that blind confidence we all know and love."

"Please." Carys looked up to the clouds, praying for enough patience to not ram Ersan through with her sword. She once again wished Laris had taken her up on the offer to accompany them. "There's no point in false modesty with just you around. You know I'm favored to win."

"Your papers are as fickle as anything. Nothing is decided until a crown is upon one of our heads."

"*My* head," Carys corrected. "Maybe we should just agree to meet back outside the city in three weeks' time—"

"No."

Carys's fingers itched for the hilt of her sword. "You know there's another place between here and Marraden. We don't need to camp the whole way."

"We're not staying in Roughwater Cove," Ersan said. "That's a pirate town."

"I think we can handle a few pirates." Carys smiled up to the gold and red canopy as she added, "A future king certainly could."

"You're goading has gotten pretty obvious in the last few years," Ersan jeered. "I miss your subtlety. And as eager as I am to be mugged, we're not going to Roughwater."

"*We* don't have to go," Carys said resolutely. "But I am."

"Carys."

"Ersan," she taunted back, mocking the gruff way he rumbled her name.

Ersan pinched the bridge of his nose. "Gods help me."

"I think the Gods have forsaken us long ago, don't you?" Carys said it in a teasing way, but she meant every word. Whatever cruel Fates brought them together, those powers were probably laughing at them from the afterlife. How twisted to put the two of them together and then yank them back apart . . . only to thrust them back together again.

Ersan opened his mouth to speak again, but Carys cut him off in a way she knew would further ruffle his feathers. "Maybe we should ride in silence."

She smiled as the muscle in Ersan's jaw popped out. Bull's-eye.

They carried on wordlessly, hours passing by as Carys first thought of all the ways she could torment Ersan on their journey, then thought of Aneryn, then Laris, then Morgan and hoped that she and the children were still doing well. But each topic kept turning back to one thing: what Adisa Monroe had said to her in that pit.

She felt stained with those words as if they had seeped through her clothes and into her bones somehow. She couldn't shake them. Carys had known loneliness, true, desperate loneliness, the kind that made her feel like she didn't exist anymore, the kind that made her *want* to not exist anymore.

And even after she found Ersan, even after she found friends who would lift her up and drop everything to keep her going, she still felt only one step from that darkness. No matter how far forward she moved, it stayed right there alongside her, just as Ersan's horse shadowed her own.

Sometimes she would forget about it. Everything would seem fine for a while and then the smallest, most innocuous thing would tip the scale and she'd be right there again, one foot in that desperation. And every time she remembered it, it came crashing down on her just as hard as it had every time before, no rhyme or reason to it, no amount of wealth or friends or even joy could make it not slam into her again just as hard.

And Adisa had voiced all that in an instant.

A knot tightened in her throat. Maybe Adisa had sensed that emptiness in her, could hear it somehow in her words, or maybe she felt it as she went clawing through her mind. Carys didn't know. But she hated how easily the witch could get under her skin and now *that* thought plagued her in the silence of their ride. Maybe Adisa's words were enough to plunge her back into that depthless despair that always walked alongside her.

Carys's hand dropped to the hilt of her sword, her other gloved hand squeezing the reins tighter in her grip. No. She could fight it. She wasn't so weak this time that she needed her friends and certainly not her Fated to keep her from losing herself again.

She nudged her horse and her mare pulled ahead of Ersan's. "I'm hungry," she called as Ersan urged his horse to pick up the pace. "How far is the inn?"

"Not long now," Ersan called.

"Good." She kicked her horse and it broke into a full canter. "I'll meet you there!" she shouted.

Adrenaline coursed through her as the cool wind stung her cheeks. Ersan called after her but she ignored him. She could outrun it all. Just keep moving forward.

THE INN THAT SAT ALONG THE CRUSHWOLD RIVER HAD A CARVED door painted in mauve and lavender flowers. Antlers were mounted above the frame upon which hung a sign naming the place: The Wandering Stag. Weary from the day's journey, Carys was eager for a cup of wine—or maybe seven—and something roasted and greasy to fill her belly.

There was no point glamouring herself in a human form, not when she carried expensive fae weaponry, and Carys wasn't about to abandon her sword and dagger for the ruse either. Ersan followed along after her as she dutifully ignored him, wishing she had been assigned this mission with anyone else—Ivar even—or better yet, alone, and hating that this desire was almost certainly the point of them all being paired.

Two children sat playing with marbles under the shade of the stable roof. The elder stable boy's eyes grew to the size of saucers as Carys rode in and paid him a gold coin to water and brush down her horse. "Aren't you . . . ?" The boy's voice quavered as he called after Carys. His sister tucked in further behind him. "The one everyone says will be Queen?"

"Carys Hilgaard." She introduced herself with a bow of her head.

The boy's younger sister gasped, her large blue eyes flitting from Carys to Ersan, who dismounted his horse with a groan and rubbed a fist down the outside of his muscled thigh. Ersan slid his cane out from where it was buckled by two leather loops under the saddle and Carys knew it was not only to assist him in standing after a long ride, but also to keep close the dagger hidden inside it.

"And who is he?" the stable boy asked.

Carys's face was the picture of seriousness as she replied, "My servant."

"I am not," Ersan said roughly. "I am her accomplice on this quest and her contender for the crown."

The boy snorted. "Well, you have my vote, Lady Hilgaard."

Carys beamed and bowed deeply to him, an honor in and of itself. "Thank you, master . . . ?"

"Brendan, my Lady," he said, his cheeks flaming to a bright shade of scarlet. "This is Corie."

"Brendan, Corie," Carys said with a broad smile, delighted that the boy joined her in slighting Ersan. "We require food and accommodation."

"The Wandering Stag would be honored to host you, my lady," he said. "My ma is the matron of the inn. I'll run ahead and see to your room"—he glanced between Ersan and Carys, his brows pinching together—"rooms?"

"Two rooms, please," Carys confirmed.

"Close together," Ersan added, stepping to Carys's side.

She shot him a dirty look, but the two children just nodded and hastened toward the stable door.

"I can protect myself just fine without you in earshot," Carys said.

Ersan cocked his head, his eyes sliding from Carys's face and down her body. "Planning on getting up to some mischief you don't want me to hear?"

Carys folded her arms and popped her hip to the side. "Maybe. Who knows?" She tipped the crown of her head toward the open door and the view of the river beyond. "I spied a few good-looking fellows and far more fine-looking ladies along the ride here. Perhaps a romantic walk along the river is in order after such a long ride."

"That's one way to get to know your future citizens."

"So long as they are *my* citizens and not yours, I don't care what you think." She swiped her braid over her shoulder and Ersan's eyes followed its swish to and fro. Turning, Carys felt Ersan's irritation rise off him as he silently followed. She pressed her lips together. Each time she got under his skin felt like a miniature victory.

The Wandering Stag was a quaint and pleasantly appointed inn with carved ceiling beams and painted floral sills in the Eastern Court stylings. The bottom floor was doing a roaring trade, though judging by the empty stables and their pick of the rooms on the floors above, the patrons all seemed to be locals. Before the Siege of Yexshire, this town was a popular destination for those wanting to escape the capital in the winter months, the climate by the river more temperate and less prone to snow. But most of the attractions that centered around leisure had gone out of business over the last many years and the late Eastern Court King didn't seem particularly inclined to help humans get back on their feet. The fae continued to thrive, fighting battles for glory and amassing more wealth, while the humans and witches toiled, collateral in the faes' many wars.

Throughout the day's ride, Carys noted how much of the Eastern Court now seemed like a ghost of its former glory. It would be one of the many things she'd need to change when she became Queen.

Carys settled into a corner booth and scowled at Ersan as he took the seat across from her.

"You can sit on your own," she said, scanning the room and finding a lone stool at the bar far across the space. "There."

Ersan was about to shoot back some sort of witty retort when the bar matron hastened out of the kitchen and bounded over to them. She balanced the stems of two goblets in one strong hand and a hefty pitcher of wine in the other.

"Thank you for being so kind to my children, Lady Hilgaard," she said, her plump rosy cheeks rising toward her eyes as she smiled and bowed. "Brendan will be talking about this forever." She set down the goblets and filled them with a practiced ease of years doing the same movement day in and day out.

When she pulled the pitcher back, Ersan put his hand on her arm. "Leave it," he commanded. "Save yourself the trips."

"Yes, my Lord," she said with a merry curtsy.

Before the matron could depart, Carys held up her hand to stall her again. She couldn't lose sight of why they were staying in this inn in the first place: the competition. And if anyone knew what beasts were afoot it would be an innkeeper who kept the drinks flowing.

"Tell me . . . " Carys paused, waiting for the matron to supply her name.

"Audrey," she offered, bouncing on her toes.

"Audrey, have you seen any creatures roaming the forests in these parts?" Carys held her hands wide. "Almost like a lion but larger."

Audrey nodded vigorously. "I haven't seen such a beast but the township about half an hour south of here has seen something terrible racing through its woods." She shuddered. "Ate half a herd of goats, it did. And destroyed the watermill on its way out of town.

Sordid business, that." She worried her lip, waving a hand between the two of them. "Is that what you're after?"

"It is," Carys said, unsure how much people knew of the rules of the latest challenge.

"You're a true hero, you know. Saving us from that thing." Audrey clasped a hand to her chest. "But you won't find it around these parts. Last I heard, it was bolting straight southward toward the southern coastline. The sooner someone puts a sword in that thing the better."

"The sooner someone puts a sword through Adisa Monroe the better too," Ersan muttered as he took a sip from his goblet. Carys kicked Ersan under the table and he scowled back.

"Thank you for the information," Carys said diplomatically, placing a gold coin in Audrey's palm. "If you hear of anything else before our departure, we'd be most appreciative if you could inform us."

"Of course, my Lady." Audrey looked back at Carys with the same wide, blue eyes as her children. "I'll go have the cook whip up something befitting of a future Queen." She nibbled the corner of her lip, debating herself for a moment before asking, "When you are crowned, can I say that I hosted you on the front signage?"

"I'd be delighted," Carys said, making the matron's smile widen further as she gleefully beelined back to the bar.

Ersan's lips curved down as he snatched his goblet and leaned back in his chair.

"Something bothering you?" Carys asked ruefully. "Don't like that your former girlfriend is about to become Queen?"

"Former girlfriend?" Ersan's eyes shot up to meet Carys's own, his head shaking slightly in disbelief. "Whether you wish it or not, we are more than just lovers."

"'Lovers' implies there was love. 'Begrudging allies'?"

"Uh-uh."

"'Mortal enemies'?"

"Carys."

"No. I'm not playing this game." She took a long sip of wine, welcoming the feeling of it burning down her throat. Gods, if he said her name in that patronizing way one more time, she would leap across the table and throttle him. "There is nothing else. Not anymore."

Ersan's voice dropped an octave. "Saying it doesn't make it so."

"Must we go round in these circles again?" Carys leaned back against the hard wood of the booth. "I'm too tired to have this argument with you right now. Let's just eat in silence."

"Car—"

"Better yet," Carys interjected, shooting to her feet. She couldn't take it anymore. Not this. Not now. They were on a mission and their continual spats only distracted her from achieving their goal.

That was the reason she couldn't take it, she told herself, not because every time she spoke to the fae Lord across from her, she felt his betrayal like a war hammer to the chest.

She found the matron's gaze from across the room. "I think I shall dine in my room," she called over the crowd, gesturing upstairs to get her message across.

The matron nodded and Carys raised her glass to cheers the air, pointedly ignoring Ersan, who just sat there glaring at her, before heading toward the stairwell. One day, she'd pin him to the wall with her dagger and demand he explain why he'd lied to her and not let him squirm out of it until he either confessed or bled. One day.

But tonight, she couldn't stomach the thought of being near him, and wondered how she was going to survive the next three weeks.

And that was without counting the beast they were chasing in the mix.

CHAPTER EIGHTEEN

They continued their ride south in silence, days stretching on without a word to each other. Every time Carys tried to rise early and leave their campsite before Ersan, he'd immediately be up as if by magic and follow her. Every time she tried to get her horse to ride ahead or turn down a different path, he'd be there right behind her a moment later. More and more his silent presence irked her. She wanted to scream into his face, but if she did that, she'd let him win this vexing little game between them. Carys was equally perturbed and impressed by Ersan's commitment to call her speechless bluff. But Carys wouldn't be the first to speak. If she had to cut her tongue out to win, she would consider it.

The southernmost town before the forests and overgrown farmlands of the Marraden province was the port town called Roughwater Cove. Carys could feel the anger rising off Ersan as she left her horse at the stables at the edge of town, but he didn't speak, didn't stop her, only followed in an increasingly brooding silence. Carys didn't have any real reason for stopping in the town other than she knew it would infuriate Ersan . . . and that seemed like a good enough reason.

Roughwater was filled with more pirates and criminals than decent people and Carys knew they'd have a hard time finding any sort of accommodation. Luckily, the town was in a perpetual state of drunkenness and a cloaked figure was so common that she was perfectly hidden amongst the throng.

Music and boisterous singing echoed out from the tight rows of buildings. Ersan let out a long sigh as they walked deeper into the crowd. Carys knew exactly what that sigh meant because he'd made the same sound for the last three hours of their ride, and it spoke a single sentence over and over:

We should be camping in the woods.

If Ersan knew her as well as she knew him then he'd know her response: *We will be camping in the woods for days, possibly weeks, before finding Fenrin. We should take all the cooked meals we can get before then.* Carys rolled her shoulders back, making her posture stronger and walking faster toward the smell of roasting duck, Ersan close on her heels.

Even packed into the crowd and with the person who knew her better than anyone in Okrith by her side, Carys had never felt more alone. It had been days since she'd used her voice at all. The chasm between her and Ersan grew larger everyday, and the wider it grew, the more she felt his absence from her life. From connection to anyone else of any kind. No matter his proximity, their souls had never been further apart. When she got back, she'd make sure Elwyn knew just how cruel it was to push the two of them together again.

Every few paces a break in the buildings would reveal the brackish waters of the Crushwold River mouth and the churning black waves of the southern seas beyond. On a clear day they might even be able to spot the hill on the far horizon that was Arboa. She wondered if the heaviest of breezes could carry with it the scent of snowflowers—a scent she secretly still yearned for more than any glass of wine or honey-eyed cake in the realm—a scent the fae lord beside her bore on his skin along with the smell of turquoise tropical waters and sun-baked clay tiles, and that she hated him for as much as she desired it. Hated him for taking the place that she loved from her. Hated him that his very scent mocked her, reminding her that she'd never feel such peace again.

Carys tried not to look, not even turn her head in the general direction for fear Ersan would notice her looking at the river. She wondered if he longed for his homeland too—so close and yet so far. Wondered too why he'd be willing to give it up even for a few weeks in the pretense of becoming King.

Relief washed through Carys as they followed the crowd round the corner and away from the riverbanks. The clamor grew louder, along with the lewd sounds of passion ringing from brothel windows. Carys was used to these places, having frequented all sorts of establishments with Hale and his crew . . . but this was different—or at least, her company was. She pushed against the tint of embarrassment, knowing she could be more brash than any man if she chose to be. Picking the nearest open doorway and beckoning firelight, she pushed through the clustered patrons lingering around the threshold with a grunt and dove into the loud music and chaos that promised to take away the thoughts of the Crushwold River and the foreign town that still felt like home.

AFTER SEVERAL GLASSES OF WINE, LOTS OF THINGS SEEMED LIKE a good idea. One such thing was how satisfying the comfort of another warm body would feel and how Roughwater was the perfect anonymous town to find one.

Once Carys had finished her dinner—and a pitcher of wine—she'd absconded from her room back down to the bar . . . where Ersan was still drinking too.

He tracked her across the bar for hours, his drunken eyes watching her like a jungle cat's. Whenever she turned to look at him, he'd be looking elsewhere, but she knew his eyes were upon her, knew it with as much certainty as she knew her eyes were blue and her sword was strapped to her hip.

Carys tried to use the time to her advantage, trying to glean any word about the beast in these parts. But the drunken gossip of the tavern had nothing to do with lion monsters. The most she could get out of one snaggle-toothed oaf was that the beast had turned inland, down the trail to the southern coast, and you couldn't pay him a hundred gold pieces to go follow it . . . not that anyone had asked him to. That information was a slight relief at least. The creature was last seen headed to an uninhabited part of the coast where it would be causing the least amount of havoc. Hopefully the beast would dine on sheep and nothing more until they could slay it and get its trophy of a tusk.

Once Carys had exhausted the potential small talk and extorting of rumors, she found herself eager to bolt from the crowded room, but Ersan's eyes were still upon her.

Adisa Monroe's words haunted her: *We both know you can be surrounded by people and still feel the bite of loneliness.* Carys felt those words worse than any curse, and an itching unrest rose within her to remedy it. After days of traveling in silence, she'd thought being amongst this rabble would make her feel full again or at least distracted from her emptiness.

She waited until the end of another song for the crowd to raise their glasses and cheer into the air. When the line of sight between Ersan and Carys was obscured, she ducked into the kitchen and out the back door to the tavern before the cheering had ceased.

The night breeze tousled her hair but the pleasant buzzing in her veins kept her from feeling its frosty bite. She kept to the main road, winding her way through the crowds of drunken men, scanning through them trying to find one who looked at least a little bit worthy of her attention. But one didn't hire an assassin as a bedfellow, as the saying goes, and if Carys wanted a *worthy* suitor, she was searching in the wrong places.

A whistle caught her attention and she paused, turning to the man leaning against a tavern doorframe, his arms folded and eyebrow arched. He was just as gristly as the other men hanging around him, but his face bore no scars so he was at least somewhat competent in a fight . . . which meant—hopefully—he'd be skilled in other ways too.

"You ladies turn more and more ferocious each time I dock in port," he said. His eyes smoldered as he scanned Carys from head to toe. "I can't tell if you're going to fuck me or cut my throat. And I like it." She felt every inch of his gaze scanning over the leathers that hugged her every curve. "How much?"

Carys's smile turned wicked as she sauntered over to him. Maybe this was exactly what she needed: to wipe the slate clean, to replace the memories of Ersan's lips with this nameless stranger and finally move on, to fill up this emptiness inside her with noise and distraction.

Carys sized up the man's muscles, tanned skin, and auburn hair. Maybe she could get the smell of snowflowers out of her head and replace it with his ale and leather polish. She didn't speak, didn't deny that she was for sale. This would be a transaction whether money was exchanged or not. He wanted Carys's body and she wanted to forget.

His hand shot out, circling around Carys's waist, and she folded into the man's arms, both enjoying his warmth and closeness and trying to push down the bile churning in her gut. She wasn't sure if it was the too many drinks or the sense or wrongness of a stranger's arms around her, but she shoved away the discomfort and lifted on her tiptoes to kiss him.

His breath stunk of ale as his smile widened and she suddenly regretted everything. This wasn't what she wanted. He wouldn't make her whole again.

"Kiss me for real," he demanded, squeezing her tighter against his chest.

Carys hesitated, warring with herself as the man pulled her in closer, bruising her body with his grip. Impatient, his fingertips squeezed as if trying to inflict pain and all of Carys's indecision suddenly turned into deep belly laughter.

Did he really think he could outmuscle her? *Her?*

He was a human, she was a fae, and a famed warrior at that. No amount of wine would give him the upper hand. *Let's see him try to outmaneuver me.*

His head dropped, his lips trying to close the distance as he said, "Come on, little doe, I know you want me."

"I've changed my mind." In one swift move Carys unsheathed her dagger and pointed the tip to the man's broad chest. "Now fuck off."

He leaned his head back in surprise as Carys eased her blade backward. He moved to escape her blade when—

His head slammed to the side and Carys's hand was knocked sideways as he fell, her dagger just missing the flesh of the human's neck. Her eyes flew to Ersan, who stood there, fuming, shaking out his hand.

"Sy," Carys hissed, the slurred nickname escaping her lips before she could take it back. "I had it under control."

Ersan's cheeks dimpled at the endearment before the sound of the man's sword being unsheathed pulled his attention away.

"You want to be a knight in shining armor?" the man said, and Carys quickly trained her blade back on him, coming to her senses.

But instead of battling him, the man shoved Ersan in front of him. "He's all yours, boys."

Before Carys could grab Ersan's arm, four men appeared, sucker punching him and dragging him down a side alleyway.

"Hey!" Carys barked out, turning and punching the man she'd almost kissed in the nose. "Only *I* get to fuck with him."

Blood poured from the pirate's nose and he took a menacing step forward, reaching for her. The man tried to catch Carys by the braid but his fingers weren't fast enough and she ducked out of his grip and ran. Her breathing hitched as she jostled her way through the crowd, trying to spot the four men who'd dragged Ersan away.

Curse the Gods, she thought—she'd just got Ersan captured by a group of rowdy and bored pirates and she was squarely to blame. Her heart hammered and a drunken giggle escaped her mouth even as she ran faster. That would teach him. Ersan being fae would give him a mighty advantage, but in a tight space, with that many humans . . . Carys's footsteps faltered. Dread pooled in her gut. What if there were more?

"Fuck." She turned the corner, spotting Ersan and the four humans at the end of the alleyway. Ersan had his dagger drawn but was on his knees. And while two of the four humans were already lying either dead or unconscious on either side of him, the other two were still taking swings. Ersan lifted his head and when he spotted Carys he looked both relieved and incredibly pissed off.

To be fair, she hadn't told him to punch anyone, and *maybe* those

159

four others wouldn't have assaulted her as the fifth dazzled her with his rancid lips. So *maybe* this wasn't completely her fault. Except, it was definitely someone's fault, and as Carys ran toward the brawl, five more humans converged on her. Shit. There were more of them.

"That sword looks like it could fetch a few coppers," one man said, slinking forward from the shadows.

Carys unsheathed her sword from its scabbard and pointed it at him. "Come have a closer look," she taunted as she dropped into a fighting stance.

Wine had turned to acid in her gut from the running and she thought she might spew onto the ground. Her vision doubled and blurred and her pulse raced as she realized she was not as in control of her body as she'd thought.

The men crowed with laughter. "One tip, love." The one with greasy blond hair took another step forward. "Be careful who serves you wine in the Roughwaters, especially if you have something worth stealing."

Carys's knees buckled and she dropped onto the dusty ground of the alleyway. "What did you do?" Her speech came out even more slurred. *Maybe definitely probably all my fault . . .*

"I didn't do anything, love," the man jeered. "But I will reap the benefits of whoever did."

A fist flew out of nowhere, colliding with Carys's lip. She knew it split but couldn't feel any pain, her face so numb she barely registered the trickle of blood dripping down her chin. A boot kicked her in the back and her hands were too slow to shoot up and catch her and she fell face-first into the dirt.

Shit.

Her fingers became pins and needles as she grasped for her dagger. When they circled around the hilt she rolled, stabbing her blade into her attacker's ankle. The man shrieked in pain, jumping back as Carys scrambled to her feet. Her vision spun as another attacker ran at her. Stomach churning and seeing double, Carys knew she needed to end them fast. She prayed Ersan was still holding his own against his attackers at the end of the alleyway. Had he been drugged too?

Her stomach lurched and Carys threw up all across the dusty ground. The men whooped with laughter, jumping out of the way of her splashing bile. The reek of wine and acid coated her clothes. She lay her wet cheek into the grime for a split second, catching her breath.

Don't stop. Keep fighting. She could hear Bri's voice in the back of her head, shouting at her to keep her wits about her. The men's distaste was a mistake, because it gave her the time she needed to scramble back to her feet, swaying like a rocking ship on a windy day.

The next man to reach for Carys found his arm grabbed and twisted round, his elbow popping from its socket. Before he could even scream, she whirled around and punched the next man square in the temple. He dropped like a bag of sand. The last attacker swept out her feet and she fell forward onto her knuckles and knees but kept her dagger in hand. When he grabbed her by the neck of her tunic she swung back blindly, stabbing and swiping at his forearm and side.

"Leave her! She's not worth it," another man shouted. "Let's go."

They stumbled down the alleyway as Carys clambered back to her feet. She turned to find Ersan at the end of the alleyway, another two bodies lying around him. A bruise had bloomed along his cheekbone and rivulets of blood poured from his nose and mouth. More blood splattered his clothes and he swayed just as violently as Carys did herself. He wiped his needle-like dagger across one of their cloaks and sheathed it back in his cane, steadying himself against it.

"I had them under control," he panted.

"Of course you did," Carys said with a wink, steadying herself with a hand against the brick wall. "So did I."

Fire filled her veins as Carys stormed down the alley toward him, weaving despite trying to march in a straight line. "If I weren't here to save y—"

She tripped on nothing, tumbling forward. Ersan caught her by one arm, slowing her fall before dropping her onto the dusty ground.

"You were saying?" He chuckled.

Carys's stomach lurched. "I don't feel so good."

"Neither do I," Ersan groaned, dropping back to his knees.

"Well, one of us has to stay awake long enough to get us back to the inn and lock the fucking door," Carys said, clenching a fist to her stomach as it panged with shooting white-hot pain. "I vote you."

"Carys?"

Her eyes rolled to the back of her head. "I think they poisoned us . . ."

She heard Ersan shout her name again, but she couldn't respond, her body going slack. She felt him trying to shake her awake but she couldn't open her eyes despite the tinge of pleading in his command. The panicked sound of her name on his lips was the last thing she heard before the world went dark.

CHAPTER NINETEEN

When Carys awoke in the middle of the night, she was still covered in sick, her leathers constricting against her clammy skin, and her weapons belt and boots still on. Ersan lay beside her, hugging a bucket in his sleep, still in his rancid clothes as well. He'd managed to get them back to the inn, it seemed, before collapsing under the potency of their spiked drinks—the same inn that had spiked their drinks. She jerked even more awake, wondering just how safe they were in this room. The door, barricaded with the dresser, seemed secure enough from her vantage, and she took a deep breath before checking Ersan's pulse, just to be safe. Sure enough, he was sleeping off the effects of the poison beside her, but he seemed in deep enough sleep that when she rolled out of bed he didn't stir.

She stretched her sore neck from side to side, touching the bruises on her face and arms. Fae were fast healers, but even with fae magic, it would be days before she didn't bear the scars of that drunken brawl. Ambling around the bed, she peeked at Ersan's face, and what she saw made her suck in a sharp breath. In the dimness of the alleyway she hadn't seen the true extent of his injuries but now . . . he looked so bloodied and brutalized that it made Carys blind with rage. She swore she could make out the perfect outline of a boot print up the side of his face that stretched to his ripped pointed ear.

Her chest rose and fell; she was possessed by an overwhelming need for vengeance. She couldn't control it, couldn't force it down. Those pirates attacked someone who belonged to her *and* it was her fault. If she hadn't been so petty, so stubborn, so arse-blindingly stupid, Ersan wouldn't look like he'd been beaten within an inch of his life right now. They'd hurt him and no one, *no one,* hurt Ersan but Carys herself.

Checking her weapons belt, she spun toward the door, shifted the dresser aside, and stormed into the night. There was a reason it was bad luck to threaten someone's Fated, and Carys was about to show them why.

AS SHE NIBBLED ON THE BUTTERY ROLL, CARYS'S STOMACH BUR-bled with acid. The stench of wine seeped from her pores and made her even more nauseated. She'd drunk enough the night before to forget more than just the scent of snowflowers. She wasn't sure she even remembered her name at one point. But the sting of her sore lip reminded her of what had happened and her bloodied knuckles reminded her what came next. She'd come close to the tip of a dagger many times in her life, but that moment in the alleyway when her vision started blurring was a fresh kind of fear she never wanted to relive.

Wandering her way down the now quiet streets, each step made her wince. She'd sustained quite a few injuries before her midnight vengeance—and even more afterward. Only the last of the night's stragglers were still out, retching into barrels and slumped on doorsteps. Her clothes remained soaked in the blood and gore of her late-night victims. She'd stumbled back just before the dawn and collapsed into sleep. Ersan was gone when she'd awoken the second time and when she checked the stables, the horses were gone too. She suspected he'd taken them down to the river to be watered properly. The stable hands didn't seem to care much for their charges.

For a minute she wondered if the horses had even been there when he woke up.

When she turned the corner and the steps down the riverbank appeared, her guess was confirmed. Ersan stood with the horses, staring out across the river in the direction of Arboa. With the heaviness of the haze, the shoreline of the other side was obscured. The air smelled of an impending rainstorm and the drop in the air pressure made Carys's head ache even worse. A big storm was coming, but probably a few more days away. She prayed they'd make it to Marraden before the deluge.

She walked slower as she neared Ersan, unsure of what to say to him. They'd both just saved each other's life, and if she'd listened to him, they wouldn't have needed to.

"I told you we shouldn't have come to Roughwater," he grumbled by way of greeting.

Carys's voice squeaked with sleep as she said, "How long have you been waiting to say 'I told you so'?"

"Well, I attempted in vain to warn you from your very first suggestion that we come here. But the 'I told you so' has been since I woke up this morning." Ersan's eyes drifted halfway to her. "Since I saw your split lip and bruised face."

"It's nothing compared to the state of you." The swelling had gone down and the dark circles under his eyes had faded from an angry red to a deep bruising blue. "I guess I owe you an apology," she muttered.

"For what?" Ersan turned back to the horses. "For not heeding my warning to come to Roughwater or for inciting a mob of drunken pirates?"

"Yes."

Ersan ignored her words and passed her the reins of her horse. "Let's just get out of here."

"I need to bathe," Carys said, waving a hand down her soiled clothes and back up to her still-blood-encrusted face.

Ersan's eyes filled with a quiet anger as they lingered on her wounds. Still, he said, "We can bathe in the Marraden streams once this place is far behind us and we don't have to fear being mobbed again."

"Fine."

"Fine."

Carys had never felt more like a teenager again than she had in that moment. She and Ersan used to have all sorts of petty quarrels. They'd fight about the most foolish things and then make up in the brightest bursts of passion. That's who they'd always been to each other—swinging between light and dark, love and hate.

Ersan cleared his throat as he mounted his horse and Carys wondered if he was remembering those bursts of passion too. Their fighting wasn't nearly as fun anymore. She wondered for a split second if Ersan might pin her against her horse and kiss her. If Carys's head wasn't throbbing so terribly and the lack of sleep starting to make her dizzy, she might not even protest. And then she'd hate herself even more than she already did. She needed to get away from Ersan, as his proximity was beginning to muddle her mind.

They rode through the dilapidated houses and toward the archway that led out of the seedy town. As they turned the corner to the arch, Ersan swore. Three bodies hung from the splintering wood archway and Carys watched Ersan as recognition flickered across his face.

"You can't be serious," he spat, twisting to glare at her. "You *killed* them? Over a few bruises?"

"They were trying to hurt you worse than a few bruises," Carys countered, trying to summon a sense of guilt and failing. A thrill ran through her as she remembered the surprise on their faces as she shoved her blade into their throats and watched the life fade from their hateful eyes. "Me too, if you remember."

"That does not give you permission to kill them."

"We're in a pirate town," she countered. "The best fighter is the law here." Her gaze stayed fixed on the bodies until they rode underneath them. "Maybe stringing them up was a bit overkill," she conceded.

"Car—"

"They hurt you," she cut in, unable to take his chastisement. Surely he of all people should understand. "If you had been conscious, Ersan," her words dripped with her barely restrained rage—some primal need in her rising to protect him again, "maybe I would've meted out their judgment as *you* saw fit. But you were so badly injured I feared for a moment that you wouldn't wake, so I made my own choices."

"So you were so concerned for me you left me to wake alone and fear for you all over again?"

"Curse all the Fates," she muttered. "And their bloody magic that compels me. It's what I could think to do in the moment. That Fated magic once more rears its ugly head. All that magic knew was that they tried to take you from me. They tried to take me from you. It is a bond beyond logic. And I took their lives for it, yes, and I don't regret it."

"If I wanted them dead, I'd have killed them myself when I woke," he gritted out.

"If I didn't follow you into that alley, you might not have woken."

"If you didn't have your fucking tongue down another man's throat—"

"Stop." She clenched her fists, wanting to scream at him. "I didn't need you to be there. I was handling it. You only made it worse. I don't need you to be my savior."

"No." His cold eyes slid to hers. "You'd rather fuck a pirate. Gods, you'd rather *die* than need me at all."

A lump formed in her throat and she couldn't speak anymore. Which was good, because the word "yes" was once more on her lips, but this time had no way of getting out. Even then, with the alcohol out of her system and the raging pressure in her head, she'd never felt number. She hated the truth in it. Carys had never felt so completely out of control and there was one thing that frightened her more than the rest: It was true. Sometimes she thought she'd rather die than need anyone at all.

CHAPTER TWENTY

A thousand unspoken conversations played over in Carys's mind as they rode without so much as looking in each other's direction—so many daydreamed arguments she won against the man next to her, so many vindicating points well made.

The signs of a passing beast were clearer in these parts. Adisa's monster had passed through days ago if the scat was anything to go by. The completion of their task was still out of reach for another day at least, probably more. Their horses weren't going to catch the creature up until it paused, especially since the beast didn't seem to be following any well-worn path. Sure enough, its trail headed straight southward as if following an invisible compass. The gait of the paw prints denoted a hasty speed too, snapped branches and trampled brambles left in its wake.

Carys prayed the monster didn't double back to any villages before she had a chance to skewer it with her blade. She also prayed all the other competitors were having an equal amount of difficulty finding their beasts and that some of them maybe wouldn't even return . . . especially the arrogant Ivar and self-satisfied Falaine. At the very least let them all have miserable journeys with awful companions; it would make her feel better about how terrible her own was going.

The air was poisoned with a thick tension that accompanied their ride until the sun was high overhead. They stopped at a creek along the coastline to bathe, water the horses, and eat some of the rations Ersan had acquired on their way out of town. Carys found a fallen log to perch on and Ersan sat on a river stone, rubbing the tight muscle down his thigh. Passing the lump of bread and hard cheese between them, their earlier barbed words seemed to hang in the air between them as they ate. All of Carys's well-rehearsed arguments seemed to evaporate into the ether.

For maybe the first time since he'd arrived at the Eastern Court, Ersan didn't track her every move. Rather, he stared out at the shoreline, Arboa a thin strip on the other side. It was like a phantom sitting on the horizon, one that Carys yearned to draw closer, like there was a hook pulling from the center of her chest. Like so many things in her life, that yearning would drive her mad if she let it—a place that once felt like paradise, a place to which she would never return.

Yet she couldn't quite push it away. She closed her eyes and breathed deeply, the scent of snowflowers drifting off the water. Probably it was just her imagination, but with that sweet floral scent came a hundred racing memories: of dark corners, of hushed whispers and featherlight kisses, of her name repeated over and over like a prayer . . . Sun-baked clay and white sand beaches, youth, excess, freedom . . . and then it was nothing but heartbreak and sorrow.

Carys's life had always been lonely—so desperately lonely. Her father kept her cooped up for most of her youth in Hilgaard castle with no friends and no family. Her mother had taken her own life when Carys was just a toddler and she had no siblings . . . that she knew of at the time.

Her father, broken with grief, retreated into the cold statue of the person the staff once spoke of with fondness. They referred to her father in the same tone as they spoke of her mother, as if he too had died and whatever husk of a person was left was a stranger even to them. Still, he hosted many parties and entertained many guests, nights filled with fleeting, surface-level conversations. No one to hold on to. No one to stick around long enough to bear witness to his unraveling.

Which meant that Carys had no one to help her deal with her own grief, so thorough was her isolation. She'd wished so desperately for someone to alleviate that crushing weight that sometimes she thought she'd conjured Ersan out of thin air. When she met the Arboan fae with his golden-brown skin, dark eyes, and cavalier grin, she was immediately entranced. But more than that, when she found him, she'd been relieved, because it meant there was, at last, someone else. So firm was her attachment that no one could keep him from her, especially not when the blue witches confirmed that he was, in fact, her Fated. She had almost laughed at that—of *course* he was. No declaration was necessary when there was no way she would ever let him go, Fated or not. He was the one person she was allowed to have. Amazingly, connecting with him also brought her to the Heir of Saxbridge, whose friendship she clung to like a lifeline. But it was nothing like the way she clung to Ersan—so desperate to fill the gaping hollowness she'd felt for so long. Once she claimed him, she thought she'd never be lonely again.

When she found out about Morgan—a sister, a *family* that she never knew about, it was shattering. It was nothing, though, to how she felt when she found out Ersan knew the whole time that they'd been together . . . that he'd held her through tears as she cried for her mother and listened to her longing for the big family that she would never have—listened to the life she ached for—all the while having the remedy to her pain and not giving it to her.

What kind of evil Goddess would curse her to such a fate?

To such a Fated?

She'd never understand it and yet here she was, sitting beside him once again. No matter how far she ran she kept ending up crossing paths with him, now staring out at the city that was once their happy place together—the place she'd wanted to live and die in, the place she'd wanted to make her own kind of family in. It sat there—the Fates gloating—across the river, out of reach physically and emotionally.

A life she'd never have.

Carys had a hundred things she wanted to ask the fae Lord beside her, but instead she found herself saying, "Do you think Collam will make a good Lord if you become King of the East?"

Ersan let out a little grumpy breath and Carys knew the exact face he'd be making—knew him, her Fated, in ways she seldom knew herself. How strange to still be tied to someone she hated; what existed between them still echoed there, seeped of color in a tainted black and white.

Strange and cruel.

"He will hate it," she added.

"As you will hate being Queen."

Carys glanced at him sidelong and then back to the view across the Crushwold. "I would make a great Queen." She tried to say it with some level of conviction. How many people had told her that over and over? And yet, it didn't fill her with any pride. It meant nothing to her at all, simply an obligation she had to fulfill.

"Of course you'd make a good Queen," Ersan said. "You were born to a prestigious Lord. You are allied to every crown in all of Okrith. You have all the training and skill to be perfect for the role of ruler"—his mouth pulled to one side—"but you'd still hate it."

"Stop talking as if you know my mind."

"Stop talking as if you believe I don't."

"You *don't*," she snapped. "You knew a childish fool. Who I've become since . . . everything I am now, is a complete stranger to you."

He propped his elbows on his knees and steepled his fingers in front of his mouth. "You'd like to think that, wouldn't you?"

"As you are a stranger to me," Carys continued, a knot forming in her throat. "A stranger you have always been, it seems."

"Car—"

"If you're not going to tell me why—and you *know* what I'm referring to—I don't want to talk about it. We keep dancing around your reasons and I should know by now you're never going to be honest with me." Ersan remained silent, incensing her further, and she stood up so quickly she even surprised herself. "We don't need to go this whole route together." She brushed the bark from her trousers, trying to busy her hands. "You trail through the foothills. I'll take the forest path. I'll meet you at Lord Marraden's manor in two days' time."

Ersan opened his mouth to speak but she turned and strode off back to her horse, praying he'd listen to her for once and leave her to her churning thoughts.

One day, they'd have their reckoning, and on that day she wouldn't be on the verge of tears when it happened. She'd be in complete control and watch as her words eviscerated Ersan to nothing but heartbroken ash.

That's what she wanted after all, wasn't it? For him to be ruined—so completely destroyed that he'd crawl back to Arboa and never be seen or heard from again? That's what she should want—for the Fated who wronged her to be punished and for her to be gloriously successful as the Queen of the Eastern Court just to spite him . . . even if she hated it.

CARYS SNAPPED A TWIG AND TOSSED IT INTO THE EERIE GREEN flames. She looked across the clearing and up into the hills for the hundredth time, making sure Ersan wasn't within earshot.

The insufferable fae Lord had listened to her . . . and also he hadn't.

He'd started his fire for the night on the foothills that perfectly looked down upon Carys's campsite, the conniving fool. His silhouette was still there on the mountainside, clustered next to the plain orange flames of his fire. He wasn't contacting anyone through the fae fires apparently—unlike Carys.

She probably should've taken the high road too—the lowlands would be easier for a beast attack—but they hadn't seen any sign of the creature that day and the last scat they'd come across had been days old again. The bloody creature was probably waiting at the very tip of the Eastern Court just to spite them. Carys would happily play the bait if it meant one less day on the road with Ersan, though she doubted she'd be visited by any beast other than her Fated in the night.

As much as she'd wanted time to think, she found she couldn't take the weighted quiet that roiled within her like the white foaming seas on a stormy day. Not for one more second could she take feeling like she was one step from madness if she didn't speak to another soul . . .

and yet, that stubborn streak still flooded through her, refusing to let the one person who could resolve that predicament any closer.

Gods, how was she meant to control an entire court when she couldn't even control her own emotions?

"I'll send you a book about it." Neelo's voice carried through the green flames. Carys only responded with a hum. The fire was quiet for a long time before Neelo finally added, "It must be torture."

That caught Carys's attention. "What is?"

"To be so close to someone you hate," Neelo said tentatively. "To be forced to be with him at all."

"It's survivable," Carys muttered, yanking at another prickly weed and popping the scraggily flower head off with her thumb.

"But don't you want to do more than survive?"

Silence lingered a long time before Carys replied, her heart unwilling to respond. She waited until she was confident there wasn't a wobble in her voice anymore. "I never deserved your friendship."

"That is a very random thing to say. And a stupid and wrong one, in case you're wondering."

"I didn't," Carys pushed.

"You did." Neelo's voice carried a considering lilt and Carys trusted the Sovereign of the Southern Court to be honest with her. Neelo didn't lie to make people feel better, but Carys still couldn't believe the truth in their words. "You continue to deserve my friendship, just as I deserve yours."

Carys chewed on the inside of her lip. "Is there any way forward for someone who was once a bad person?" she mused aloud. "I was a bad person, Neelo." She thought of how she'd just nearly gotten Ersan killed out of sheer stubbornness and her brutal means of retaliation against his attackers. "I probably still am. Why are we even friends? Why, when I'm so awful?"

"You give yourself too much credit," Neelo said, a hint of amusement in their voice. "You forget the people I grew up around."

Carys plucked another weed from the ground. "Yeah, and you didn't want to be friends with any of them either." She dropped the leaves of the weed into her fire one by one. "So why?"

"Because I saw you beneath all of that," Neelo said like it was obvious. "The actual Carys. You wore that other person like a dress that never fit you right. I saw under that."

"You saw under my dress?" Carys teased and was satisfied to hear Neelo's snort of laughter from the other side. Getting Neelo Emberspear to laugh was harder than pulling teeth from a chicken. It was one of the biggest points of pride that Carys managed to do so regularly. In that moment of levity, she decided to ask the question she'd been mulling over for days, the one that prompted her to contact Neelo in the first place. "How badly did it hurt when you took the tea?"

Neelo's tsk sounded through the fire. They knew which tea she spoke of—the one that would stop Carys's bleeding forever. "No worse than one of your cycles, I'd say," Neelo muttered. "Though your cycles have always seemed like you're being disemboweled with a flaming sword, so that's not saying much."

"Great."

"Do you want to take the tea?" Neelo's question was slow and careful. "I always wondered why, with such terrible cycles, you didn't."

Carys didn't know how to respond to that. The weight of it feeling bigger than anything she could say with simple words alone. She glanced back up to the flickering orange fire on the hillside.

"Something has always held me back," she murmured. But now, with Ersan there on the foothills probably staring down at her green flame even as she spoke, she wished with all her heart that she didn't feel so conflicted. In fact, she was downright furious with herself. Why couldn't she just do this? Why couldn't she just end it?

"You know . . ." Neelo hedged. "Not bleeding doesn't make you any less, just as it didn't make me any more."

Carys's mouth pinched. "I know."

"Good."

Taking the tea was probably the right decision, she'd thought so since her first bleeding, but . . . she thought of the many years she'd endured it, just in the hopes of little brown-eyed children, their hair a shade lighter than their father's own, their faces a perfect mixture of her and him. The smell of Molly's hair came to the front of her mind. She blamed that hypnotic scent for all of her irrationality. After what Ersan had said to her that morning, there should be no more question in her mind, and yet, it lingered there, breaking her more with every season.

Neelo wasn't much of a conversationalist but the relief of having them on the other end was so great that Carys found herself saying, "Thank you."

"For what?"

"For being here."

"Always," Neelo said and that made Carys's eyes prick with tears. She held in the sob that threatened to escape her lips. "I'm guessing you rise with the dawn tomorrow. Don't you want to get some sleep?"

She cleared her throat. "I don't think I'll be doing much sleeping."

"Rest for a little," Neelo offered. "I want to finish reading this book anyway. I'll sit here with you."

"How many books do you have there beside you right now?"

"Three."

"Cutting back, I see."

"Something like that."

Carys stretched out her cloak like a blanket and lay down beside the fire, edging instinctively closer though she was too numbed from the day to feel its heat. "Don't you want to be with Talhan right now?"

Neelo's soft breath sounded from the other side of the fire again. "I want to be here. Reading a book. With my friend."

"Like we used to do," Carys said, tucking her pack under her head like a pillow.

"And like we'll do many more times in the future," Neelo added.

Their words made Carys twinge with sorrow. Why did it hurt so much to think of the future? She sometimes wished the future didn't exist at all. She couldn't bear to feel this much emptiness as acutely as she did now another day, let alone months, years.

"Carys?" Neelo's voice was so soft she'd thought for a second that she'd imagined it.

"Yeah?"

"Hang on," Neelo said. "Promise me you'll hang on until we do this again."

A tear slid down Carys's cheek, one she didn't even feel welling, then another. She felt its warmth, tasted its salt on her lips, and it was the first time she felt anything in her body all day. Neelo's words rattled her. Whatever mask she usually wore was slipping enough so that Neelo could sense it even through the fae fire. And it scared her to know that her friend worried about it, made her worry even more about herself. Maybe it was that serious. Maybe she was that desperate . . . just like her mother had been. Maybe she just wanted this empty feeling to end.

"I'll try," she whispered back, her voice breaking. "Whatever you're reading . . . can you read it to me?"

Neelo was quiet on the other end of the flickering green flames for another breath before they finally said, "'He'd always smelled like damp earth and woodsmoke—a bonfire after a rainstorm . . .'"

CHAPTER TWENTY-ONE

The next day Carys rode as far as she could, hoping Ersan would give up and break for camp before her. Neelo's words hung over her like a thundercloud the whole day, and, as the sun set and she rode into an abandoned township, she thought it had finally happened—she'd truly lost her mind.

Carys dismounted her horse and wandered through the peculiar deserted streets. What was this place? Nothing was marked on her map. How long had this town been abandoned? She ran her hand along the crumbling stone wall and feared for a moment that perhaps this whole place was a twisted hallucination. Nothing felt real anymore—not the stone beneath her fingertips, not the whistle of the wind, not the stones crunching beneath her boots. Maybe she wasn't real anymore either.

The eerie windowless buildings watched her like the gaping sockets of a skull. The stillness all around her was horrifying. Everything was forgotten and overgrown, and she thought about how this place that was once a home, once filled with memories, with families and laughter—now all gone. They seemed to echo there, still embedded in the stone, singing on the wind.

The mist lifted, revealing a fountain in the city square. A long, rectangular reflection pool now covered in a thick layer of green algae. The stones of the fountain were overgrown with moss but it was the same shape and size as one she'd seen before and she wondered again if this place was just a memory.

It reminded Carys of the Saxbridge fountain she'd once swam in with Remy and Bri. She could still hear the laughter, still feel the sense of fullness and vibrancy in her life; that lingering pain within her was so easy to ignore back then. The mirth and joy, the battles and bloodshed, it all diluted that pain, never erasing it but dulling it somehow.

If Morgan were there, or Bri, or Remy. They would've held her. Hugged her. Their hands finding her shoulder or linking arms together. They would've instinctively just known. The feeling of that physical absence left her bereft. How quickly this isolation warped her mind. Even with so many loved ones propping her up, in their briefest absence she could still slip, foundationless without them.

Carys knew she could call upon any one of her friends and they'd be there before the words even came out of her mouth. But she wouldn't rob them of their joy, not for her pathetic sadness, one she should've grown out of years ago. She shouldn't need their help at all. She should have been made of stronger stuff, and embarrassment warred with shame within her along with that nagging little notion that asking for help and deserving it were two different things entirely.

But Neelo's reaction gave her pause. She didn't want to worry anyone—and telling them that she wasn't sure if she was walking through a twisted manifestation of her memories would most certainly cause them to worry. So she ambled to the fountain and sat there, wishing she could reach out to someone, and knowing that she wouldn't.

She thought about her mother and wondered again if the former Lady Hilgaard somehow cursed her to this fate. If that sticky sort of sorrow ran through her veins too. Her father had always told her she'd inherited her mother's melancholy, but Gods, it ran so much deeper than that. Carys had thought it was her mother's heartbreak that had pushed her over the edge, and perhaps the shame of that too, but as Carys got older, she began to suspect that her mother always had that tumultuous undercurrent flowing below the surface and just didn't have any of the people Carys had in her life to pull her through. She hated how unpredictable and erratic it was. Hated that for all her accomplishments and all her friends, she was here in this depthless pit—*again*—hated how easily she could swing from famed warrior to heartbroken child.

Her hand hovered above the water, sensing, aching to feel the memories of happier times vibrating out of the stillness—of Remy's laughter, of Bri's jokes, of Talhan's hugs . . . A water bug danced across the surface of the water and Carys's eyes pricked with tears.

This whole place—this abandoned, haunted place—was still filled with more life than her own broken soul.

The sound of a twig snapping made her jolt, snatching her hand back. She knew it was him before even looking, knew with an unsettling certainty. Of course her mind would conjure him out of the ether. Of course he'd want to twist the knife deeper. Of fucking course.

"You either followed me or . . . you're not real." She wanted to tell him to go away again, to leave her alone, but she couldn't bring herself to do it.

The sound of Ersan's pack hitting the earth cut through the quiet before his boots came into view. Followed her then . . . if she could trust it. She couldn't know for certain. The world around her prickled with the numbness of a limb gone to sleep, as if part of her she knew existed but couldn't be felt anymore.

Carys stared at her palm, feeling the little pinpricks dancing across her skin where it had hovered above the water. What was there keeping her tethered to existence anymore? She'd never felt more adrift. Part of her wanted to cut that final string and just let herself float away.

Ersan sat and didn't say anything for a long time, his presence dropping into the depths of her mind like a heavy stone. Finally, Carys realized she'd been staring at her hand for several minutes and lowered it, resting her arm in the gap between them.

"I shouldn't—I don't need you to be here," she whispered, her bottom lip wobbling in a pitiful way.

"I know." Ersan's voice was so deep and quiet, his words rumbling straight from his chest like a roll of distant thunder.

"I don't want you to see me like this."

"I know."

"I just need *someone*, though." Carys's voice cracked. "Someone to hold me. Someone I can feel their skin against my own." A tear trailed down her cheek. "If only to remind me that this is real. That I'm not already gone. That I still exist."

Ersan's hand slowly lifted as if debating whether to move before his fingers threaded through her own. The contact shot lightning through her, as if reawakening her in a painful shock.

"You are not your mother," he whispered and a small sob escaped Carys's lips. "I never could understand how—"

"Good," she cut him off. "I pray to all the Gods that you never know what it means to understand why someone would do it. I pray that even the people I hate most never truly know what it is to understand a choice like that."

He could hear all the words unspoken, see straight to the core of her, even now. "Wherever you disappear off to, Carys, I'm coming with you. Even in this." A burning knot lodged in her throat, her very soul trembling at that promise. "Hate me all you want. You don't get to die without me."

His fingers squeezed tighter and that small gesture—just the feeling of his warm skin and the weight of his words—made the dam break and the tears flood down her cheeks. Only with his warmth did she know how frozen over she'd become. *I don't have to feel all this darkness alone.*

Ersan's other hand lifted to the back of her neck and he turned, pulling her face into his shoulder as he gently cradled her head. His fingertips pressed into her skin more at the sound of her sobs, as if it pained him too to hear them. Her forehead pressed against his warm neck, the contact grounding her further back into her body, painfully pulling back the frostbite in her soul.

She melted into him, unwilling to hold herself back any further, collapsing against his chest. His arms banded around her and he held her tight, letting her wring out the sorrow, the pain of losing him, her family, and in the process, herself.

It wasn't until her sobs eased that Ersan's hand squeezed her own and he pulled her to a stand.

"Wh—"

"Come with me," he said, tugging her into the overgrown road and toward an abandoned building across the square. Refusing to release Carys's grip, he grabbed his pack from the path with one hand and kept walking. He kicked open the door and stepped onto the creaking floorboards. "We'll shelter here tonight."

"But—"

"We'll shelter here tonight," he said again, more adamant.

Carys was too broken to protest any further. Whatever energy she'd had to push him away was gone in that moment; she was too raw to put up a fight.

He unbuckled his cloak and tossed it onto the floor in the far corner. Then turned to Carys and unbuckled hers, leaving it beside his own. When he reached for his tunic and hauled it over his head, Carys finally found the words again. "What are you doing?"

Ersan reached for her own tunic and began untying the strings down the front before his hand dropped to her weapons belt. His fingers stilled as his eyes found her own. "Let me hold you," he whispered. "Please."

The pleading in his voice made more tears fall from Carys's eyes. He seemed just as desperate to feel his skin against hers and Carys didn't know what came over her, but the need was too strong. Her hands flew up and she frantically undressed herself until she was bare as Ersan shucked his boots and did the same.

When he was stripped down to only his undershorts, he sat on his cloak and reached for Carys, tugging her by the hips to lie down beside him.

The feeling of her bare skin pressed against his own sent lightning through her, pulling another sob from her as she buried her face in Ersan's chest. One strong hand fanned across the small of her back, the other cradling her head.

His lips dropped into her hair as he murmured, "I'm here. I've got you."

She wept, shattering more with every sob, safe in the knowledge that Sy would never let her drift away. And that's who held her now, not Lord Ersan, but Sy, her friend, her lover, the one who saw her so fully in a way she both hated and craved. This moment was too raw for him to be anything else to her. No more defenses could safeguard her from the truth of this. Not here, when everything felt for a brief flicker safe and warm and whole.

She didn't know how much time passed from one bout of tears to the next, but slowly the tension in her body eased and she melted into the warmth of Sy's soft skin. The stiffness in his hands relaxed too and he began to idly run his fingers up and down her back in leisurely strokes like he'd done so many times before. Carys's cheek rose and fell against his chest, Sy's heart beating in a slow steady rhythm under her ear that lulled her to sleep. His gentle hum vibrated through her body and the exhaustion of the day finally caught up to her and she yielded to sleep.

CHAPTER TWENTY-TWO

The manor at Marraden would have appeared to be deserted were it not for the flickering of candlelight in the windows. Paint peeled from the splintering wood door and years of heavy rain created permanent white streaks along the roof pipes and down across the cracked glass windows.

No one greeted them. No guard or gatekeeper stood watch at the creaking iron fence overgrown with weeds. Carys couldn't help but think of Hilgaard castle. Did her old family home look like this now? Was any of it left after it had gone up in smoke? The memory of the place had warped over the years until the only things that remained clear in her mind were little snippets: the coral-colored roses her mother had planted to ramble up the hedge, the blues and reds of the stained glass windows creating patterns across the ornate carpets, the hiccupping sound her father made when he was trying to stifle his tears . . .

In many ways, she was glad it was gone. She never wanted to return to that place—or that feeling—again. But no matter how far she ventured, it stayed with her, lived within her. The horror of that life in that big, beautiful home still filled her with the same aching hollowness.

Sy's hand landed on Carys's knee, snapping her from her thoughts. She looked down to where his gloved hand touched her leg and echoes of the way he'd held her flooded back in, filling up that hollowness again, and when he pulled his hand away that rising warmth snapped back to frost so quickly it gave her whiplash.

After a night's rest, her wall had come back up again, and still, even within her mind he was no longer Lord Ersan Almah, but only Sy. Whatever other steps closer she'd come to Sy, she stepped back again, fortified by a good night's sleep. He may have held her, may have even cared for her the night before, but he was still a liar, and none of his compassion would change that. She needed to protect herself from his charms even more now when her body felt so dangerously desperate to be back in his arms.

The manor door creaked open and a hunched old fae stumbled out. His once fine clothes were tattered, his spectacles off-kilter on his long crooked nose, and his countenance entirely unwelcoming even as he croaked, "Lord Almah. Lady Hilgaard. Welcome."

Sy waved to the stooped old lord. "Greetings."

Lord Marraden only gave the barest of nods in response.

"I'm sleeping with my dagger under my pillow tonight," Carys muttered, dismounting her horse.

"I thought you did that every night?"

Carys shot Sy a look. "I think we should've camped in the woods again."

"You were the one who wanted as many cooked meals as you could get," Sy countered, glancing up to the darkening sky and then back at Lord Marraden. "Besides, one of the Southern storms is rolling in. Can't you smell it in the air? We've got a couple days before we'll be able to make any headway again."

The Southern storms brought viciously high winds and days-long deluges of rain that felt like the oceans were falling from the sky. Carys didn't blame Sy for wanting to seek shelter and this was the only dwelling that they knew of so far south.

Sy's voice dropped an octave, careful to not be heard by Lord Marraden who lingered in the doorway like a canktanerous shadow. "It's only for a few nights until the storm passes. I think we can survive one grumpy lord."

Lord Marraden made a pointed cough from the doorway, but Carys doubted his old ears could hear them.

This was one of the many things about the lives of fae Lords and Ladies that Carys hated. These important houses all carrying on the pretenses of hospitality and importance even when they were falling into ruin. How many of these grandiose fae did her father host as they traveled through the South even as he mourned the loss of his Fated? How many fake laughs and faux pleasantries had Carys had to bear throughout her childhood? Worst of all were the pitying smiles of strangers apologizing for her mother's death as if they played any role in it. Guilt—that was probably it—that they didn't do more to help the former Lady Hilgaard while she was still alive. But even if they had known, Carys doubted they'd have acted any differently; only in hindsight did they pretend to care.

It was not the sort of legacy Carys had ever wanted to uphold. She'd rather let her castle burn to ash than continue the family tradition . . . But Carys was only beginning to realize she'd well and truly inherited the Hilgaard ways after all: pretend you're not suffering until it kills you.

A bedraggled stable hand ran out, taking the reins of Sy and Carys's horses, while another unbuckled the packs off their mounts and hastend inside. Carys kept her eyes trained on the weary servants and she realized that Lord Marraden had been speaking to them but she hadn't heard a word. As Carys dismounted, Sy stepped behind her, herding Carys to the door like a wayward sheep as if she might turn and bolt rather than receive the Lord's hospitality.

Lord Marraden extracted a crumpled handkerchief from his pocket and honked his congested nose loudly into it before pulling the handkerchief back to inspect its contents.

"Nope." Carys swiveled around and Sy grabbed her by the shoulders, steering her back to the door.

"Just deal with the creepy old fae for one night," he whispered behind her as thunder cracked in the distance, "maybe two, so I don't have to sleep in the pouring rain."

"This may be the nicest thing I've ever done for you," Carys muttered even though they both knew it was a lie.

The forests around the eastern cliffs were sparse, without any caves or thickets dense enough to create shelter from the rain, let alone a heavy storm. They'd either have to double back and waste all of the progress they'd made, or they'd have to drown on dry land hoping to find Fenrin in the middle of a bloody storm. Neither of those were an acceptable option.

"Lord Marraden." Carys stepped up to the old lord as he took her hand, kissing the back of it with wet lips that made Carys's stomach clench. She tried—and failed—not to pucker her face. "So kind of you to host us."

"Of course, Lady Hilgaard," he said, inspecting her with watery eyes before extending his hand to Sy. "How good of you to tour the Eastern Court so thoroughly before claiming its crown. Any child of Matthias Hilgaard has the full support of the house of Marraden." He released Sy's hand and stepped back, granting them entry. "Lord Almah, you look well." They stepped inside the dimly lit hallway, the curtains flailing in the breeze before Lord Marraden shut the door. "Seems like you made it just in time."

Thunder rumbled as they moved through the house. "Indeed," Sy said.

"I've had the chef cook something special for your arrival." Marraden coughed into his sleeve, a wet hacking cough, before gesturing to the stairwell. "But first, I will point you to your room."

"Room? Singular?" Carys asked with a frown.

Marraden's rheumy eyes widened. "You two are Fated, are you not?" He exchanged confused glances with them. Had he not heard of their falling-out? Did he not know Carys had been off fighting with Hale for the past several years? "Your father spoke so proudly of the two of you." He clapped a hand on Sy's shoulder as if that pride was his own. "You were the son he never had."

Carys noted the way Sy tightened at the action. It was no secret Sy and her father had been instantly close and she knew her father heartily approved of him. But this was the first time she'd considered that Sy had lost someone important to him too—the only father figure he had left. Did Sy mourn her father's loss just as much as she did? If he did, he didn't show it.

Bitterness tinged the thought until it clouded out all else. She knew it would be unfair to wonder if her father loved her as much as he loved Sy, but she knew for certain her father *trusted* Sy more than her. And that, she couldn't so easily forgive.

"I think my Fated is tired," Sy said, placing his hand on the small of Carys's back and guiding her up the stairs.

"Yes, a little weary under the eyes," Marraden agreed, waving a knobby finger under his own generous bags.

Carys wanted to counter that it wasn't from exhaustion but rather the remnants of two black eyes from nearly being killed by a band of pirates. Instead, she stepped out of Sy's touch, hiding her contempt with the fake laugh she'd perfected. She climbed up five steps before she muttered under her breath, "You're sleeping on the floor."

"I know," Sy said through a tight smile.

"I'll let you get settled in," Marraden called from the stairwell. "I'll see you at dinner."

As soon as he turned down the hall Carys's smile vanished and she stared daggers at Sy. "Don't do that again."

Her stomach twinged and her face flushed as she rushed up the final steps and turned toward the only open door in the long hallway. She raced past the peeling wallpaper as dread mounted at the familiar telltale squeeze of pain in her lower back.

Fuck.

THE ROOM WAS NOT A ROOM AT ALL BUT RATHER A SUITE WITH A formal front lounge, a bedroom through gilded doors, and a bathing chamber beyond with a clawfoot bathtub that was begging for someone to soak in it. Apart from the few cobwebs clinging to the ceiling and the tattered edges to the upholstery, the room still carried the weight of opulence of a bygone era.

"Perfect." Carys marched through the lounge and into the bedroom. She grabbed her pack off the trunk at the foot of the bed, hefting it up and marching back to the tufted velvet sofa.

"Wh—"

"You take the bed. I can sleep out here," she said, dumping her pack onto the sofa.

Sy grabbed the other strap of her pack. "You take the bed. I will sleep out here."

"I don't need your chilvary—"

"Gods, do I know it," he spat as an impromptu game of tug-of-war ensued.

"Unless you'd like to request Lord Marraden to appoint you with your own accommodations?" Carys offered with mock sweetness, finally wrenching her pack back from his hands.

"We'll take turns," Sy groused, relenting. "You take the bed tonight and I will tomorrow."

As her lower back twinged, Carys thought better of her stubbornness. Her impending dilemma would be easier to conceal behind a locked door and closer to the bathing chamber.

"Fine." Carys hefted her pack back on her shoulder and pulled the gilded doors shut behind her with more force than necessary. Snatching her pack up in the air, she dramatically dumped its contents across the bed.

It wasn't fine. Nothing was.

She riffled through her belongings until she found the vial she'd been searching for. Her "just in case" vial, one she'd prayed to all the Gods she wouldn't need on this trip. She scowled at the label of a crescent moon and flower—too soft and feminine for what its purposes truly were: pain relief—one of the most potent kinds around. She clasped her fingers around the bottle tighter. One of these tiny little vials was enough to knock her out for a full day, enough that she wouldn't know her own name and probably wouldn't rouse from sleep at all. She stared longingly at the vial and cursed.

No, she couldn't take this here. She needed to be on alert. Sedating herself wasn't an option.

The cramping in her back grew, blossoming up to her shoulder blades and shooting down to her legs. For most fae in Okrith, their seasonal cycles were nothing more than a minor inconvenience: two days of bleeding and then it was over. For Carys . . . it felt like two days of her body being ripped in half. She was a soldier—she'd broken bones, been shot with arrows, stabbed straight through with a blade once, and nothing—*nothing*—was more painful than her cycles. There was nothing cyclical about them either. She couldn't time them to the moons or seasons or to any date like the other fae did. The bleeding came and went sporadically, less frequently than others' and always catching her off-guard. And when it came, it was the worst sort of surprise.

From her first bleeding onward, Carys slowly began to understand that her body wasn't exactly built like those around her. She put on muscle quickly, sprouted coarse hairs on her top lip and chin, and parts of her seemed slightly larger than others'—not that she'd spent much time in the soldiers' camps comparing parts, but she noted it, and for the most part no one cared or thought much of it at all . . . except for times like this. These crippling erratic cycles that snuck up on her at the worst imaginable times.

Maybe this one wouldn't be so bad, she lied to herself. She told herself that every time.

Carys thought to the days before, of the merciless slaying of those pirates, of her broken-down sobbing . . . and frowned.

She'd never met another fae in all of Okrith whose cycles were so debilitating. To be fair, not every fae wanted to talk about it, but she'd discussed it with enough of her friends to know her case was rare. She couldn't believe humans had to cope every month. Luckily, the brown witches had a good supply of elixirs that could pull her through the worst of it, but their blessing was also their curse: the elixirs were too powerful to take and still keep her wits about her. And in this strange place at the end of the Eastern Court with one of Adisa's monsters on the loose, she couldn't be out for a whole day.

"Goddess strike me down," she muttered, throwing handfuls of clothing across the bed.

Squeezing the vial, she paced back and forth across the room and debated what she should do. Could she hide it? How? She didn't know if stubbornness alone could get her through this one.

A knock sounded at the door.

"What?" she snapped, whirling toward the sound.

"Are you getting dressed for dinner?" Sy's muffled voice called through the door.

"Shit." She dug through her clothes. "Give me a minute!"

"Please don't tell me you brought a dress with you," Sy jeered. "Don't waste your energy freshening up for Lord Marraden. He's staler than weeks-old bread."

Carys let out a surprised laugh as she continued digging through her pack to find her underwear. Whatever material the brown witches wove into it was a secret they held tightly, but it was the most absorbent material—magically so. Most fae only needed two pairs to last them a whole cycle: one to wear and one to wash.

Carys carried six with her always.

Her fingers slid across the satin outer layer of fabric she wore and grabbed the balled-up pair, quickly stripping to the waist and swapping them out. She jumped back into her trousers as Sy knocked again.

"Just go without me," she growled. "I'll meet you there in five minutes." He tested the door handle, pushing it open and peeking inside. She knew she should have locked it. "Sy—" Carys snarled, buttoning her trousers. "Seriously?"

"I was just checking some monster hadn't eaten you," he said with a mischievous look. His eyes scanned around the room and across the bed to Carys's scattered belongings. "You live like an animal."

"I didn't ask for your opinion."

"And yet here you are, receiving it." He cocked his head, eyeing Carys up and down too, and she wondered if he could sense what she was doing by the sharpness of his eyes in his otherwise playful expression.

"Let's just eat," she grumbled, breezing through the door and past him as he watched her like a riddle he wanted to solve. "I'm exhausted and want to get to bed."

Maybe she could make it through dinner and sleep through the worst of it. Maybe she'd be able to hold it together and no one would ever know. Maybe if she found an excuse to keep her distance over the next two days Sy wouldn't smell the blood on her or notice it in the bathing chamber and worry . . . Gods, he knew more than anyone how bad they got.

With each step, pain shot up her legs and her stomach turned to acid. All those "maybe"s fell away as her loose hands turned into fists, fingernails digging into her palms. She took a sharp breath, and then another, willing herself to hang on. Maybe she could take one sip from that vial? Maybe one drop wouldn't make her act suspicious? Maybe . . .

This can't be happening. This can't be happening, she told herself over and over like a chant, as if saying it enough times would make it true. How in the Gods am I supposed to be Queen when I can't even function during this?

Each step, each breath, hurt a little more than the last and she was certain her panic was bringing on the pain faster than it usually arrived. No, normally she'd have hours, if not days, of warning. She needed to relax.

Wine.

There'd be wine at dinner. She'd have a few glasses and calm the fuck down. There was still time before her flow got out of hand and the pain grew to the point of crushing.

For so long she'd been so numb, so desperate to feel anything other than that emptiness inside of her, but as each step felt like a hot poker in her back, she wished she felt nothing at all again.

CHAPTER TWENTY-THREE

Everything about Lord Marraden's house had a tinge of foreboding that Carys couldn't tell was from her own panic or from her honed instincts. She kept her linen napkin screwed in a fist in her lap, leaving her upper body above the table completely serene as her hand gripped the napkin until her knuckles were white. Every instinct told her she needed to keep her wits about her. What if those pirates from Roughwater tried to exact revenge? What if Adisa Monroe had some plan up her sleeve? What if the monster they were searching for attacked? What if this manor came alive and tried to eat them?

But despite all of the reasons to stay on alert—even the ridiculous ones—her mind kept drifting to that vial in her room.

One harried servant made several trips from the kitchen to deliver them their meal and Carys wondered where the rest of the manor staff was.

As if reading her thoughts, Marraden said, "There's nothing to keep the young ones here anymore. I think Mary's grandson is the only member of my household staff under fifty." He watched the older human maid scurry back to the kitchens. "This used to be a lively town. Now, the younger generation has all gone off, either to more lucrative trades further north or conscripted into one of the late King's many armies."

"He had humans in his armies?" Sy leaned forward across from

Carys, staring down to the head of the table where Marraden sat. It seemed a silly formality that they should sit so far apart from the head of the household, forcing them to raise their voices to an uncomfortable pitch just to converse.

"Cannon fodder," Marraden said, lifting his napkin to cough into it. "Gedwin Norwood feared the North and kept his armies full with young ones to bulk out his numbers. He didn't care what happened to them."

"Just like he didn't care for the fate of his eldest son." Carys's voice came out sharper than she intended, as if it was a great exertion just to speak, and she noted how Sy's eyes snapped to hers at the sound.

Shit. She didn't want him to know, didn't want him to sense her weakness. She also had no bloody clue how she was going to keep it from him either.

"But Hale Norwood is not a Norwood at all," Marraden blustered. "It makes sense now why the late King thrust him into so many harebrained battles. But Gedwin only succeeded in making Hale a hero for all of the trials he endured and survived." The Lord dabbed the corners of his mouth and returned to his soup.

Carys pushed the chunky potato slop around with her spoon, thinking fondly of all of those trials she'd endured by Hale's side—one wild adventure after another. She'd lived a lot of life over the past several years as a member of Hale's crew. They'd become legends of sorts—unkillable, some would say—but Carys had seen members of Hale's army die too many times to count. A wash of blood-drained faces clouded her mind, some close to her, others she didn't even get to learn their names—humans like Mary's children—sent to pad out Hale's numbers while giving him no real advantage against a fae army. But between Carys, the Golden Eagles, Hale, and their ragtag crew of humans, they'd managed to outmaneuver even the North's highly trained soldiers through grit, sheer willpower, and a little mischievous ingenuity.

The conversation dawdled on, Carys lost in the memories of battles long gone. What had happened to her? She used to be mighty.

She used to be worthy of a crown. One look at her long braid and the armory of weapons she wore and people would know—she was Carys Hilgaard, famed warrior and member of the Crown Prince's inner circle. Her fame was now the only thing bolstering her in the competition for the Eastern Crown. She didn't feel like that person in her soul anymore—didn't feel strong, resolute, fierce. She felt weak and broken, even more so as the growing pain swirled in her gut every time she shifted in her seat. Soon there would be no position that would bring her relief, and she needed to be in her room with the door locked and a knife under her pillow before then.

The courses were swapped out again and again, Lord Marraden trying to show off with the mishmash of sumptuous fare, but Carys couldn't bring herself to eat more than a polite mouthful of each. She knew Sy tracked her every movement, her every bite that she did not take. She hated how perfectly tuned into her he was, even after all this time. He could read her poorly hidden secrets like an open book. She probably reeked of fear too. Maybe he could smell her panic from across the table as easily as he could see it in her too-widened eyes.

She reached across the table for the pitcher of wine, her muscles tightening up her back like a corset pulled too tight. Sy intervened, reaching the pitcher before her hands could graze the handle and rising from his seat.

"Allow me," he offered, bending to refill Carys's goblet nearly to the brim.

Her lips pressed into a smile at the unseemly serving size. Maybe he thought she was nervous for another reason . . . or maybe he knew. Either way, Carys gulped down her third goblet of wine and wiped her mouth with the back of her hand.

Lord Marraden gaped at her, his mouth open and his spoonful of peas hovering midway to his mouth.

"The wine is delicious, my Lord," Carys offered sheepishly, trying to act a little more demure. The warmth of the wine spread through her limbs in tingling pinpricks like stepping into a too hot bath. Now, with this pleasant lightness that spread through her from the drink, was her chance to make her escape to her room before things got worse.

She already knew she'd be warring with herself all night whether or not to drink from that vial.

"You've spent too many years on a battlefield, Lady Hilgaard," Marraden admonished lightly with a tsk and continued eating. "And away from the guidance and wisdom of your father. I always admired him. He was everything a good lord should be."

"Indeed," Carys agreed a little too quickly, feigning a yawn and stretching her arms out beside her. "And I fear I'm growing weary from the journey."

Sy moved to stand and Carys lifted a hand. "I know Lord Almah was looking forward to after-dinner drinks with you in your study, Lord Marraden." She grinned at Sy as he was forced to hide his frown. That would buy her enough time for him to think she was asleep at least. "I'm sure he'd love to reminisce about my father with you. The two of them were so close, after all."

"Delightful," Lord Marraden said.

"Splendid," Sy replied, though his face said it was anything but.

"Have a good night, gentlemen," Carys said, rising from her chair and offering them each a quick bow before she hastened out of the room, sharp fire blossoming low in her belly with each dreaded step.

PAIN.

Such blinding unending pain.

Muscle pulled from bone, her whole body shattering, her mind trembling as her stomach lurched. Carys hurled the pitiful bites of her meal onto the carpet before she could reach for a bucket. Her hand gripped that vial tighter—so tightly she thought she might crush it in her grip.

She couldn't lose control. She needed to keep on guard in this strange house in this strange part of the realm. This couldn't be happening.

A light rap of knuckles sounded on the door and Carys cursed all the Gods as she groaned into her pillow. She took a deep breath—and then another—trying desperately to put on a calm yet grumpy voice as she said, "I'm trying to sleep."

"Carys." Sy's voice was slow and rough, tinged with a snarl of command that made Carys know he wasn't going to easily walk away. The doorknob rattled. "Come to the door."

"Exactly how many drinks did you have?" Carys growled. "Go sleep it off, Sy."

"Carys," he said again, enunciating each word with biting authority. "Open. The. Door."

She wanted to shout, "Fuck off," but couldn't. Her legs were pins and needles, her body trembled worse than a trapped rabbit. She opened her mouth for a sharp retort but instead she stifled a cry, her hands fisting into her sheets until her nails dug holes into the fabric.

Gods, she was going to die. This was going to kill her.

She was so lost in her pain that she barely registered the door being kicked in, the splintering wood flying across the room as Sy let out a string of curses. But he was there and the tightening muscles in her seemed to release ever so slightly as he rushed to her side. His scent and warmth swarmed her and her muscles eased even further.

"Fucking Gods," Sy barked. His hand swept the hair back from Carys's sweaty forehead. "Why?" He sounded like he was going to punch his fist through the wall. "Why didn't you tell me?"

"I'm. Fine," Carys panted between each breath.

"Clearly."

"Leave me."

"No."

"Leav—"

Sy's hand dropped to bracket Carys's jaw. He turned her face to meet his storming dark eyes as he growled, "No." His thumb swept across her cheek, trailing down her shoulder, arm, and to her clenched fist. "Why haven't you taken this yet?"

Her whole body shook with restraint, the pressure mounting within her from every side. Her stomach lurched again and Sy shifted to the bed, dodging the bile that splattered across the floor as if he was expecting it. This wasn't his first time seeing her like this. He held back the strands of hair that had fallen loose from her braid as she emptied the contents of her stomach.

Carys rolled over, curling into a ball, her fist still white-knuckled around the sleeping elixir in her hand.

Sy grabbed her fist and tried to peel her fingers back from the bottle.

"I don't need it," Carys gritted out. "I can't sleep for two days in this place. I need to be on guard."

"Gods curse me," he said, finally freeing the vial from her pathetic grip. "Your stubbornness will *kill* you."

"I have to be ready!"

"To what? Bleed and moan at our enemies?"

"That's not funny! What if there's another attack? What if an army of violet witches is marching toward us as we speak?" Carys moved to sit up on her elbows and Sy's hand roughly shoved her back down by the shoulder.

"There is no army," Sy snapped. "We're on the hunt for Fenrin, possibly with a small retinue, but nothing I couldn't handle without you."

"Cocky."

"I can handle it."

"You forget there's monsters," Carys countered.

Sy stared at her, letting out a sharp frustrated breath as she continued to fight him with her last vestiges of strength. "I can handle a few monsters too if I must."

Carys pushed against the hand on her shoulder but Sy easily pinned her down. She moved to struggle against him again when another blinding wave of pain shot through her and she ground her teeth, grimacing as she clutched her stomach.

Sy yanked the cork from the vial and brought it to her lips. "Drink this. Now."

"I need to—"

"You need to drink this and stop being so *you*." His mouth dropped to her ear. "I will protect you," he promised. "In your soul you must know, I will *always* protect you." His breath skittered across her hair. "Now drink. Please."

The pain had muddied her mind until the entire room was spinning and the only thing she could do was bring her lips to the glass. Even if it killed her, she needed it to stop.

"Good," Sy whispered, sweeping her stray hairs back behind her ear.

Pain lanced through her and she cried out, flailing as if fighting off an invisible foe. Sy grabbed her, pulling her up against his chest, his arms constricting around her. Carys tried to fight him as if he was the pain coursing through her, scratching and clawing and beating against his chest, but his arms simply tightened that viselike grip and he dropped his mouth to her ear.

"Hold on," he murmured. "It's nearly passed. Hold on."

Her whole body coiled tighter, her muscles contracting so viciously that she thought they might snap her in half. A cry of pain rose up from her chest and Sy's lips found her own, swallowing her scream.

"Hold on," he murmured against her mouth.

The feeling of his lips anchored her against the maelstrom of suffering. The wave of pain crested within her and then began to ebb, the feeling of it releasing so incredibly blissful that she thought she was high on witching brew.

The elixir started to work its magic quickly from there, the muscles in her arms and legs loosening to jelly and her racing heart slowing to a steady rhythm. But when Sy moved, Carys's hand flew out and her fingernails dug into his arm.

He let out a rough laugh as he continued to prop himself up long enough to grab a pillow and tuck it under his head. Then he lay back down beside her, shuffling in close until his body was flush against her back, his warmth radiating into her as sleep beckoned closer. Sy's hand slid around to Carys's belly and her hand held his there, fingers interlocked.

How many times had they lain in this very position? How many beds had they fallen asleep in just like this?

And as powerful as the sleeping tonic was, Sy's voice had a magic all of its own as he dropped a kiss to Carys's temple and whispered, "Rest, love. I'll protect you."

And she finally did.

CHAPTER TWENTY-FOUR

She awoke to her stomach growling and the sound of rain pelting against the windowpane. She smelled the heady scent of snowflowers wafting on the air and knew she was back in Arboa.

Carys's eyes flew open and she stared at the peeling filigree wallpaper. No. This wasn't Arboa.

The memories of the day before flooded back to her. Had she slept all night? A day? Two? The cramping in her back was still there but a mere echo of what it had been. She shifted in the sheets, realizing there was a smooth satin nightdress against her skin and not her riding leathers . . . She rolled over to take in the disheveled room, her eyes instantly landing on the Arboan Lord sitting at the desk, his back turned to Carys as he wrote on a sheet of cream paper.

Her eyes drifted down to the floor, noting the carpet had been cleaned of her sick. She lifted her hand to the back of her head, her fingers sliding down her freshly braided hair.

"How long have I been asleep?" she croaked and Sy immediately swiveled around.

A mixture of relief and happiness suffused his normally guarded face. It only lasted for a split second before he returned to his usual brooding, but Carys saw it there—the same expression he had when they were young.

"A day and a bit," he said, swiveling his chair and sitting back down.

Carys's thoughts were still clouded by sleep—and probably the potent elixir too. Everything felt foggy and distorted, her world contorted along with her judgment. She didn't feel well enough to play her usual games. She lifted a hand to massage her temple and said, "Gods."

"How do you feel?" Sy's words were careful and his eyes assessing.

"Mostly better," Carys assured him. She shifted, feeling the blood pool between her legs as she changed to a seated position. She wondered if he'd cleaned her or simply changed out the thick blanket placed beneath her. The sound against the windowpane pulled her focus. More rain pinged across the glass, accompanied by the rattling of hailstones. "The Southern storm?"

"The worst has passed," Sy said, staring at the ceiling. "There's a few more leaks that need patching and half the forest to be cleared out of the front lawns, but no real damage to the manor. The rain should be light enough for us to head off tomorrow by Marraden's estimates."

Carys suddenly remembered their host and wondered what he thought of her day-long absence. "What did you say to Lord Marraden?"

Sy shrugged. "That you weren't feeling well and needed some rest."

"And?" Carys prodded.

The corners of Sy's mouth pinched as he relented. "And that I ordered you to remain in your chambers."

"Of course." Carys rolled her eyes, knowing there was more to that conversation but feeling too exhausted to push further. It was probably a wise lie. Marraden wouldn't question the instructions of someone's Fated, but still, if the old fae thought Carys took orders from anyone, he clearly didn't know her at all. Lords, fathers, Fateds. Even within the hierarchy of beings in Okrith, fae had a hierarchy of their own. And men valued the opinions and loyalties of other men to the detriment of all else.

Carys lacked the energy to verbalize that particular diatribe, however, and simply let out a disparaging hum. She reached for the glass of water on her bedside table and swigged down the entire thing in one big gulp. Grabbing the pitcher beside her glass, she refilled it two more times.

"Thank you," she murmured at the fresh pitcher of water, not meeting Sy's stare.

He waved it off as if it hadn't meant everything to Carys to be protected by him, to be safe enough in her trust of him, even through her hatred, that she knew he'd battle a dragon just to let her sleep.

"It gave me time to catch up on some long-overdue letters." He gestured to the paper strewn about the desk, his fingertips stained with black ink.

"Have you written to all of Okrith?" Carys teased.

"Four of those pages are for a single letter to Collam." Sy's eyes crinkled as he spoke of his younger brother. "I've had many adventures to tell him about . . . and many more reminders and instructions for him as acting Lord of Arboa."

Carys's mouth curved. "Poor Collam." She could only imagine the litany of detailed orders that were on those pages. Sy cared deeply about his city, some might say pedantically so. He wouldn't want a single person to be let down by his absence and it made Carys question again Sy's decision to compete for the Eastern crown.

"He'll learn in time," Sy said.

Carys noticed the hint of scorn in Sy's voice and pressed her lips together to hide her knowing smile.

Collam would hate it—acting as Lord when he'd rather be in his studio painting. But they all had lives not of their own making now. Carys was destined to be a great ruler—or so everyone kept telling her. Her father raised her to be a lady of the highest nobility. He would've turned in his grave if she'd not entered the competition for the Eastern throne, and been only slightly less appalled if she wasn't crowned. She wondered if Sy vied for the crown to win her father's approval too. Were they both still scrambling to win the respect of a ghost?

She was molded to be Queen from her appearance and her wealth to her fighting prowess and political connections. It should be everything she wanted her life to be. There would be no hiding out in the blooming fields, just as there'd be no hiding out in the paint studio for Collam. Greatness called each of their names, and they were forced to listen to it, no matter how much they wanted to turn away.

Another wave of cramps hit her and Carys curled in on herself.

Sy shot up from his chair and rushed over.

"I'm fine," she groaned. "It's nothing compared to what it was. By tomorrow it'll be gone."

"Do you want more pain relief?"

Carys shook her head. She couldn't take another day's worth of the sleeping tonic. She knew she'd feel better soon enough. She lifted up on her elbow and Sy's hands hovered on either side of her shoulders as if she might fall over even prone in bed.

Carys snorted. "I'm not made of porcelain."

"I know." He dropped his hands, his eyes searching her face with a concern he couldn't seem to hide. He'd seen these episodes before, but two nights before had been one of the worst she'd ever experienced, and it was clear that it had rattled him. "What do you need?"

Carys sniffed the air and wrinkled her nose. "A bath."

Sy's eyes instantly heated, his fingertips slowing their trail down Carys's wrist to her palm, and Carys knew he was thinking of the same lustful memory she was. It hadn't been intentional to trigger such memories between the two of them, the word had just tumbled out, but now she knew it instantly evoked a spark. Before, when the worst of her pain had subsided, there was something else that always relieved the tension of Carys's cycles . . . something far more enjoyable than sleeping for two days. She thought of the many baths they'd shared together, of Sy's eagerness to make her feel better in the way only he knew how.

A whole conversation seemed to pass between one breath and the next as Carys's fingers curled to Sy's touch. He seemed to debate with himself whether this was a good idea or not. Carys forced herself not to think about it too closely. It was a physical thing, it didn't need to be anything more . . . at least she could try to keep it from being anything more. Her mind and her heart clashed blades again, warring with each other, but as her muscles tightened again she forced all thoughts away.

She lifted her eyes to Sy and said, "Go draw us a bath."

She let the word "us" hang between them as Sy rose from the bed and did as she commanded.

CARYS GINGERLY WALKED ACROSS THE UNEVEN TILES INTO THE bathing chamber. The clawfoot bathtub sat in the center of the tiled room, a fire roaring to life on one side and a basin and towel rack on the other.

As Sy walked in, Carys's pulse quickened and she bit the inside of her lip. What in the Gods's names were they doing? Sy wore a secret smile that tugged at the corners of his mouth as if he knew exactly what Carys was thinking. Were they really going to do this? She knew she'd hate herself for it in another day, but right then, she didn't care. Her body still ached and she wanted to be flooded with the warmth and pleasure that she knew awaited her with his touch. Consumed by a need to take her pain away—and sate her ever-growing desire—she knew the second she commanded Sy to draw them a bath, it would only lead to one end.

Still, she moved slowly, awkwardly, as if Sy hadn't seen her naked a thousand times before. Sy wandered to the fire as Carys fumbled with her chemise. He picked up an iron and stoked the fire before adding another log. With a final decisive breath, Carys whipped her chemise over her head. She pulled her sodden undergarments down, streaking her legs with red as she stepped out of them, her body feeling both exhausted and filled with flames all at once. She needed to stop overthinking this, battling her mind still groggy from the sleeping potion. Maybe once it was out of her system, she'd be filled with regret. Whatever small voice was trying to shout at her from the recesses of her mind would have to wait.

She stepped into the hot water of the bath, stifling the soft moan as she sunk under the surface. With his back still turned, Sy grabbed a towel off the rack and brought it to the fire. Carys's eyes tracked him silently as he wrapped one of the stones sat beside the fire into the towel. He spun the hot stone into the fabric like a parcel and brought it over to the bath. His eyes remained glued to the tiled floor.

"Here," he murmured, dropping the towel-covered stone behind Carys's back.

The water rose higher, covering her peaked nipples. When the fabric hit Carys's lower back, she groaned. Leaning back into the bundle, it was so hot it was almost painful, but she felt her muscles blissfully release at that heat and she melted further into the tub.

Sy placed a kiss on her temple, his expression so soft and tender compared to his normal countenance, as if he needed to be sure of the relief coursing through her.

"Thank you," she whispered, leaning her head back against the porcelain.

"Enjoy your bath," Sy said.

He was trying to do the noble thing. She supposed she could just pleasure herself like she usually did around her cycles these last many years. It would still bring her some amount of relief.

Sy pushed off from the tub to stand and Carys's mouth fell open. He was really going to leave. The Sy from their past together would've never been so chivalrous and it reminded Carys once more of how much time had passed, apart and alone, yet how much the two of them had grown in each other's absence. But right then she didn't want the reformed version of Sy. Right then she wanted her roguish lover who always seemed eager to get between her thighs.

Carys's hand shot out, confusion knitting her brows together. Sy's gaze dropped to where her hand held his to the bath's edge. "Stay."

"Carys," Sy warned. "Think about this. I don't want you to hate me for the rest of this journey."

"There's so very many reasons why I hate you already," she countered, "but this won't be one of them." Sy grinned, shaking his head at her, and Carys added, "Please, Sy. Help me."

She knew it was a low blow, to use his nickname, to let him think that she was warming to him when really she was just desperate for release. Add it to the list of strikes against her soul that the Gods would tally. She knew she'd already be denied passage into the afterlife.

Sy stared at her for a long moment, frozen, but clearly debating with himself. Finally, Carys added one more nudge to push him over the edge. Her fingers constricted around his hand, giving it a little tug as she whispered, "Do you want me?"

Sy's gaze fell to the floor, his dark hair falling across his brow and into his eyes.

"Do you want this?" Carys found herself asking. There was only so far she was willing to push, suddenly second-guessing that perhaps he didn't want her the way she wanted him. Maybe the tricks of her youth no longer worked. Maybe she'd wagered on his desire mirroring her own and had miscalculated. Even the evidence of his arousal straining at the seam of his trousers wasn't enough to know for sure. She cleared her throat. "It's okay. I can handle this on my own."

"No." Sy's eyes flared. His face morphed to pure lust as he said, "Let me assist you."

Assist you. That's what this was. He was helping her—a kindness as a friend, a fun one, but nothing more.

Yeah, right. But Carys did need him for so many reasons and she was too tired and foggy to put up the many layers of defense around her weary heart. Let them have this moment, the fallout would be tomorrow's problem.

Sy slowly pulled loose the laces of his shirt and then reached back to pull it off revealing his chiseled chest. Gods, he was far more carved of muscle now than his once lean form, his chest more dusted in dark hair. Carys swallowed, her eyes savoring each of his slow, deliberate movements until her whole body ached.

His belt was next, letting his trousers pool around his feet, and her eyes fell to the outline of his hard cock before glancing away. Her cheeks were on fire and her throat dry. She had the sudden urge to lick her lips as Sy perched himself on the edge of the tub. He shucked one boot and then removed his wooden foot, boot and all. The muscles in his arms bulged as he held his weight up to remove his undershorts, balancing on one leg, and Carys had to clasp her hands together under the water to keep from letting them rove all over his body. He swung his leg into the tub behind Carys, his arms straining as he held himself up. He balanced with a practiced ease as he brought over his half limb and shifted off the edge, and slowly lowered himself down. He hissed at the scorching heat of the water.

Carys pulled the hot stone from her back and moved it to her front, holding it low on her belly, and she felt her insides clench. This is what she needed—to muddy the waters between her pain and her pleasure.

Sy's muscled thighs bracketed Carys's own, his arms snaking around to her belly and splaying out across her warm flesh. She leaned back into him, savoring once more the feeling of his skin. She dropped her head to his shoulder and his lips skimmed across her cheek.

His fingers circled her belly, drifting lower until she was writhing beneath him to get that hand exactly where she wanted it. Water lapped up the sides of the tub at her movement. Sy let out a little grunt as she moved her hips, his length hardening further against her back as she moved over him.

She felt his smile against her skin. "Do you want me to touch you?" he asked as if the answer wasn't already abundantly clear.

"Yes," she panted, arching her back to get those fingers lower.

Finally, Sy obeyed, his fingers dropping to the hair between her legs, sweeping down her center and parting her flesh. Her moan echoed across the tiles as Sy's middle finger skimmed her swollen, throbbing bud. Sy's other hand pulled her tighter to him, keeping her from slipping across the tub.

His fingers deftly circled her, stroking up and down and swirling in just the way he knew she liked. Slowly he built that pleasure inside of her one moan at a time. Gods, she missed this. He touched her like he was in her mind, knowing right where to rub and stroke to keep her teetering on the edge of pleasure. After all this time, he still knew exactly what she needed, intuiting every breath and moan.

Carys turned her face in toward Sy's neck, breathing thick gasps against his skin. A deep sound rumbled in his chest as she shifted and her ass rubbed over his cock, taunting and torturing him with each rock of her hips.

With a possessive growl, his fingers dropped lower, dipping inside her molten core. Carys moaned as he filled her, making her inner walls clench around him. He massaged his fingers in and out, tinting the water pink as he moved.

"That sound," Sy groaned, dropping his thumb to her swollen bundle of nerves and making Carys cry out again. "Gods, the fires I've walked through hoping to hear that sound again."

Carys ground her hips, riding Sy's fingers, chasing that flicker of ecstasy that was just beyond her grasp. She needed more, needed the fullness only he could provide.

That his fingers were never going to quite achieve.

"I need all of you." Grabbing his wrist, she pulled his hand away and rose up on her knees. She reached between her legs and took hold of his throbbing cock, stroking him until he groaned before positioning him at her entrance. Sy's fingers found Carys's hips, digging into her soft flesh as she slowly lowered herself onto him. He sat up further, his forehead resting between her shoulder blades as his hot breath skittered across her wet skin.

She rocked her hips, moving him inside her torturously slow. Sy's fingers gripped her tighter, pulling her down further onto him and bucking up until he was buried deep inside her. Carys gasped, throwing her head back at the feeling of him fully seated within her. Her senses exploded, her pulse ratcheting up, as she lifted up and down again. Sy let out a breathy groan and thrust his hips up, meeting each of Carys's movements, and her hands shot out to grab the edges of the tub to keep from tipping over.

"Gods," she moaned, lost in the sensation. It felt so good. Every ache and pain completely forgotten now as she dove beneath the waves of rapture.

One hand gripping Carys's hip released and skimmed its way around, stroking over that throbbing button until her vision was spotting with stars. She moved faster, crimson water sloshing over the sides of the tub. Sy met each of her movements with a punishing pump, moving faster, harder, harder, until . . .

Her entire body seized as a scream pulled from her lungs, a string of curses interwoven with gasps of pleasure as she tipped over the cliff inside her. Over and over she tumbled, her body clenching around Sy as he spilled into her with his own growl of release.

The whole time, he never let go.

Her body prickled with a million tiny bolts of lightning, her orgasm shattering her until she was spent and collapsed backward against Sy again. His fingertips trailed up and down her legs as the final echoes of pleasure clamped around him.

She didn't want to move, didn't want to come down from that high, didn't want to face the inevitable conversation that was surely to come after. So Carys simply leaned back into him, enjoying the perfect fit of their bodies together, and remained silent, pretending it was just like it used to be between them for a little while longer.

CHAPTER TWENTY-FIVE

Carys pretended that it was out of propriety and politeness that she accepted Lord Marraden's invitation to dine with him for lunchtime, but the thinly veiled truth was she wanted a buffer between herself and Sy.

To his credit, Sy hadn't said a word about their shared moment in the bath. He had made himself busy in the sitting room in the hours following—with what, Carys didn't know—so that she could get dressed in peace. But the anxious questions began to burble up within her in that silence: Was he ashamed for giving in to his baser instincts? Was he mad at Carys for encouraging his lust only to immediately ignore him again? What was he thinking? What did she *want* him to be thinking?

What had *she* been thinking?

Gods. She'd really fucked up. Just for a moment of pleasure. Just to soothe her pain—pain that was almost at an end. Except, maybe that wasn't exactly true. Maybe her cycle was over, but she was still in pain, wasn't she? The echoes of that pleasure still pulsed through her body even hours later. The fact she felt loose and sated for the first time in longer than she cared to admit made it clear she certainly hadn't been completely well.

Carys pushed her roast chicken around her plate with her fork, barely lifting her gaze to make eye contact with Lord Marraden and catching Sy's attention from her periphery. She focused on the details around the room, from the elaborate molding to the cranberry garland centerpiece. Her eyes snagged on the tapered candles, trying to focus on the spitting flame on the left one instead of the fae across from her. The bottoms were dipped in a black wax and earthy scents emanated from the bits of herbs within the candle, the flames crackling each time it burned down to another clove or sprig of rosemary.

"It's good to see you are feeling better, Lady Hilgaard," Marraden said, glancing between Carys and Sy. He nodded to her plate of boiled potatoes and roast chicken. "I had the cook prepare a blander fare for you today"

"Ah," she replied. "That explains the bone broth soup." She offered him a half smile. "I appreciate the care you've taken of us since our arrival." Marraden nodded, looking all too pleased with himself. "And I apologize that we didn't get to spend more time together during our stay." She hooked her thumb at Sy. "It was his fault."

She knew without looking that Sy would be frowning at her.

"You're off already?" Marraden's bushy eyebrows shot up. "The storm has barely rolled out. It's still raining. I thought tomorrow, perhaps—"

"Unfortunately, we must make haste. This is, sadly, no pleasure trip." Yet even as she said it, she blushed, and Carys glanced at Sy for the first time all day. He glowered back at her for a split second to let her know he noted it. Was he mad she had been ignoring him? Or just mad that she clearly regretted the thing she explicitly promised him she wouldn't regret? If he truly knew her that well, then he should have known she'd lie to get her way, regardless.

Sy put on that pleasant diplomatic face—a mask he wore too easily—and turned to Lord Marraden, saying, "Yes. A terrible shame." He gestured around the dining room. "We'd love to come visit your beautiful home again sometime."

"Beautiful." Marraden blustered, looking up to the cobwebs in the corner of the room, then laughed ruefully. "I may be old, but I'm not blind. I know this place has fallen into disrepair." He reached across the table and placed his weathered hand atop Carys's own. "But with a new Queen—and King," he quickly added, giving Sy a repentant look and Sy frowned again at Carys instead of the Lord, as if his comment were her fault too, "I hope that will be rectified. With new industry and new hope for the people of Eastern Court, no longer under Gedwin Norwood's thumb, no longer a factory for war, but for commerce and art and peace, perhaps the southern regions of the East will flourish once more?"

"I pray to the Gods it is so," Carys said in her practiced, courtly manner.

"And perhaps I will curry the favor of the future Queen?" Lord Marraden gave her hand a light squeeze before letting it go. Carys placed her hand back in her lap and wiped the clamminess off on her napkin.

Ah. There it was. He wanted money from the crown.

"First I must win a place on the throne," Carys said. "Then we may speak of favor."

"Yes, yes, of course." Lord Marraden waved her statement away as if he wasn't the one who'd just brought it up. "How about some dessert while your horses are readied?"

"Dessert at lunchtime, how decadent," Sy said, patting his lips before spreading his napkin across his lap again. "But I fear we must—"

"You Arboans have strange eating times," Lord Marraden prodded, clearly trying to goad Sy into further conversation. "I don't think I could ever wake in the middle of the night to feast."

Sy opened his mouth to interject but Carys beat him to it. "It is the best time of day to do so in such a hot climate."

"You can't seriously enjoy the two sleeps?" Lord Marraden asked, clearly taken aback by such a concept. He studied the candles, watching as the wick burned down toward the black wax, his eyes dilating in the flicker of the flames.

"I do," Carys said resolutely. "I like the afternoon rest when the sun is still high and it is too hot to do anything productive. I like rising to watch the final rays of the sunset, bathing in the cooled waters of the stream, and dining without a litany of insects descending upon me." She set her utensils down with a loud clink. "And I like going back to bed in the cool midnight hours to sleep until sunrise."

Lord Marraden cocked an eyebrow. "Then why don't you keep to such traditions here?"

Her voice dropped low. "Because here is not Arboa."

"You sound like you'd be better appointed as the Queen of Arboa than the Queen of the Eastern Court." Lord Marraden let out a scratchy laugh that Carys and Sy didn't match.

A moment of silence passed through the dining room and she could feel the weight of Sy's eyes on her like a brand. She'd always loved Arboa. She still loved Arboa. Even if she hated its Lord . . . well, mostly hated him.

Carys feigned a titter of laughter, breaking the awkward silence. "Perhaps I've had too much wine." She stood and hastened to the dining room door that led out into the foyer. "I think we should be on our way before we lose the light."

She tested the door handle, but it didn't budge. Lord Marraden leaned back in his chair and steepled his fingers, watching the dark smoke billowing from the candles now, some new herb catching the flames.

Carys tested the door again, she must have imagined . . . no. It was locked.

She whirled around to Marraden, who remained the picture of contemplative innocence as her heart began to race. Something was wrong—very wrong. "What is the meaning of this?"

Sy bolted to his feet, his hand dropping to the dagger on his belt. "Why is the door locked, Marraden?"

"Have dessert with me and I'll tell you," he said, his voice slow and antiquated.

"No," Carys snarled. "Open this door. Now."

A maid came in through the doors from the kitchen and Carys and Sy exchanged glances and then both moved toward the kitchen exit at the same time. The maid set a cake on the edge of the table and yanked back the knife that sat beside it, holding it out toward them. Carys's eyes lifted from the tip of the maid's knife to her glassed-over eyes.

Carys pulled out her dagger, her brow furrowing as she said to the human maid, "You can't be serious."

"I can't let you leave, Carys Hilgaard." Lord Marraden's voice was filled with an eerie singsong and she glanced over her shoulder to see his dulled eyes, the same dulled, soapy sheen as the maid's.

"Shit," Carys muttered. To Marraden, she said, "Is that you, Adisa?"

Lord Marraden cackled, a dark and feminine laugh. "The Lord was most pleased with the cigars that arrived to him this morning . . . and the new tapers too. He shared them with his whole staff with a little encouragement."

"I'm guessing a certain purple flower laced those cigars?" Carys growled, twisting to the inky smoke billowing from the candles. "Still enjoying your pit, you old crone?"

Marraden—Adisa—cackled again. "I'm loving my time. Two mostly filling meals a day. Plenty of solitude. And time to play my little games with you, Carys. I told you, my mind can be anywhere." Marraden reached across the table and knocked over one of the candles. Sy quickly doused the flame with his drink. "No one will suspect me of your deaths." Marraden stood and walked over to the other candle, plucking it from its holder and walking over to the peeling paper on the far wall.

"Don't." Sy took a step toward him and Marraden lifted the candle higher.

"You perished in a house fire. How sad. How unheroic." Marraden's sadistic, lamenting face made Carys shudder. She kept her knife trained on the maid beside her as she watched Marraden set the peeling wallpaper ablaze. "But these old, unkempt manors . . . it was inevitable. One fallen candle and the whole place is in ashes."

The old, dry wallpaper sucked in the flame like a drowning man gasping for air. The whole wall erupted into flame in the blink of an eye, licking toward the ceiling and spreading across the walls.

In a split second, Sy threw out his fist and clocked the maid square in the temple. She went down hard.

"What are you—"

"We've got to get out of here," Sy said, yanking Carys through the swinging kitchen doors. "Now!"

Carys looked back at the sliver of Marraden visible through the kitchen doors. He stood stock-still, staring at the growing flames as smoke circled him. "We've got to help him."

"He's trying to kill us!"

"It's not him. It's—"

Sy grabbed Carys by the back of the neck, swinging her face around until it was inches from his own. "It is too late to save him," he gritted out, slowly, plainly, his eyes imploring her to hear him. "We're leaving. Now." He blinked back the sting of smoke as the room filled with billowing shadow, his eyes landing on the far windowsill. "We'll jump out the window and run to the stables. Go." He shoved Carys hard toward the sill, jolting her out of her shock.

They ran to the window and shoved open the sill. The pane groaned, the wood swollen with the heavy rains. Ersan climbed through first, tall enough that he could lower himself down onto one leg, keeping his wooden one at a right angle to keep it attached. Carys swung one foot through the window when a heavy mass collided with her and she was tackled to the side. Her wrist smacked the ground and her dagger went flying from her grip. She kept her wits, though, and scrambled for her sword on the other hip as the stable boy clawed at her face. He attacked her with wild abandon, but he was small and untrained. Carys shoved him backward and with one boot to his chest, he went flying across the room.

Sy screamed her name. She stumbled to her feet, moving toward the window when the boy rose again. The door swung open and another two staff members appeared, getting between Carys and the window.

"Get the horses," Carys shouted, spotting the peek of Sy's face between the three bodies. "I'll find another way out."

"Hurry before this whole place goes up in flames!" Sy shouted back.

Like she was about to dawdle. Carys looked into the three faces, dulled eyes and wicked smiles. Was Adisa watching her through every one of them? She took another step back to the side door into the hall. The three servants tracked her, taking a step for each of her own. Carys grabbed a bottle of vinegar from the shelf beside her and hefted it across the room. It shattered against the wall, staining it with brown liquid, and while the three heads turned in its direction, Carys kicked the kitchen table over and bolted.

She raced into the smoky hall, but the front door was already consumed with flames. She turned toward the back, but thick black smoke billowed from there as well. All of the exits were in flames.

"Shit," she hissed, twisting toward the stairwell. The whole space was dark with smoke now, her eyes tearing and a hacking cough escaping her mouth.

Carys darted up the stairs, taking them two at a time, her footsteps thundering above the hiss and crackle of splitting wood. A hand snapped out between the railings and seized her by the ankle. She let out a surprised cry as she fell forward, smacking into the hard wood. The air knocked out of her along with a sharp pain, and she wondered if she'd cracked a rib. Her chin had definitely split open, judging from the sting and trickle of blood. But she kicked herself free and didn't stay down long, crawling up the stairs just as an elderly servant rounded the bottom step, appearing from the haze like a monster. She scrambled up the steps after Carys, grabbing her ankle again and yanking her down the steps.

Thud, thud, thud, she clawed up her legs.

Carys grabbed her other knife from her thigh belt and spun, stabbing straight through the woman's hand and impaling her palm onto the step. The servant yanked at her hand, then the hilt of the knife, but couldn't pry it free. She didn't cry out, just seemed to stare at the blade and her hand dumbly. Carys clambered up to the top of the steps, watching in horror as the smoke consumed the dull-eyed servant who watched Carys like a predator tracking prey until the flames finally consumed her.

Carys's stomach roiled and she gagged at the stench of burning hair and—in a moment—cooked meat as the servant writhed beneath the flames. But she didn't speak, didn't scream, as if being burned alive was only a hindrance to her plans.

As Carys leapt to her feet, she prayed that Adisa's magic had fully taken over the woman's mind and suppressed her own consciousness. Carys hoped with everything in her that the servant wasn't awake and aware inside of that mind-controlling curse in her final moments, but she also couldn't wait and find out.

She sprinted down the long hallway and back to her chambers, yanking her tunic up over her nose. She threw open the first window and quickly threw the packs out to the ground. She heard a horse whinny and then Sy swear. Carys peeked her head out the window to see him with their two horses hastily saddled, standing halfway down the entry road.

"Leave the fucking packs," Sy shouted, even as he dismounted his horse to collect them.

Carys climbed out the window carefully, the moss-covered shingles still slick from the storm. Prickles of rain misted through the air. She sat on the sloping roof, searching for her best path downward.

Sy pointed toward the trellis leaning against the second window ledge along. Carys lifted into a crouch and released one hand from the roof toward the next ledge. A shingle came loose beneath her boot and slid out from under her, her legs stretching into a split as she swung her weight to the next window along. Sy released another litany of curses.

Carys made it to the trellis, which wobbled and creaked with every tentative step. She only made it halfway down before the thing started bending, bending, the wood whining.

"Carys . . ." Sy warned.

Carys leapt just before the wood snapped, hitting the ground with a roll to break the impact of her fall. She somersaulted back up to her feet with a bounce and Sy's eyebrows shot up as he buckled the final pack and remounted his horse.

Carys looked back at Marraden's manor one last time. Flames erupted from all of the bottom floor windows now and she looked up to see the face of Lord Marraden watching from the second floor, pouring brandy over himself, silhouetted in smoke. Her mind flashed to the stable boy and the faces of all the servants. No one ran. No one fled from the building. Marraden—Adisa—watched them with a smile as if pleased she and Sy had escaped or perhaps she was delighted at all the lives her evil soul had claimed that day. Carys's stomach turned into a hot knot again and she thought she might spill the contents of her lunch all over the wet grass.

She saw the old fae, drenched in liquor, go up like a lantern's wick.

"Carys." Sy's voice snapped her attention back to him. "Get on the fucking horse."

Her hands shook with unrestrained rage. That witch was still able to get her claws into Okrith even from her pit, still destroying the world even from her cage. That stable boy was only a child. She killed. Unblinkingly and with abandon. And Carys felt even more bolstered to find the amethyst dagger and plunge it into Adisa Monroe's cold violet heart herself. She would avenge each and every one of the people Adisa had stolen from the world.

Carys mounted her horse and grabbed the reins, determination coursing through her as she nudged her horse forward. The horses seemed all too keen to get out of that place and took off at a gallop down the road.

Carys glanced over at Sy, who seemed equally rattled and filled with rage. It would be another day of travel to make it to the southern cliffs but their adrenaline and anger would spur them onward. It was time to kill that witch once and for all.

CHAPTER TWENTY-SIX

The ride was miserable, the day heavy with mist, not quite raining but wet enough that Carys's clothes were soaked through within an hour. The bracing winds were so cold that they seeped into her bones. She was sure her fingertips were turning blue underneath her leather gloves. But there was nowhere to turn back now, no point of shelter. The only thing they could do was keep going.

As they rode further toward the coast, the trees became sparser, their branches now bare, their red and gold leaves blown off in the storms. The forest yielded to brambles and then fields of green and golden grasses stretching out to white cliffs, and beyond that, the ocean.

Sheep grazed along the southern cliffs and they passed a couple lone farmhouses far off toward the east—too far to seek shelter in. Luckily, the storm continued to blow out to sea as they rode, as if they were shepherds herding it out toward the cliffside.

"Should we talk about it?" Sy finally said and Carys knew he didn't mean Adisa's attack or the house fire.

"No."

"Carys," he said with a frustrated sigh. "Look at me."

"I'm focusing on the trail."

"We almost just died," Sy pointed out. "*Again.* And yet you can't talk to me about what happened in the bathing chamber? As if we hadn't done that a hundred times before?"

"Exactly. We have done it all before," Carys countered, keeping her eyes fixed on the horizon. "So there's nothing to talk about. If you can't handle a little adventure, maybe you should just go back to Arboa."

"You're such a child."

"You're such a fool." Her chest heaved and she pushed her horse to ride faster. "He calls me childish. *Me*," she muttered to herself even though she knew Sy was still well within earshot. "After burning down Hilgaard castle and—"

"You and I both know I didn't burn down the castle!" Sy shouted, clearly exasperated by the same argument they'd had for many years. "It was already on fire when I got there. There was a lightning storm!"

Carys rolled her eyes. "And you just decided to run into an already burning building?"

"I did!"

"Why?"

"I was drunk."

"Ah." Her shoulders shook with bitter laughter. "Well, that explains it."

"I was trying to get something," Sy spat, his horse catching up with her own, and Carys relented, allowing their horses to match a meandering pace again.

"What would you possibly run into a burning castle for? Gold? Treasures?" Carys asked. "Any more secrets you'd like to share with me?"

"Yes," Sy said, making Carys's head lift with surprise. By the time she caught herself, it was too late, she was already hooked into his stare. All of the emotions of the night before flooded through her in a mighty gust.

"Bri has always thought you went in for my engagement ring," Carys said. "The one I threw back in your face after I found out about Morgan. But I know you wouldn't have been so foolish. You could've bought another one." Sy gave the barest nod. "You shouldn't have gone back in at all."

Carys's eyes dropped to his boot. It was clicked into the stirrups by an interlocking contraption that Sy invented to keep his wooden foot from dangling and accidentally kicking the horse. Memories of the night of the fire flashed back into Carys's mind: of her blind rage, of seeing the castle ablaze, of finding Sy, his ankle trapped beneath a burning beam, the fire already having scorched past, of the hate and heartbreak that filled her as she stared down at him, of the betrayal in his eyes as she turned and walked away.

"I'm sorry I left you there," she muttered. "I knew you weren't in danger of being killed in the blaze, if that's any consolation."

Sy huffed. "And if you thought it would kill me?"

"I'd have dragged you out of the flames and left you just outside the house," she said.

"You were angry," he said, as if it was understandable to abandon your Fated to suffer, trapped and alone. "Even if you had helped me, my foot was already shattered," he added. "It was already too late."

She sucked her teeth disdainfully. Carys knew she was wrong for leaving him there, just as Sy was wrong for lying to her. "Don't make excuses for me."

"I'll do as I please." Sy let out a rough chuckle at Carys's scowl. She held Sy's dark gaze, losing herself for a moment in the intensity of his stare, of all they'd been through, before he said, "The thing I was looking for? I found it."

Carys's voice was breathless as she asked, "What was it?"

His eyes dipped to her lips and back up to her eyes, seemingly debating if he should tell her, but finally he said, "Your mother's ring."

Her body reacted of its own volition, tears welling in her eyes. Her hand pressed down on the center of her chest to stop her body's traitorous wave of emotions. She took a deep breath to stop the tears from spilling and she hated the softening look in Sy's eyes.

Carys had used to wear that golden ring all of the time. It was a simple band with diamond-patterned etching. The bottom was smooth, thinner than the top from years of wear. Apparently it had been her grandmother's gift to her mother when she was a little girl and her mother had wanted to gift it to Carys when her fingers were big enough to wear it. Or at least that's what her maids would tell her. She never knew if it was a well-spun lie. She'd left it behind that night of her father's death—the night she'd fled the castle and Sy and her entire life. It hadn't matched her dress, so she'd worn another one instead. She let out a bitter laugh at the memory. Carys had debated turning back for it many times, ordering someone to dig through the ashes in the hopes it hadn't been taken by Arboan bandits, but over the years she accepted that it was lost to her forever.

Sy's eyes tracked Carys's every facial expression. "Where is it?" she finally asked.

"It's safe in Arboa," Sy said carefully.

Carys's expression hardened again. "Why didn't you tell me? Oh, never mind—because you don't feel you need to tell me anything."

"We weren't exactly speaking."

"You could've given it to Neelo to give to me."

"I could have . . ." he hedged. "But as the years went on it got harder and harder. Your forgiveness started feeling ever increasingly further out of reach. And besides, back then I still thought . . ."

"Still thought what?"

He lifted his long lashes up to meet her gaze. "I still thought one day we'd be together again."

"Well, you were wrong."

"Was I?" he asked, leaning further in the saddle to maintain their eye contact.

Carys broke their stare, the feeling of looking into those dark brown eyes too painful. She battled herself, pulling in two different directions as she debated what to say. After all this time, even if she hated it, it was still the two of them.

"Yes," she said more resolutely. "You were wrong."

"Why?"

"Because everything you do hurts me!" she shouted and from her periphery she could see him flinch. "Even your kindness. It hurts that sometimes you care. It hurts that you'll never tell me why . . ."

They crested the final hill and all of the storming words and swirling thoughts vanished from her mind at what she saw. A lone tree twisted over the edge of the white cliff and there, hanging lifeless from a gnarled branch, was Fenrin.

THE SIGHT OF HIS HANGING BODY HIT HER WORSE THAN A KICK TO the gut. She wanted to cry, to scream, but only burning tears filled her eyes, stymied by her rising fury. Fenrin was a good person, pulled into the center of a raging storm, and here he was at the edge of the world, gone.

They were too late. Was this his punishment for trying to warn Aneryn before Adisa's attack? Had Adisa used him in every way and now was done with him, discarded him like she had Cole? One thought rose above the rest: he didn't deserve this end.

Sy murmured words to her but she didn't hear over the roar of blood in her ears, each heartbeat painfully thudding in her chest, each breath a whoosh of air across her ears. It wasn't until Sy's hand touched her cheek that she snapped back into the present, her wrathful eyes finding his.

"We need to cut him down." She was barely able to get the words out over the lump in her throat.

"I don't think that's a good idea."

She unsheathed her sword—wishing she had her shorter blades, but they would be buried in the ashes of Marraden's manor now.

"We need to cut him down," Carys pushed again.

Sy grabbed her shoulder, yanking her back with enough force to draw her attention from Fenrin's dangling body. "I know this is a terrible shock. I know you're hurting," he swallowed and she knew he was thinking about what she'd just told him on their ride, "but think like a soldier for a second," he demanded. "Use your training. Look around you. She knew where we were. She knew where we were going.

"Adisa expected us to find this."

Carys's eyes shifted from Fenrin's body to Sy's face and then finally she forced herself to look around at the environment. They stood at the edge of the white clay cliffs, undulating up and down the rocky shoreline. Sheep grazed in the far distance, barely white specks amongst the green—a beautiful pastoral landscape were it not for the body dangling from a lone tree.

The tree's roots emerged from the white soil, clinging desperately to the side of the cliff. Its lean trunk was twisted into a hook, clearly battered to the side over years of enduring the southern storms. One lone gnarled branch emerged from the trunk, hanging over the precipice of open air. Carys shifted her weight and leaned to peer over the ledge. Sy's grip tightened on her shoulder again. It wasn't a sheer drop, but rather a steep slope of loose shale, broken seashells, and large stones.

"It's not a trap," Carys said, pulling free from Sy's grip. "It wouldn't kill us to fall."

"But it would hurt. A lot," Sy said, staring at the slope of rocks far below. "They left him there specifically to deter anyone from cutting him down."

"I don't understand," Carys whispered, the wind sweeping her voice away from her. "He was the key to her prophecy—'the smallest seed.' Even Aneryn agreed with Adisa's vision—Fenrin on a throne."

"Visions change," Sy said.

"There has to be more." Carys shook her head. "And even if the vision changed . . . why like this?"

"You're asking that of a witch who just had a whole household set themselves alight," Sy pointed out. "She's lost herself to madness. This is erratic violence to scare us, not strategy."

Carys's heart thundered in her chest as she stared at Fenrin's limp body. How was she going to tell the others? How would she tell Remy? If Aneryn ever woke, how would she tell her? Carys's eyes dropped to the dagger on Fenrin's belt. "Gods."

"Is that . . . the amethyst dagger?" Sy took another step toward the tree. "The one that can kill Adisa Monroe?"

"It can't be. Why would they leave it on him?"

"Because this is a trap," Sy muttered again. He turned back to the horses as if seeking confirmation that something was amiss, but the two mares continued to graze, unbothered.

"Maybe Adisa Monroe doesn't need it anymore . . . " Carys hedged. "Maybe she's found another way to harness her power. Maybe her accomplices don't know that this dagger can kill her. Or maybe she's content to die as a martyr now that others have taken up her cause?"

"Or maybe the dagger can't kill her at all and it's just a useless relic." Sy took another tentative step. "Maybe all the rumors about it were lies and they left it here to taunt us, to show us how futile this search was after all."

Carys shook her head. "Then why the attack in Marraden's manor?" She squinted her eyes against a beam of sunlight that burst between the thick layer of clouds. The last of the storm was rolling out to sea now and the heavy blanket of mist was lifting off the land. The swells beating against the shoreline eased a little more from one breath to the next. "What if Fenrin was trying to stop the attack on Marraden? What if he found a way to fight back again just as he did in Wynreach? Maybe he was slipping too far from Adisa's control and she killed him for it?" She turned in a full circle but there wasn't another person in sight for miles in any direction. "Did Aneryn See this? Did she know her lover would die this way?"

"Maybe that's why she was willing to dabble in such ancient magic," Sy replied. "Maybe she was too desperate to save him and got in over her head."

Carys flipped her sword over in her hand, fiddling with the hilt as she debated what to do. The answer was still the same.

"We need to cut him down . . . and we need that dagger. If there's any chance it can kill Adisa Monroe, we need it." Sy stepped forward but Carys cut him off with the raising of her hand, saying, "I'm going," as he opened his mouth to protest. "There are many things you're better at than me, but climbing trees is not one of them."

He couldn't deny that he'd struggle more than Carys shimmying across the lean trunk. "Be careful."

Carys sheathed her sword back in her belt and began pulling herself up the tree. The whole trunk wobbled, the branch bending further as she hugged its narrow girth.

Sy sucked in a sharp breath, holding his tense hands out in midair as if he could magically keep the tree from tipping.

"Shut it," Carys snapped.

"I didn't say anything."

"But you were thinking it."

She could feel the tension rolling off Sy, the tightness in his every muscle and the sharpness in his eyes without even looking. Carys inched further, the bough creaking as she got closer to the noose. The branch dipped further and further until she was pointing toward the ground. Slowly, she reached a hand back to unsheathe her sword again, the bough wobbling further with each of her movements. Ever so slowly, she extended her blade out to the rope—

Crack!

The sound registered in her ears before she felt her stomach lurch. She lost her grip as the branch snapped and her hands shot out as she fell, grabbing for the amethyst dagger even as she plummeted. Her hand snagged on the dagger's hilt and she jolted, her shoulder socket barking in pain. The branch creaked and cracked again, dangling from the tree. Fenrin's body swayed wildly.

"Hang on!" Sy screamed, just as the dagger slipped from Fenrin's upturned scabbard and Carys plunged down the cliffside.

CHAPTER TWENTY-SEVEN

The air rushed out of Carys as she collided with the unyielding slope of hard stones. Adrenaline coursed through her, delaying the pain that she knew was soon to follow. Her body slid across the rubble, scraping her back and arms, until she came to an unceremonious stop against a large rock halfway down the cliffside.

Carys shook out her hands, then feet, curling her fingers and toes. Nothing felt broken, at least. She thanked the Gods for the thickness of her leathers and the braid at the back of her head that protected her skull from cracking into the stone.

With a groan, she sat up, spying the amethyst dagger by her boot. She grabbed the hilt, rubbing the cloudy amethyst stones with her thumb, then froze. What if the blade had been poisoned like the others? The metal of the blade shined at least, more than the poisoned cutlery in the Western court had during their investigation of Queen Thorne's assassination.

She remembered how Cole had demonstrated the power of the poisoned metals and she dropped the tip of the dagger to a thorny weed poking out from the shale. When it didn't immediately wither into ash, she sighed and stuck the blade through her belt.

Sy appeared from the edge of the cliff, holding the reins of his horse with one hand.

Carys frowned as she waved to him, trying not to wince at the movement. If she hadn't cracked a rib on the steps of Marraden manor, she definitely had now. "I'm alive."

"Barely," Sy muttered, throwing down a loop of rope from his saddlebag. "Grab on."

Carys crawled over to the rope, opening scrapes on her hands along the sharp rock and seashells as she went. Crimson stained across the rough burlap of the rope as she looped it over her head and threaded her arms through.

With a click of Sy's tongue, his horse walked backward and the rope went tight, hoisting Carys by the armpits. The rope groaned against her leathers, hauling her across the bumpy terrain and up the white cliffside. She grabbed on to the dense clumpings of grass clinging to the clay and pulled herself the last few feet as Sy leaned over and grasped the back of her belt, pulling her over the edge. They tumbled, rolling across the long grass until Carys landed roughly on top of him.

Sy's arms bracketed her body, his hands pressing tightly into her back, his dark hair dusting into his eyes as he stared up at her.

"You can let go now," Carys said, a smile pulling at her lips.

Sy seemed reluctant but he let go, his eyes drifting over her shoulder as he released her.

He froze.

Carys whipped her head toward his line of sight and her stomach dropped further than when she plummeted off the cliffside.

There. Hanging from the tree. Was an empty noose.

"Where did he go?" Carys scrambled to her feet and yanked the rope from around her. She circled again, seeing no one across the rolling hills. She darted to the cliff edge and peered down.

No one. No body. No Fenrin.

Sy's horse whinnied and reared up. Carys spun again, watching as her own horse bolted off with a keening neigh. Sy held tight to the reins of his horse, shushing it as he rubbed a steady hand down its nose.

"What is spooking them?" Carys searched for something, anything, but the hills were bare.

The hills were bare.

"Where have the sheep gone?" She pointed toward the distant hills just as an earth-shattering roar split the air.

"What in the Gods' names . . ."

A golden spot lifted over the horizon, running unnaturally fast in their direction. Carys blinked as the shape came swiftly into view. One of Adisa's monsters, the same one she'd come face-to-face with that night in the witches' quarter . . . and she had a terrible suspicion that the monster and Fenrin were one and the same.

"Shit," she shouted, whipping around and darting in the direction of her bolting horse. "Run!"

Sy mounted his horse in one swift step as Carys ran past him, chasing down her own horse.

The beast roared again, this time its closeness shaking through Carys's chest. Fuck. She wouldn't get to her horse in time.

Sy whistled and Carys turned to the sound, seeing him galloping toward her. Holding the reins with one hand, he leaned down and extended his arm. Without thought, she clasped his forearm and leapt, letting him yank her around onto the back of his horse. It felt like he pulled apart her sternum, her ribs screaming in protest at the jerk of being pulled up. Her chest crashed into his back, her chin colliding between his shoulder blades and splitting the freshly scabbed wound there open, but her arms snaked around him, clinging on as the horse bounced her up again.

Sy shouted and kicked his horse with his calf and the horse doubled its already racing speed, darting over the hills. Carys thanked all the Gods for Sy's skilled horsemanship and all those summers spent racing bareback through the blooming fields. She peeked back over her shoulder, her neck smarting with the whiplash.

The beast was gaining on them. The lionlike creature the size of their horse ate up the distance between them. In a few more bounds, it would be sinking its curling tusks into the flank of their mare.

Carys stared into those vertical pupils, yellow eyes glowing as if Adisa Monroe herself was watching through them. Then Carys remembered . . . in the forests of Swifthill, she'd discovered with Bri that one thing seemed to control these beasts.

And she was wearing that one thing on her belt.

She gripped the amethyst dagger tightly, careful to not let it fall from her grasp as she pulled it free.

"Stop!" she screamed, holding the dagger out to the beast.

The creature's legs seized at her command, locking as it skidded to a halt, kicking up a layer of clay and grass as it finally came to a rest.

"Yes!" Carys cheered, watching the beast stare her down with just as much ferocity, but it didn't move.

Their horse carried on its flight, catching up to Carys's horse, which was bolting down the same path worn into the field.

"Don't let go of that dagger," Sy commanded, leaning over and snatching the reins of Carys's horse.

"That's amazing advice," she muttered, finally turning to face forward as they curved around the bend and the beast fell out of sight. Her hand splayed across Sy's muscled torso and she pulled herself flush against him, giving him a squeeze before loosening her grip.

Sy reached down for his sword.

"What are you doing?" Carys called, shoving his hand down until he released his weapon.

"We came here to slay the beast, not flee from it," Sy shouted. "If that dagger can immobilize it, then it shall be an easy kill."

"We can't." Carys shoved Sy's shoulder again, kicking the horse to keep its speedy gait.

"What?" Sy didn't try to turn the horse again. "If we don't return with a tusk, we are forfeiting our place in the competition. We need to kill the creature. What are you thinking?"

"I'm thinking about Fenrin."

"Did that beast eat Fenrin?" Sy asked, having to shout over the thunder of the horse's feet.

"I think that beast *is* Fenrin."

"Like the Norwood prince? Gods."

"It's the only explanation," Carys shouted, her outstretched arm aching with each jolt of the horse. "I can't kill him. I won't." She scrutinized the dagger in her hand. "Returning with this dagger was our mission too. Surely, Elwyn will understand."

"You may be her friend, but I don't know if she will be swayed into such blatant favoritism," Sy said.

"We might have the only tool to save Okrith in our possession," Carys pointed out, finally allowing her arm to lower and cradling the blade in her grip. "What if this dagger possesses the magic Adisa claimed? Do you think it will work on her?"

"I don't know," Sy said gruffly as they raced toward the forest. "But I *do* know it will feel really good plunging it into Adisa Monroe's heart, regardless."

CARYS HUDDLED CLOSER TO THE FIRE, THE ECHOES OF THE AT-tack still playing over in her mind. Not just the beast, but earlier, at the manor. Every crackle of the spitting wet firewood was the start of a roar, every whine of the wood was the start of a scream. Her teeth chattered and she pulled her miserably wet cloak tighter around her, staring longingly at her garments draped on a spit above the fire. How long before their clothes were warm and dry and she could cover her naked body in more than cold, wet wool?

One more night. One more Gods damned night and they'd be back at the Wandering Stag. They'd pushed the horses to the brink of collapse to ride as far as they did that day. But with the heavy clouds, when the sun set, the forest was so dark they could barely see a foot ahead and were forced to stop. The Southern storm may have rolled out to sea, but the turbulent autumn weather still brought with it more rain clouds and a bitter, gnawing cold.

Part of Carys wanted to double back, to see if the beast had changed back into Fenrin. Maybe they could find a way to capture him and bring him back to Wynreach? Maybe he was able to control himself in his witch form? But Carys knew it was too risky. She had no way of knowing what the creature might do and even with the amethyst dagger in her possession, she couldn't risk it.

Sy had disagreed. Every hour of their trek back northward had been a bitter battle. Carys was already planning how to convince Elwyn to let them remain in the competition, while Sy wanted to turn back and make sure that beast was, in fact, Fenrin, because if it wasn't, they'd just let the easiest path to the crown slip through their fingers. Still, Carys couldn't risk it, couldn't kill the monster only to have Fenrin's body appear. Two things existed at once: she wouldn't kill Fenrin, and she wouldn't withdraw from the competition either. No, the best course of action was to return to Wynreach and kill Adisa Monroe with the dagger. Then—hopefully—all of her curses would be broken, Fenrin would be free, and Carys's decisions would be justified to the people of Wynreach.

Carys's trembling hand held the amethyst dagger under her cloak. The frigid metal made the bare skin on her side ripple with gooseflesh, but she didn't want to let it go. This dagger was their salvation . . . not only from Adisa, but also to remain in the competition, or at least, she prayed it would be.

"You sound like you're playing Arboan cymbals the way your teeth are clicking together," Sy said. "Here."

"Don't." Carys held a hand up to him as he shifted onto the log beside her. "I'm fine."

Sy frowned at her and kept his cloak wrapped around him but shuffled closer to Carys's side. She secretly prayed that even through their cloak layers his warmth would find her and ease her shivering.

"The fire's growing stronger," Sy murmured, holding his hands out to the flames. The larger logs hadn't caught alight yet, the flame still working its way up toward the larger pieces of wood. "You'll be okay in a minute."

"I'm okay now," Carys muttered.

Sy shook his head, reaching into the folds of her cloak and placing his warmed hand on her knee. Carys jolted at the contact of his heat against her cold wet skin. She bit down on a moan threatening to rise from her throat. Gods, that felt so good.

When Sy shifted to remove his warm palm, Carys's hand shot out and held his in place. Sy snickered, shaking his head at her stubborn antics, before taking his other warmed hand, snaking it into her cloak, and placing it like a brand against her side.

Carys hissed through her teeth, her chattering subsiding as her frozen shaking ebbed. She let out a little hum of relief.

"This isn't exactly a comfortable position," Sy said with a chuckle, trying to pull away and Carys holding his hands down.

"I don't care."

"Of course you don't."

Keeping his hands in place, Sy shifted off the log and knelt in front of Carys, shuffling closer, pushing his cloak back until his shoulders met the inside of her thighs. Carys's lips parted at the contact, her eyes hooding with desire as she stared down at him crouched between her legs.

The hand on her knee slid up an inch. Then the hand on her side followed, heat dancing higher and spreading through her limbs.

"What are you doing?" Carys asked, admonishing him with a shake of her head.

"You know exactly what I'm doing," Sy replied with a wicked grin. His hands slid up another inch, his thumb on her side skimming the underside of her breast, and Carys's mouth opened wider. "I'm cold and I'm trying to keep us warm."

She tried to laugh but it came out all breathy. She licked her lips and swallowed. "That's one way of putting it."

Sy's mouth dropped to the inside of her knee and he placed a warm kiss there. "Do you want me to stop or keep going?"

His lips whispered higher as his hand did the same and Carys arched into his touch. Gods, she knew exactly how it would feel, how deft he could be with his mouth and fingers, and Goddess of Death strike her down, she wanted to feel that way again.

Sy's hands stilled, his teeth testing the fleshy inside of Carys's thigh, making her moan. "Do you want me to stop?" he asked again with taunting slowness.

"You know I don't," Carys panted and Sy smiled against her skin.

"Gods, do I know."

"Then *keep going*," she pleaded, making him chuckle.

"Such a commander."

"Such a tease," she countered.

Sy glanced up, his eyes hooded with lust, a mischievous smile curving his lips. "I'm going to make you wish you didn't say that." His hand dropped from her breast to her other thigh and he spread her legs wide, yanking her forward and dropping his mouth to her core.

Carys let out a shocked gasp as Sy feasted on her, the intensity of his tongue making molten heat pool between her legs. "Gods," she groaned, her eyes rolling back as her hands dove into Sy's dark hair and held his mouth against her.

His tongue lashed her up and down and she ground into his mouth, little groaning breaths escaping her with each sweep of his tongue. Her chest pounded and her stomach fluttered as she rode his mouth.

Sy's hand skimmed up her thigh and his fingers trailed to her entrance. His fingertip circled her, dipping in an inch and then pulling out again. Carys writhed beneath him, desperate for his fingers to enter her, and finally he acquiesced. His fingers pushed into her so torturously slow, each inch making Carys's breath hitch. He didn't even get them all the way in before she was exploding around him, her orgasm taking her by surprise. She ground against his tongue, riding each wave of sudden pleasure.

When Sy pulled back the look in his eyes was nothing but feral. He yanked free the pin holding his cloak together and then unclipped Carys's own. The burgeoning fire now raged behind them and Carys's skin felt flushed with heat. Sy's hand whipped out, circling Carys around the waist and pulling her from the log down onto his waiting cock.

She moaned as he thrust inside her, her core fluttering with the echoes of her last orgasm. Groaning, Sy dropped his head to Carys's chest, taking her nipple into his mouth. He sucked on her as she rolled her hips, delighting in the fullness of him inside her. She wrapped her legs around him, letting him fill her deeper. His teeth tested her nipple, making her cry out.

The sound of her cry unleashed him and he pulled out of Carys so suddenly that she let out a frustrated cry. But then he was flipping her over so that her stomach lay flat against the fallen log and her ass high in the air. He grabbed her hips and lined himself up to her throbbing core. In one thrust, he filled her entirely and she cried out again, pushing back against him. He pulled all the way out and then thrust back in again, rolling his hips over and over and pounding into her until she was seeing spots. Her nails clawed into the earth, digging lines into the soil, desperate to hang on as he rode her faster and faster. Each pump made her rise closer toward another orgasm and she knew from Sy's erratic movements that he was getting closer too.

"Gods," he groaned. "You feel so good."

Again and again he thrust into her so deeply, so completely, that she forgot everything except for the feeling of where they joined.

"Yes," she cried out. "Yes!"

Her sounds of pleasure broke the last of Sy's control and with a barked cry, he released into her, his fingers scoring into the flesh of her hips so tightly she knew she'd have bruises for days. But none of that mattered, not as Carys tipped over that ledge inside herself again, an orgasm roaring through her louder than the roar of any beast. Her cries of pleasure tore through the forest, so rough they made her throat raw. With his one final, sated pump, she collapsed across the log and Sy pulled out of her, dragging her back down into his lap.

Her body went slack against his, her back to his front, his arms and legs encircling her as they stared at the fire now full of life. She dropped her head back against him.

"Warm now?" Sy murmured into her ear.

Carys hummed. "That was very effective."

She felt his stubbled cheek smile against her temple and she leaned into him further, not wanting to think about anything in that moment other than his smooth skin and warmth that still somehow felt like the safest place in the world.

CHAPTER TWENTY-EIGHT

They arrived at the inn so late at night that they had to wake the matron to get a room. She tried to rouse herself and put on her merry disposition but she was clearly exhausted. Carys had just put out her hand and told the matron to give her the first key and they left the drowsy matron to sleep.

Carys barely had the energy to shuck off her wet boots and sodden tunic before she collapsed into the soft bed. She didn't budge or protest as several minutes later Sy climbed in after her. He wrapped his arms around her, hauled her back against his warm muscled chest, buried his head into her shoulder, and they both instantly fell asleep.

In the morning light, with her need for sleep sated and finally, actually warm, Carys was suddenly keenly aware of the intimate position they'd fallen asleep in. She peeled Sy's arms from around her and ever so slowly rose out of bed so as not to wake him. Buttery sunlight filtered in through the window. They'd forgotten to draw the curtains and there was no point drawing them now. Carys sighed in relief at the sight of the sunshine. Finally. It wouldn't be another day of traveling through the cold mist and rain. Her clothes would finally remain dry for the last day back to Wynreach.

She tugged on the strings of her tunic, pulling the neckline tight before tying it in a clumsy bow.

"When's the last time you were touched?" Sy's sleep-addled voice drifted from the bed.

She snorted. "A day ago," she said in her raspy morning voice. "You've already forgotten our fireside tryst?"

"Before the competition, I mean." Sy sleepily rubbed the heel of his hand into his eye "When was the last time before then?"

Carys didn't turn, spying him in the reflection of the foggy, warped mirror. "Does brawling count?"

Sy chuckled and shook his head

"Bri hugging me."

"No," he corrected, hugging the pillow and dipping his face further into it. "When was the last time you were touched *romantically*?"

"Seriously?" Carys's shoulders tightened when he hummed, her fingers pausing on her shirt strings for a split second as she debated whether or not to tell him the truth.

Truth, the voice inside her whispered. The morning was too quiet, the days before too raw and real, for her normal, cavalier lies.

"You know the last time," she murmured. "It was with you."

Sy sucked in a breath and Carys cringed, looking back out the window, not wanting to see the surprise on his face. "But you said—"

"I know what I said," she muttered, thinking of how she'd taunted him with talk of her many lovers. "I say a lot of things to get under your skin."

"You're too good at it," Sy replied. "I'm just surprised, is all—"

"Don't pity me," Carys snarled, snatching her weapons belt off the dresser, needing the weight of her sword and the blade she newly acquired from Sy's cache on her hips. "There's no desire I can't take care of by myself."

"Like I said, Car," Sy said into his pillow. "You're too good at lying."

"Yeah, well." Carys gritted her teeth and hastily buckled her belt. "I guess that makes two of us."

She snatched her satchel off the dresser and whirled for the door. Sy bolted up, grabbing her wrist as she tried to skirt around his side of the bed in the tight space. Carys paused as his thumb swept down the inside of her wrist.

"What happens now?" he asked.

"Now we convince Elwyn to let us return to the competition." Carys swallowed. "Now we fight for the crown."

Sy's fingers pressed in tighter, an urgency and yearning just below their tips. "That's not what I meant."

Carys pulled her wrist from his grip. "That's all there is," she whispered. "That's all that's left. You took the rest from us with your deceit, and you're never going to explain yourself, are you?" She pinned him with a look and when he didn't answer she rolled her eyes with a huff. "See?" She headed to the doorway again.

"You're going to hate me forever, aren't you?"

"Yes," Carys hissed. If only hate could be an exclusive feeling. She wished her hate would crowd out the rest of her feelings. What she would give for it to be a singular emotion within her, but the others were still there too: longing, friendship, desire, even happiness . . . coalescing into a bitter agony that kept her circling Sy's world with a gravity all his own.

"If I can't have you at least let me cure our loneliness," Sy called. "Let us at least be together in our hate."

"Don't," Carys said. "Don't torment me like that. You'll ruin this."

"Ruin what exactly?" He rose off the bed, his presence so strong that Carys backed up until her shoulders hit the wall behind her. Sy swarmed forward, crowding her in as he spoke. "I went from being the love of your life to someone you only let hold you when you're on the verge of collapse."

"Yes," Carys said tightly. "And no matter how much I tried not to let you in, I knew the moment you entered this competition that you'd find a way. But being with you hurts me just as badly as being apart from you does, maybe more so because you're never willing to give me reasons why you created this chasm between us. And yet, every direction I try to run from you, you are always at the other end."

His eyes dipped to her mouth. "Some might call it Fate."

"Some might call it a curse," she countered, her voice rising with untethered fury. "The worst sort of curse because I am Fated to an unrepentant liar."

Sy's eyes flared. "And I am Fated to a stubborn fool."

"I hate you," she shouted, fire pumping through her veins.

Sy's hand snapped out, grabbing Carys by the jaw and pinning her to the wall. "I hate you too," he growled, and kissed her.

Her back slammed against the wall, her breath consumed by Sy's hungry lips. He kissed her with such a deep, burning need, his fingers constricting around her throat for just a second before drifting down her body to her belt. Carys was already fumbling for his belt in return.

She needed him. Desperately. Always.

This is what they did. This is all they were to each other. Fighting and fucking were the only two things they'd ever gotten right.

Sy grabbed Carys by the braid, spinning her around. "Don't move," he rasped in her ear as he tugged her trousers down. He yanked off her boots and she stepped out of her trousers, kicking them across the floor.

Her fingers splayed over the peeling wall as Sy slowly rose from his crouch. He trailed his lips up the inside of her calf and Carys's legs trembled with anticipation.

"Tell me you hate me." Sy's whisper tickled up the inside of her thigh. He stood, wrapping his wrist around Carys's braid again and yanking back her head with a bite of pain. She listened to him freeing himself with his other hand and her eyelids shuttered as he trailed the head of his cock between her legs. "Say it."

"I hate you." Carys's words ended on a gasp as Sy thrust into her. She arched her neck back, being pulled further by her braid until her head rested on Sy's shoulder.

"Good," Sy growled.

Carys writhed against him and Sy released her braid and shoved her chest forward, pining her hard against the wall, lifting her hips further into a position he already knew would drive her wild. Gods, he felt so good inside of her.

Ever so slowly, Sy pulled out. Each slick inch of him lit up Carys's insides like a bolt of lightning. She let out a frustrated moan, wanting to be filled again, wanting more, faster, *harder*—her body keening for release.

Sy's lips found the shell of her ear and he whispered, "Now tell me you missed this." Carys tried to push back, to take more of him, but he tugged on her braid again and she stopped with a snarl. Sy stilled, waiting, and she knew he'd wait all night for her reply, just to torture her even if it tortured him too. He'd deny them both the releases they so desperately craved just to make her say those words. This is what he did. He never played fair—not where her heart was concerned.

"I missed this," Carys groaned and Sy pushed into her scorching wetness again, moving inside her until her eyes were rolling back and she was shaking with need.

He rolled his hips in a torturously slow rhythm, in and out, as if savoring every sound she made, every panting breath.

"I missed this too," he murmured. "I hate you and I miss you. I wish I could always be buried inside of you and I wish I'd never see you again. I want you to forgive me and I want you to hate me forever all at once and—" He groaned, his hips moving faster of their own volition.

He thrust up into her faster and harder, bucking her into the wall until the only sounds that filled the room were their heaving breaths and the sound of their slick skin slapping together. Carys's toes curled as her fingers desperately clung to the wall, her knees ready to buckle from the building pleasure that was poised to send her toppling into euphoria.

"Yes." The word hissed out of her teeth as he kept moving inside of her.

She felt all of that wild pendulum of emotions when it came to Sy too . . . and it frightened her. Even then, even as she was desperate to come undone, she needed to put some distance between them again, if not in body than in soul. She needed him to know that she didn't play fair either.

"Gods," Carys moaned, the building sensation growing greater with every breath. "Yes. Ersan."

Sy stilled again and Carys let out an indignant cry as he pulled out of her. He spun her around and she instantly reached for his wet cock, trying to put him back inside of her.

Sy took a step away out of her reach.

"What are you doing?" Carys snarled.

"Even buried inside of you, you still call me Ersan," he seethed, taking another step back toward the chair beside the fireplace. "Even then you won't let me anywhere near those old wounds, will you, Fated?"

Carys blinked. Over the last several days there'd been no space in her mind for Lord Ersan of Arboa—only Sy. She didn't know exactly when she'd stopped calling him Ersan in her mind, but it felt like forever ago now . . . but he didn't need to know that. The fae standing in front of her was only Sy still, but he couldn't ever know it. She wanted desperately to keep her guard up. She swallowed, hating the way he'd eased his way back into her life and past all her defenses. Where once she was resolute to keep him at arm's length, now she was fucking him again? How had they gotten back here?

Ersan dropped into the chair behind him and began stroking himself, the action incensing Carys further. That was not how this would end.

"I told you, *Lord Ersan*," she said, marching over and straddling him. She lined him up with her entrance and hovered there. "We hate each other and we miss each other and I am too tired and horny to make sense of it anymore. Now stop pouting and fuck me."

Sy smirked, grabbing Carys by the back of the neck and pulling her lips to his as she lowered herself back onto him. He groaned as she sheathed him into herself, lifting his hips to meet her aching core.

"Can you hate someone and still want to be with them endlessly?" He panted, dropping his hands to Carys's hips as he bounced her up again. "Why? Why must you torture my every waking breath?"

She gasped, the feeling so overwhelming her thighs began shaking and that rising need in her building up to its precipice again.

"At least you're not alone in your suffering." Carys moaned, her voice barely more than a feral rasp as she rode him harder and chased her release.

Sy leaned forward and took one of her nipples into his mouth, sucking on the budded peak. As he swirled his tongue over the tight, pebbled skin, he pushed her over the edge. Carys cried out, her body clenching around Sy as he thrust up into her, battling her tight muscles two more times before he followed her over the cliff. Her climax roared through her, so strong she had to cling to Sy's shoulders for fear of floating away. Wave after wave of ecstasy shot through her until she thought she might be drifting into the ether.

Sy dropped his sweat-beaded forehead to Carys's chest and took deep sips of air. His fingers pressed into her flesh as if he couldn't bear the thought of releasing her.

When her quick breaths finally slowed, Carys climbed off of him and walked back to her discarded clothes. The window snagged her attention and as a farmer leading an ox walked past, she ducked down, suddenly wishing she'd closed the curtains after all. She hastily pulled on her tunic and popped back up, sheepishly waving at the farmer, who gave her a lingering look. Sy chuckled, saluting the man from the window by his chair. Carys threw her boot across the room at him.

"Carys," he called after her as she padded toward the bathing chamber. She paused and glanced over her shoulder at him. "Whatever this is, I don't want it to end after tonight."

Her face softened for a split second, and then bracketed with pain. She didn't know if she could ever forgive him, let alone truly *love* him, but the very basest parts of her soul needed the comfort of his body at least. No. *No.* She knew whatever this was building toward would only break her apart again and even worse than before. She'd barely survived the first time, she didn't think she could do it again—to let her walls down, to *trust* him, only to discover she was the fool once more. After all her hard work getting herself into a good place the last several years, she was slipping right back into this darkness with him again.

She held his deep brown eyes as she said, "I don't want it to end either, Sy." He smiled as she said his nickname by accident, and then painfully watched it fade as she added, "But I can't do this."

She couldn't do any of it anymore—not this game with Sy, not her ignoring her past . . . not her quest for the crown.

CHAPTER TWENTY-NINE

C arys had taken off ahead of Sy on the last stretch of road toward Wynreach and Sy hadn't tried to keep up for once. She wondered if he felt as low as she did herself, like her heart had been freshly stomped on all over again. There was nothing more to say between them. It seemed like Sy had finally given up all his fight, resigned to the fact that they could never truly reconcile.

When Carys arrived at the stables, one of the stable boys ran out with a letter for her, while another ran inside to alert Councilor Elwyn. A smile broke through Carys's gruff expression when she saw the letter was written in Morgan's handwriting. She hoped it was filled with details of the children and everything they'd been up to. She needed some good news. Gods, she missed them.

She'd barely dismounted her horse when the stable boy ran back in to inform her that Elwyn was in a meeting and she should await the Councilor in her private chambers.

"Tell the Councilor that I have it," Carys said to the boy. "She'll understand what that means."

Carys gave the anxious boy a pat on the shoulder and he beamed as if she'd just knighted him. He turned and raced out of the stables.

She couldn't wait to see the look on Elwyn's face, the relief she'd undoubtedly feel knowing that they possessed the ancient witch talisman at last. With the amethyst dagger, Adisa Monroe's days were numbered. Okrith would finally know peace.

But Carys didn't feel any of the ease or joy she should have felt in that moment, not as the stable doors opened and she knew Sy's horse rode in behind her. She gripped the letter tighter in her hand and strode off into the palace without looking back. Even one glance and she thought she might crack. One imploring look might stop her faltering resolve. But she was fighting on behalf of her younger self now, the one who almost didn't survive his betrayal, the one she promised would never feel so broken again.

As she wandered the narrow hallways, Morgan's letter clutched in her grip, she finally accepted how close she'd let him come again. She feared the free fall that would come if she didn't excise him from her life before it was too late. Forcing her eyes to remain glued to the letter, she raced away from the brewing storm at her back.

Carys,

I'd say I hope this letter finds you well but, judging by young Collam's sour mood, I can assume you've been causing some form of havoc or another. Please tell me you didn't go to that pirate town, as Collam suggested? Collam writes to his brother so frequently—perhaps you could learn to acquire such a skill.

Carys snorted and shook her head at the page. Leave it to Morgan to admonish her even in written form.

I've never known a place to be like Arboa, not even in travelers' stories. The people here are kind, the food is abundant and delicious, and I'm even beginning to get used to the two sleeps. Maybe a love of Arboa is in our blood, sister. Everything here smells of sunshine, ocean air, and snowflowers—just as you said it would. I hadn't believed you. Nor had I believed you when you said the people would be kind to a halfling, but again, you were surprisingly right for once . . . must be a fluke.

The children grow bigger by the day, as does my belly. Matthew has been learning to fish and Collam has been teaching Maxwell how to paint. Molly is just happy she doesn't have to share a room with her brothers anymore. The local girls have taught her how to braid flowers into her hair and I'm constantly plucking flower petals out of her sheets.

Magnus has taken a carpentry job here teaching the local woodworkers. It pays three times what he made in Wynreach. I still can't believe it! They offered him a permanent position—

Sucking in a sharp breath, Carys realized she was gripping the letter so tightly that the edges were crumpling.

But don't worry, Car, he won't be taking it. We've waylaid our departure by a few weeks, but I know you would kill me forever making this place my home. Once Magnus's current course has ended, we will be heading back to Wynreach.

A lump in her throat formed as Carys's eyes misted. It read very much like Morgan was giving up her happiness—*her family's happiness*—only because of Carys's spite. Her feet started steering toward the castle, even as she read on. She couldn't let Morgan throw away a good life just because it would pain her. Gods, she needed to let Morgan know straightaway before she packed up the children and moved back. Carys could imagine it now: the children crying, not wanting to return, all of their new adventures stripped away, cursing their aunt for making them return to a life they'd outgrown.

No. She knew she wouldn't do any of that, knew Morgan would take all of the blame and protect her sister's heart in the process.

Carys couldn't allow that either. It was her turn to take care of Morgan after all the many years that Morgan had taken care of her. Carys nearly tripped up the stairs as she took them two at a time.

She'd go straight to Elwyn's chambers and deliver the amethyst dagger and write Morgan a letter while she waited for Elwyn to arrive. She read on.

> I worry sometimes, Car, that I've pushed you too hard toward the Eastern crown. I only did so because I thought it was what you truly wanted but now, being here, I'm wondering if that was wrong. You know there are many ways to help the humans and halflings, don't you? You don't need to sit on a throne to make a difference to this world. (If I'm being ridiculous, ignore this.)

Carys barked out a laugh through her tears.

> I only want you to know that whatever direction you want to be heading in, I will support it. There are many ways to be a good person, Car, and you are a good person.
>   I hope this letter finds you well and you've returned to Wynreach in one piece. I love you higher than the God of Stars and deeper than the Goddess of Ocean Waves. Everything will be all right.
>   Morgan x

A sob escaped Carys's lips and a maid at the end of the hall jumped and turned in the other direction before Carys could apologize. She wiped her cheeks with her sleeve and sniffed, trying to not look so pathetic. Curse her sister for knowing the exact words to say to cut her to the very bone.

She doubled her speed up the spiraling stone steps toward Elwyn's chambers, feeling more certain with every step of what she must do.

"YOU DID IT, CARYS," COUNCILOR ELYWN SAID, PLACING A HAND on her décolletage as she breezed into the room and stared down at the amethyst dagger placed on the center of the council table. "You really did it."

When Elwyn looked up from the dagger, though, the buoyant look on her face fell. Judging from her dismay, she clearly already knew what Carys was going to say.

Carys looked to the table covered in the tusks of slain beasts and she prayed not a single one of them changed form upon their death. "I failed in my mission," she said. "And I hereby withdraw from the competition—"

"Carys—"

"But I ask that you allow Lord Ersan to remain," she continued, balling her hands into fists to force the words out. "It was under my directive that the beast was not killed. It was Fenrin, I'm sure of it, and I couldn't allow anyone to kill him, beast or no. These are the complicated choices you've tutored me to make. I ask you to take this dagger in place of a tusk and allow the Lord of Arboa to remain and not be punished by my choices."

Elwyn looked aghast, the statement washing over her, her expression scrambling to keep up with the thoughts clearly racing through her mind.

It was a hollow whisper when she spoke. "You're *leaving*?"

Sy had been right and Carys knew it deep in her bones from the moment he'd said it: she'd hate being Queen. He spoke the truth into being and now she couldn't unhear it. It was never the future she wanted, only one she was told she should want, an assumption that first her father and then her friends had made that she went along with out of a misplaced sense of duty. She thought of Morgan's letter, the final piece of permission she needed to make a choice for herself and not for the public good. Carys didn't need to sit on a throne to fight for people like Morgan. She could find a way to do the right thing and honor her own truths as well. Like her decision to not kill Fenrin, to give Aneryn and Laris the continued hope that he might one day return to them.

"Laris," Carys asked as she scanned the prize tusks. "Is she well? Did she return? And Aneryn? Has she awakened?"

It took Elwyn a moment to answer. "Laris has returned safely, still champion to Aneryn while she continues her endless sleep."

The relief of that sentiment was short-lived as Elwyn's watery eyes lifted to hers.

Carys's throat had constricted as she'd watched the joy leave Elwyn's face, and Carys wished in that moment she could take back what she was about to do, but couldn't. In a split second, Elwyn had gone from gaining the tools to defeat an evil witch to losing her future Queen.

Elwyn reached behind her, feeling for the head council chair and dropping into it. "What happened on your quest southward?" she asked breathlessly, her brows pinching in confusion.

Carys sighed, her eyes wandering from where she stared out the window, and took the seat beside the Councilor. "Does it matter?"

"It does when the future you'd hoped for gets pulled out from under you. I would accept the dagger as a task complete in place of the tusk, you know this. But I fear it doesn't matter." Elwyn's words carried no heat, only disappointment. Tipping her head, she assessed Carys with her gray shrewd eyes. "We were so close over these past seasons since King Norwood's death. You pulled this court through more than they'll ever know." She gestured around the room. "You lifted me up from silenced wife to this esteemed position and made me believe I had the knowledge to lead the council."

"You did and you do," Carys said, placing a gentle hand on Elwyn's forearm. "But I don't."

"That's not true."

"Maybe I have the knowledge for it," Carys said, her voice cracking. "Maybe I have the title and the connections and the acclaim . . . but I don't have the spirit. My soul was meant for smaller titles and warmer skies, Elwyn. I'm sorry."

"That's that, then. If you speak the truth, then I wouldn't wish to stop you," Elwyn said, resigned. "I suppose with you gone the people's votes will now be tied between Falaine, Ivar, and Ersan."

"Not Ivar," Carys interjected. "I don't like the idea of Falaine with a crown either."

"And yet you're leaving." Elwyn chuckled. "Falaine is insufferable, but at least she has potential, unlike Ivar. If not Ersan, then I hope to sway opinion toward her."

"And Aneryn?"

"Aneryn was a favorite of the witches to be sure," Elwyn said. "But despite Laris's clear devotion, she cannot keep the people's faith the same way Aneryn could. If Aneryn does not rise before the final trial, then I fear the likelihood of her garnering any votes is low." Elwyn sighed and waved away the train of thought as if it was a cloud of smoke above her. "It is not for you to fret over anymore."

"I'm sorry."

"Don't be. You will be so very deeply missed by the people of Wynreach, though," Elwyn added. "I hope you know that."

Carys hung her head, grateful that the Councilor didn't push her further. She must have seen the resoluteness in Carys's eyes and knew it was futile. Elwyn's soft weathered hand landed upon Carys's own and she gave it a squeeze.

"I will miss you too," Carys murmured.

"Just because you don't want to be Queen doesn't mean you can't visit," Elwyn huffed, waving off the notion and making Carys crack a smile. "In fact, as head Councilor, I insist upon it."

In that moment, Carys realized Councilor Elwyn had become a sort of mother figure to her—chiding her to visit more just like her sister did. Elwyn was the kind of family Carys had longed for as a child. The Councilor was tough as nails and often stoic but she was thoughtful, attentive, and she cared for Carys just as much as Carys cared for her. Carys felt secure in that moment that Elwyn wouldn't let go of her, that Carys would remain in the Councilor's life whether Carys liked it or not. She offered Elwyn a conspiratorial smile as she said, "I will come visit you. I promise."

"Where will you go?"

"I need to go back to the Southern Court." Carys sighed, toying with the end of her braid. "I need to see the ruins of Hilgaard castle for myself—face the night of that fire that still burns in my mind. I need to say farewell to the place like I should've done years ago. I need to pray over my parents' graves." Her voice grew quiet. "I need to forgive them. And myself."

"And where will you go from there?" Elwyn asked and Carys

shrugged. "Saxbridge, I presume? I could see you sitting on the council there. Or perhaps Swifthill? You certainly have friends in the highest of places. I know you'll find somewhere exceptional to settle down."

Carys shifted in her seat, already knowing there was only one place that had ever felt like home. But she couldn't exactly go back to Arboa while Sy was left behind to become the Eastern King, which seemed much more likely now that she was withdrawing from the competition and Aneryn was still in her trance, or maybe . . . With Sy gone, maybe Carys could help Collam rule Arboa, and any time Sy came to town she'd just go visit friends . . . it was clear Morgan loved Arboa so much that she wanted to stay there too . . . maybe, *maybe* it could work.

Carys dropped her head into her hands. First her family's ruins, then the rest of her problems. "I don't know where I'll go after Hilgaard castle. I just know I need to be there right now."

Elwyn clicked her tongue, seeming to divine all of Carys's harried thoughts.

Carys tipped her head to the dagger on the table, eager to change the subject. "Will you do it now? Can I be there?"

"The people deserve to see Adisa's end," Elwyn said. "After all the city's been through, they need to know she's really gone. Let the image of her death assuage their ever-growing fears."

"Every moment she breathes is a moment too long, Elwyn," Carys implored. "She is a danger."

"She's trapped in an inescapable fortress."

"And yet it is not enough," Carys pushed, slamming an angry hand on the table. The tusks rattled across the surface. "She can travel through minds. Now that we have the dagger, she might get desperate. We might force her hand. Maybe we should burn the blooming amethyst flowers, take the seeds as she feared we might do. Take the last vestiges of her power just in case—"

"She doesn't even know we have the dagger," Elwyn said coolly. "She just continues her humming as usual. Whatever plan she could create, it'll be too late." With a sigh, Elwyn rose and picked up the amethyst dagger. "We'll execute her tomorrow at midday in the amphitheater. Wynreach needs this. Perhaps we should hold the last trial at the same time? Let the victor be the one to wield the amethyst dagger? It would make an excellent crowning story. One for the history books." She worried her lip. "No, perhaps that it's too rushed. Regardless, you should be there, Carys. This is your victory, crown or no."

Carys shook her head. "As tempting as seeing Adisa Monroe's demise is, I will be on the first merchant vessel leaving the city at dawn."

"I would ask why you're in such a rush to leave this place, but I think we both know the answer already," Elwyn said.

Carys sighed; she knew it was cowardly, but when she told Sy she couldn't do this anymore, she'd truly meant it. This was her breaking point and no amount of holding her through the night would fix it. She placed her elbows on her knees, holding up her head as if it was too leaden to hold itself. Everything felt too heavy. She needed to keep moving, the momentum made her feel lighter. For once she felt resolved in that, at least. She was finally ready to take the hard steps to take care of herself, and she now knew she didn't need Sy to hold her together anymore. She'd find the right people, the ones who were ready for her to lean on them when she needed. She wasn't afraid to need people anymore, but she now knew leaning on Sy would pull her down into the fathomless depths of their messy relationship in the process. And she deserved the truth from Sy. If he wouldn't give it then she deserved more than a Fated like him.

She prayed Sy was already asleep in his chambers and that she would be gone from the city before he awoke. After everything that had happened between them on their trip . . . she couldn't bear to face his disappointment when he realized she was leaving even if she knew it was the right choice. She wondered if he'd known from the silence of the last day's ride together. He'd pled his case, he'd tried to get through to her, and she'd chosen to pull away because without trust their whole bond was built on smoke.

"I'm glad you know your mind well enough to make this choice, Carys," Elwyn said tentatively, pulling Carys back into the room.

"But?"

"But I hope you realize that you don't have to carry every burden on your own." Elwyn pinned her with a knowing look. "I hope you find the place and *people* that make your soul at ease. And I hope you aren't running away rather than running toward something better."

"I don't know which I'm doing most of the time either," Carys said, making Elwyn chuckle. "All I know is that if I just keep running long enough, I'll find the next thing to run toward."

Elwyn placed her hand on Carys's shoulder. "If you don't pause for long enough, the next great thing in your life might already be behind you." Carys frowned and Elwyn carried on. "You should go say goodbye to Aneryn before you leave, at least." Elwyn frowned, grabbing the amethyst dagger from the table and sheathing it in her waist belt. "She may be asleep but I know you'd be mad at yourself if you didn't say goodbye to her anyway."

"You're right." Carys nodded as she stood and wrapped Elwyn in a tight hug. "Thank you. For everything."

"Be well, Carys Hilgaard," Elwyn said, squeezing her back. "May you find the life you've been searching for."

CHAPTER THIRTY

S he sat beside Aneryn's bed in the same position she had weeks ago. "I'm sorry," Carys whispered to her. She pulled the amethyst stone out of her hip pocket and considered it. The leather of her trousers had bent and molded around the little stone. "I'm sorry I couldn't give this to him." She tucked the stone back into her pocket and set her hand atop Aneryn's still-flickering blue fingers.

Aneryn wore a fresh chemise, her lips freshly applied with salve, and a bowl of fresh-picked berries sat beside her like an offering on an altar—a green witch's offering. Knowing Laris had recently visited upon her return made it the tiniest bit easier to leave, knowing that Aneryn would be cared for, knowing the woman Aneryn loved was there and determined to pull her through.

Ehiris chirped a mournful weak sound, so different from his normal screeching. The hawk too seemed to be fading along with the hope that Aneryn would wake. "I'm sorry I couldn't save him from this. I'm sorry I didn't turn back for him." Tears choked Carys's voice and she squeezed Aneryn's hand tighter. "And I'm sorry I won't be here to tell you all this when you wake."

She stood and turned toward the door, setting an intention to message the Northern King, Renwick, and tell him what had happened. It was time that he knew of Aneryn's fate. By the time he inevitably arrived, Adisa Monroe would be dead and Carys prayed to all the Gods that Aneryn would be awake.

The crushing weight of failure pushed her down further with every step. She didn't help Aneryn. She didn't save Fenrin. Choice or no, she didn't become Queen ...

She stared straight ahead as she walked out of Aneryn's room, not looking back to see the sleeping witch one last time. She paced down the flight of stairs to her old bedroom wing and walked blindly into her room, feeling for a match to light her candle. When she struck the match aflame, she jolted, noting the shadowed figure on her bed. She'd been too lost in her storming thoughts to sense him. Carys reared back, taking her candle with her as her gaze darted to Sy's dark brooding eyes.

"You're running away again." His voice was deep and wrathful, each of his words smacking Carys across the face like a slap of cold wind. "I don't know why I'm surprised."

"Let me guess, Councilor Elwyn happened to casually suggest that I was getting my things," Carys said, setting her candle back on her beside table. Sy didn't confirm it, but she knew it was true. Elwyn wouldn't have been able to help but nudge them together one final time. The Councilor's comments about running away echoed in her mind. Of course, she'd push Carys to be her best self, to say goodbye, to do the awful thing of facing her choices head-on.

Carys turned, opening her dresser to shove the clothing she left behind into her half-filled pack. Gowns, jewels, all of the things she thought she might wear in the days leading up to her coronation—just like all of the plans she'd left behind on their quest southward. She didn't think she'd be shoving them into her worn leather pack like this, but it seemed like a fittingly graceless end to her time in the competition. "You said it yourself, I'd hate being Queen."

"I did," Sy said. "But I didn't think you'd be leaving here like this."

Carys's braid whipped around to her back as she spun her head. "Like what?"

"In secret." Sy dropped his elbows onto his knees and rubbed a hand across his stubbled jaw. "With your tail between your legs."

"That's not—"

"Without me." Sy kicked the bed frame hard with his boot as he shot to his feet. "I didn't think you'd be running out of this competition without me, Carys."

She bristled, packing the rest of her bag and buckling it with shaking hands. She set it against the door and shot Sy an accusatory glare. "I thought you said you were only here for the crown. I've secured your place in this competition with Elwyn. Tusk or no, you are allowed to remain and claim the throne you came here for."

Sy shook his head, nostrils flaring, his rage filling the room until she thought he might combust. "You know I'm here for you," he rumbled. "Only for you. I thought you'd reconsider what you said in that inn, it was too soon for me to push that hard. I knew it was a mistake the moment I said it, the moment I watched your face fall like that. I wish I could take it back, but we were heading somewhere, and now . . . now you're just running away from us again."

"There is no us!"

"That's not true, Car."

That lump formed in her throat again. "Sy—"

"Now I know nothing is given that can't be take away. Even the Fates themselves can steal away a gift they've given." He balled his hands into fists. "Even the person you trust your soul with can rescind their love."

"That's rich coming from you, you traitorous, lying piece of shit." She stabbed an accusatory finger into his chest. "You never truly let me go, did you?" Carys glared at him. "Except, neither did you ever truly fight to make your lies right or get me back."

"Is that not what I'm doing now?"

"No!" she shouted, not caring if the entire castle heard. "You still haven't told me why you kept Morgan from me."

"I've been trying!" he barked.

"Bullshit," she snarled. "There's been nothing from you every time I've brought it up."

"Because you say all I do is hurt you and this," he said quietly, "the truth, will hurt you worse than all of the rest of it. You were already so broken down. I didn't want to be the hammer that shattered the last piece intact."

"You should have thought about that when you dashed my trust against the stones all those years ago." Carys curled her lip at him. "Not that I'm some porcelain doll."

"You're not." She started to turn and Sy's hands lifted, trying to stall her. "I'll tell you now. Let me explain myself."

"It's too late, Sy. It's far too fucking late," Carys seethed. "There is no belonging together anymore—you have to know that, right? So why are you still hanging on when everything between us has withered and died? When you *killed* it? Because you think you own me? Because you think you have the right?"

Sy took a menacing step toward her. "The right?"

"Yes. Look at you, a Lord and his Fated conquest. You think the Fates gave you the right to keep coming back." Carys stiffened, her hand inching closer toward the hilt of her sword, but Sy was already too close for her to draw the long weapon. "That's why you still hang on, isn't it? Because the Gods said you should care."

"I care because you were the first person who ever loved me!" he screamed inches from her face. "I care because you were the first person I ever loved in return. You are the only direction I know how to turn. You are my rising sun, my guiding star, my entire heart. You are my Fated, damn it."

"'Fated' is a word and nothing more." Her fingers drifted lower until she felt her knife on her belt. She didn't know why she reached for it. What exactly was her plan? Kill him for saying he didn't want to let her go because he loved her?

"I don't need the Gods to tell me how to feel about you. I don't need Gods or Fates or any magic at all. I only need you and me." His chest heaved. "I would burn Okrith to the ground for you, Carys, you know that."

"That is meaningless."

"Meaningless?"

"It only feeds your own rage." She placed her hand on his chest and shoved him backward. His hand snapped out and covered her own, holding her palm to his heart as if he couldn't bear to not be touching her. "You know how you really prove your love? Hearing me now, letting me go, winning this war within yourself, now, *that* is truly love."

"Carys . . ."

"You know what words have meaning, Sy? 'Trust.' 'Loyalty.'"

"I am sorry for not telling you about Morgan. The Gods know I wish I could take that back." Sy's fingers tightened over her own. "But I know by now I could apologize another thousand times and it would never matter one whit to you. I'm ready to answer now, though. The question that has torn us apart: *Why?*" He took a step closer, his hand still holding hers against him, until they were so close that his breath brushed across her cheek. "Are you finally ready to hear it?"

"I've been ready this whole time," Carys gritted out. "It is only when I stop needing an answer that you wish to give it? I'm ready to walk away, *finally*, answers or no."

"Then ask me," Sy urged. "Ask me why I never told you about Morgan, why I kept your father's secret."

"I know what you're doing," she seethed. "Trying to make me furious enough to fight? Goading me into letting you stay even at the tip of my blade? Baiting me into another bout of fighting and fucking? I am done with these games, Sy. *Done*. So go on, let's finish this once and for all." Carys's whole body shook and she knew Sy could feel the tremble in her hand, but she forced herself to meet his eyes as she asked, "Why?"

Sy lowered his face until his eyes were in line with Carys's own. "Because your father loved you and he thought the truth would break you just as it did your mother." Carys threw her head back and it smacked against the door, her mind reeling. "And if it didn't break you, he feared you'd cast Morgan out, stop the funds he was sending, leave her destitute."

The sister she'd wanted nothing more than to exist and her father thought she'd abandon her . . . and Sy clearly did too if he was so willing to keep the lie.

"That's ridiculous," she spat.

"Is it?" Sy asked, pinning her to the door with his chest, trying to hold her in place so that she'd finally hear him. "You threw wine in the faces of witches and treated your human servants like dogs just like your father taught you to do. You were every bit a burgeoning fae Lady: arrogant, elegant, and quick to anger. Even now, long after you've eschewed the courtly life, you have a fiery temper and are un-afraid of killing those you believe to be your enemy." Carys broke his gaze, thinking of that pirate town, hating the truth in his words. "You think it's really so unbelievable that he thought you'd not delight in a halfling sister? A secret older sibling who might threaten your very inheritance, let alone the stain on the Hilgaard name."

Carys shoved Sy away and this time he retreated a step. "All this time thinking I was on the side of good." Carys shook her head. "But my father thought I was so much of a monster that I'd hurt my own sister?"

"Your father was your hero. It was self-serving of him to want to remain a hero in your eyes," Sy said bitterly. "He didn't want you to look at him the way your mother had. He didn't want to see the be-trayal of his actions in your eyes."

"And *you*?" Carys hissed. "You agreed to hide his secret for him? You agreed to keep his secret from *me*! The one person you're meant to hold above all else."

"He convinced me the truth would hurt you," Sy implored. "And I was so desperate for him to approve of me as your Fated, for him to *love* me as a son, the approval of a father I never had that yes, I'm ashamed to say, I kept his lies. But I am not the cowardly boy who needs a father's approval anymore nor are you the girl who joked of drowning halflings in the river."

"I never—"

"You did," Sy cut in. "Whether you meant it or not, you did. And after all you said to me about my own brother over the years, I had reasons to believe you'd hate the truth of your own sibling." His eyes tracked her hand as it reached for the doorknob. In one swift movement he took a step into her again, unsheathing his knife and stabbing it into the wall. Carys jerked, feeling the tug on her hair and realizing he'd stabbed her braid into the wood. "You need to hear this," he growled. "You are not the same person you were when your father died. I'm sorry I let your father make me believe that the truth would take you from me like it took your mother from him. I'm sorry that I'd rather risk you *hating* me then not existing in this world at all. I was young and I was scared and I *needed* you to be okay." She tried to shake her head but her hair caught again, tears welled in her eyes. "Neither of us are the same people. I'm ashamed to say I didn't see how strong you were back then. Please, *please*, we need to forgive ourselves and each other of who we once were." A single tear rolled down her cheek, then another, and she hated him for forcing her to cry in front of him. "I, for example, am no longer the sort of person who would think it wise to keep secrets from a fearsome, stubborn warrior who can easily keep yearslong grudges."

Carys huffed a laugh as she reached back and pulled the knife from her braid. "You're still as brash as ever." She threw the knife across the room, the blade impaling into her bedpost.

"As are you," Sy added with a smirk.

Carys's eyes roved his face for a split second and then they both shot forward at the same time. His hands bracketed her face and he pulled her into a deep burning kiss. His warm lips collided with hers, enveloping them in their warmth. She tasted the fear-tinged urgency, the way his hands clung to her as if he was afraid she'd slip through his fingers again. Carys melted into him for one brief, indulgent moment, trying to tell him all the things she couldn't say, then she pulled away.

Sy's forehead rested against her own, his eyes welling with tears.

"I need to think." Carys's voice cracked as she grabbed her pack. Sy took a step to follow her and she added, "Alone."

"Car—"

"I won't leave the city." That was the best she could do. His face flashed with pain but he bowed his head. She wished she could promise she'd return to him, but her whole soul was breaking and she needed to figure out what this new truth meant. She turned and raced as quickly as she could out of the palace, willing herself not to shatter into a million pieces until she reached the palace gates.

CARYS COLLAPSED INTO MORGAN'S ROCKING CHAIR, SOBBING INTO her hands as she rocked back and forth. Morgan's house was dark, devoid of the life and warmth that normally filled the space. Carys didn't bother lighting a candle nor starting a fire, she just simply collapsed into her sister's chair and wept.

She mourned the years gone by, mourned the person that she was and the relationships she'd lost. Carys had outgrown her old life, needing more than the remote castle had to offer, needing more too than the poisonous relationship she had started with her Fated. She and Sy had both grown into different people—better people. Sy cared about Arboa now more than drinking wine and stealing horses for midnight rides through the blooming fields. He cared about his duty to his people and he cared about his duty to his younger brother . . . A new wave of tears hit her. But Sy still cared about his duty to her, that much was clear now.

He'd kept those secrets to protect her in his own twisted, misguided way. He'd acted out of fear of losing her and in doing so lost her nevertheless.

Her father was a convincing man, a leader in every room he stepped in. Every fae in Okrith who came across him jockeyed for his approval. Carys had looked up to him with blind regard for so long and yet, she couldn't accept that Sy had done the same.

She understood now why Sy didn't tell her about Morgan, and Gods, she hated that she understood. She had been so conceited back then that it made her wince to ever fully remember it. If Aneryn hadn't mentioned her past behavior, Carys would probably still think of herself as the wounded one.

Two things existing at once: both victim and villain. She didn't deserve her father and Sy's lies but neither had she exactly been a trustworthy person back then. She very well might have cut off Morgan's funds or wanted to keep her secret for appearances or been thrown into such a deep depression by the truth of her father's actions that she couldn't claw her way back out. Maybe the two weren't such exclusive notions: heroes and villains, good and evil, right and wrong. Maybe each of them would always be a little bit of both.

Her mind flashed to the pirates in Roughwater hanging from that archway—even as a child in Hilgaard castle, she was skilled with a blade. It wasn't so far-fetched to believe she would have cut down anyone standing in her way. And sister or no, she had cared about being fae, was so proud of who she was as if she'd done anything to ever earn it. It wasn't until her father's death that she realized she didn't deserve any of what she had—not the praise for her money, her beauty, her standing in the world. And when her father died, she knew she needed to do more than inherit his land and titles, that her life needed to be more than the sum of her ancestor's misdeeds. She told her father that on his deathbed, Gods curse her; she told him that she needed to do more with her life than just be Lady Hilgaard.

And *that's* when he told her. When he trusted she'd grown just that touch more he felt was necessary. With his final breaths, he told her she had a halfling sister in Wynreach. To find her. To protect her.

She recounted the moment he told her over and over as she cried. He was going to die with that secret. It wasn't until she confessed that she was ashamed of the person she was becoming that he decided to tell her the truth with his last breaths.

She'd thought he'd told her out of pity—to give her someone to comfort her in her loneliness, replacing one family member with another. She thought he'd told her out of concern for Morgan.

It was only now, alone in that halfling sister's house, that Carys realized her father didn't tell her about Morgan out of pity. He told her out of pride. In those last moments he'd seen she was worthy of knowing and he trusted that she wouldn't hurt Morgan when she found out. That he was willing to admit to her his secret shame. That she was strong enough to withstand the truth.

That grieved her worst of all. It was only on his deathbed that her father was truly proud of who she'd become.

She understood now. Gods, she understood. And if the roles

had been reversed, if she'd been the foolish youth with a Fated who seemed to spit upon every person who was slightly different, who had such dark moments and bouts of hopelessness—she would would have kept that secret too. And in some strange way, she knew Sy did it to safeguard her own heart, as if he could keep the ugly truth of who she was from her. Maybe he knew she'd get there in time. Maybe he was planning on telling her when that day came. Maybe he wanted to ease her into the idea just as he had with Collam.

Collam. Tears spilled anew. She used to say the worst things to Sy about his little brother before she'd finally met him and all those hurtful things disappeared with a single one of Collam's smiles. Carys had implied on more than one occasion that Sy should have been embarrassed to have a bastard younger brother and a halfling's son at that. She wiped her nose on her sleeve, huffing at the irony. She'd run off to become part of Hale's—*the bastard prince's*—crew and she'd seen the way that nickname had haunted him. Gods, she'd threaten to kill anyone who'd called him that when only a few years prior it would have been her whispering those things to other courtiers in a ballroom and laughing and laughing . . .

She thought to what Neelo said, about her wearing that personality like an ill-fitting dress. She'd repeated the words she'd heard around her unquestioningly for most of her childhood. That's how highborn people spoke, how fae spoke, how her *father* spoke. She sniffed again, her nose running like a waterfall, nothing soft or poetic about the way she sobbed. Her own father had spoken about the fae as if they were superior to all others . . . and yet he had a secret halfling child. Maybe he had even loved Morgan's human mother. Now she realized he only said those things for the benefit of the people around him, just as Carys had done for the benefit of him. That he'd never said such things when it was just the two of them. Yet that didn't excuse him, either. How could her father blame her for hating halflings when he was the one who taught her to do so?

Everything was falling apart inside her—her entire life seeming to warp and twist under this new lens of understanding.

Deep down she knew the biggest reason why Sy didn't tell her was out of fear. He was afraid it would break her like it had her mother. She mourned the loss of her mother anew—a woman betrayed by her Fated, a woman too fragile for this world. The pieces finally were starting to fall into place. Her mother must have learned of Morgan's existence and it had thrown her over the edge. Was it so far-fetched of Sy to believe Carys's reaction would be the same? Sy already had felt her falling into that bottomless pit of despair. So many times he'd tried to hoist her out of it. And that was before, when life was seemingly good. When her father was still her faultless hero. When her mother had taken her life for reasons unknown. And Sy would have feared that bottomless pit that seemed to follow Carys like a shadow, loved Carys too much to let her fall.

When Lord Hilgaard confessed to Morgan's existence and told her that Sy had been the one overseeing her funds all those years, the betrayal was so strong it blotted out everything else. Only now could she see why: her father had been afraid and ashamed, scared of Carys hating him for it the way her mother had, terrified of what she might do, and he had roped Sy into these misbeliefs under the guise of fatherly love.

A fist pounded on the front door and Carys jolted. Wiping her face, her first thought was that Sy had followed her, that he couldn't wait any longer for her to think and grieve. She marched down the narrow hall and threw open the door, finally ready to accept his apology . . . and what's more, to apologize herself.

But when she opened the door, it wasn't Sy standing there, it was four crowns of Okrith: Remy, Rua, Bri, and Neelo.

"I knew everything would fall to shit without me," Bri said with her cavalier grin. "You look awful."

Before the sob could escape her lips, Bri shot forward and pulled Carys into a fierce embrace. Remy and Rua quickly circled her from either side, pressing her into the center of a fervent group hug.

"We've got you," Rua murmured.

"We're here," Remy said, dropping her chin onto Carys's shoulder.

"Is this real?" Carys sobbed. "How are you here? How did you know to come?"

Neelo stepped up onto the stoop, a stack of books in their arms. The gift of books was undoubtedly their version of a hug. They nodded their head to Carys in greeting instead of joining the knot of hugging arms and Carys blinked back tears to nod back.

Carys dropped her forehead to Bri's shoulder, soaked with tears. "Gods, I needed you. I needed your help. I'm sorry I didn't ask for it." Her chest heaved as she finally said the words she'd been holding in for weeks, wishing to all the Gods that she'd said them sooner.

"Come on." Bri pulled back, wiping a tear from Carys's cheek. "Let's go to Lavender Hall."

CHAPTER THIRTY-ONE

They sat with their backs to the crumbling gray stone on the circular rooftop of Lavender Hall. The dilapidated violet witch temple had been abandoned nearly a century ago but it had become the place where Hale would come with his friends to escape the hateful eyes of his court. Carys had many nights sleeping on this rooftop under the stars, some so drunken or so fogged and exhausted from days of trekking that they were only a blur in her memory. But she knew she'd never forget this night.

"I can't believe you captured her," Remy said, shaking her head.

"We will say farewell to her onslaught of terror tomorrow," Carys said with a hollow bob of her head. She couldn't feel any joy in the victory.

Rua squeezed the hilt of the Immortal Blade on her hip. "I think it would be fun to test just how indestructible that dagger makes her before her execution."

"Absolutely not," Remy said, just as Bri said, "Good idea."

Bri passed the nearly empty bottle of wine to Carys. "This conversation could do with some more wine."

Rua rolled her eyes. "Then you should've been the one in charge of bringing the drinks."

Carys took a long swig from the wine bottle, letting the liquid burn down her throat before setting the bottle on her knee. "How did you know to come?" she asked, glancing around the group from one sheepish face to the next until her eyes landed on Neelo, staring a little too intentionally down at their book. "You sneaky fucking book-worm."

"You just said you should've asked for help sooner," they said with a shrug.

"They were worried about you," Bri insisted. "When I got their message, I came straightaway. We all did."

"Did you all come? Lina? Tal? Hale? Renwick?" Carys's eyebrows shot up as she glanced between the four of them. "The others are all here too?"

"At the palace, waiting for Adisa Monroe's execution," Remy said. "We thought we should all come as a show of force and a unified Okrith . . . but really we just came to see you."

"And to see Aneryn," Rua added, giving Carys a sharp look. "We would've come much sooner if we'd known she'd been in a trance for nearly a *month*."

"It was a very stressful month," Carys amended. "I thought I'd find a way to heal her before now," she added with a sniff.

Remy elbowed her sister. "You're making her cry."

"She was already crying," Rua gritted out.

"I'm sorry I didn't tell you," Carys said, clearing her throat. "How's Renwick doing with the news?"

"He hasn't killed anyone yet," Rua said. "So he's practicing a con-siderable amount of restraint."

Remy pulled her cloak over herself like a blanket and leaned her shoulder into Carys. The warmth of that contact made the tension in Carys's shoulders ease. She hadn't realized how taut her muscles were until they loosened—she felt that with her emotions now too: how every color flooded back into her, more brilliant and harrowing for better or worse. She thought it made her weak to let anyone else help revive all those colors within her . . . now she knew each of these friends painted their own mark on her soul.

"Do you think that Aneryn will wake when Adisa is killed?" Remy asked.

"I think she'll wake," Carys said. "I hope so."

A long silence passed between them before Bri spoke. "Why didn't you tell us, Car?" Her golden eyes narrowed in concern and Carys knew she wasn't talking about Aneryn. "Why didn't you tell us it had gotten this bad?"

A fresh bout of tears welled in Carys's eyes, her whole body slack with exhaustion, and she leaned further into Remy, dropping her head onto her friend's shoulder. Remy lifted her hand and gently wiped Carys's tears.

Carys took a shuddering breath. "I didn't want you to worry."

"We'd be a lot fucking less worried if you'd told us sooner," Bri snapped. "This is Ersan's fault—"

"No. Yes, but no." Carys couldn't wipe her tears fast enough as more fell, springing forth at the sound of Sy's name. "This wasn't his fault." Remy's arm came around her shoulder, pulling her closer. Without looking up from their book, Neelo passed her a handkerchief. "Did you know? Did you know why he didn't tell me about Morgan?" Remy and Rua instantly shook their heads, Neelo's lips pressed into a thin line that told Carys they definitely knew, but Bri simply paused. "Did you know, Bri?" Carys pushed again, her face falling.

Bri swallowed. "I'd suspected it was to protect you from doing something you'd regret." Carys blotted away more tears. Gods, had she seen it in her too? "And perhaps protecting himself too . . . I didn't know you well before you joined Hale's crew," Bri said. "But I heard tales of your father my whole life. He sounded like a formidable man. One even a grown warrior might be afraid to refuse, let alone a wayward young Lord."

Remy and Rua's eyes darted back and forth, tracking the conversation with rapt attention.

Carys shook her head. "I withdrew from the competition."

"Good," Bri said at the same time Remy, Neelo, and Rua made noises of agreement.

Carys gaped at the three of them. "What do you mean, 'good'? I thought you all wanted me to be Queen?"

"We wanted you to be *happy*," Remy said, echoing what Morgan herself had told Carys in her letter. "And you seemed so focused on the Eastern crown, we thought that's what you wanted . . . but it clearly isn't."

"And what do I want?"

Remy smiled softly and turned her gaze up to the swollen moon low in the sky. "Do you know what tonight is? It's the Harvest Moon."

"Don't tell me you brought a candle," Rua grumbled, rolling her eyes.

Remy laughed. "I did." She nudged Carys with her shoulder. "Come pray with me."

"You enjoy your witches' prayers." Rua stretched her arms and yawned. "We shall enjoy the rest of the wine."

"Here. Here." Bri raised the bottle of wine.

Rua plucked one of the books from beside Neelo and shifted closer to their side. As Carys turned to head back down the ladder after Remy, she noticed that Bri leaned over to whisper something to Rua and Rua nodded.

"No plotting without me," Carys scolded.

Bri placed a hand on her chest in mock offense. "Me? Never."

Neelo tossed another book into Bri's lap and then flipped the page of their book. "We'll just read while you're gone."

Carys snorted. "I missed you fools."

Bri winked as Carys descended the ladder. "We are very missable."

THE FULL MOON FOLLOWED THEM THROUGH THE CITY STREETS. Remy looked beautiful basked in its glow, serene and calm in a way Carys had never seen in her before . . . and envied. Everything within Carys felt like it was being tumbled by a giant wave—complete upheaval; if her mind could just stop spinning for more than a single breath, maybe she'd be able to grasp on to a feeling.

Maybe this Harvest Moon would actually help her in its own way too. The witches prayed to each of the full moons and they believed each moon carried with it its own sort of magic. The Harvest Moon was said to be the one night they could commune with the dead, hearing the whispers of their ancestors through candlelight. But that was a witch tradition . . . Carys didn't know if she'd hear anything when she listened to the flames. Still, standing beside Remy, feeling her calm presence, made Carys feel steadier and she was grateful to her friend for bringing her along.

The witches' quarter was made of all curving lines, winding paths, and domed rooftops—homage to the moon and the womb and the twisting flames of their magic. Fae architecture felt rigid and cold compared to the earthly beauty of the witches' and she wondered if it was why Remy added so many witch touches into her palace in Yexshire . . . little did she know, her Fated was part witch too. How strange these royals, Remy and Rua raised by witches in such different ways, Hale and Renwick both with witch blood they never knew about. The legacy of witch magic was upheld and funneled through them more than they ever knew.

"I'm sorry about Fenrin," Carys said as they walked down the side alleys of Wynreach.

"He's not dead," Remy replied, straightening her shoulders and becoming regaler with every step. "There's still hope."

"He turned into a lion monster." Carys bit her lip at the indelicate way she said it.

"We've come back from worse," Remy countered with a chuckle. "How many times were we faced with unbeatable odds and prevailed? I know sometimes you can't see all of the things we've overcome, all of the dark places we climbed our way out of . . . but we have and we will again."

Her words were so gentle, so motherly, it made Carys want to be wrapped up in her hug. It wasn't so long ago that their roles were reversed and she was the one pulling Remy out of those dark places.

Carys sighed. Remy was right. And the following day, the biggest threat to Okrith would be dead and maybe all of her ancient dark magic would go along with her. Carys wouldn't be able to let out a full breath until Adisa was dead. Yes, she was locked in an impenetrable pit. Yes, the people needed their vengeance. And perhaps, Elwyn needed to win their favor with a public execution. Nevertheless, Aidsa's power still existed on the banks of the Crushwold River and her well of magic had not yet run dry. Drink or no, it would be a sleepless night. Carys would rest once the witch was gone.

They came to a little grassy knoll lined with trees and bushes and Remy dropped to her knees on the soft grass. She pulled a totem pouch out from her pocket and loosened its strings.

"You still carry that with you?" Carys asked, crouching beside her.

"I was raised by witches. I carry their magic in my blood," Remy said simply.

"So does Rua." Carys scolded herself internally for being so derisive. Her friend had invited her along on this prayer to pull her out of her own despair; Carys didn't need to pull Remy into her angst with her.

Remy poked a hole in the ground with her pointer finger, swirling it to widen it, then produced a stubby candle from her totem pouch. "Rua and I had very different childhoods," she said. "Both challenging. Both filled with heartbreak. But I had two things she didn't have."

"What?"

"Heather and Fen," Remy said, her voice thickening as she spoke their names. Heather had been like a mother to Remy, raised her, protected her, and ultimately died for her. It was only after her death that Fenrin learned Heather was acutally his aunt and that she'd been protecting him from Adisa Monroe too.

She laid out her totems in a long line in front of her candle and then lit it, murmuring a soft prayer in Mhenbic. Carys took Aneryn's stone from her pocket and laid it in the line of totems beside the miniature bottle of silver sand. She had a sense that if Aneryn was awake, she'd have wanted to bring it out to bathe in the full moon's glow. Better for Remy to have it anyway. She'd know how to care for a witching stone.

"What do we do now?"

"Stare into the white of the flame," Remy said. "And listen."

Carys pressed her lips together, wondering if she'd hear anything at all. She didn't have any witch magic like Remy did, but maybe her proximity to her would—

She heard a whisper from the flame. She blinked and it was gone. Straining to listen, she stared again at the flame, trying to make out the sound. A warm smooth voice whispered not aloud, but into her mind. A voice she did not know.

"*You are a seedling growing in the ashes,*" the voice said. "*If you need to burn one life down to grow another, my love, do it, but don't forget who you truly are either. Don't forget all the sacrifices that brought you here.*"

Carys kept straining to listen, little snippets of words and sayings in the witches' language that she couldn't quite understand. She heard laughter and screams but she kept her blurry eyes focused on the flame. And then she heard two final words as clear as a single pluck of a harp string: *Be loved.*

The flame extinguished and they both rocked back on their heels. Remy dropped her hands to the earth, tears spilling down her cheeks and dripping into the soil. Her shoulders shook with unrestrained emotion and Carys instantly knew from her friend's reaction whose voice she heard from the flames: Heather.

Carys wrapped her arms around Remy and pulled her into a tight embrace. Carys enjoyed being the one who gave the comfort instead of being the one who needed it. She was forced in that moment to be the strong one if only to remind herself that she was, in fact, strong. In some strange way she was grateful for her friend's burst of emotions and Carys's instinctive reaction to them—another gift that her friendship with Remy had given her. The kindness she struggled to show herself she could so easily pour into Remy . . . because Remy was far worthier of it. Carys slung her arm around Remy's side and held her until Remy's tears had ebbed.

They were all hurting in some way or another. Sometimes in short sharp flashes, other times in nagging continual waves, but it felt comforting to know she wasn't alone in it. Maybe she'd swung harder into the darkness than the others, maybe her well ran deeper, but she wasn't alone in that either.

"I'm okay." Remy wiped her cheeks and sniffed. "We can't all be falling apart."

"Sure, we can," Carys said, elbowing her.

They both chuckled and Carys stood, offering Remy her hand to help her rise. Remy quickly collected the totems and her unlit candle and put them back in her pouch. She pulled the drawstrings tight and tucked it back in her pocket before taking Carys's outstretched hand.

They ambled back toward Lavender Hall, but slower this time, each silently contemplating what they'd heard.

"'A seedling rising from the ashes,'" Carys mused as they passed a gap in the buildings and the moonlit Crushwold River came into view. "The seeds . . ." She paused, staring down at the river, and Remy halted beside her.

"What are you thinking?"

"Adisa Monroe had wanted us to collect them for her. She was adamant that we not destroy them . . ." Carys cocked her head and stared at the darkened shoreline. The purple flowers had all wilted now, the seed pods would be emerging soon, and once those pods matured and fell . . . another year's crop of blooming amethyst would be seeded. "When does the blooming amethyst go to seed?"

"I have no idea," Remy said. "Why?"

"I think Heather wants us to burn it," Carys said.

"What?" Remy's brows pinched together. "What exactly did you hear?"

"I think that message that came through the candle fire . . . I think it was her way of telling us to burn it all before the seeds can rise from the ashes." Carys glanced at Remy's wide eyes. "You think I'm crazy, don't you?"

"I . . . I don't think we heard the same thing. Heather was telling me to be resilient. To remember my past but to make my future better." Remy shifted her weight, staring out at the water. "But destroying the amethyst flowers before another year of crop could be produced is wise. Without more of that flower, any of Adisa's allies that might still exist wouldn't be able to pick up where she's left off after her ex-

271

ecution. That flower is the conduit to all of their power. Of course we should get rid of it."

"I'm glad you agree," Carys said with a grin. They walked the quiet streets, Lavender Hall hovering above the skyline beside them. "I'll go—"

When they curved down the final street, Carys froze.

There, leaning against a temple column, was Sy.

CHAPTER THIRTY-TWO

C arys stood there frozen as Remy gave her arm a squeeze.

"You okay?" Remy asked and Carys numbly nodded, never breaking from Sy's intense stare. Remy gave her one last squeeze in acknowledgment. "You are strong, Carys," she whispered. "Good luck."

Carys felt more exposed and raw with each of Remy's steps toward the temple. Remy quickly skirted past Sy back into Lavender Hall.

Sy's hair was unkempt, tousled to the side, his eyes ringed in red as if he had been crying, the stubble from the journey southward still present on his scruffy cheeks, but he stood with the same stoic command he always did. When his right cheek dimpled he shifted from Lord of Arboa to her childhood friend again with that barest of movement.

"I didn't know how long it would be until I saw you again," he said. The way he rubbed his fingertips together by his sides was the only indication of his nerves hiding below the surface, but his words were deep and slow. "I would've bet all of Arboa's gold that it would've been days, weeks, months, but definitely more than a handful of hours."

"I think we're getting a little bit faster with each fight." Carys's lips pulled up in a smirk that didn't quite reach her eyes. Everything within her was still so exposed—shame, anger, love, a torturous vulnerability as she reflected on their past together. "How did you know I was here?"

Sy pulled a piece of paper out of his pocket between his pointer and middle finger. "I was summoned by the Queen of the Western Court."

Carys glanced up to the flat-topped roof of Lavender Hall and three heads instantly dropped from view. "I'm going to kill her." Sy chuckled but didn't move. Finally Carys forced herself to say, "But I'm glad you came nevertheless. We need to talk." He bobbed his head, dark hair falling across his brow and into his eyes. "But not here," Carys added, shaking her head at the rooftop, where she knew her friends were just waiting to pop up again.

Sy pushed off the temple column and slowly walked after her as Carys turned back toward the way she'd came, winding through the streets down toward the river. Laughter and song filtered their way over from the more boisterous parts of town, accompanied by the gentle sound of water coming from the river up ahead.

Carys knew as she walked that this was what the strength of their love truly was—not the battles and swords, not the wild fights and shouting matches, not the hysterics and dramatics of their youth. *This*—walking side by side along the river, hearing each other even when it was hard, *trying*. This was what really tied them together more than anything. They'd fought the worst sort of monsters within themselves to end up here in this quiet, real moment.

They walked for a long time in silence, unsure of what to say and even more, how to say it.

It was Sy who finally broke the silence. "I should have—"

"Yes, you should have." Carys held up her hand and he stopped. "But I understand now," she said and Sy's shoulders caved in as if the weight of carrying her hatred all those many years was finally released.

"I never thought I'd hear you say that," he murmured, his voice thick with emotion.

"Neither did I," Carys said and they both let out a soft laugh. "But I understand why you didn't tell me. I wish I couldn't understand why . . . but I do." A knot formed in her throat, hard as a rock, but she forced herself to keep speaking. "I've been trying so hard to prove to Aneryn that I am more than my past. That the sum of my actions is greater than my youth. Hoping, praying, that she will see me as I am now. To not forever hold me at arm's length for my past mistakes . . . and yet, that's what I've done to you every moment since the night of that fire."

"I'm ashamed I ever thought it was right to keep the truth from you," Sy said.

"My father was a convincing man."

"But I should have been wiser, stronger. I should've known as I do now, that you could handle anything." Sy cleared his throat. "You are the one I should've been loyal to above all else and . . . in some strange, warped way I thought I was taking care of you." He shook his head. "I wanted to give you more time. He fell ill so quickly. I-I thought I could protect you from it. And when you found out . . . I thought it was easier if you just hated me instead of him . . . and then it just got harder and harder to ever make it right again. At some point I stopped even dreaming of doing so. It started to feel right that you hate me forever."

The hill sloped steeper down to the river, turning into small steps that they took two at a time. They stopped and sat on the lowest steps, just before they reached the pebbled shores of the Crushwold River. Carys kicked her legs back and forth, her feet skimming over the withering amethyst flowers that covered the shoreline like a blanket. Sy sat beside her, his shoulder and legs brushing against hers. The riverside was quiet. Torches dotted down the esplanade but not a single person roamed it. Even the docks at the other end of the city were dark.

A single tear slid down Carys's cheek as she stared out at the currents of the midnight river.

Without looking, Sy reached over and found her hand, taking it in his own just as he had when he'd found her at that abandoned fountain. The memory flickered through Carys, the warmth of Sy's hand bringing all of those feelings back to the surface. She squeezed his hand and he squeezed hers back.

"I withdrew from the competition," Sy said. Carys snapped her head up to him. "Elwyn was already waiting for my resignation," he added with a soft chuckle. "She knew it was never truly where I wanted to be."

Carys's words thickened with tears as she asked, "Where do you truly want to be?"

"With you." He glanced at her and wiped her tear away with his thumb. "In the same place you truly want to be," he whispered.

Her eyes roved his face. "Arboa."

"Arboa."

When he reached to wipe another tear his hand lingered, his palm bracketing Carys's jaw and keeping his gaze hooked on her own. "You are the first and only person I have ever loved, Carys Hilgaard. I didn't think it was possible, but I love you more still. You are a hero, warrior, leader, and aunt, sister, and loyal friend. You take each one of those roles with the utmost care. My only wish is to add Fated to that list again." Tears poured down Carys's cheek and Sy added his other hand, pulling her closer until her forehead rested against his own. "All I want is to be yours again and for you to be mine."

"I always was. I always will be," she said, grabbing the back of his neck, pulling him closer until their lips were a hair's breadth away. "I'm sorry it took me walking through such darkness to see our love with such light." She took a shuddering breath. "I love you with every ounce of my soul. Your pain is my pain. Your joy is my joy. Your fire is my fire." She spoke the words like the wedding vows they never got to say to each other.

Sy nodded, as if hearing every thought in her head, his eyes searching her own until his gaze settled on her mouth. Tears welled in his eyes as he ever so slowly leaned in and bridged the distance between their lips. His kiss was warm and soft and all-consuming. Whatever bond their souls had known before was nothing compared to the intensity of that moment. He claimed her with his softness for once, not with bitterness and anger and longing, and Carys melted into him, her hand roving up his back and into his hair, fusing them together into one.

His fingertips pressed into her tighter as he took a deep breath and she did the same, filling her very essence with him. Her hands roved up his muscled shoulders and dove into his hair as she lifted from her seated position and straddled him. One of Sy's hands wrapped around her waist, the other cupping the back of her head as he shifted forward and lay her across the river stones.

The hard rocks bit into Carys's back and Sy stalled as Carys winced.

"Come on. I know a place," Sy said, hoisting her to her feet. He eagerly dragged her down the esplanade toward the fae quarter as Carys laughed into the darkness of the night.

THEY DIDN'T CUT INLAND BUT RATHER STAYED ALONG THE ESPLA-nade until they reached a beautiful townhouse that sat right along the Crushwold River. An archway cut through the building and the esplanade continued through it. The other side sat right above the water, the top of it built up on stilts to avoid any rising waters.

"What is this place?" Carys asked as Sy fumbled behind a planter box. He produced a bronze key from the soil behind a bunch of marigolds and lifted it up in victory.

"A friend's holiday home."

"What friend?" Her words drifted off as she surveyed the townhouse.

As they pushed through the door, she saw that it was gorgeously decorated; sumptuous fabrics dotted the room and embroidered tapestries hung from the wall. Dust cloths covered most of the furniture and portraits.

"Where exactly are this house's owners?" Carys asked, turning around the room.

"It belongs to the Hemarr family," Sy said.

"Hemarr? As in the family that owns half of the mines around Silver Sands Harbor?" Carys's eyes widened. "Bern's family?"

Sy nodded. "One and the same."

"Huh." Carys inspected the surroundings with new eyes. "Figures."

Bern's family lived luxuriously traveling from one court to the next. It didn't surprise her that they owned one of the most beautiful townhouses she'd ever seen and left it mostly vacant.

"How did you know that key was there?" she asked.

"I ran into Bern tonight on my way out of the castle," Sy said. "He is staying in the palace as an honored guest."

"And he told you where he hid the key to his house?" Carys asked incredulously. "I mean, that does sound like something he'd do, but I didn't think you two were such close friends."

Sy arched a brow at her. "Why do you assume you know Bern better than me?"

Carys frowned and Sy's face split into a grin as he threaded his fingers with hers and pulled her toward the stairs.

"I didn't come here to fight with you," he said, tugging her up the stairwell.

"But we're so good at it," Carys teased.

"We're better at something else."

Carys's rough laugh was cut short as they entered the first room on the left. A giant bed sat in the center of the room with satin sheets and far too many pillows covering the quilted duvet.

"Way better than river rocks," Carys said, taking in the room.

She turned to say more but Sy's lips descended on hers. His hand lifted to cup her cheeks and pull her in closer.

"I love you," he murmured against her mouth. "You are woven into my very own soul." He peppered kisses across her jaw and up to her ear and whispered, "I'm sorry my lies drove us apart. Every day without you was the worst sort of torture. I only hope now you feel as complete as I do when I'm with you, my Fated, my everything."

Carys's throat tightened, her hands clawing at Sy's tunic, wanting to feel his skin.

They stumbled over to the bed, fumbling with each other's clothes. Their lips remained interlocked, their tongues tasting the other as a frustrated groan escaped Carys's mouth. Gods, she needed him in every way.

She frantically kicked her boots off and Sy smiled against her mouth as she shimmied out of her trousers. Sy's clothes disappeared just as fast until he was bare except for his booted wooden leg. He stepped out of his clothes puddled on the floor.

Sy took a breath to scan down Carys's body, his cock hardening with each passing heartbeat. When his eyes lifted to Carys's, his gaze was molten, his eyes hooded with desire. That look made Carys throb with need.

"Turn around," Sy commanded.

Carys's brows knitted together in confusion and the slightest flicker of intrigue but she did as he commanded. She felt Sy stalk up to her, his fingertips sliding up either side of her arms and leaving ripples of gooseflesh in their wake. Then they lifted from her skin and grabbed the leather cord that tied the end of Carys's braid. He deftly untied the cord and combed his fingers through Carys's hair. She tilted her head back and shook her hair free.

"There," he murmured and took a step back.

She turned to face him again, her hair spilling over her shoulders and falling to her sides. This was her, bare and vulnerable, ready to be seen without any masks.

They reached for each other at the same second, Sy practically tackling Carys onto the bed. One rough calloused hand cupped her ass and pulled her higher up onto the soft satin plushness. Her loose hair splayed across the pillow like a sunburst behind her head. His hips nestled between her wet thighs, his other hand skimming up her side. Sy's fingers swirled around her nipple, making a soft breath escape from Cary's lips.

The tip of his hard length brushed against Carys's sensitive skin. He dragged himself over her swollen bundle of nerves and then replaced it with his fingers, circling her in torturously slow circles that made her whole body tighten and melt all at once.

"Sy," she whispered and those swirling fingers paused.

His hand drifted higher and bracketed her jaw. He forced her gaze up from his lips to his eyes just as he pressed himself to her entrance again. His expression was filled with raw emotion intermixed with burning lust.

"I'm sorry I hurt you," he murmured. "I'm sorry I continued to hurt you. I'm sorry I was too afraid to tell you the truth."

"I'm sorry I pushed you away all these years," Carys replied as Sy pushed into her an inch and her breath hitched.

"I love you," Sy said, inching deeper inside her as his voice ended on a growl, his words so thick they were barely more than a rumble as he filled her. "I never stopped loving you."

Carys gasped as he pushed the rest of the way inside her, her core pulsing with the fullness of him. Her words were half moan, half cry as she said, "I never stopped loving you."

Sy's head dropped at that and his lips collided with Carys's again. He rolled his hips, pumping in and out of her in easy rolling thrusts. The sensation made Carys's eyes roll back, her fingernails clawing down his sides, relishing in the sweet, slow building inside her.

"Gods, I love you," she barked and Sy let out a rough laugh as he began moving faster.

His hand cupping her ass lifted her higher as he drew up onto his knees. Carys wrapped her legs around Sy's muscled torso and he drove into her deeper and deeper, the angle making her whole body skitter with lightning.

"You are mine," Sy rasped, his movements becoming faster and faster, driving Carys higher to that precipice inside her. "You and me, Carys. Always."

"Always," she cried out, her chest bouncing with each hard thrust.

Her hands fisted into the bed sheets, her body completely at Sy's mercy as he rode her over the edge. She screamed out his name, her soul shattering apart and fusing together again.

In two more hard thrusts Sy followed her over that edge, releasing a loud groan that she couldn't tell was her name or not; all she knew was it made the euphoria pulsing through her veins carry on and on until she was gasping and clenching around him again and again.

Sy collapsed back down beside her and gathered her into his arms. His lips found the shell of her ear and he placed a gentle loving kiss there. Carys's cheek pressed against his sweat-slick chest, their heavy breaths making their whole bodies rise and fall. Sy's hands idly stroked down her spine as he hummed into her hair.

"This," he said softly. "More than Arboa. More than my reflection. More than my name." He breathed her in deeply and pulled her closer. "This is when I am certain who I am. When you are in my arms."

Carys lifted onto one elbow and planted a soft smoldering kiss on Sy's lips. "I wish we could stay here all night," she said as she traced the lines of Sy's torso.

He arched his brow. "Who says we can't?" Carys paused and Sy continued, his fingers flaring at the base of her spine. "You're not getting on that ship tomorrow morning still, are you?"

Carys considered him for a second before saying, "No, I'm going with my friends to watch the end of that violet witch's tyranny and then we will both announce we're stepping back from the competition to the people of Wynreach."

Sy smiled and lifted up to bridge the distance between their mouths again. Carys leaned forward into him, feeling his newly hardened cock against her thigh. She lifted a wicked eyebrow, smirking like a cat, drunk on lust. She brushed a quick kiss across his lips and rose.

"Where are you going?" Sy asked, swiping his hair off his face and watching the swish of Carys's hips. Carys's hair covered her like a blanket, wrapping around her shoulders in a blond shawl, Sy's scent wafting off her.

She paced to the ornate wardrobe and pulled back the dusty drop cloth. Reaching into the top drawer she grabbed a candle and a piece of flint, lighting it. Only when the warm orange glow covered the room did she really know how dark it had been in the room. She grabbed a rusting oil lamp from another drawer, filling it with the viscous liquid, and lighting it aflame.

"Carys . . ." Sy warned. "What in the Gods' names are you doing?"

Carys pinched the handle of the creaking lamp and sauntered naked over to the window, pushing it open with her hip. She leaned halfway out the window, staring at the giant clumps of wilting burning amethyst along the riverbank. She held the lantern out the window, watching the flames grow higher.

"I'm burning down our old life," she said, repeating the words that Heather had spoken to her through the witch candle, "so that we may grow a new one. A seedling rising from the ashes."

She dropped the lantern and it hurtled down to the rocky riverbank below, fire spraying from it like a dragon's breath. Sy ran to the window, appearing beside her as he gaped down at the growing fire that caught the dried scrub of the withering flowers. A line of flames spiderwebbed out from where Carys dropped the lantern and heady floral smoke curled into the air.

"What if something other than amethyst catches fire?" Sy asked, frowning at the spreading flames.

"The flowers cling to the waterline," Carys said. "Then the riverbank is all rock for a long stretch and then a wide stone esplanade beyond that before any of the buildings. It won't spread beyond the flowers." She leaned her bare shoulder into Sy and his arm came around to her waist. "But it will destroy the source of that witch's magic once and for all. When the city awakes tomorrow morning another violet witch threat will be neutralized."

"And if your friends at Lavender Hall spy the smoke?"

"They will see from their vantage point what I have done," Carys said. "Remy and I were planning on doing just this before you turned up and . . . distracted me."

Sy smiled and kissed her shoulder. "My favorite kind of distraction."

Carys turned to give Sy a mischievous look before leading him by the hand back to the bed.

CHAPTER THIRTY-THREE

S moke filled the distant sky as they sat in the autumnal chill that even the bright bursts of midday sun couldn't seem to ease. After her night with Ersan, Carys felt bolstered about her decision not to leave on the ship at dawn and instead attend Adisa's execution. She'd spent too much of her life running away from her choices, never owning up to them and facing them head-on. She needed to close this chapter of her life properly. Her presence would be part of a unified show of strength against Adisa and it would convey to the people of Wynreach that it was time for them to move on from the idea of Carys as Queen.

Carys didn't sit with the others, though. Elwyn had insisted that she sit on the platform alongside her—a final display of their unity and a farewell to the people of the Eastern Court. For a long time, Carys had been a symbol of hope for them, of a future without a tyrant king, and she regretted she had to step away from being a symbol for them in order to be a real person for herself. But a new king or queen would be found, a better one surely. She glanced to the remaining contenders, who sat in the second row behind the Okrith royals. Falaine Fowler would be infuriatingly smug about her win, given she would have probably been the late King Norwood's choice of successors after his sons. But despite her dubious connections and general self-satisfaction, her actions showed she wouldn't be another fae tyrant.

Still, Carys hoped it would be Sava or Alwyth . . . but in truth, it didn't matter.

Carys would still lobby the courts to continue to bring more equality to the humans, halflings, and witches of Okrith. Using her connections as leverage, she would become a thorn in the side of whoever claimed the Eastern throne, and Elwyn would be there to steer them on the right path as well. Morgan was right—she didn't need a crown on her head to make a difference in this world. She could honor the life she wanted and do work Okrith needed too.

The four crowns of Okrith were all in attendance. Carys stared out at the faces of Remy and Hale, Rua and Renwick, Neelo and Tal, Bri and Lina—the final couple looking far more hungover than the rest. Even the silver-haired courtier, Bern, was in attendance sitting beside Rua and murmuring something to her that made her lips quirk into a smile. Rua gripped Renwick's hand tightly even as she carried on conversation with Bern. The Northern Court King looked like his jaw was about to snap from how tightly he clenched his teeth and Carys knew why: Aneryn. The blue witch who was like a sister to him was still asleep in the castle behind them. Carys knew how intently Renwick would watch this execution, how quickly he'd flee from his seat when the witch was finally killed, running to Aneryn's side to see if she finally woke up. Carys noted Laris wasn't in attendance either, probably holding watch at Aneryn's bedside.

On the other side of Bern was Sy, who joined in the conversation that seemed surprisingly amusing for such a somber occasion. When Bern locked eyes with Carys, he winked and she blanched. Whether Sy had told the courtier what had transpired in his townhouse or whether Bern had simply guessed it, she didn't know. But she'd be slapping Sy for it later either way. How strange, two people she knew so well separately were close friends in their own right too. She frowned down at Sy from her elevated position, which just made him smile wider.

So bloody pleased with himself.

Elwyn gave a long speech to the crowd, filled with words of justice, vengeance, a new dawn for Okrith. The crowd hung on her every word. They sat along the same bench seats of the amphitheater as they had for the first trial, but this time, the spectacle would be much more horrific. Elwyn brandished the amethyst dagger, holding it skyward as the crowd cheered and she turned toward the tunnels beneath the theater commanding, "Bring out the prisoner!"

The crowd erupted, the sound so loud it shook the creaking wooden platform that Carys sat upon. Four guards marched out ahead and another four behind, at first obscuring the silver head of the robed figure. Chains rattled from her bound feet and hands, her hair hanging like a blanket across her face, but then Adisa Monroe lifted her head and the steely look from her weathered face was enough to make the entire crowd hush. She was marched up the steps of the platform and shoved down into the seat beside Carys.

She did not continue her eerie humming, but neither did she seem the least bit frightened—all hard edges and merciless expression. Elwyn carried on her speech about glory and sovereignty and Adisa spat onto the wood.

"Fae may have walked these lands before the witches, but it is the witches who will walk this land still after you are long gone." The crowd's attention snapped to Adisa even as Elwyn carried on her speech.

"I honestly expected more fearsome final words, Adisa." Carys leaned over, staring down at the witch's bound hands. "I thought you'd be determined to go out with a bang."

Adisa cackled and the crowd's eyes darted to her again. Elwyn's hands gestured in bigger sweeping swoops as she spoke, her voice growing louder to try and keep the crowd's attention.

"I'm glad I stayed for your death," Carys added.

"Looking forward to having your little witch friend back?" Adisa muttered from the corner of her mouth.

"So it's true?" Carys asked, trying to keep her expression neutral and not seem too eager. "Aneryn will wake when you die?"

Adisa tipped her head from side to side as if debating telling her. "She'll need to be awake if she is to marry Fenrin and become his Queen." Carys glared at the witch as her lips thinned into an evil smile. "Our goals are not as dissimilar as you think, Lady Hilgaard."

"You kill people."

"As do you," Adisa countered. "You're about to kill me, for instance. You're fighting to protect your people as I am fighting to protect mine." Adisa glanced out at the crowd and then back to Carys. "Violet witches will have our sovereignty. We won't live under your fae control any longer. In fact, you won't be here at all. I'm reclaiming this continent for witches and witches alone."

"So you'd slaughter all the fae?"

"Everything I do is for the good of my kind."

"You turned your grandson into a monster," Carys quietly seethed.

"You must admit it's quite extraordinary." Adisa grinned. "I have advanced us a generation with this magic. My coven was too cowardly to ever let me try. They wouldn't bring me the subjects I needed to test out my theories."

"So you experimented on your family instead?"

"That stubborn Norwood Prince was the first who survived," Adisa said in an oddly proud way. Carys's frown deepened. She had no love for Augustus Norwood but even he didn't deserve to be used in such a way. "How appropriate to take the lion—the proud symbol of his family's reign—and twist it against them, don't you think? Who better to destroy this court than its own prince, though . . ." her smile widened, "he did take a fair amount of torment before we got it right."

"That's what you had Cole doing in the Southern Court, wasn't it?" Carys asked. "Making these monsters?"

"Cole was a disappointment."

"You tortured him!" Carys protested. "Is Fenrin the only one of your descendants that you care for? Your obsession with your youngest heir has blinded you to the rest of your family."

"Fenrin will carry on the legacy of our people," Adisa said. "He will expunge the fae and humans and become king of all the witches. He will bring us glory."

"Through mind control," Carys snapped.

Adisa rolled her eyes as if Carys's complaint was a minor point. "The smallest seed *will* be king," Adisa said. "I have Seen it. And once the bloodshed is over, the youngest in my line will bring a peace and prosperity to Okrith the world has never known. He will rule over everything with our magic. Okrith will be one, an amethyst kingdom, a land just for the witches. The smallest seed will finally make the witches free." Her eyes slid to Councilor Elwyn. "He is the true owner of that dagger."

"You speak as if you care for all witches," Carys said. "What do the other covens think of all this?"

"It doesn't matter what they think," she sniffed. "Look at what they've done. Look at what's happened to the witches over the last centuries. Witch magic was once dark and ruthless. It is time it becomes that way again. Making healing balms and praying to candles in the moonlight is nonsense. We used to be mighty! And if we need to kill a few witches to pull the others in line, so be it."

"A few?" Carys balked. "How many people do you plan on killing before you see your ambitions for the lunacy they are? How many people have already died at your behest?" Carys shook her head. "The blue witches in the North? The Western Court coup? And if your plans for Saxbridge had come to fruition, the carnage would've been unfathomable."

"Unfathomable only to you."

Carys laughed bitterly, and nodded out to the Crushwold River on the horizon. "Do you see that smoke in the distance? We've burnt every one of your precious flowers. The ones you were so desperate for us to save. The seat of your power has ended, Adisa, along with your life."

Adisa cocked her head, staring out at the swirls of smoke that curled into the air. A haze drifted across the city, blanketing it in a sheen of gray. Adisa's shoulders shook, more and more until she threw her head back and she released a wicked cackle.

"Why are you laughing?"

You are a seedling growing in the ashes, a voice whispered into her mind, the voice twisting and warping until it wasn't foreign at all but that of Adisa Monroe. *If you need to burn one life down to grow another, my love, do it . . .*

Carys froze.

"I'll let you in on a little secret, Lady Hilgaard." Adisa lowered her head and pinned Carys with a look, her eyes filled with an evil delight as Carys's heart pounded in her ears. "I have been pushing you to light that fire since the day I arrived in Wynreach." A scream rent the air in the far distance, then another, the crowd bolting to their feet as Adisa leaned in and whispered, "You know how we violet witches love to start a spark. Now let me show you what I can do with a city on fire.

"Oh—and thank you for inviting all your other little kings and queens."

And with horror, Carys looked to where her friends sat, certain they were all exactly where the amethyst witch wanted them.

CHAPTER THIRTY-FOUR

The crowd scattered, some leaping to their feet, others stumbling up the stands, trying to reach the highest point. The five gates that tunneled out of the amphitheater lifted and a sea of bodies swept in. Some human, some witch, some fae—they marched with vacant expressions, their eyes dulled and expressions hazed. In their hands were every manner of weapon from candlesticks to kitchen knives to splintering chunks of firewood.

Carys's stomach plummeted to her feet and her heart raced as the cursed mob turned toward the stands. They hacked and cut through the crowd with an unsettling calm. Many were dressed like the dockworkers and fishermen who lived closest to the river where the amethyst smoke was thickest.

Those people probably had taken in lungfuls of Adisa's poisoned smoke. Now, they were attacking their friends, family, neighbors, and lifelong acquaintances, but they didn't see anything other than what Adisa commanded them as they attacked with brute force and impassive faces.

Horror filled Carys's body. This was all her fault. Guilt would storm her like a mighty wave later, but first she needed to act.

"Elwyn!" Carys screamed, leaping to her feet and rushing to the stunned Councilor, who stood motionless at the end of the dais. "Give me the dagger. Now!"

Elwyn turned, her face bone white with dread, and she proffered the dagger with trembling hands, right as a piercing roar shuddered through the amphitheater. Then another. And another.

The wobbly wooden beams of the dais quaked with each roar. Carys whipped her head in the direction of the sound just in time to see five mountain lion beasts tear through the tunnels and slam through the crowd like battering rams. The gates slammed down behind them, locking people in, all apart from a single gate still lifted behind her.

Before Carys had time to brace, one lion collided with the dais and she went flying. Her stomach lurched as the wood disappeared below her feet, her arms and legs windmilling with the sudden free fall. She twisted even as she fell toward Elwyn, reaching for the amethyst dagger, reaching for salvation, but lost her in a dust cloud kicked up by the beasts.

Carys landed hard on her side. The air whooshed out of her lungs and she guessed she'd probably refractured her already injured ribs. She sucked in a sharp breath that stabbed into her side and let out a pained curse.

Get up. Get up. Get up.

She couldn't lie there dying in the dust. She willed herself, knowing at any moment she was either going to be trampled by another beast or crushed beneath a hundred fleeing feet. The screams and roars were overpowering, rendering Carys unable to hear even her own heart racing in her ears. Cries of pain and barked commands and pleas for rescue and screeches of the dying. She blinked through the cloud of dust, searching which direction to run. Where were the others? Where was Elwyn? Where was Adisa? And where was the dagger to end her? But most of all she searched for one person: his wide-brimmed Arboan hat, his starched white shirt.

Carys stared out into the sea of bodies, finally spotting one she recognized, lit up like a beacon amongst the rest. Remy's whole body flickered in red, her amulet flashing as she held out her hands, holding aloft the iron barriers that separated the bottom levels of the amphitheater to the top. She used her red witch magic to keep the makeshift blockades up and keep the humans who managed to flee to the top of the stands from the cursed mob below. Hale stood beside her, fighting in a circular dance around her to keep her protected from all sides. He moved with ruthless efficiency, hacking and slicing down everyone who got within arm's reach of his Fated. His teeth were bared and he growled as he moved, fiercer than Carys had ever seen him in battle before. But in battle he'd been protecting only his name and comrades; now he was protecting his Fated. She saw his fear-tinged movements and knew he wouldn't let anyone—even these cursed innocents—get anywhere near his Remy.

Rua stood a few paces off from her sister, holding the Immortal Blade in a double grip. Renwick stood back-to-back with her, his sword drawn and a look of pure wrath on his face that matched his Fated's. White air bent around Rua, her hair lifting into the air. She hesitated, her eyes darting through the crowd of faces, knowing that the cursed humans were just as innocent as the humans they were slaying. Renwick shouted something to her and she clenched her eyes shut for a split second but then moved, slicing the Immortal Blade through the air and felling a whole row of humans.

Bri and Lina stood further into the fray, their battle-axes barely visible through the press of bodies. Bri barked something out that Carys couldn't hear but it was clearly meant for Rua because upon hearing it, Rua swung her sword and a lion beast dropped to the dust.

The air stunk of bile and the coppery tang of blood—a smell that made Carys's senses focus, her heart slow, her training kicking in. She had just been dropped into the middle of the largest battle of her life and she couldn't discern who was friend or foe. Her eyes landed on a heap of silver robes and her heart leapt into her throat.

Elwyn.

She darted over to the Councilor, fighting the jostling crowd trying to flee the carnage. Elbows and shoulders rammed into her, shoving her to and fro as she reached Elwyn. Carys dropped to her knees beside the Councilor and rolled her over. A cut sliced across Elwyn's temple, weeping rivulets of blood, and her right leg bent at an unnatural angle, but her eyes flickered with enough awareness for Carys to know she wasn't mortally wounded.

Another roar split the air and Elwyn jolted. Carys searched the crowd being herded around the amphitheater in wild chaotic patterns as the lions chased them, snapping them up one by one.

"Where is the dagger?" Carys shouted to be heard above the screams.

"Gone." Elwyn's lips trembled as she spoke. "She took it. She-she's gone. Vanished."

"Fuck!" Carys screamed.

Another roar ended on a keening screech and Carys looked up to see the nearest beast's head rolling across the theater toward her. There was only one weapon that could've cut straight through the monster and she thanked the Gods for the Northern Court Queen and her Immortal Blade in that moment. Another throng of people pushed into them and Carys shoved them away before they stepped on Elwyn.

"You need to get off the floor before you get trampled."

"I can't walk," Elwyn said, her whole body shaking, and Carys was reminded that, for all her stoicism and calm in crisis, Councilor Elwyn was not a soldier. She didn't know a battlefield and she was just as ill-prepared to handle the shock of a sudden attack.

One rusty gate to the tunnels out of the amphitheater screeched and lifted into the air. Carys's shoulders drooped in relief. The mob must've pried it open. They had a way out now.

She shifted one hand under the Councilor's shoulders. "This is going to hurt, sorry." She slid her other arm under Elwyn's legs and the Councilor bit down on a scream, but a broken leg would heal . . . only if she got to safety before a lion beast trampled her.

The crowd of fleeing people at her back came thicker and faster again, shoving her this way and that as Carys followed the flow of people out the only open gate. She ran, carrying Elwyn in her arms, trusting that the rest of her friends would be able to handle the mob behind her. First, she needed to get Elwyn to safety. She ran through the city streets, trying to keep her feet under her as the stampede pushed her onward, picking up momentum as the streets began to slope.

She hadn't heard the roar of a beast for several minutes and she prayed the Immortal Blade had cut them all down.

They careened downhill toward the river . . . toward the wall of haze and blooming amethyst smoke that would control the minds of whoever reached it.

"Stop!" Carys screamed, pulling up short and almost getting bowled over by the crowd behind her. "Don't run that way!"

"Leave me here," Elwyn said, her eyes widening at the encroaching smoke. "You must stop them before the whole city is cursed."

Carys turned to the nearest door and kicked it in—a cobbler's shop. She set Elwyn behind the countertop, obscured from street view, and grabbed a hammer and a shoehorn and passed it to Elwyn. The Councilor arched her brow at Carys but accepted the makeshift weapons nevertheless.

"Stay hidden," Carys instructed. Elwyn gave a shaky nod and Carys turned to the door.

"Carys?" Elwyn called after her. "Queen or not, you are a savior of our people. The East will never forget it."

Carys swallowed the lump in her throat, the split-second look between their eyes saying everything: they didn't know if they'd see each other again. This could be it for both of them. Carys didn't have time to tell Elwyn everything she'd felt in her heart—that Elwyn had been like a mother to her, a guiding figure in her life, a friend when she'd needed one. She didn't have the time or words for her deep gratitude but she knew she didn't need them, because the way Elwyn looked back, it was clear that she already knew.

Carys turned toward the racing mob, shutting and barring the door behind her, just as another roar shook through the city.

"Fuck." One of the beasts must have gotten away from the theater and the reach of the Immortal Blade.

She ran down the main street, the press of bodies lighter now as most had fled. Carys's eyes followed Cobblers Row and down the street to the docks, her stomach tying in knots at the sight. People ran full tilt in their panic toward the smoke-lined sky, and right around the fish markets, when they hit the haze, they stopped—so sudden, so bone-chillingly terrifying, the way one after another they stopped, and turned around. All of the people following their loved ones to safety were suddenly faced with the glassy eyes of their impromptu attackers. Mothers cut down their own children, friends turned upon friends, the sight permanently branded into Carys's mind. The battle lines were drawn in ashen smoke, and still, more people raced straight into the fray.

"Toward the markets!" Carys screamed. "Run toward the markets!" She ran as fast as her legs could carry her, sprinting downhill toward the ever-advancing line of smoke.

She watched as one by one more and more bodies became cursed, more sudden soldiers in Adisa Monroe's unwilling army. She got to the front of the crowd and pulled out her sword, smoke at her back, holding it out at the people running toward her as she gestured wildly with her other arm for them to turn. The wide-eyed crowd started turning, the ones behind following suit, but Carys didn't have time for the panic to ease, not as the newly cursed humans ran for her.

She knew she had two choices: run or turn and face them and end up killing more people who were also the victims of Adisa Monroe. Her hands tightened around the hilt of her sword as she watched the faces of the cursed humans advancing on her—one no older than ten. She couldn't do it. She couldn't kill them.

Running, then.

She turned and bolted down the opposite street away from the markets. A wave of relief crashed into her as the cursed humans chased after her and not the stampede running toward the markets. She darted through the chaos. Houses burned, filling the sky with even more smoke. Glass and bodies were strewn about the streets. Every person she passed she wasn't sure if they were cursed or not. Who needed her protection and who the sharp end of her sword?

She caught a flash between the buildings, seeing the steady stream of people fleeing the amphitheater. It dawned on her all at once. The attack was perfectly orchestrated too: the one gate that had been opened for people to flee perfectly funneled down the main streets into the awaiting smoke. Adisa Monroe was leading her puppets to the slaughter. Carys prayed the witch hadn't gotten far, that she and the dagger were still nearby enough for them to have a chance. If only they could kill Adisa, the curse would be snapped and the people released.

Carys led the cursed humans on a wild chase through the city, her heart hammering and legs aching as she ran and ran and ran without stopping.

She turned the last corner and slammed straight into the side of a giant mountain lion monster.

CHAPTER THIRTY-FIVE

The beast roared and Carys didn't have time to think, letting her instincts kick in. She unsheathed her sword as the creature turned to snap at her. Lunging forward, she stabbed the sword deep into the lion's side. When the lion jolted and took off, Carys held on tight to her hilt and shot forward, her shoulder socket smarting with the sudden force. She swung her leg around the beast, trying to hold on as the creature yowled and fled. It shot through a network of packed buildings trying to fling Carys off but Carys didn't let go. With each of the beast's steps, she worked her blade deeper, attempting to sever the creature's spine. The beast bucked beneath her and she kicked it with her boot as if it was a stubborn stallion.

By all the Gods, she was riding a monster through the city.

Glass shattered over Carys's head and splintering debris clung to her hair as the beast ran wild, bashing through the fine houses of the high-class fae and winding its way back toward the castle.

Blood poured from the creature's wound, coating the street and stippling Carys's face in specks of hot crimson. With each city block that the beast's paws chewed up, its steps slowed.

"Come on," Carys growled, twisting the sword as the creature's steps slowed further. "Die."

But when the lion stopped, Carys realized it wasn't the wound that was slowing it down at all, but the person standing in the middle of the open square.

Bern stood on the lip of a fountain, staring wide-eyed at the beast. But it wasn't fear in his pale eyes, it was utter broken sorrow. What in the Gods' names made him stare that way?

The beast padded another step closer to him.

"Fight it," Bern said, his throat bobbing. "Please, Gods. Fight it." His voice was thick with feeling and Carys's brows knitted together in confusion. "Fight it, Cole."

Carys froze, releasing the hilt of her sword and dropping to the cobblestones in a crouch.

"Cole?" she asked and the beast snarled as if in response. Was this beast, this monster, Cole Doledir? Had Adisa Monroe changed her brown witch descendant just as she had changed Augustus and Fenrin? Had Carys just delivered a killing blow to Fenrin's uncle?

She shook her head. "How? How can you tell it's him?"

Bern's icy blue eyes never left the lion's. "It's him."

The beast took another step as if in response and Carys's chest tightened, a burning knot forming in her throat. Could Cole hear Bern? Had they all been awake and alert within the confines of this beastly prison?

The city square was desolate apart from a few fleeing street cats. Carys and the beast had drifted to a part of town that was either abandoned or the residents were hiding still as statues. The screams and shouts were far in the distance; the castle looming above them seemed empty as well, as if all of the guards had fled their posts out into the city to help the mob of cursed humans.

A soft little breath escaped the beast's snarling maw, shaking its whiskers. Carys startled, pulling her gaze from the high turrets of the palace. She'd nearly forgotten for a split second about the placid beast while straining to listen to the distant screams. The streets around her were so eerily calm. The haze of amethyst smoke drifted away from their direction toward the other parts of the city.

"Easy," Bern whispered, his voice catching as his eyes welled.

The beast lowered onto its haunches and Bern's trembling hands dropped to his sides. Carys's mind flashed back to Silver Sands Harbor, Bern's hometown. He'd hosted them at the library at Silver Sands and he and Cole seemed to have become fast friends in that time. If it hadn't been so soon after Bern's Fated had passed away, Carys might have even assumed they were more . . . maybe one day they could have been.

A sudden scream had them all startling and a woman ran into the square, chased by three glass-eyed humans. Carys whirled toward them, unsheathing a knife from her thigh belt. The sound of the woman's screams made the beast roar again. Carys turned in horror, watching the lion rise up and swipe Bern across the chest, ripping open his flesh as he fell backward into the fountain.

A scream pulled from Carys's lungs, but she whirled back to the glass-eyed humans, sensing them about to collide with her. She tripped the first one, knocked out the second with a quick blow to the temple, and kicked the third through a glass window. One, two, three. There was no time to delay, no time for fancy moves, she needed them incapacitated and the woman safe as quickly as possible so that Carys could turn her attention back to the beast behind her.

Never turn your back on a threat. It was only a useful lesson when there was only one threat.

When all three humans were down and the woman they were chasing fled back through the alleyways, Carys spun around, ready to train her dagger back on the monster, but what she found instead . . .

Cole Doledir knelt covered in blood. The caked gore on his lanky flesh was so thick that Carys barely noted he was naked. He crawled on trembling limbs toward the fountain. His blond hair was speckled burgundy and his watery blue eyes were bloodshot and hollow. Carys's bloody sword that was once impaled in the beast's side now lay discarded at the lip of the fountain.

The muscles in Cole's arms strained and his teeth bared on a garbled scream as he grabbed Bern's lifeless body. He fished him from the fountain and hoisted him onto the ledge. A horrible broken sob shook through him as Bern's head flopped onto his bare leg. Cole's shaking hands tried to cover the gaping wounds slashed across Bern's chest. Blood gushed between Cole's pale fingertips. His cold eyes lifted to Carys as he uttered, "Help me," in a broken plea.

Carys's eyes welled, the vision of the two bloodied figures—one witch, one fae—blurring with her tears. She took a hollow step forward when she heard a piercing screech in the skies. She looked up just in time to see a hawk dive down, dipping its talons into the fountain before swooping up again. Its screeches again pierced the air.

"Ehiris," Carys whispered, watching the bird circle round.

One of the knocked-out humans behind her gasped. It was the sharp sucking sound of someone breaching the surface of water after nearly drowning, so loud and sudden, like coming back to life. Carys turned back to the human and her eyes again lifted skyward.

"What in the Gods' . . ." Her voice trailed away, breathless, her body numb as a wall of sapphire fire moved through the alleyway and its blue flames scorched into the square.

She squinted through the flames, holding aloft her dagger as if she could fight off the strange inferno . . . when a figure appeared from within its blaze.

"Aneryn!" Carys sobbed, her knees threatening to give out with relief as the blue witch walked out from the sapphire flames.

Aneryn's eyes were filled with brilliant blue light, cerulean flames licking up her hands, the air bending strangely around her as if charged with the static of her magic. Had Adisa Monroe been killed? Had Aneryn's curse been broken?

Aneryn seemed *possessed* by this magic, unseeing, unhearing, her eyes glancing over Carys as if she didn't recognize her at all. She marched straight to Bern.

Cole held up a trembling bloodied hand as if to stop her but Aneryn just shot him a look and Cole's body went slack at the touch of her flames, slumping back along the stone fountain lip. Aneryn's flickering sapphire hands lifted skyward as if pulling from the charged air around her. More blue flames glittered with specks of silver and golden lightning, shifting around her and moving *into* her. When Aneryn dropped her hands back down, the whole space exploded with blue flames and lightning. Sparks sizzled and bent around her, their heat scorching on her skin but it did not blister or boil. With each wave of flickering fire, Carys felt stronger again, as if the flames were healing her wounds.

Carys cowered against the inferno, holding up her arms to protect herself from the bright sparks and scorching heat. When the flashing subsided, she blinked through the ever-growing blue flames, trying to find Aneryn, but what she saw instead . . .

There, lying along the fountain's lip, were Bern and Cole, wounds vanished and only thin pink scars striping Bern's torso. His chest rose and fell in rhythm with Cole's.

Thick salty tears streaked down Carys's face. Aneryn had saved them. The humans who were once glass-eyed all rose to their feet, confused and crying. Had Aneryn found a way to break Adisa's curse?

The smoke of the burning amethyst flower drifted closer and more sparks of lightning emanated from Aneryn's hands.

"The castle walls." Aneryn's voice was severe and strained. Her hands shook with the force of her magic as her blue flames battled the amethyst smoke, trying to push it back and out of the city. Ehiris screeched from the skies. "Give him the stone." Aneryn gritted out every word, a trickle of blood trailing from her nose and her knees buckling. Her shins cracked into the cobbles and Ehiris screeched again, but Aneryn kept her hands aloft, fighting back the smoke. What she had done saving Bern and Cole had probably taken a lifetime of power already and still she fought. "Save him, Carys. Save them all."

"Aneryn!" A distant voice cut above the sound of roaring flames. It was a broken, desperate scream. "Aneryn!"

Renwick. He was searching for her.

Aneryn thrust her hands forward and her flames advanced, rushing through the city and beating back the smoke. Wherever it touched, bodies surged back to life and wounded people rose to their feet, healed. Tears spilled down Carys's cheeks at the sight.

Aneryn's arms shook with the force of her magic. "I can only hold it for so long," she gritted out.

"No." Carys wept. "Aneryn, please."

"Go, Carys." Aneryn's pleas ended on a shriek and her magic flared again. "Kill Adisa. End this." She panted and rasped out, "Goodbye, my friend."

Carys let out a sob, tearing her gaze away from Aneryn and running to the fountain to pick up her bloodied sword.

With a keening distressed cry, Ehiris swooped down toward Aneryn. Her fire-filled eyes darted toward her hawk. "Don't," the word came out as a scratchy snarl, but Ehiris didn't heed her warning. As the bird circled back for her, Aneryn's power flared and the bird let out a final screech before plummeting out of the air.

Aneryn didn't blink, didn't scream, the force of her magic making it impossible for her to move as she battled the amethyst smoke. Carys's heart cracked as Ehiris disappeared beyond the line of buildings, but she didn't have time to mourn him.

With a final "Goodbye, my friend," she gripped her sword tighter and ran just as Renwick Vostemur turned the corner and fell to his knees, letting out a final, broken scream of his little sister's name. He'd found her, but he was too late.

CHAPTER THIRTY-SIX

Tears streamed down Carys's face, blurring her vision as she weaved through the streets. Whatever Aneryn had harnessed to save Bern and stop Adisa's smoke, it was going to kill her. Renwick's screams echoed in her mind, chasing her up the hillside, but she couldn't stop, not as Aneryn's final plea clanged in her ears: *Save them all.*

The castle was only two blocks from the ornate houses of the fae quarter—the beauty of the buildings sitting in stark contrast to the carnage that lay all around her. Carys's rough breaths shredded her lungs as she pushed faster and faster, leaping over bodies and shattered glass to get to the castle. The cobbles were slick with blood, the chaos and damage of another beast evident from the bloodbath left behind. Some eyes still blinked, some limbs still twitched, others lay hollow and vacant as they bled out onto the stones. Each body she ran past took another ounce of her soul. She couldn't stop . . . maybe Aneryn's fire would reach them in time . . . maybe the only salvation would be in saving the city as a whole.

Carys held her knife tight in her grip as she ran, trying to prepare herself for what new horrors she might see when she reached the castle wall.

But nothing could prepare her for the sight when she reached the final parapet, entering the narrow path between two battlements. She skidded to a halt. On one side along the castle walls stood four glowing figures like menacing gods come to reap their final vengeance. Red, blue, brown, and green—the leaders of each coven—the witches of Okrith had come. Baba Morganna stood to the front of the group, her whole silhouette shimmering in crimson fire, her hands poised as if readying to rip down the castle wall across from her. And on that castle wall . . .

Carys's whole body doused in ice as she took it in: Remy weeping on her knees, the amethyst dagger held to her throat.

And the person holding the dagger splattered in blood?

Fenrin.

Adisa Monroe stood by his side with her hand on his shoulder and her chin held high as she grinned coolly at the witches across the way.

A line of others knelt beside Remy, some Carys knew: Bri, Neelo, Rua; others she didn't—though they were all clearly important to the coven leaders watching, their witch magic flaring and yet frozen with indecision. Swords and knives were held to the throats of those kneeling alongside Remy, both by a line of guards and random castle staff. They were too far above for Carys to judge the glassiness of their eyes, but she knew from the way they stood, cold and unflinching, that they too were cursed.

One who stood shoulder to shoulder with Fenrin she recognized, though, holding a knife to Bri's throat: the Lord of Arboa.

"Sy." Carys's voice cracked.

She was already running before her brain caught up, feet eating up the last stretch of cobblestone before reaching the steps of the palace wall.

She didn't know how many steps she leapt up, her mind focused on getting to the top before one of those daggers was pulled across her friends' flesh. Her face burned with rage, her body chilled with fear—the two emotions warring to take pride of place above the constant din of panic in her mind. Step after step. Sweat poured down her temples and trickled down her back, soaking her as she darted up the steep winding steps and onto the wall.

Adisa Monroe had moved to the wall's edge, staring down past the descendants of her once sisters and out to gaze over the burning city like the conqueror she was. Her eyes snagged to her left where Carys knew Aneryn's blue fire was sweeping through the city, cleansing the poisoned smoke and healing the cursed mob. Carys only prayed that Aneryn kept going, kept fighting, just as Aneryn knew she would do the same.

To the end.

"Stop!" Carys screamed, pulling the gazes of her friends. "Don't do this!"

Adisa's sharp eyes pulled from the cityscape to gaze at Carys, the coven leaders giving her only a passing glance. Adisa threw her head back and cackled.

"Not dead yet, Car," Bri said with a smirk, eliciting Sy to yank her head back by her hair.

Bri cringed but didn't wipe that grin off her face. Carys gave her a look, imploring her with her eyes that now was not the time for her smart tongue and antics.

Her gaze lifted to Sy, who looked straight ahead. Carys's stomach dropped to her feet. She wanted to call his name, run to him, but Adisa Monroe held up her hand and the line of cursed guards seemed to straighten.

"No!" Carys screamed.

A brilliant flare of magic emanated from the coven leaders across from them.

"Go on, Morganna," Adisa goaded. "Pull down this wall. Kill me and your precious Queen along with me."

"We both know that wouldn't kill you," Morganna seethed.

"No." Adisa picked at her fingernails and laughed. "It wouldn't. Nor would any of your magic stop me and my blade." Adisa sighed, shaking her head at the elder witches. "Such a pity you can't see. All of this is for *us*. For *our* kind."

"We will stop you, Adisa," Baba Airu said, her blue flames swirling like a tornado around her so that only flickers of her appeared through her magic. "Just as our ancestors stopped you before."

"Have you Seen it, sister?" Adisa chuckled. "I doubt it."

"I once Saw a world in which you ruled," Airu said and Adisa perked up at that. "Miserable and alone, killing first the fae, then the humans, then one coven after the next until you had nothing but your vengeance and hate to keep you company."

"You blue witches were always so bleak." Adisa clicked her tongue. "Still, you have Seen my victory, haven't you?"

Airu shook her head. "It fades like water through my fingertips now." Airu tilted her ear to the sky as if listening to the sweetest whisper. "I've Seen you die too, Adisa. Such a fitting end, the one who strikes the final blow."

Adisa huffed and waved them off. "If you've come here to do something, just do it, then," she said with a scowl as if the coven rulers were nothing more than a pest. "But you can't, can you?" She waved at the witches with a laugh. "What are you going to do, Visello? Bake me a cake? I have no wounds that need your healing, Omly. The only one who could actually stand against me is Morganna and we all know you won't, not when my dagger can evade all of your red magic. Not when I am about to slaughter the ruler of your court."

Tears streamed down Remy's cheeks. Her broken bow sat discarded in front of her and the red stone around her neck strobed with magic, but there was nothing she could do with a knife held to her throat—no magic faster than the amethyst dagger. Carys remembered Remy knelt in such a similar position not so long ago, watching as red witches were cut down before her. Carys had been there that night, tucked into the shadows, hiding as a servant. But this . . . this seemed less shock and more broken sorrow—to have her best friend be the one to take her life. It was the cruelest thing Adisa could make Fenrin do.

"Fen," Remy sobbed. "Please."

"Fenrin was never yours to mourn," Adisa said to Remy, grabbing her by the chin and forcing her to meet her storming amethyst eyes. "But he will be the one to end you." She released Remy's chin and Fenrin's blade pressed tighter to Remy's throat again. Carys caught Adisa's attention from the corner of her eye. "Why aren't you kneeling?" she asked as if Carys's presence was a minor inconvenience. She snapped a finger at Sy. "Lord of Arboa," Adisa called. "Release the Eagle and kill your Fated."

Carys froze as Sy turned his haunted eyes on Carys and booted Bri forward. Carys let out a broken whispered, "Sy," before he advanced on her.

Sy trained his dagger on Carys, his cloudy eyes looking straight through her.

"Don't make me do this," Carys growled, shaking her head at him. "Please, Gods. Don't make me do this, Sy."

She turned her dagger on him but already knew she couldn't plunge her steel into his heart. If it was between her and him, it would be her. She couldn't do it. Wouldn't. Wouldn't end him. Not after everything she'd already done to hurt him. Not after the self-hatred she'd finally redeemed him of. Not after they finally had gotten through to each other.

Sy struck first and she dodged, swiping at his side but refusing to make a killing blow. She tried to disarm him, kept trying to get one step ahead, kept trying to anticipate all of the ways he normally fought. But this wasn't him. Sy wasn't in this fight. Or at least . . . Carys prayed he wasn't there just under the surface, watching as he tried to kill his Fated.

Carys connected a blow with his jaw and Bri let out a whispered, "Yes." But didn't move from where she lay belly down on the stone, not when Fenrin still had his blade pressed into Remy's skin.

Where was Hale? Where were the others? Were they even still alive? Carys tried to focus on the sharpened blade darting at her over and over but her mind kept going off to the others. Would any of them make it out of this alive? Would the city burn to ashes? Would Adisa Monroe set the whole world on fire?

Sy's blade pierced her side and she gasped, the scream lodging in her throat as Sy twisted the dagger between her ribs and her knees buckled. Deep. Too deep.

"Carys!" Bri screamed. She tried to scramble to her feet and two guards grabbed her by either arm as she struggled and flailed.

Carys had the strange sense of wanting to comfort Bri then,

even as pain ignited in fiery blossoms within her. She couldn't take a breath, each pull of her lungs shooting more pain through her body. She coughed a wet hacking breath, blood splattering across the stones.

"Watch how easily she dies," Adisa said with a smile. "You fae are pathetic without the aid of our witch magic, eh, Omly?"

Baba Omly's brown witch magic flared, a powerful blast shooting across the space and washing over them, but without her elixirs and potions, it only stymied the blood loss.

Adisa shook her head, merely amused as she nodded to Sy and said, "Continue."

Carys's cheek slammed hard into the stone floor, blood spraying again as her teeth cracked. Sy's knee landed on the middle of her back and she let out a pained groan as he yanked his dagger free and held it to her neck.

"Watch now, Lady Hilgaard. Watch what true power is," Adisa said, turning toward Remy. "Watch as the life fades from your friend's eyes. A life she never should have had. A life stolen for her by the life of a brown witch."

"Heather loved her," Bri screamed, thrashing against the guards' hold. "You, on the other hand, seem willing to sacrifice everyone but yourself." She spat at the witch's feet and one of the guards punched her across the face so hard her eyes rolled back and she collapsed.

"The reign of fae has ended," Adisa said, lifting her hand higher, and as she did, Remy whirled.

She spun around and shot to her feet, but instead of running away she turned in to Fenrin and threw her arms around him. She sobbed into his shoulder and even though Fenrin's eyes remained hollow, his arms trembled and then closed around her for a split second. Carys couldn't tell if she'd imagined it or not, but it seemed as if Fenrin whispered something to Remy before he blinked, his mind resetting, and shoved her back to her knees facing him.

Remy let out a broken sob, tears streaming thick and fast as that dagger tip pointed to her throat again, but she kept her bloodshot eyes trained on Fenrin.

"Please, please, please," she whispered. "Remember."

A surge of bodies stormed toward the battlements. The mob of cursed humans had reached them. They darted up the steps as Carys took a shaking breath. In another moment, they'd be overrun, the castle walls filled with Adisa's vengeful puppets. There would be no fighting them all off, not as wave after wave reached the castle.

"Kill her, Fenrin," Adisa commanded, the sound of the mob making her voice rise to a shout.

"Remember the blackberries," Remy whispered. "Remember the castles we would build and the kings and queens we would become. Remember all the love that kept us going. Remember Heather."

Fenrin stood motionless, the tip of the dagger pressed to Remy's throat. Carys blinked, blood weeping from the cut on her brow into her eyes. She spat blood onto the stones, trying desperately to hold on to consciousness.

"Please," Carys whispered, staring at Fenrin as Sy's blade pressed tighter to her throat. "Please."

The entire world seemed to fall silent. No screams in the distance. No caw of gulls in the sky. Even the Fates themselves seemed waiting with bated breath to see if Fenrin would kill the Queen of the High Mountain Court.

Fenrin's ocean-blue eyes stared unblinkingly at Remy for a breath. And then another. And on the third, he flipped the dagger over and gave Remy the hilt.

If Remy was surprised, she didn't show it. She instantly grabbed the dagger and shot to her feet, driving it straight up through Adisa Monroe's chin and into her skull.

The witch only had a moment of confusion, a frozen second of horror, and then a waterfall of crimson fell as Remy yanked the amethyst dagger free.

The violet witch gasped, trying to make a wet "S" sound as she reached for Fenrin. He opened his clenched hand, revealing the amethyst stone that Aneryn had in her grip when she fell into her trance, the one Remy had taken along with her other totems the night before. Carys didn't know how Remy knew to give it to him, that final embrace a cover to slip it to him.

Adisa gaped at the amethyst stone. She mouthed the words "But—but he's—" until only a garbled choking sound came out of her mouth, and she fell hard against the ground.

Carys tried to cling to consciousness as Remy's foot stepped on Adisa Monroe's wrist, halting the witch's feeble attempt to grab for Fenrin. Remy's gaze was hard as she watched the life bleed out of Adisa Monroe's glowing amethyst eyes, just as the angry mob poured onto the castle walls.

"You're wrong, Adisa." Remy clutched her belly and frowned down at the witch. "He is no longer the smallest seed."

CHAPTER THIRTY-SEVEN

Carys awoke on a cold stone floor and blinked up at the hazy gray sky. She took a pained breath and then another before she heard the groans and cries from all around her. Shifting her head even slightly to the left made her whole body twinge with pain. Her mouth was dry, each swallow burned as if she'd been screaming . . .

The memories of the attack on Wynreach flooded back into her and she shot upright.

The first word rasped from her lips was, "Sy."

There seemed to be only one brown witch far in the distance tending to the rows and rows of injured lined up along the stones of the castle courtyard. What had happened here? What happened after Adisa died?

Then her eyes focused and she rolled over to stare into the lifeless pale eyes of Councilor Elwyn. Carys gasped sharply as she reached her shaking hand to Elwyn's pallid face. She tapped her cheek and the Councilor's head lolled to the side. Her eyes scanned down Elwyn's body to where her dress was shredded open, her insides hanging out onto the stone floor, flies already swarming her innards, the blood no longer flowing.

"No," Carys mouthed, a voiceless sob cracking her open. "No."

With trembling fingers she closed the Councilor's eyes. Where was this? Where were the healers? Why was no one helping them? Where was everyone?

She swept the hair off Elwyn's face as tears spilled down her cheeks. She needed to get up, needed to find the others, but could barely move, barely breathe, and now Elwyn was gone. Was the city gone with it?

Get up, the earth seemed to call to her, a sudden wind whipping her hair, and Carys rolled to her side.

A sharp pain blossomed in her side as she stood, limping down the rows of bodies, many already dead. The carnage was horrific and bile rose up Carys's throat as she forced herself to scan one after the other for her friends' faces.

She glanced back at Elwyn one more time before she turned down another row of bodies. Carys reached for her belt but there were no weapons hanging from it. A trickle of blood trailed down her side, soaking a line down her trousers and into her boot. With each step, more blood flowed.

The more she looked at the dead faces, the more she knew what this was—she too had been forced to make these choices in many battles: this is where they put the ones so injured they weren't going to make it. Had she been brought out here to die? Did they think she wouldn't survive her wounds? Her body discarded next to her mentor and friend? Carys's hand splayed against her side as blood seeped between her fingertips. Maybe she would die here still.

"Sy!" she rasped again, her voice too shredded to rise above a whisper.

She limped faster, scouring the faces of the dead and dying, and a terrible thought rose to the front of her mind: if Sy were alive, he'd have found her by now.

Tears welled in her eyes as she reached the final body. None of them were that of her Fated or her friends. She prayed to all the Gods that Elwyn was the only one lost to her. Carys stumbled through the archway and into the castle. More wounded citizens of Wynreach lined the halls; others ran through the chaos screaming the names of loved ones.

Carys found the first person who seemed clear-eyed enough to ask. "Ersan," she pleaded. "Of Arboa." The elderly man blinked back at her. "Where is he?"

The man shook his head as if he'd never heard that name before. She wondered if he was in shock or if his ears had gone from the fires and explosions and roaring beasts. Tears streamed down her face as she hobbled into the great hall. Brown witches rushed from table to table making poultices and mixing elixirs. Not a single one stopped to look at her as she pushed through them to the other side.

The crowd at the other end of the grand hall was so thick, she could barely push her way through it. People were screaming and shouting to be let in to see the brown witches but two guards barred the doors. One roughly grabbed Carys and shoved her into the hall.

"You wait your turn," the guard barked.

Carys's brows knitted together, more blood weeping from her wounds, as she was jostled down the normally serene hallway. She sucked in a wet breath and bent over, coughing up blood that splattered onto the frantic boots of the people milling around her, but no one seemed to even care. When she lifted her head back up, she caught sight of her reflection.

The person staring back at her looked nothing like her. She was caked in gore, her hair matted and loose, her skin so covered in dust and dirt that not a single section of her hands or face was uncovered by the grime. Whoever found her probably had no idea who she was.

She was pushed to the back of the group and she barely had the strength to fight against the fray to pull herself into a side hallway. Each step became harder and she leaned a hand against the splintering wood shelves to keep herself upright. The other side led out to the fields and the palace woodshop, and Carys had a strange urgency to get to the open field. She needed air and space, needed to get there before her eyes went dark. If she died in this hallway, she'd never be found. A twisted little voice grew in the back of her mind that this would be her final resting place—to die under the open sky, staring out at the city.

Her hands were so slick with her own blood she could barely twist open the doorknob. It took all of her energy to turn the handle but once she got it, the door sucked open in the breeze and banged against the stone wall.

The field before her was empty. The woodshop sat in the distance, its windows and shutters drawn apart as people darted in and out of the far door. They carried armfuls of wooden trinkets, looting the shop under the cover of the chaos.

How appropriate, Carys thought, that I will die amongst thieves.

She leaned limply against the doorframe as she stared out to the city. A gasp caught in her throat at what she saw. Half of the city was on fire . . . but it did not burn. Blue flames rose up between the buildings, the brilliant sapphire burning away the gray amethyst haze, which now was barely a thin strip on the river line.

More tears fell as she stared at the surreal and beautiful sight. Aneryn had done it. She'd saved the city. Carys wondered if there was any chance the blue witch was still alive or if the fire burned on even after she died. Was this Aneryn's final gift to Wynreach? Carys noted how it covered more of the human and witch quarters than that of the fae, but was slowly creeping up toward the castle and the highborn fae areas as well. More tears fell as Carys prayed Aneryn's powers would reach all of the bodies still alive in the castle before they too were lost.

Some of the city still looked intact. Carys had to squint to see the collapsed buildings and certain areas flattened by rampaging beasts . . . but Wynreach wasn't gone. The city hadn't been razed. People still lived. Adisa had done her worst and still hadn't won. Carys's legs gave out from under her and she slid down the doorframe. More than any curse could claim Fenrin, there was a claiming even more powerful and profound—the people he chose to call family. Adisa hadn't been prepared for the love between her witch heir and the High Mountain Queen—that some bonds were stronger than any magic.

With her final thoughts, Carys prayed they lived, prayed that the crowns of Okrith flourished and that they built a better world from the ashes in which they were all crowned. Her eyes fluttered closed, the pain in her side easing to warmth and pleasant numbness. The air turned sweet, the smell of sun-baked clay and snowflowers. She heard Sy call her name and welcome her into the afterlife.

A soft smile pulled at her lips as she heard him call her name again. And again.

Her eyes shot open and she saw Sy running for her. His white shirt was splattered red with blood, his face was caked in dirt, but it was him, he was alive.

He bolted and stumbled, nearly falling to Carys's feet as he grabbed her tightly and pulled her into a fierce hug.

Words hurt as they formed in her mouth and she said, "Don't worry." She took a shuddering breath. "Even in the afterlife I'll keep on running in your direction. My soul will always find yours, Sy."

"Carys," he begged, his bloody hands finding the wound he himself had inflicted. A cry caught in his throat. "Please. I'm so sorry. Why didn't you stop me? I know you're a better fighter than th—"

"I couldn't do it. I couldn't let you live with your actions, just as you couldn't let me live with mine." Carys winced and Sy let out another cry. "Take care of my sister."

"No." Sy shook his head, his tears spilling down onto Carys's rumpled tunic. "You will take care of her yourself. You have to meet your newest niece or nephew. You have to teach them to be as fierce as their warrior aunt." He held the full weight of Carys's head in his hands. "Hang on. I'll find a brown witch."

"There's too many to save."

Sy shook her. "You're more important," he insisted.

"I'm not." Carys lifted a weak, bloodless hand and wiped her thumb across Sy's bottom lip where a tear clung. "Bury me in Arboa."

Sy's face crumpled, his jaw clenched and his teeth bared as he struggled to breathe against his anger and pain. "No."

Carys glanced one last time at the sky, now filled with brilliant sapphire flames, and said, "I love you."

Sy sobbed her name and Carys dropped her forehead into his shoulder, just as she had done sitting on that fountain a moon ago, and let herself melt into him.

"Help!" he screamed. "Help us!"

"I'm here," a smooth, warm voice said. Sy let out a growl but the voice cut him off. "I'm a friend."

Carys's eyes squinted open, her vision blurring but she could make out the features. "Morgan," she said, reaching up to cup her sister's cheek.

"I'm not Morgan," the woman said, her eyes flaring the deepest shade of purple and then flickering to bronze. She placed both of her flame-covered hands on Carys's chest. "I'm Evelyn, her mother."

CHAPTER THIRTY-EIGHT

W hen she cracked one eye open it was to a room of people again, but they weren't dead and dying, they were laughing around a card table. Carys blinked her bleary eyes at them. A long hall table appeared to have been pulled into the center of her bedroom—a much larger chamber than the bedroom she'd stayed in during the competition. Her friends crammed around the table, passing bottles of wine and shouting at their cards.

A chest rose and fell at her back and she realized she was lying back against someone and she could tell by the scent who. She nuzzled back against him, humming to herself as the hand stroked her arm up and down. Her hair smelled fresh, her clothing the softest silk.

A kiss dropped to the top of her head and Sy murmured, "Thank you for being too stubborn to die."

Bri's head snapped up and landed on Carys's peeked-open eyes. She kicked her chair backward and bolted over to Carys, pulling her off Sy's chest and wrapping her in a fierce hug.

"You stupid fucking bitch," Bri sobbed. "Don't do that to me."

Lina walked over and rubbed Bri on the back. "Easy, love," she said to Bri. "You don't want to reopen those wounds." The Western Court Queen offered Carys a warm smile as she squeezed her wife's shoulder reassuringly.

Bri's grip only eased slightly. "I thought I watched you die," she said, her words muffled against Carys's fresh braid. "Even when your fever broke, I feared we'd lost you."

Carys lifted her chin from Bri's shoulder, taking every face into account: Remy, Hale, Rua, Renwick, Neelo, Talhan, Bern, and Cole all sat around the card table. Tears welled in her eyes as she looked each of them over. They were all there. All well in fresh clothes and clean hair. One by one they drifted over to the bed. Some looked unscathed, others looked like they'd barely made it out alive. Hale had a black eye, Talhan a split lip, and Renwick's eyes were so bloodshot, probably from his screaming, she could barely see the whites . . . and then she remembered. She heard Renwick screaming Aneryn's name over and over.

Carys scanned the room again, bolting upright.

"Whoa," Bri said, steadying her by the shoulders. "What is it?"

"Where's Aneryn? Where's Fenrin? And Laris?"

Bri's fingers squeezed her shoulders. "They're alive. They're alive," she repeated in a reassuring tone. "Breathe."

Carys's shoulders drooped. "She saved us," she murmured. "She saved all of us."

Sy's arm banded around Carys's waist, careful to avoid the wound bandaged at her side. "Not all of us," Sy said.

Carys froze and she twisted to lock eyes with Sy. His lips pulled up to one side, his eyes sad, as Carys asked, "Who?"

Sy pressed his lips together and swallowed, his eyes roving her face. "Ivar, Prestev, Falaine . . ." The way his voice drifted off made Carys understand the next he would name. "Elwyn."

"I know."

Sy's brows pinched together and Carys dropped her head into her hands. "You know?"

Her shoulders shook with the force of her cries. "I woke up next to her. My body dumped with the others."

Arms circled around her: Sy, Bri, Remy, Rua, one by one they all gathered around her in a bundle of warmth and comfort.

Grief warred with the relief that so many had survived, many more than she had ever hoped. She was alive, but her joy was bittersweet.

Elwyn should've been there to see this victory—to see the better world that she'd fought so hard for.

Carys finally had enough strength to ask, "How did she die?"

"The shop that you left her in caught fire during the attack," Remy said. "She managed to flee back to the castle but it was overrun with cursed people."

Rua swallowed and stared at her hands as she added, "She did one thing before she went, though."

"What?" Carys asked.

A soft sorrowful smile played on Sy's lips and he said, "She picked the competitor to win the Eastern Crown."

CARYS SAT BESIDE ELWYN FOR A LONG TIME WHILE SY LINGERED IN the doorway. Carys knew he'd stand there and wait all night if she needed him to, just so she could say her goodbyes. The coffin Elwyn lay in was beautifully carved—the story of her life etched in every inch.

It would be another few days before the royal woodworkers finished their burial carvings on her coffin and then she would be laid to rest in the palace cemetery. Carys made sure they gave her pride of place with a petrified wood statue above her burial place. She would be forever remembered as a hero—not of magic, not of sword, but one of hope. She pulled her people through an impossibly difficult time and gave them hope for a brighter future. Elwyn led with calm and stoicism, a picture of reassurance in uncertain times, and Carys was determined to make sure everyone remembered what she'd done.

Carys's fingers trailed over the carved wood, her smile soft, her soul raw. Elwyn had led Carys through the darkest times too. Carys wished Elwyn could see her now, finally feeling so full—full of sorrow and of joy and of every feeling in between, that empty void within her filled to the brim. Elwyn always had faith she'd find it again—a full life—had even let her walk away from the crown in the end because it was clear Elwyn knew it wasn't where Carys's heart truly belonged.

She felt Sy's warm silent presence at her back and finally turned to him with a nod. He walked over and offered his elbow for Carys to take. He'd clung to her side the whole walk from her chamber up to the top floor of the castle, where Elwyn's body lay. Sy had helped her back into some clean clothes and Carys opted for a billowy loose tunic that wouldn't brush the wrapping around her chest that covered her wounds. Each flinch and wince of pain, Sy flinched too, the guilt so potent in him that Carys tried to school her expression and hide her affliction.

She hobbled down the covered bridge that led to the western wing of the palace, trying not to lean so heavily on Sy but he was practically carrying her. They got halfway down the bridge when something in the courtyard to the left caught her eye.

"Aneryn." She gasped the witch's name but Aneryn was too far below to hear her.

Aneryn knelt, her shoulders slumped, her head hung low. A little feathered body lay in front of her: Ehiris. Another hawk was held in between Aneryn's knees and she held a dagger in her hand.

"Gods," Sy muttered as he took in the sight. "Is she going to try to perform the *midon brik* on her hawk?"

Carys gaped down at Aneryn, shaking her head. "I . . . only if he's still alive. I don't think she can swap her bird's life with another after they have truly gone . . ."

"Who knows what she's capable of," Sy said. "She just healed half the capital with her magic."

Carys glanced back from the way they'd come. "Those who remained alive when her magic reached them," she said, thinking of Elwyn's pale, lifeless face.

Carys's heart leapt as she caught sight of a mop of blond hair on a tall frame. Fenrin walked out from the corridor and leaned against the stone pillar beside Aneryn—a small figure with raven hair peeking out from behind him. He stared down at his boots, seeming to wait for Aneryn to make her choice. He murmured something so soft that Carys couldn't hear and Aneryn dropped her dagger and released the hawk. The bird took to the skies with a screech and Aneryn crumpled forward, dropping her head in her hands.

Fenrin dropped to his knees and gathered her to him, saying something into her hair. Laris came around to Aneryn's other side, wrapping her arms around her back and dropping her chin to Aneryn's shoulder. The three of them intertwined as Aneryn's hands flickered with sapphire as she pulled them tighter, her shoulders shaking with silent sobs.

Carys shook her head thinking of what Aneryn had been through, the life she'd lived, the horrors she'd endured to end up where she was—to finally allow people to love her.

Sy tugged on Carys's elbow. "Come on, let's get you back to bed. Fenrin said you shouldn't be walking around yet," he added, brushing a tender kiss to her temple. "He said Aneryn had a message for you when you woke, but that she was still coming back to herself and needed time."

Carys's eyes shot to Sy. "What message?"

He smiled. "He said to tell you: 'I'm glad you're finally awake, friend.'"

"I'm glad she's awake too." Carys's eyes misted as she stared out at the city beyond the courtyard. "She'll make a better queen than any of us," Carys said.

"That she will."

She gave Aneryn one last look, her heart softening at the way she and Fenrin intertwined, grateful that the blue witch finally had someone she could lean on. Aneryn had been the one propping up so many others her whole life, had sacrificed herself to save the city, even, and was powerful enough to survive it. It felt good to see her leaning on someone else. Now, she had two consorts to keep her propped up. Carys glanced at Sy, letting him take more of her weight. It felt good to lean on him too.

"I guess her visions were right," Carys said, clenching her jaw to keep from groaning as another sharp pain shot through her side. "And Adisa's too, just not in the way she had imagined."

"What do you mean?" Sy asked, his sharp eyes missing none of Carys's discomfort as she walked.

"Both Adisa and Aneryn said they Saw Fenrin on a throne," Carys said with a pained smile. "Little did they know it was as King Consort to Aneryn."

Sy hummed. "I wonder if she knew."

"I don't think she did. I think she thought she would die saving the city." Carys shook her head. "Adisa wasn't wrong. *The smallest seed shall be King.*" Carys's eyes welled again with happy tears and she cursed her body for being so quick to swing into emotions now, but she was grateful for it too. "I wonder if that means Remy will have a boy."

Sy paused and blinked at her. "The future King of the High Mountain Court."

"I'm going to be an auntie again," Carys added with a smile.

"Speaking of," Sy said. "I sent word to Collam to tell Morgan that you're okay." Sy dropped a kiss to her loose hair. "She was about ready to commandeer a pirate ship to get to you."

Carys laughed. "That sounds like her."

"The baby is coming any week now," he added.

Carys turned toward him. "We need to get back to Arboa as soon as Elwyn is laid to rest."

"Don't you want to wait for the coronation?"

"I'm guessing all of the others will be present," Carys said. "They can represent me. I missed the newborn days of all three of the others. I can't miss this one." She scoured the courtyard and to the crowd beyond. "Will her mother come too?"

Sy's brow crinkled. "Who?"

Carys's eyes widened as she searched Sy's confused expression. "When I was . . . dying," she said and Sy winced. "Was there a woman?"

"I carried you to the head of the brown witches, Baba Omly herself," Sy said. "She healed you. She said it was a miracle you hung on that long."

Carys shook her head, trying to reconcile the vision she had. "I guess I'm just that stubborn."

Sy chuckled. "I love you," he said.

"I love you." Carys leaned in and brushed her lips to his. "Take me back to Arboa. I'm ready to go home."

CHAPTER THIRTY-NINE

She stood barefoot on the sun-baked tiles, warmth radiating into her soles. As she leaned over the balcony, she stared out at the city of Arboa, still tropical and blossoming even in the depths of winter. The breeze danced through her hair, bringing with it the heady scent of snowflowers and the salty brine of the ocean.

A hand landed on one side of the balcony by her waist, careful not to skim the exposed skin of her bare-backed dress even though her wound was now fully healed. Sy's other hand reached her other side and he leaned in until his chest brushed against Carys's back, enveloping her in a warm embrace.

She'd barely had time to step into the billowy dress and tie it up at the neck before heading back to the balcony to stand in the Arboan sunlight. A smile tugged at her lips, still swollen from another bout of lovemaking. Sy's lips dropped to Carys's shoulder, pebbling her skin in the echoes of their last heated encounter. Carys's body rolled like a wave as Sy's chest rose and fell with a deep, long sigh.

Gods, she felt that sigh in every ounce of her soul. She'd been taking a deep breath like that every few hours since arriving in Arboa. Every time she caught a glimpse of the ocean or the floral breeze hit her face she'd remember again—she was really here—and her whole body would sigh again.

For the first time in her life there was a feeling of calm—of rightness and fullness and completeness—that she'd never once known before. And in that moment Carys knew she didn't regret the years of heartbreak and darkness that led her to this calm, steady joy. If she and Sy had always stayed together, she didn't know that she'd have ever found it within herself.

She toyed with her mother's gold ring on her finger as she leaned her head back on Sy's shoulder and tilted her cheek against his own, needing to be in contact with him from crown to foot. Her eyes trailed from the mouth of the Crushwold River and in the direction of Wynreach, too far upriver to see.

A soft smile played on Carys's lips. She would one day travel back to Wynreach just to see Aneryn in her crown, but right then she was glad she hadn't stayed. The urgency to get back to Arboa was too strong. She imagined Aneryn sitting on a throne, though, as clearly as if she had the witch's Sight, her two consorts beside her. It mirrored the rightness she felt every time her bare feet stepped on Arboan soil.

"She will make a good and fair ruler," Carys murmured. "She will make sure everyone in her court is cared for."

Sy dipped his head, his chin pressing into Carys's shoulder. "Not all fae will be happy about three witch rulers."

"Not all fae are their people," Carys countered. "The fae of Wynreach saw what Aneryn did for them, *felt* what she did for them. She gave them their minds back. She healed incurable wounds. She saved their lives and all of their family members when she could have just saved the humans and witches, even when she thought she was going to die saving them."

"The way she conjured that firestorm was incredible," Sy said. "If it had been a moment later . . ."

Carys's fingers threaded through Sy's own and pulled his hands from the balcony to wrap around her waist. They both knew what would've happened if Aneryn's fire magic had been a moment later—Carys, and all of the others in that courtyard, would have died.

"The way Fenrin fought Adisa's mind in the end was incredible too," Carys said, thinking of the way Fenrin's whole body trembled trying to fight the witch out of his mind. Carys still didn't know if that

323

small amethyst stone had been imbued with magic or just a token of Aneryn's love, but whatever it was, it snapped Fenrin from the spell and she thanked all the Gods that Remy was brave enough to hug him and slip it in his pocket.

The warm breeze swept up the hillside to the balcony in another gust that tousled the gossamer curtains on either side of them.

"It still feels strange, though, knowing Adisa wanted Fenrin on the throne, and now he's there, even as King Consort," Sy said. "Do you think their children will have full violet witch magic like she prophesied?"

Carys shrugged against him. "Who knows. Maybe it will be Remy's child with the violet witch magic, maybe none of them, but it won't matter."

"Why?"

"Because whatever powers those children possess, they will be raised by good people who will show them how to use their powers for good." Carys pulled Sy's arms closer around her. "The five crowns of Okrith are finally at peace."

Carys turned in Sy's arms and he lifted her by the back of the thighs, perching her on the balcony railing. Her knees hugged his hips, her hands clasped behind his neck as he leaned in and kissed her slowly, savoring the feel of that deep, slow kiss. His tongue licked into Carys's mouth and she opened for him, her hands diving into his hair.

"Ew, gross," a little voice called out and Carys leaned around Sy to find Molly hanging on to her mother's skirt.

"Sorry," Morgan said, holding up a hand over her elder daughter's eyes, her other arm cradling newborn Maeve. She turned to leave as Molly interrupted again, asking, "Did you say yes?"

Sy tensed his grip on Carys's hips and Morgan cringed.

"Sorry. Sorry," she muttered, giving her daughter her infamous "be quiet" stare. She bounced tiny Maeve in her other arm and Carys had the overwhelming urge, despite her near-nakedness, to offer to hold her niece again. "We're going. We'll talk later."

She waved at them, hustling out of the room and back to their dwellings at the eastern end of the grounds.

Carys dropped her forehead to Sy's chest and laughed.

"I suppose it was never going to truly be a surprise," Sy said with a grin, kissing the top of Carys's head. He reached his hand into his pocket and pulled out a ring. "I wasn't worthy of your answer the first time I asked you," he said. "Nor was the ring."

Carys chuckled. The ring he'd proposed to her with when they were teenagers was a gawdy ruby so large it weighed Carys's whole hand down. But now, Sy brandished a delicate golden ring, the band perfectly matching her mother's ring. A burst of diamonds sat atop the band, shaped like a blossoming snowflower.

Carys stared out to the array of blooming fields that circled the city in every direction like the beaming rays of a midday sun. In the late autumn, the petals had all dropped, scattering like a white carpet across the fields. Even the dots of the bare brown bushes still looked beautiful like speckles of dark paint upon a white canvas. Looking down at the ring brandished in Sy's hand, Carys smiled.

"Carys Hilgaard," Sy said, dropping his forehead to her own and holding the ring between them, the moment so small and delicate and perfect compared to the grand gestures of his last proposal. "Will you marry me? Will you be the Lady of Arboa? Will you rule over this city and my heart for the rest of our lives?"

Tears misted in Carys's eyes as she stared down at the ring. They'd come so far to get to this moment. They'd fought such monsters both in the world and within themselves to arrive here. Carys reached a hand out, cupping Sy's cheeks, and stared into his welling eyes as she whispered, "Yes."

Sy closed the distance between their lips, enveloping her in a burning kiss as he slid the ring onto her finger.

"Did she say yes?" Collam's voice called from below the balcony.

Carys and Sy laughed against each other's lips and Sy shook his head. This was the life she'd always wanted, always dreamed of—a big family, surrounded by the people she loved, the joyful chaos of a full house. She loved this life they were building together, the life of their own choosing.

She pulled Sy closer, kissing him again as she murmured, "I love you," against his lips.

"I love you too," Sy said, his arms constricting around her tighter.

"Sy! Did she say yes?" Collam shouted.

Sy broke their kiss and pulled away with a laugh. "I knew I shouldn't have told anyone." He rubbed the back of his neck but his giant smile belied the frustration in his words. "They have a little surprise party set out down in the gardens and I fear they're going to keep pestering us until we go."

Carys shook her head and laughed, threading her fingers between Sy's own and enjoying the feel of her new ring upon her finger. "Let's go," she said with a smile. "I'm ready for our story to begin."

CHAPTER FORTY

ONE YEAR LATER

T he ancient tree stood proud in the center of the clearing, ribbons of every color waving from its gnarled branches. The tree once filled with only red ribbons now bore every hue of the rainbow—each ribbon a prayer for a fallen loved one. The boughs, so laden with every color, were a sobering reminder of how many lives had been lost since the Siege of Yexshire. On the one-year anniversary since the Battle of Wynreach, they gathered to remember the fallen.

Carys stared up at the purple ribbon she hung for Elwyn. The bright new ribbon waved gently in the wind, standing out clearly amongst the sun-bleached fabric and bringing life back to the crooked old branch. Carys took a step back, and then another, emotions choking her throat as she stared at the ribbons—so many, *too many*—so much grief and remembrance and joy of life danced along each branch.

"It's my turn," Bern said, holding his hands out to the baby balanced on Remy's hip. "I haven't held Raffiel all morning."

Carys smiled as the child reached out to his uncle, tipping fearlessly away from his mother and landing in Bern's arms. The smile that lit up Bern's face was enough to shatter a heart and put it back together in a single breath.

Sy's arms wrapped around Carys, pulling her back against his chest. His chin dropped onto her shoulder and she leaned into him as they watched the tree and the ribbons waving in the breeze.

"He will be ten years old before his feet ever touch the floor," Hale said as he slid his arm around Remy's waist, but his smile belied his words.

"There will be more babies to dote upon soon enough," Lina said, her hand rubbing her swollen belly. Bri leaned in and kissed her wife on the temple, her hand covering Lina's own with a proud smile. Any week now, their child would be born. Carys couldn't wait to see how parenthood would change Bri. Already, her friend was nesting, becoming even more broody and protective of her wife and Carys knew Bri would love her child fiercely—just as Carys would herself, albeit probably more sensibly than Bri. Carys already had to talk Bri out of having a baby-sized battle-axe made in her child's honor.

"I sent you a tale of fables to read to them," Neelo said, clutching a book between their hands, their thumb rhythmically rubbing the edges as they stared up at the waving ribbons. "Never too early to start."

"I think we'll be visiting Saxbridge for more books too." Bri inclined her head to Neelo. "Rumor has it you're building a children's library in your old gambling hall."

Talhan beamed at his Fated. "We both suspect there will be many more royal children visiting our court in the future." He glanced halfway to Rua, and Neelo elbowed him, and they both went back to busying themselves cutting more lengths of ribbon to hang on the prayer tree.

Carys smiled as Renwick gathered Rua closer into him even as she gave him her best glare. The Northern King simply chuckled, the sound more familiar every season to Carys's ears.

Their lives had never been more full, more full of laughter, and joy, and family, but as Carys stared at the tree she knew that joy came at a great cost.

Blue flames flickered across Aneryn's fingers as she hung a blue ribbon onto the tree. Fenrin and Laris stood a single step behind her, arms around each other, watching her with such quiet pride. They were the true embodiment of a King and Queen Consort, as if they too knew their greatest accomplishment was in finding her. Carys didn't know which of Aneryn's loved ones she prayed for as she whispered her Mhenbic words and hung her sapphire ribbon.

So many had died, thousands that would be mourned or prayed for. This day had become a day of mourning and celebration across the entire continent. In each of their capital cities, people would rise with the dawn to grieve the decades-long wars between their courts. As the day went on though, the mourning would morph into a celebration of life, of survival, of peace at last. The streets would be filled with people, but the rulers of Okrith decided to gather here in the middle of the jungle to celebrate just between themselves.

Carys grabbed another violet ribbon and hung it on the stubby new shoot that curved off the ancient branches. She hung it for the humans of the Eastern Court, the ones who'd been slaughtered a year ago in the carnage of Adisa's mob. Even with Aneryn's magic, so many hadn't survived—whole families gone with no one to mourn them.

Carys still sometimes felt Adisa's shadow, her memory lurking in the quiet and darkening the corners of her mind as if the witch might come back from the dead again. Aneryn had assured Carys that Adisa Monroe was gone for good, but every time Carys smelled the faint wafting of amethyst perfume she still cringed.

Sy seemed to sense the direction of her thoughts and pulled her closer against him.

Carys had returned to Hilgaard castle with Sy by her side. She'd laid fresh flowers on the graves of her parents and said her prayers. And she did the one thing that had weighed her down like a stone for so many years: she forgave them. They weren't the family that she needed. They never could have been. But she'd been wrong to believe that she would never find this either.

Aneryn gave her a wide-beaming smile from across the clearing, her eyes filled with tears as she nodded and mouthed the word, "Yes."

Carys shook her head at Aneryn with a laugh. She'd been foolish about a lot of things.

"Look at them," Sy whispered into Carys's ear, her skin tingling with the feel of his warm breath. Carys looked from Remy and Hale, to Rua and Renwick, Lina and Bri, Talhan and Neelo, Aneryn, Laris, and Fenrin, before settling upon Bern bouncing Raffiel in his arms. Sy's murmured words rumbled through his chest and into her back. "How many years did you mourn that you'd never have people in your life like this? And yet, here they are."

She thought for so long that she'd need to stand alone, apart, be independent of any support or aid or love—that somehow that independence would make it easier to find connections, but she'd had it all wrong. Needing people, letting them in, allowing them to carry some of the weight, offering to carry it for others—that was the true meaning of family. She'd tried so hard to not need anyone and yet, it was this messy, loving, chaotic connection where it all really lay.

"I know now, we'll only find a way forward together," Carys whispered, leaning into Sy.

"As one family."

DRAMATIS PERSONAE

Remini (Remy) Dammacus, fae with red witch magic, Queen of the High Mountain Court, Fated to Hale Norwood, sister to Rua

Ruadora (Rua) Dammacus, fae with red witch magic, Queen Consort of the Northern Court, Fated to Renwick Vostemur, sister to Remy, wielder of the Immortal Blade

Hale Norwood, fae, King Consort of the High Mountain Court, illegitimate prince of the Eastern Court, believed to be son of Gedwin Norwood but disproven, raised as the step-brother to Augustus Norwood, mother Kira Ashby

Gedwin Norwood, fae, deceased King of the Eastern Court

Augustus Norwood, fae, prince of the Eastern Court, youngest son of Gedwin Norwood, ally to Adisa Monroe

Abalina (Lina) Thorne, fae, Queen of the Western Court, Fated to Bri

Briata (Bri) Catullus, fae, Queen Consort of the Western Court, Fated to Lina, twin sister to Talhan Catullus, nicknamed the Twin Eagles or Golden Eagle when alone, member of Hale's crew

Talhan Catullus, fae, twin of Bri, nicknamed the Twin Eagles or Golden Eagle when alone, member of Hale's crew

Carys Hilgaard, fae, one of Hale's crew, childhood friend of Neelo

Neelo Emberspear, fae, Heir of Saxbridge, only child to Vitra Emberspear

Vitra Emberspear, fae, Queen of the Southern Court, mother to Neelo

Renwick Vostemur, fae and part blue witch, King of the Northern Court, Fated to Rua, son of Hennen Vostemur

Hennen Vostemur, fae, deceased King of the Northern Court, father to Renwick, ordered the Siege of Yexshire and the annihilation of red witches

Cole Doledir, brown witch healer, former head healer to the Western Court Queen

Adisa Monroe, immortal ancient violet witch, searching for her youngest heir to take over Okrith as King of the witches

Heather, deceased brown witch healer, surrogate mother figure to Remy and Fenrin

Fenrin, brown witch healer, head healer to the High Moutain Court

Rish, green witch, personal witch attendant to Neelo Emberspear

Aneryn, powerful blue witch. Former personal witch to Renwick Vostemur. Partner of Fenrin and Laris

Red Witches, power of animation

Blue Witches, power of Sight

Green Witches, power of growing plants and making delicious food

Brown Witches, healers

Violet Witches, power to control smoke, scents, and incenses

ACKNOWLEDGMENTS

I can't believe our journey through Okrith has come to an end! Thank you to everyone who has supported this series. *The High Mountain Court* started this whole crazy journey and helped me actualize my lifelong dream of being an author.

Thank you to my amazing husband and gorgeous children for your patience, support, and encouragement during the writing of this book. I love the life we've built together and love you to the moon and back.

Thank you to my Mountaineers for celebrating my books both online and out in the world. You are the most amazing group of readers!

Thank you to my Patreon members for supporting me and pushing the direction of my writing in so many amazing ways. I love the novellas we create together and the ideas we share! A very special thank-you to Audrey, Jaime, Kristie, Lauren, Linda, Marissa, Alyssa, Amy, Ciara, Crystal, Drea, Emily, Hannah, Kelly, Katie, Mandy, Latham, Sarah, and Virginia! I so greatly appreciate your support!

To my writer friends, thank you for lifting me up through the writing of this book. Thank you, Kate, for being my book wifey and for always having my back. *You better be moving to Australia ASAP.*

Thank you to Treece for being an amazing VA and keeping Team A.K. going. I love working with you and so appreciate all of your ideas, creativity, and support!

A.K. MULFORD

Thank you to my amazing agent, Jessica Watterson, for all of your support and for championing my stories out in the world. I love working with you and look forward to many more bookish adventures in the future!

Thank you to the whole Harper Voyager team! It has been a pleasure working with you all on this book. Thank you to my amazing team who worked on this series for all of your insights, creativity, and talent. A big thank-you to my editor, David Pomerico, for taking on this series. It is wonderful working with you!

Thank you to my gorgeous fluffballs, Ziggy, Bruno, and Timmy, who will never read this for alas, they cannot read. Thank you for all the biscuit making when I was stressing out!

If you've read this far, wow! I can't believe this journey has come to an end. Remember: no one decides how bright you shine but you.

Turn the page for a sneak peek
at the second book in *The Golden Court* trilogy . . .

A Sky of Emerald Stars

A SKY OF EMERALD STARS

SADIE

The wagon tilted precariously to one side, turned, and then tilted the other way as we switched down the back road toward Valta. Maez and I were both turning green as we sat on the couches getting tossed to and fro. Nesra's pass was a long steep ascent but at least it was steady. This road was a short, sharp nightmare.

When the wagon finally leveled out it took me a second to feel like we weren't still moving. My stomach roiled and my hands shook.

"Fuck that road and it's grandmother," Maez snarled.

"Never again," I groaned, clutching my gut.

Navin knocked on the wagon door. The stairs were lifted and locked for the rocky journey and they rattled with each pound of his fists. "I'm heading into town for some food," he called. "Come find me at Jevara Vanesh when you're ready."

Jevara Vanesh. It meant "the roasting pig" in Valtan, a restaurant or inn, I presumed.

As I took more queasy breaths and fanned myself, I noticed that the air in the wagon was starting to turn more humid. The sweat on my brow wasn't only from nausea but also the heat. Maez's short hair curled at the temples, her face flushed. We'd dropped so far in altitude over the course of the day, the Valtan heat had started to seep into the cracks of the wagon.

I pulled back one of the windows above my head and a wall of heat blasted at me. "Ugh," I grumbled, looking back and forth between Maez and my clothing of thick furs and leathers. Maez and I exchanged glances as we both started disrobing and went searching through the trunks of abandoned clothes for something lighter to wear.

When we stepped down off the wagon I stifled a gasp as I craned my neck up toward the sky. In the far distance were mountains floating amongst the clouds. The bottoms of the mountains were diamond-shaped rock—the darkest iridescent black, like a raven's wings. Far below the floating mountains were circles of shade and turquoise pools of water. I'd heard of nomadic groups that would spend each day following the trail of shade from the mountains' shadows. I shook my head. It would be the only way to survive in such an unwelcoming environment. Unlike the lush, pastoral landscapes in the sky.

The floating mountains were called Upper Valta, where all of the Onyx Wolf pack lived. The biggest mountain at the center of the cluster was the capital of Rikesh. I gaped, unbelieving that anyone could reside in the sky like that. Long rope bridges tied the floating mountains together and my already sore stomach twisted at the thought of riding across them with nothing but open air beneath us.

I lowered my gaze to the desert that stretched out on the ground below. It seemed like a wasteland of deep golden sand. No cities popped up in the distance, no other signs of life except for those from above. The teeming verdant green and sharp onyx stone of the mountains above sat in stark contrast to the rolling sand dunes below. Behind us was what appeared to be the only low-dwelling village in all of Lower Valta.

The town was built near vertically into the sandstone cliffside. Little darkened square windows cut into the stone and crisscrossed pathways led up to the higher buildings. Donkeys pulled carts up and down the narrow roads as people darted to and fro between the shade of the buildings. There was no greenery apart from the plants that sprung up from a lean waterfall that poured from the cliffside down onto the top of the township, like a miniature oasis amongst a sea of sand and beige.

The few people who moved from building to building all wore

337

broad hats and lightweight, pale clothing to keep cool from the scorching sun.

"So glad Briar packed my fur hat and woolen cloak," I muttered, "considering we're going to be in the scorching heat for most of this trip."

Maez let out a half snarl beside me at the derogatory mention of her mate. "You'd have frozen your tail off in Taigos, you ungrateful fool."

She fanned out the billowing white shirt she wore over her half vest and fitted linen trousers. Her weapons belt was still strapped to her waist but it was the only thick material in her otherwise desert-appropriate attire. I, on the other hand, wore similarly light fabric . . . but over the top of my fighting leathers. I wasn't going to risk being stabbed just to keep cool. My bandoliers of knives were all hidden within my clothing now. For all intents and purposes I was dressed like a human civilian, far more stealthy than Maez's weapons belt, though I knew I might boil alive for the choice.

"Come on," Maez said, elbowing me and taking a step out of the shade of the wagon and into the sunlight. "Before we shrivel up. I need to eat something greasy."

The first step into the sunshine felt like stepping too close to a fire and I fought the urge to retreat into the shade. Behind us, four giant posts poked up from the earth, a shade sail hanging above it. Navin had parked the wagon under the sail alongside many other wagons and carts. There were feeding troughs and water—a makeshift barn. But a wooden barn would've probably been impossibly hot and equally easy to catch aflame. One spark and the whole thing would burst into an inferno. This place seemed teetering on the precipice of a firestorm.

I forced myself forward as the sun seared every inch of my exposed skin and I grimaced at the brightness. The sand was baking in the sun's heat and I felt like I was being cooked alive both from above and below. If the makeshift barn had been even a few more paces away from the shelter of the township, I might've collapsed from heat exhaustion right then and there.

Wearing my hidden leathers was a bad fucking idea. The regret mounted with each step through the burning sand but I also didn't want to turn back when the shade of town was so close. I had half a mind to strip naked right in the middle of the desert, which in hindsight would be far more suspicious than wearing a sword on my hip.

When we reached the arched doorway to the township, we entered a corridor that tunneled into the hillside and traveled up through the shadowed town. The relief of the shade was so great I wanted to let out a moan.

"How does *anyone* live in this fucking town?" Maez groaned, wiping the back of her sweaty neck.

An old man carrying a tray of glass vials stopped short and frowned at her.

Maez grimaced. "Apologies," she said in her best Valtan accent.

The man blustered off, shaking his head and muttering something about Damrienn.

"He knows where we're from," Maez whispered to me.

"What did you expect?" I waved to her bright red face and my sweat-soaked tunic. "We look like we've just been dunked in the ocean. All of the people around us look fine with the heat," I said as Maez desperately fanned herself. "At least we pass for humans of Damrienn."

"For now," Maez muttered. "Any more of this heat and I might go completely feral."

We wandered further down the main corridor, passing a cart of fans made from woven palm leaves.

"Here," I said, plucking two off the cart and passing the woman a crover.

She eyed it suspiciously, turning the foreign coin over twice to make sure it was real. Then she nodded and kept walking.

We frantically fanned ourselves as we kept walking and Maez started to loudly start talking about our family's farm and visiting cousins in Valta. It wasn't the worst ruse, but she was certainly overselling it.

"How about we just be quiet humans," I muttered out of the corner of my mouth.

"Why yes, cousin!" Maez said loudly and laughed for the benefit of the family passing in the other direction. I elbowed her hard in the ribs. "How my cousin loves to jest," she tittered.

"By all the fucking gods," I spat and stormed off ahead of her.

Off the main vein of the town were narrower corridors, some bustling with people, others quiet. With Maez hot on my tail, I followed the Valtan signs up and up toward the top of the town, following the words "Jevara Vanesh," along with the symbol of a plate and spoon drawn next to it.

My stomach rumbled more with each step upward, the smell of roast meats and spiced nuts drifting down the tunnel. When we finally turned from the main hallway into the restaurant, all of my relief disappeared.

Navin sat in a far corner booth, wide-eyed, with a knife pressed to his throat.

And the person holding that knife?

My father.

ABOUT THE AUTHOR

A.K. Mulford is a bestselling fantasy author and former wildlife biologist who swapped rehabilitating monkeys for writing novels. She/They are inspired to create diverse stories that transport readers to new realms, making them fall in love with fantasy for the first time, or all over again. She now lives in Australia with her husband and two young human primates, creating lovable fantasy characters and making ridiculous TikToks (@akmulfordauthor).